RETURN
OF OUR
COUNTRY

BY

DAVID M. BURKE

"We have 15 billion in gold in our treasury and we don't own an ounce. Foreign dollar claims are 27.3 billion dollars.[1]"

"History will record with the greatest astonishment that those who had the most to lose did the least to prevent its happening. Well I think it's time we ask ourselves if we still know the freedoms that were intended for us by the Founding Fathers."

If we lost freedom here, there's no place to escape to.
This is the last stand on earth.
- Ronald Reagan

It is well enough that the people of the nation do not understand our banking and monetary system for, if they did, I believe there would be a revolution before tomorrow morning.
- Henry Ford

ISBN: 978-0-578-69968-4

Website: davidburke.us
Email: davidb1author@gmail.com
Twitter: @dmburkeauthor

Cover design and layout by Norm Williams, nwa-inc.com
Edited by Katy Light, editsbykaty.com

Printed in the United States of America

ACKNOWLEDGEMENTS

Many thanks to Norm Williams and Julie Nielsen for all the help with formatting, publishing, cover art and always being there.

A special thanks to Boyd Craven author for conducting very helpful free seminars for new authors.

I would like to also thank the authors of the books I reference and whatever source gave me the premonition that led me to write this book.

PROLOGUE

1963
VIRTUES TO DIE FOR

The explosive thrust sent the president's head forward. Another shot, from a different direction, jolted his head back as blood and brains splattered on the top of the trunk. A bullet entered Governor Connally's back, and ripped through his body before exiting just below his nipple, then continued clean through his wrist and lodged in his right thigh. Panic stricken, those inside the vehicle ducked down, except for the President's horrified wife who, in her panic-stricken state, reached for a section of the President's head, which lay on the trunk of the open top convertible sedan. As she picked up the piece, she somehow reasoned that her husband — the President of the United States — the most powerful man in the world — could be put back together.

The crowd was in a panic. Some took cover on the ground. Others ran. One woman slowly lowered her camera. She had been filming. Her mouth hung open.

* * *

Thousands of miles away, self-centered Lord Rothmayer, one of the wealthiest men in the world, studied his television screen as the scene unfolded.

He turned to his brother and his nephew, who would eventually take over the family business. His raspy voice resonated through the room. "There, it's done. I told you we'd handle it."

Several months before that, the President of the United States had eliminated the Federal Reserve. The US treasury had been printing the country's money. The President had printed enough cash in those few months to fund the entire US economy for more than a year. To that day, the Treasury continued to print. But, that would all stop now.

Rothmayer was the family patriarch. He had personally taken charge of the hit on the President. He glanced back at the television for a brief second before resuming eye contact with his brother.

He pressed his hands to his knees to help himself stand. "That should put an end to it for our lifetime," he said.

The aristocrat turned to his nephew and added, "But you may have to deal with this the next time."

The established patriarch of the family businesses pointed at the TV. "You need to never let what he wanted to do happen, or that will be the end of our way of life."

This family was the largest owner of the Federal Reserve. Tomorrow, the very next day after the president's assassination, those dollars the President had printed would all be recalled. Every bank in the US would keep the dollars as soon as they came in. They'd practically all be confiscated within a year or two. And the families who owned the private Federal Reserve would all be back in business. They'd be printing Federal Reserve notes on overtime, starting tomorrow. The media would be busy covering the assassination and they'd never cover the Federal Reserve. It had all been arranged.

Rothmayer's tone softened and he said, "By the way, how is little Amstel?"

CHAPTER 1

MODERN DAY, ELECTION YEAR, WASHINGTON DC

Adam Youngeagle moved to his left as the man came at him. With his left hand, the Vice President reached out and met the attacker's gun hand, placing his thumb on the back side of the assailant's hand, between the ring and pinky fingers. Adam's right hand came up and supported his left. With lightning speed, he gripped the gun hand and twisted the attacker's wrist inward towards his bicep with a downward thrust, causing the man to lose his grip on the gun. Now at the man's left side, Adam maintained control of the hand, and brought his left leg up behind the man's shoulder and took him to the ground with a thud, executing a nice arm bar. Adam torqued the man's arm.

The trainer barked, "Okay, nice move, but get up. We can't have you take a man to the ground and stay there. As soon as you hit the ground, you need to complete your move and bounce up."

The trainer was direct. He wanted Adam's moves to be subconscious in the unlikely event he ever had to use them.

Adam knew this highly skilled opponent wasn't as easy as the others with whom he'd previously trained. This guy fought the disarm the whole way and it took longer to complete the proper torque.

Since being elected to the office of vice president, Adam had been working out routinely here at the White House athletic center. The Seventeenth Street address was right across Pennsylvania Ave. from the White House. It served as the primary physical fitness center for the employees of the Executive Office of the President. The head of the facility had discreetly brought in this world class trainer, along with some of the most notable MMA and martial arts competitors in the country. Adam used this as his primary workout facility to hone his skills while staying in shape and relieving stress.

Adam stood dripping in sweat and acknowledged what he already knew. "Understood, get out of the situation and make my way to safety."

The trainer nodded once. At first, he hadn't been keen on the idea of training a politician. He was sure he'd have to water down his regimen. But after the first workout with Adam, he had realized Adam wanted anything but that. Wanting to build his already exceptional skills, Adam enjoyed a competitive workout and the excitement helped him maintain a steady routine without boredom. Since going to a regular gym wasn't an option any more, Adam now had the trainers come to him. Usually, it was in the early morning like this, before it got crowded.

The trainer smiled and reframed his previous comment with a lighter tone, saying, "train like your life depends on it."

"Got it." Adam smiled and faced off with the man in front of him again.

The next time around, Adam disarmed the man, bounced up and jogged a few feet away, simulating his getaway. Their training usually ended with something practical, like Adam getting out of a situation.

They had been training for an hour and Adam had worked up a strong sweat. He took his workouts seriously. He wasn't one to socialize much once the sparring started.

Krieger was standing nearby watching. He looked at the clock and said, "Sir, it's about time."

Colonel Don Krieger had become a friend to Adam. Originally brought on by the president to head up security when their election campaign started, Krieger and Adam now worked very closely together. Wearing multiple hats, one of Krieger's areas of authority spanned overseeing the president and vice president's personal security. Being an ex-Marine Special Operations commander who had seen many special operations missions before leading the largest military base east of the Mississippi, Colonel Krieger had grown to respect Adam. Ever since there had been an assassination attempt on Adam and George in the Grand Canyon of Pennsylvania, Krieger's respect for Adam had begun to grow as he'd watched Adam grab a gun from a downed man and engage in the ensuing firefight. Then, a few months later when Adam had been kidnapped by those trying to derail the president's bid to be the first non-politician to become president of the United States, he had seen how Adam had fought off the assailants. When Adam had gone missing, Krieger had watched the recorded footage from closed circuit cameras in the hallway. Adam, the vice presidential candidate at that time, who had a legitimate black belt in a few different styles of martial arts, took out four trained assailants. He would have gotten away, if the last one hadn't stuck him with a tranquilizer in the leg.

Adam was the president's voice of reason on economic issues. He had written about the demise of the middle class and was the foremost voice of the needs for the resurgence of the middle class. That's why there were many that didn't want either him *or* the President to win the reelection. The globalists were genuinely afraid of what they'd do in a second term.

Adam glanced at the clock. "Okay, that's all for today fellas."

After waiting for Adam to do his usual fifty sit-ups with a forty-five-pound plate behind his head, Krieger escorted Adam to an adjoining room, where he took a call. Adam rolled his eyes as he listened to the House Majority Leader explain why they needed to spend so much more money than they had the previous year. It was obvious that the Majority Leader was saying that the president would not get support from the establishment to cut costs. Unfortunately, he was right. Adam and the president weren't in a position to cut spending. Actually, the plan was to cut massive amounts of waste and run a surplus after winning the election. Until then, it was spending as usual. Adam hung up. He needed to keep moving.

* * *

Adam stood in the shower, letting the warm water run down his back. His thoughts wandered. The president had been recruited by some in the military. It was actually the marines. They knew the country was about to fall to the hands of the globalists.

But no one knew Adam. He reflected on how grateful he was to be the vice president. President George Carnegie had met Adam through some others while Adam was living in an unfurnished apartment in a barn in northern Pennsylvania. Adam had built his family's failing business to over one hundred million dollars in revenue and over that in profits in just under fifteen years. Then, through a series of ill-advised moves, uncontrolled spending and paying well connected people too much, the family business was lost. Adam hadn't ever been given the stock he was owed, so he had to go to work for other people. He wasn't suited for that.

Adam knew he wasn't alone in his economic struggle. After a few years, he understood the plight of almost every other working person. He'd been a top producer at the jobs he'd had, but it didn't matter. Only politically correct and well-connected people got ahead. There was no use being a top producer in corporate America, the culture had changed too much.

Then providence had smiled on him. Now, Adam was the vice president. He and the president had fought the establishment tooth and nail. The establishment had used every trick in the book and invented a few new ones to stop them. But the president was a stud. He was a master at engaging people during his rallies and getting his messages out. Sure, Adam fed him some key talking points, but the president was the one out there tirelessly engaging the people, and dealing with politicians and the media.

Adam had a different role in the administration. Working behind the scenes, he did more of the dirty work than anyone would ever know. That was fine with him. Together they had given the country many wins and more importantly, hope.

The country was being attacked by an enemy that, until he and the president had got into office, had been content to devour the country slowly. But, now with the president and Adam having so much success, the globalists were in a full out panic and had suddenly begun using tactics never before deployed. They shamelessly yielded the power their positions afforded. They knew that behind the scenes, the president was lining up charges to take them out legally. Record numbers of politicians from both parties had already retired rather than face prosecution. They knew the heat was coming. Now, the deep state feared what the president would do to them if he was reelected.

For that reason, Adam understood that the establishment would attack them with something new. He thought, *what will these globalists do next?*

Adam turned around, letting the water run down his head and the front of his face. Then he shut the hot water off quickly. Ice cold water sprayed out. His muscles tensed and he took deep breaths. Ending his showers this way invigorated him.

He turned off the faucet and wiped the water from his face. It was time to head to the office. He had some things to address before he and Krieger had an interview to do.

CHAPTER 2

Six hours ahead of DC, it was midday, and the transformed city of London was bustling with activity. The head of the world banking empire, Amstel Rothmayer, felt a sense of satisfaction as he stared out of the window of his opulent penthouse suite. Amstel Rothmayer was the nephew of the man who'd ordered the hit on Kennedy after President Kennedy had got rid of the most lucrative and risk-free cash flow the world had ever seen, the Federal Reserve.

He turned and looked over to the Senator who was seated at the opposite side of his desk, then up to one of the large television screens on the wall. The height of the stock market didn't settle well with him. It created overall wealth and brought hope to the middle class of America. Even worse, they were beginning to realize that the globalists were working within the US government to put higher taxes and regulations on industries. They were realizing that, years ago, when the trade barriers had reached a tipping point, those businesses had left the United States and moved to the globalist properties where they had no environmental laws, no labor, health or safety laws, and could pay people little. It was a windfall for Rothmayer and his cohorts, but the middle class was beginning to realize that the elites were prospering by moving from country to country using these techniques.

Rothmayer and his family, along with their banking partners, had transformed most of Europe into a socialist society and had controlled both political parties in the United States for decades. Through shell corporations, funds, and a variety of other legal entities, they quietly controlled well over half of the wealth of the world and paid almost no taxes. His life of luxury included houses no president could afford, and lands and private islands where he could indulge all of his cravings for women; the younger the better. Who were others to say what was an appropriate age? Others had no authority over him and his kind. He was free to do what he wanted on his private estates around the globe, but now he needed to be more cautious in the United States.

He could sit back and enjoy himself, but his way was shameless human nature, craving more, taking more, a true Darwinian, survival of the fittest. In his sixties now, he had worked all his life to bring the United States under his total control.

Rothmayer had a strong sense within him that he wasn't accustomed to. The president of the US had said publicly that the Federal Reserve was the biggest current threat to the country. Luckily, he and other banking families and their business partners owned controlling interests in the media, and very few of the working class saw the president's comments.

But, with the rise of alternative media that used the internet and cell phones to share their messages, globalists had begun to lose control over information to which the working class was exposed. This necessitated that he used untraceable money and connections to control that information. It was working to a degree, but they needed to take it to another level before the president took further action.

The senator, whose trip to London was cloaked in fake reasons, just sat there and waited for the money. Amstel Rothmayer hadn't acknowledged the senator for a few minutes. He was bought and paid for. Rothmayer had enough on him that he need not worry about the senator ever betraying him. Rothmayer, after all, didn't want to end up in a US federal prison himself. The senator had come to feign negotiating, supposedly to improve relationships in the wake of some of the President's trade moves. But he wasn't here to make the United States bigger and stronger. Heck, he'd never stay in office with that platform, because there would be no money for his election campaigns. His money came from those who would only give to enriching themselves. That didn't mean enriching the wealth or culture of the middle class.

Although it was minimal so far, resurgence in the United States wasn't supposed to happen. It was the damn president. President George Carnegie and Vice President Adam Youngeagle had immediately begun reducing regulations to stimulate the economy. When the economy exceeded or surpassed three percent GDP growth, globalists worked feverishly to stop the surge.

Established political families realized the risk being posed to their aristocratic positions due to the president's initiatives. Fearful of being voted out of office, they passed watered-down tax breaks for the middle class and a reduced corporate tax rate so they could later claim that they were helping them. In truth, it was a pittance compared to what they had taken from the middle class over the previous decades and it was only temporary.

The president, George Carnegie, undid many executive orders from the previous administration and implemented some of his own. On the heels of numerous resignations and some new blood in Congress, the establishment used their media and unfounded investigations to distract the President and the public from the true reason he was in office: to save the middle class.

With the mid-term elections over, the president focused on several items to remind citizens that he knew what they wanted and needed. He had played the political game long enough. He was talking about what he would do during his second term. His announcement that he would push for the repeal of the seventeenth amendment was a shot across the bow. He tweeted and explained in speeches that establishment politicians had control over Congress, and that many had amassed hundreds of millions, and recently over a billion dollars, of wealth at the expense of the middle class.

Businesses across the country were preparing for the president's planned proposal for the next phase of tax reductions. It would lower taxes even further for companies who proved that a majority of their stock was owned by middle class American citizens. This possibility sent the president's approval rating to an all-time high.

Because of these bold moves, the country was seeing a resurgence few had thought possible.

George and Adam's policies would create that revival and change the social outlook to nationalism for at least a hundred years, but this was unacceptable to the globalists. Unacceptable to Rothmayer.

These globalists, led by Rothmayer, had worked for decades to design and implement the progressive movement, a diabolical scheme to ignore the constitution and allow them to capture the country's wealth. One of their strongest tools, the Federal Reserve, was increasing interest rates in an attempt to thwart the resurgence, but the president was taking control of the Fed.

Devint Sordid, the right-hand man for the globalist banking families, had orchestrated a number of false flags; real incidents that happened but the media reported reasons other than what he and his associates had composed. The Las Vegas massacre they'd orchestrated was blamed on a lone gunman. In reality, Sordid had proved that they could orchestrate mass casualties and pull out before being discovered.

A man entered the room and placed a sheet of legal-size paper on Rothmayer's desk and said, "And my Lord, the last of the trucks have arrived."

Rothmayer had requested to be notified when the last of the gold was transferred to their multiple holding places. This gold was untraceable. It was money he and his kind used to manipulate governments and entire economies. It had no record; no taxes were ever paid on it, and it was their flexibility, their way of having black operations. This brought a feeling of security to the aging aristocrat. He nodded deliberately, signaling for the man to leave the room.

Rothmayer slid the paper to the other side of the desk, signaling for the senator to pick it up, saying, "There you go. That should be enough money."

When the US fell, the rest of this nationalist resurgence around the world would also wither away and the world would be theirs to control.

The globalist bankers, in the name of the Federal Reserve, had taken similar economic actions in the past. The lengths they would now go to would depend on if the president could be forced into submission.

Congress was still mostly controlled by those who had been compromised, and they were keeping the spending up. That would feed the globalists' operations.

However, a senator had been secretly made aware of the president's plan to run a surplus, and frighteningly to him, it was viable. This couldn't happen. If the middle class saw a surplus and a surging economy, giving them more discretionary spending, all accomplished by a real estate billionaire who had never been in politics before, the ruse of taxing and high economic spending that had taken them decades to instill into the beliefs of Americans would be shattered. Plans for bankers to have global economic control would be set back fifty years. This couldn't happen. Rothmayer would ensure it *wouldn't* happen.

The senator placed the paper in his upper left suit pocket, and would keep his jacket on until he returned stateside.

Rothmayer was being proactive. He had several things in process that would most likely bring down the president - and that cowboy of a vice president, Adam Youngeagle, with him.

The one thing that keeps the spirits of elites up is knowing that they have not played all the cards in their hand. They are about to cunningly reach into their sleeves and play their Royal Straight Flush. After over a year of planning, they were about to kick off their well-orchestrated plan to bring the economy to a screeching halt. That was only the first phase.

CHAPTER 3

Adam leaned back in his chair, feeling enthusiastic about the day. His main office in the Eisenhower Executive Office Building was a short walk from the White House athletic center, and right across the street from the White House. It housed the President's Executive Office staff, including the office of the First Lady, Colonel Krieger's office and Adam's working office, which was much larger than the office he had at the White House. It also housed offices of Management and Budget and the Special Agent in charge of the presidential and vice presidential Secret Service Protective Division.

The majestic building looked like a magnificent, rich mansion. Featured in countless movies, it was well recognized. Originally the State War and Navy Building, it had been built in phases and had taken twelve years to construct in the late 1800s. The richness of the interior decorating was unparalleled anywhere in Washington. The thick molding and chair rails that decorated the rooms were exquisite. Paintings were all chosen to preserve the historical significance that the offices commanded. Even the hallways were marbled with magnificently adorned pillars every fourteen feet and crown moldings a foot in height. Every stairway and balcony showed the richness of the country.

It had been two hours since his early morning workout, and Adam just finished all the calls he had to make. He was scheduled to interview someone that afternoon, but he knew Colonel Krieger would be downstairs in the CIA offices, listening in on the preliminary interviews of the new recruit for his team, so Adam thought he'd pop in unexpectedly and listen in, before his lunch with Gabby.

He sat back reflected on the intimate lunch he had planned with the President's press secretary. He visualized her blue eyes and how they lit up a split second before her smile. He pictured that smile and the shape of her lips which she always moistened with some shade of red lip stick. He thought about her perfect nose and her auburn hair hanging smoothly to her shoulders. Gabby was gifted with a complexion that her native American grandmother had bequeathed her. Adam knew she would be beautiful for decades to come.

Being that Gabby was the press secretary, they had plenty of reasons to meet. But Adam was having lunch brought into his office. It was easier that way, and they could have more freedom with their flirtatious glances and looks than when they were out in public. Adam and Gabby had kept their relationship a secret and, although Adam suspected the president knew, they never spoke about it. Their first kiss had been the night before the election, and their relationship had started after the election. After working side by side throughout the campaign, they'd become good friends and knew each other well. Gabby was the first to mention that they must keep their relationship from the press. The media was going after the president with everything they could muster and the last thing he needed was a scandal. Not that it would be a scandal, they were both single. It was just that Gabby knew how they operated, and they'd turn it into something they would use as a tool against the president. Besides that, and because of her extensive media experience, Gabby had been instrumental in managing media relations during the campaign. At that time, she had used Adam's looks and fitness to make him one of the most eligible bachelors in the country. It was a major help with the woman's vote and he also had a great approval rating with men. When he was kidnapped and then escaped, she'd used those exploits to help increase his approval ratings even further and she wanted to keep it that way going during the reelection campaign.

* * *

A half hour later, Adam slowly opened the door and entered the room where Krieger, his newest recruit Mindy, along with an HR Director and another women Adam didn't know, were listening in on the interview process through the speaker phone. This was the far right of three adjoining rooms being used for the interview process. It was the listening room where people could judge the responses of the interviewee and take notes. The room directly to the left served as a buffer or intermediary area to the next room, where the interview was taking place. Even though the rooms were sound proofed, it was standard operating procedure to have an unoccupied room between the person being interviewed and those listening, because most of the rooms on this side of the hallway, including these, had adjoining doors. It was convenient too. When this interview was over, Krieger, who was the next person scheduled to interview Davis, simply had to walk down the hallway to the interview room. This setup allowed addition people to listen to the interview process, and come and go as their schedules allowed.

Surprised, the HR Director stood and said, "Mr. Vice President."

Adam instantly knew they must be on mute, but glanced at the speaker phone to see the lit button to be sure. He had already established a reputation for being the most approachable and friendly VP ever. Because of this, and his well-publicized exploits leading up to the election, the respect they had for him was genuine. He motioned for them to stay seated and said quietly, "Hi, Val, good to see you," and he made an open-handed gesture to the other woman along with saying, "Hi."

Speaking in a low tone, Valerie offered a quick introduction. "Mr. Vice President, this is La Juan."

Adam smiled directly at her and said, "Nice to meet you."

Adam took note that Krieger had two women with him. *Krieger's always thinking.* It was good practice at any time, and especially with some of the allegations going around Washington these days. Having three people there at all times ensured that the perception was one of open professionalism.

The interview process was as much a formality as it was to ensure there weren't any surprises. Krieger would conduct the next interview of Davis, even though he had known Davis for years and had talked to him about the opportunity. Then, an hour after Krieger finished, Adam would conduct his own interview of Davis, a man he already knew.

Adam sat next to Krieger at the conference table. He knew Krieger always personally interviewed everyone on his team. Adam leaned over to Krieger and quietly said, "I figured you'd be here, and thought I'd just stop by and listen in."

Davis was a shoo-in as the next addition to the team which would work closely protecting Adam. Krieger was not only responsible for the Presidential and Vice President's personal security, he was quietly increasing the staff of two teams which were looking into nefarious deep state operatives and some of the unsavory characters that had infiltrated the government and other areas of society. One team was a privately organized black operation out of the control of the US government. Their mission was working in the field tracking HVTs (High Value Targets), better known as terrorists. They tracked those in the US, uncovering their network and, where necessary, disposing of those plotting terrorist activities and those conducting deep state activities. The other team was on the grid, protecting the president and vice president.

Krieger had gradually replaced the presidential detail with his own hand-picked team. Because he knew the deep state had infiltrated even those directly around the president, he was extremely careful with his vetting process, leaning heavily on those he had worked with in the past. He wanted to ensure that every person on his team was a patriot.

CIA field operative Sumner Davis had been working undercover for Sergeant Major Briggs on an operation that was being shut down at the end of the month. The previous administration had been trucking illegal immigrants of questionable character across the border, with rumors that something else was being mixed in with their shipments. The operation had stopped trucking illegals since the new administration took office, and they had recently been told they were being shut down. Davis, just back in town, had sent a message that he wanted to relay something personally to Briggs. Briggs was out of the city and had asked Davis to give the information directly to Krieger at the end of his interview. Davis had uncovered something of such grave importance that he didn't want to use electronic devices to disclose the information.

Krieger and the others calmly listened. Davis showed exceptional knowledge and people skills.

As the interview was winding down, Krieger looked at the time on his phone. Turning to Adam, he said, "Sir, you may want to head back upstairs. That drill starts in a half hour, and there'll be some extra eyes around here."

The CIA had scheduled an exercise simulating an infiltrator in the facility. Krieger wanted Adam back in his office before the exercise began. He was privy to the exercise, although it wasn't his to command, because it was a CIA operation.

Ever since December 19, 2007, when a fire had broken out on the second floor near the ceremonial office of Dick Cheney, the CIA had begun drills for suspected infiltrators. According to reports filed by the fire department, the fire had been electrical and may have started in a closet, but there were rumors that a disgruntled individual had been stalking the building.

As Adam stood to leave, through the speaker phone, he heard a knock on the door of the interview room. In the interview room, a heavy-set human resources person stood and walked towards the door.

The door opened and those in the interview room saw the man who had knocked was carrying a box. *Gun!* Davis thought to himself. A split second later the first shot ripped through the HR person's head, splattering a bloody mist in the air and sending the dead man to the ground in a heap. Another shot followed and hit a second man as the box fell to the floor. The man entering the room moved forward. Davis saw another man over the shooter's shoulder just as the third shot felled the second female HR person.

The tap in her head left no doubt in Davis's mind that *this was a hit*. He knew why and knew he had nowhere to go.

* * *

Krieger, recognizing the sound of suppressed gunfire through the phone, had already unholstered his gun.

They listened in shock as the scene played out as if in slow motion.

* * *

As his mind worked at an extreme speed, Davis moved to position himself behind a rather stocky man who instinctively stood. The big man jolted as he was hit.

The fourth person went down from the second shooter.

The assassins were now inside the room, determined to finish their mission. They were proficient in their shot placement, professional in their movements and in the way they held their suppressed weapons.

* * *

Krieger barked at one agent who had drawn her pistol, "You stay here with the vice president." Pointing to the other female agent, who had just won the short-range pistol shooting competition, he commanded, "Mindy, you come with me, stay close."

They immediately advanced through the door and into the middle room. Krieger's hand cupped the door knob to the interview room. "On my count."

* * *

Davis's thoughts were interrupted by a burning sensation. He'd taken a shot that had come through the thick man behind whom he had taken refuge. Well-schooled in evasive positioning, it didn't give the man a clean shot. Falling back, his strength weakening, he couldn't hold the body of the office worker any longer and he collapsed backwards with the large limp body half on top of him.

So, this is how it's going to end ... they've got me ...!

I never got the chance to tell Krieger how the globalists were about to make their move to taken control of the country.

* * *

Krieger looked at Mindy, who immediately nodded. He turned the knob.

CHAPTER 4

Amstel Rothmayer turned from the window of his penthouse at the global banking headquarters on the outskirts of London to hear the answer to his question. The patriarch representing the globalist banking empire needed some reassurance from the one other man in his office.

Alexander Sordid had funded the hit that was taking place at that very moment in Washington.

He assured Rothmayer, "We've taken care of all the loose ends, with one exception. One man left for Washington and our sources tell us he placed phone calls where there was something of importance he wouldn't discuss. He wanted to debrief his superiors in person immediately upon his return."

"And you suspect he knows something?" Rothmayer asked.

Sordid disclosed, "We believe he works for the new administration somewhere under Colonel Krieger. He infiltrated our trucking operations after getting through the screening."

"I see," Rothmayer said in a low, concerned tone. Being the leader of the globalist bankers, he wanted to know about the most important deception since his ancestors had started the Federal Reserve. He knew Sordid funded a trucking operation that had brought illegal immigrants into the United States during the previous administration. The President had put an end to it, but his concern wasn't their knowing about bringing illegal immigrants from terrorist countries into the US, that had leaked out a long time ago. It was what they were taking *out* of the country on those same trucks and buses that he was concerned with.

"He's at the Eisenhower building. He has an interview with a superior officer this afternoon. We are taking care of it," Sordid said forcefully, knowing it wasn't an ideal setting, but it had to be done.

Alexander Sordid was a self-made billionaire. What most people didn't know was that the wealthiest banking families had helped bankroll his ascension to power and, even today, continued to funnel money to him. With Sordid playing a public role, the banking families could remain off the radar until they completed their takeover of the United States. Then, when the US fell, they'd have an open path to controlling the global economy.

The banker acknowledged, "I assume you'll handle it similarly to the last one."

They had assassinated one other person in a federal building in Washington. They had kept it out of the media. The government had no incentive to broadcast that one of its secure buildings had been infiltrated, and these men surely didn't want anyone to know. Those assassins were never caught, and both had been killed shortly afterwards.

"Similarly, yes. The guns are already planted, and they don't know who hired them."

The Senator had left the banker's office a few hours ago. After a brief hesitation, the banker asked, "The senator give you the information?"

Sordid nodded. "It was in his best interest."

The banker understood. "Is The Cleric taking care of it?"

Sordid nodded. The Cleric was his main person on the streets orchestrating the civil unrest, bribing politicians and working with the deep state within the government. It was a nice arrangement. The globalist bankers, headed by Rothmayer funneled money to Sordid. He in turn, funneled money to The Cleric and others like him. The Cleric had a residence in the USA and did the dirty work. This way, Sordid himself had less exposure and the bankers, especially Rothmayer, had virtually no exposure. Sordid wasn't the only person doing this, but because he was one of the more well-known, the banking families compensated him extremely well. He was fine with that.

"Will we be able to get them out?"

Sordid answered, "Everything's taken care of. We have an exercise scheduled and, in the confusion, they'll be able to get out with the first responder teams." He knew the banker didn't want details, just to know that there would be no loose ends.

That handled, it was time to talk about other pressing issues. Sordid and the banking patriarch got together infrequently, and when they did, the old man wanted to discuss key initiatives. After all, he had funded tens of billions in black gold and dollars in order to achieve their objectives.

"What about the budget and, specifically, the president's plans to run a surplus?" The banker asked.

This was the primary concern of the banking families. The Senate minority leader had informed them that the president planned to run a surplus. The president had been in office long enough now to realize how simple that would be. He began disseminating it among a few of his top aides. The president planned to make other countries pay their remaining fair share of the NATO budget, saving almost four hundred billion, and then enact the cuts that the Citizens Against Government Waste (CAGW) published, which would 'save taxpayers $336 billion in the first year."[2]

The president also planned to cut 250 billion that was illegally being funneled overseas without authorization. He'd learned this from the team he'd created to review the NSA database. That made a significant surplus without any real cuts to anyone in America, almost guaranteeing the support of the American people.

If the president continued undoing the unfair tariffs other countries had put on the US and if he made new deals, he could run a billion-dollar surplus in a second term.

The banker bellowed, "That can't happen!"

Sordid appeared confident. "Understood. It won't."

They both knew their history that, *in 1821, when reliable tariff statistics began, nearly all imports (95.5%) were taxed, and duties imposed equaled 43.2% of the total value of all imports and 45% of the dutiable value.*[3] These tariffs were the means by which the US counteracted countries that manipulated the currencies.

But, as the economy matured, the US instituted better environmental, health and safety and labor laws. As time went on, these bankers wanted to exploit these regulations in the US, so they began paying off senators. Congress largely gave up on setting the details of US trade policy. Starting in 1934, it delegated to the president authority to negotiate trade deals with other countries.[4]

They had also learned that the president planned to run a trillion-dollar surplus by implementing a fair trades surplus act. According to PEW research, World Bank data, 2018, the Tariff rate, applied, weighted mean, all products,[5] can increase government revenue by at least another 250 billion by just having ten to twenty percent of goods come back to the US to be manufactured.

Sordid added, "The senator has assured us that he and his companions will not allow any of this at this time. He has assured us we're good until the election."

"I understand. The part that's unsettling is that the president has gotten to a few of the senators and they've turned on us." Rothmayer hesitated and then continued, "We're okay for today, but how long will it last?"

Up until now, no citizen had reached the office of president without the total support of the globalist bankers. George Carnegie was the first.

Rothmayer then changed the subject to something more current. "I see the social media programs are in place and they appear to be working. What about the president? He appears to be starting to investigate it."

Sordid knew the president had done several internet searches of himself and found that the good things he was doing were being filtered off the first pages.

"He won't get congressional support," Sordid said, referencing their control over Congress.

Rothmayer continued, "What about the possibility of an executive order?"

Sordid nodded in agreement. "He could do that, but soon he'll have too many other things to worry about. Even if he did, we have men on the inside, and we'll have it worded so we can get around it. If he forces the issue and gets specific, we'll mobilize resistance and law suits."

"How are the funds holding out for marketing?" Rothmayer was referring to the funding for the media. Most of the mainstream media had lost well over thirty percent of their viewership, and Sordid had to find creative ways to keep them propped up financially.

"We've been able to fund them until the next budget. The President's so busy he didn't know anything about the increased funding being funneled to us in the last extension. That may become an issue if someone catches it next time," Sordid answered.

"That's one area where we can't take any short cuts, so ensure they're well supported."

Sordid nodded. "Of course."

Sir Rothmayer had other banking issues to take care of. He got up. "Let me know when that last loose end is taken care of." He meant he wanted to know when the man on Krieger's team who had possibly found out too much, had been terminated. "I'll be expecting good news very soon. This is going to be a very busy day."

"Yes, it is, a very busy day," Sordid agreed.

Neither man could imagine what was happening in the Eisenhower building at that very moment.

CHAPTER 5

Krieger exploded through the door with his shoulder and took a step to the right, his weapon at the ready and Mindy to his left. The man on the other side of the conference table was in his sights. Krieger squeezed the trigger twice.

These two men had shot everyone in the room, and Krieger had targeted the man who was advancing to finish Davis off with a head shot. Only the deep state would attempt something like this, here and now, and though they may not have known it, they were mere feet from the Vice President.

His heart rate surged and pumped extra oxygenated blood through his entire body as he moved right, knowing he didn't have enough time to squeeze off one more shot before the second assailant squeezed one off at him. Mindy set her sights on the second man just inside the doorway. Her perfectly placed shot hit the man mid-chest, sending him back into the corner of the room against the door jamb. She maintained her foot placement. Following him in her sights, she completed her short burst of three 9mm slugs to the man's chest.

Krieger's man had sprayed shots as he fell backwards.

Scanning the room, Krieger saw an image in the closing door. He yelled, "Watcher!" That was their term for someone doing overwatch, or in this case, someone watching the hallway to ensure a safe exit for the two inside.

"Secure the room," was all Mindy heard as Krieger rushed towards the open doorway.

Two rooms down, the agent assigned to stay with Adam was guarding the door to the adjoining rooms. She failed to notice as Adam opened the door into the hall. A man was running directly towards him. With no time to evade, Adam cocked his left hand and sprang from the security of the doorway to execute a perfect C strike with his open hand to the upper part of the man's throat. He followed through with all his might. The man's feet flew into the air over his head. Adam continued to follow through until the man was horizontal with the ground. Then Adam executed a hammer-fist strike to the bridge of his nose, sending the man's head cracking against the marble floor.

Adam sensed something coming at him, then he heard shots and his whole body jolted.

The force of a 200-pound man hitting him hard disoriented Adam. He went from being on one knee, finishing off the first man, to being knocked over with another man on top of him. Adam's adrenalin surged. He exploded to stand. He took a deep breath and his knees remained flexed; he was ready to move in either direction. As his lungs filled with air, he realized the man at his feet wasn't moving and hadn't latched on to him.

Adam saw blood on his suit. He rubbed his hands over his chest; no pain. Krieger had charged down the hallway and had his gun pointed at the man on the floor. Adam realized Krieger had shot the man as he was charging towards him, and the man had fallen on Adam in a heap. Krieger bent down and turned over the hitman. He was dead.

Krieger pushed the top and bottom of his belt buckle together, completing the connection for his speaker. His voice resonated with urgency through his microphone to the person in charge of all his communications. "Mauricio, get the whole team down to the basement. Shots fired, code red — this is not a drill. The vice president is at risk."

Krieger pulled out a set of carbon steel hand cuffs and cuffed the man Adam had downed. He stood and shook his head, looked at Adam and said, "They must have had two men watching the outside of the door." He realized he had only seen one, solidifying that these were trained operatives.

A moment later, the agent from the conference room Adam had been in ran past them. She went down the hallway, broke open the glass case full of bullet proof vests, grabbed a few and ran back up the hallway to Adam and Krieger. Handing one to each, she said, "Here put these on."

Upstairs on the first floor, no one paid any attention to the long-term CIA agent casually walking out through security on his way to the street.

CHAPTER 6

Within seconds, Major Mauricio appeared at one end of the hallway. He ran to Krieger's aid. Support began pouring in behind him.

Krieger ordered, "Get the vice president up to the second floor and stay with him."

"Roger that," Mauricio replied.

Krieger added, "And secure the area. The vice president was not here, and he was never in any danger, understand? I want a full blackout on this."

"Understood." Mauricio turned and looked at the soldier to his right. "Alvarez, you come with me."

Mauricio turned to escort the vice president to the secure elevator.

Krieger had just flipped the unconscious assailant over like a child when Mindy poked her head out of the interview room urgently called down the hall for him. "Colonel, Davis is hit bad, but he needs to talk to you now. He wants to tell you something."

Krieger thought, *what was the reason for a professional hit like this? Who set it up and why? Davis was an undercover truck driver who had transported illegals across the border in the previous administration, although that wasn't exactly above top-secret intel at this point. It was known in the right circles and had stopped. It must have been something else, but what?*

Krieger came through the doorway and directed Mindy, "Don't let anyone in here yet."

"Affirmative," Mindy said, then added, "The room's secure, sir."

After Mindy had pulled the dead administrator's lifeless body off Davis to check his condition, Davis pleaded to speak with Krieger.

Krieger knelt next to Davis. Blood from Davis's cough spewed onto Krieger's suit.

Davis strained to speak. "You know about the trucks bringing illegals over the boarder?"

Krieger nodded. He knew Davis didn't have much time. He could see Davis fading as his breath gargled with blood. "We know, don't talk… save your strength."

Davis squeezed Krieger's lapel and pulled him closer with his last bit of strength, and hissed, "Gold, they were taking the gold across the border."

This was something else, something totally different.

Krieger asked, "What gold?"

Davis wheezed, "They were taking gold across the border in trucks and buses. Illegals coming across were a diversion… It was the gold."

Krieger was startled. "They were taking gold out of the country in the trucks… then they brought illegals in?"

Davis nodded. His strength was fading, and his eyes had started to close.

Krieger passionately questioned, "Who… who was orchestrating this?"

Davis pulled Krieger closer. He whispered a message, then wheezed his last breath.

Krieger stood, actuated his speaker phone and said to Mauricio, "After you secure the Vice President, get a local team here immediately. Quarantine this area and get it cleaned up in twenty minutes and keep the place secure until the scene is clean."

The CIA had the best equipment in the world to clean up a crime scene, and they could do it in under half an hour.

Krieger pondered Davis's last comment. *"They're pulling the trigger."*

"They're pulling the trigger."

* * *

George opened the door and stepped out on the Truman balcony. It was dark now. The president stood, legs apart, his hands on his hips. The expression on his face was fraught with anger. This was a character seldom seen by anyone. He looked past the south lawn of the White House and gazed out to the Washington monument. Not only had he underestimated the number of deep state operatives, he hadn't understood that they'd be working hand in hand with him pretending to come to his aid, while at the same time undermining him, leaking key information. In addition, all their fake news took time to counter. It was all designed to slow him down so he wouldn't expose what life could be like if the country were run by patriotic people who had the nation's best interests at heart.

If he succeeded doing what he wanted to do in his second term, he'd expose that Washington was almost totally infiltrated by globalists. He'd expose that lower taxes and an agenda to strengthen the nation would give people a dramatic improvement in their lifestyle. Doing that would change the political landscape towards nationalism for decades to come.

He had just begun to understand the significance of the money that politicians and deep state made on kickbacks, making themselves rich, and he had gradually been exposing it to the people using social media. These payoffs were massive, and included past presidents, vice presidents, the speaker and countless others. With a second term, he and Adam would bring these people to justice.

The warm Washington breeze came from the North Atlantic current. It smelled fresh and clean.

George thought. *It started before I was sworn in, and it continues ...*

Right after George had taken office, someone had tipped off ISIS about the whereabouts of a SEAL team that was going on a rescue mission. The SEAL team had flown directly into an ambush.

It had been hard for George to make those calls to the parents, knowing that someone had leaked the whereabouts of the team to ISIS. Of course, he couldn't reveal that information.

The terrorists had hit the SEAL team and taken only one casualty. The rest had got away clean. The SEALs' backup teams had responded quickly, but the orchestration of such a precise attack suggested more sophisticated planning and execution than a typical ISIS attack. Even the way the team had been called to that area was beyond suspect. It defied SEAL protocol. George couldn't talk about that either. It was obvious that something had been set in motion to reduce his stature, but it hadn't worked.

There were only a few people who knew about it, and Adam had used that to talk George and Krieger into finding the leakers and bringing them to justice — officially or unofficially, depending on what they found.

George's mind focused back to the present as Adam was leaving a meeting and heading over to the White House. George was anxious to hear Adam's perspective of what had happened at the Eisenhower building that day.

The President reached into his pocket and pulled out his cell phone. He saw a tweet from the Deplorable Pet Lover @petluvers4Trump. He read it and smiled. He followed a few people through dummy accounts which forwarded tweets to another dummy account he regularly accessed. The President had a passing thought about replying, but decided not to. He was busy and needed to think. As he shut his phone off and put it back into his pocket and thought to himself, *one of these days I'll retweet this guy.*

He looked up at the night sky to the north and noticed a royal blueish hue dancing around in the distance. He froze, and focused on it. He was too far south for the Aurora Borealis. A moment later the colors vanished.

The President stood there, feeling that there was something more he needed to do.

Little did he know that the deep state had planned to escalate the civil anxiety.

* * *

Loud cracking shots echoed through an auditorium in the heartland of the country, and things appeared to happen in slow motion. The ball bounced freely as the high school basketball game came to a sudden stop. Fright fueled the players' endorphins.

The shooter fired indiscriminately as he sprayed his hate. In the instant it took people to process what was happening, shots also echoed from the opposite side of the gymnasium floor. It was an orchestrated attack by two coordinated assailants.

Players and fans scattered. Many leapt off the stands and scurried out the doors.

Several in the thickest parts of the crowd succumbed when lead ripped through them. Panicked, the crowd flooded towards the edges of the bleachers. There was a mad rush to get to the nearest exits with no thoughts of who they were trampling. Women carried or shielded the young.

In seconds the extended magazine was empty.

He's reloading another magazine! A teacher stood frozen in this fleeting moment of turmoil while people flooded over the bleachers all around him.

Jim Burnor had been a teacher at the school, but had never seen this man before. When Burnor realized what was happening, he pulled out his small Sig Sauer P229, the same handgun plain clothed secret service use when they're guarding the president. While in a moment of uncertainty, he felt another man stop right next to him.

Marquis Williams, whose flight instinct had overtaken him, had jumped off the edge of the bleachers and was headed towards the door when he noticed Burnor standing with his gun in his hand. The big ex-teacher was obviously frightened and contemplating engaging the men.

Their eyes met. People literally bounced off the large former teacher as Williams pulled out his hand gun. As the sea of bodies squished through the gymnasium doors behind them, Burnor looked at Williams's Smith & Wesson M&P 9mm. Burnor nodded. He pushed forward. Williams followed.

"Former teacher," Burnor offered.

Marquis nodded. His throat chocked up. No words came to his already dry mouth. He swallowed hard. He turned his attention back towards the active shooter. It had only been seconds since the inception of the attack, but the damage was piling up. Every second counted.

What Williams didn't know was that coming in late and sitting at the edge of the bleachers had saved his life. Now a spirit of responsibility had overtaken him. This middle aged, soft-spoken black man understood that there was no other country on earth to defend. Nowhere else to be free.

They both ensured that they had one in the chamber. Simultaneously safeties went off.

There was a distinct sound of an empty magazine. They didn't have time for words. With widened eyes meeting, they nodded and ran out onto the wood floor. Williams turned right to engage the closer assailant. His target had already ejected his empty magazine. It hit the floor. A replacement was in his hand. The sight and distinct sound of the magazine being slapped into place sent a shiver of fear through Williams's entire body. With the wall in the background of his target, this father of two began firing.

Meanwhile, the former teacher knew he must take the man at the other side of the auditorium. He barreled forward across the gymnasium floor, closing the distance, his pistol held out in front.

Burnor saw the rage in the face of the black-haired assailant shooting into the crowd. He kept the pistol pointed forward. He wasn't as agile as he used to be, and the gun bounced uncontrollably. He had gotten his concealed carry permit and had gone to the range and the woods around his cabin several times a year, but that wasn't enough for him to become anything more than an average shot.

Without steadying his weapon, Burnor squeezed the trigger prematurely. The assailant heard the shots whiz by. He turned the barrel in Burnor's direction. Jim, as if in slow motion, saw the barrel of the terrorist's gun was about to point right at him. Instinct took over and the former fullback dove forward and bounced hard off the parquet gymnasium floor. He came to a sudden stop. He gasped out air. His move was graceless, but gained him a fleeting second. Shots tracked over his head. His eyes had closed from fear. He forced them open, squinting. The sights were lined up as if by divine intervention or sheer luck. Saying a prayer to himself, he suddenly felt a calmness. His thick hands engulfed his pistol. He steadied. Shot twice. The stunned assailant jolted back.

Never having seen a man shot before, Burnor wasn't going to wait to see what happened. His strength kept the sights almost in line. He realigned slightly. Squeezed… squeezed.

Automatic shots projected well over Burnor's head and through the ceiling as the assailant fell back. His shots punctuated the distant wall in a constant flow until the last were fired as the terrorist folded violently into the bleachers. He went limp.

In the meantime, Williams had taken the other assailant by surprise. He had advanced and crouched to sturdy his shooting position. As the terrorist finished a sweeping motion from left to right, he had seen Williams. As the dark-haired man's eyes widened, Williams had shot true, hitting him in the abdomen. Williams followed through with a few more shots, squeezing the trigger. Williams had no idea how many shots he took, let alone how many had hit the man.

Finally, there was no more gunfire. Only chaos. The smell of burnt powder filled the gymnasium.

Each man instinctively looked around to check for other terrorists. There were none. Simultaneously, across the gym from each other, the teacher and Williams's eyes met again. They slowly stood. The terrorist Burnor had engaged was draped over the first row of bleachers. He was perfectly still. But Williams's target was still moving. Burnor jogged towards Williams. They advanced on the terrorist who was gulping for air and bleeding out on the floor.

Williams kicked the foreigner's gun further away. The terrorist was breathing heavily. The teacher recognized that the man was of mid-eastern descent. Then it registered that in the scurry of screams and shots, it was the words "Allah Akbar" that the man had shouted. The teacher knew the true meaning: "Allah is greater than your God or government."

Williams had never thought he'd be in this position. But he had prepared himself just in case. He took another step closer to the man who now had a kind of sick look of happiness on his face. The terrorist mouthed something Williams couldn't understand, then smiled.

Standing a step behind Williams, Burnor offered, "He says death to the infidels."

Then Burnor watched as Williams reached into a concealed carry holster and pulled out a clip. Williams bent down and showed the man the bullets in his magazine. Then he whispered something over the terrorist.

The terrorist's face immediately transformed as an indescribable look of horror filled his eyes. He tried to lift his head. He tried to scream but only gasped and sprayed out blood. He gasped again. The strain on his neck muscles relaxed a bit. His face went motionless with his eyes open. Williams stood up.

Williams stepped away, and turned towards the teacher.

"What did you say to him?" Burnor asked.

Williams stepped closer to Burnor and held up his magazine. "I showed him my clip and told him what was in it."

Burnor raised an eyebrow. "Why?"

"You see that?" Williams pointed to the filling inside the hollow points. "What's that?"

"It's filled with an all-natural filling, based in pig fat." Williams, still holding the magazine, explained further. "If you're in a situation where you're in a terrorist attack and you shoot a Muslim terrorist with it, their Koran says if they die with the pigs they go to hell, so instead of getting 72 virgins, they get the opposite. I like to think that's 27 Bubbas, or something like that."

Williams became solemn. He added, "I bought these as a gimmick." His eyes gazed down to the bullets, as the reality of the situation had just hit him. "I never thought I'd use them."

Burnor said, "The school wanted someone to volunteer to carry a gun. I never thought... Where can I get this?"

"27bubbas.com," Williams said softly.

The teacher nodded. He was fully aware that, in history, these tactics had been a deterrent to radical Muslims throughout time.

Burnor added, "If enough of us get that filling, they'll stop these attacks, because they won't want to go to hell."

Williams shrugged, not knowing what to say. He was a humanitarian caught in a situation he had never imagined. He could only muster, "Whatever works."

Burnor's eyes rose. "Can I have one of those bullets?"

A crease deepened between Williams's eyes. "Sure." He ejected the top one from the magazine he still held in his hand.

Taking the bullet in his hand Burnor nodded. "Thanks. I'll be right back."

People were scurrying around now and coming out on the floor. Williams watched as the teacher rumbled back to the original assailant. He watched as Burnor took the tip of the hollow point and made the sign of a cross on the dead man's forehead. Burnor stood straight for a second, then turned and jogged back to Williams.

"He'll lie with 27 bubbas too."

Williams nodded and extended his hand. "What's your name?"

"Jim Burnor."

"Well it's nice to meet you, Jim, I'm Marquis Williams."

People began tending to the wounded. Both men were dazed as they were surrounded by grateful survivors. Neither wanted appreciation. They just wanted to get out of there. They could hear police sirens in the background.

Thank God for the men in blue. Today everyone would be glad to see them.

* * *

Gabby froze, mesmerized by the report. A text had just alerted her to turn on the TV. She heard, "School shooting," and then watched as two young men carried a bleeding woman to the paramedics. The local reporter was horrified at the devastation, and continued her report. "The heartland of America is rocked today by what appears to be another mass shooting."

As Gabby watched, she remembered hearing an Imam say that it was acceptable to attack schools because of their political correctness and teaching of the disgraceful American ways.

Minutes later, she pushed the 'off' button. *OMG, what next?*

Little did she know, less than an hour away, an Imam watched. Now he would sit back and enjoy a moment of solace knowing what was about to take place in a major city.

CHAPTER 7

Suddenly, every light in the city went out. Mohammed Adair opened the door, stepped outside, and marveled at the total darkness. He took in a deep breath, as if to signify the sight brought him new life. The prototype EMP equipment had radiated its direct energy pulse from the top of the building. It had done the job it was designed to do. Adair felt tremendous satisfaction. The EMP pulse emitted by this equipment was extremely small compared to an EMP explosion. This type of EMP could be targeted directionally. That was the beauty of it. Adair wasn't even sure if it would take out most of the city, but it did. These EMP devices were getting smaller and the technology was becoming directional and could now be concentrated on a small area as well as a large area. Being that this operation coincided with the school shooting just hours ago, the physical and emotional impacts on the softening country would be tested.

Mohammed Adair was extremely excited to have been given this assignment, to be in charge of this EMP device. It was an honor to be chosen, and to be trusted to select the highly trained six-man team which was now part of the UN peacekeeping unit embedded within the US.

He had earned his stripes. He had worked his way up through the ranks in London and Germany as a youth. For the past ten years, he had worked in the US on a myriad of assignments with progressive responsibility. It was always for the same organization and for the same cause.

Adair gave a short command to his men in their native tongue. The team packed up the equipment and headed to the waiting truck. No one had noticed the old relic driving into position earlier in the day. The old vehicle had been chosen because it had none of the electronics of modern vehicles. It was impervious to an EMP.

Before getting into the vehicle, Adair looked around and listened. Not only was it pitch black, there wasn't a moving car or truck in sight. He cocked his head. He didn't even hear the train. He looked up to see a plane flying northwest in the distant sky. It was obviously out of range for the power of this EMP device. Adair had a passing thought that he hoped the impact of the device carried far enough to reach the municipal water supply, but that was a few miles away. That may be too much to ask. Still, this was the most successful blow to a city in years. He would be handsomely rewarded.

He got into the passenger side of the old truck, and the driver started it up. These older trucks were made before there was enough electronics to have an impact. Now they would be the only vehicle on the road.

* * *

The blackout was the cue.

Moments later, doors opened at several locations across the city. Armed disruptors flooded into the streets. They were dressed in local attire, some in high school jackets. Others were in sweatshirts and hats from local colleges. They appeared to be part of the community, though most had come into the country across the southern border. Most had been trained in Somalia, and others on small islands. They immediately broke into storefronts. Their mission was to loot and make it appear that their activities were spontaneous gatherings of people in emotional disarray. These were the talking points already drafted to give to the media.

A few minutes later one of them noticed a pretty young black girl. She had beautiful smooth skin and an exceptional structure to her face. In neatly fitted clothes, she appeared to be focused on her college studies, which would take her out of this neighborhood forever. She watched as she had when other crimes took place in her neighborhood. That was her naïve mistake. This was not a normal crime. These weren't young men from the area.

They grabbed her. Her friend screamed at the assailants, so they grabbed her as well, and dragged the girls inside. Under the shadows of dim emergency lighting, they began violently having their way with the girls. In their culture, this was one of the benefits of being a male in power.

In short order, locals joined the trained soldiers. Looting and pillaging escalated across the city. Soon there was a spontaneous escalation and the naive locals outnumbered the trained foreigners; everything was going as planned.

When high-pitched sirens shrieked in the distance, the trained men left that location. The locals took the fall if they were caught. These men were ordered to spread out to increase the radius of the impact. When locals joined in, they were to leave and go another block or two to spread the chaos.

The trained disruptors had instructions: when they received the signal from their overlook, or at the appointed time, whichever came first, they were to drop everything, shed their outer layer of clothes, put on the new hats they each carried in their pockets, disperse and walk peacefully back to their assigned safe houses.

A short time later, the globalist-controlled media received their talking points. The fake story line was that social injustice was the cause of the riots. The stage was set.

The plan had worked perfectly.

* * *

Back at the White House, George had just finished conferring with Adam about the shooting at the Eisenhower Building when the news of the blackout broke.

Adam knew NERC (North American Energy Regulatory Commission) strictly enforced all of their procedures, and failures do occur. But, with everything else going on, his instincts told him there may be some dirty work afoot.

George questioned the Secretary of Energy. "How many people are out of power?"

Secretary Perry was non-committal. "We're still assessing its impact; it could be up to a half a million, possibly more."

The president immediately wanted to know, "Is this an act of terrorism?"

"We have no evidence of that sir. Any conjecture would be purely speculative at this juncture." The secretary paused. "However, if you're asking my opinion, Mr. President, I'd say that it exhibits all of the traits of something sinister."

The secretary turned to the attorney general, who had just briefed him before this meeting with the president.

The attorney general began to explain. "About an hour after the blackout in New York, Chicago erupted in similar violence. But they didn't have a blackout. There was practically no media coverage of the problems in New York and even if there had been, our sources tell us the disruptions started in more than one location. To me it looks like an orchestrated event."

The president turned to the granite presence standing in the corner of the room. "Colonel Krieger, can you and Sergeant Major Briggs look into this and start thinking about countermeasures just in case?"

Krieger understood this was a directive and not a question. "Yes sir, affirmative on both counts."

CHAPTER 8

Krieger's pounding fist sent thumping sounds reverberating through the president's bedroom. "Mr. President, we have a situation."

It was the very next morning and, because of the events from the previous night, George had gone to bed late. He woke abruptly. *The last time Krieger banged on my door like that was when seven politicians were found dead on the steps of the old Senate building.*

Inhaling deeply, George glanced at his wife who simply nodded with a smile and rolled over with a pillow covering half of her head.

He sat up, turned toward the door and said, "I'll be right there."

Krieger receded to the sitting room, where Adam and Gabby were standing. Moments later George appeared.

"Good morning, Mr. President," Gabby greeted.

"Morning Gabby, Adam… Colonel."

"Mr. President," Gabby began, "we just received word that OPEC announced they will no longer accept the dollar for payments of their oil."

George looked from Gabby to Adam. "I'm surprised, with the American family connections they have. What does this mean?"

"That's not all," Adam added. George had responded too quickly for Gabby to finish.

Adam nodded back towards Gabby for her to continue.

"Several other countries seem to be following suit, and the futures markets are down over a thousand points."

As press secretary, Gabby was giving the background already being reported. They needed to frame the presentation for the media. She had been with the president from the beginning of his campaign, and he trusted her judgement and instincts implicitly.

"What's your take on this?" the president asked her.

Gabby continued. "My gut feel is that this isn't coincidental. We've made plans to drill more oil on federal land. Our contractors are building the pipelines quickly in order to capitalize on the incentives in their contracts. The oil cartels know we can drop gasoline prices, and they'll be well under current rates… possibly in the two-dollar range with our reduced regulations and new mini-refineries. We're already exporting a lot of oil. It won't be long before they're unable to afford to funnel oil money to terrorist organizations. We're decentralizing global oil power and taking all that economic power and giving it back to the middle class. They know it, so this could be retaliation. But it still doesn't make sense."

"What doesn't make sense?" George asked. He needed clarification. It made sense to him.

"You'd think they'd want to maximize their profit from us as long as they could," Gabby said.

George thought for a second and nodded in agreement. "You're thinking there may be more to it?"

Gabby needed more information. "I'll make some phone calls and see what I can find out."

George looked from face to face. "What else do we know?"

Gabby cocked her head. "I thought this was unrelated, but now I'm not sure. The ambassador from Germany called a press conference."

George looked to Adam. "Call them and see what they're going to talk about."

"I just did, in your name, Mr. President."

George knew that was the best way to get them to respond. But he saw disappointment in Adam's eyes. "The ambassador wouldn't talk to you?"

Adam shook his head. "Not at this time, sir."

They both knew that meant Germany wouldn't speak until after they made their announcement. Germany had become a primary spearhead for the globalists, who had taken over the government. They had allowed the country to be flooded with a socialist Islamic culture. It was part of the globalists' plan. Some of the German people had awakened, but it was too late. Like the

French, their middle-class lives were gone. Their citizens were captive within their own countries. Demonstrations and riots left little hope for change.

Gabby offered, "The press conference is scheduled for seven o'clock, before the market opens."

The implications of the unknown resonated through the room. They all knew that an early morning press conference was deliberate. They were usually orchestrated to give the media time to spread whatever the globalists wanted them to. They'd spread their fake news to millions during the morning rush hour. George's eyes narrowed in contempt.

* * *

An hour later, Adam was in the situation room with the president, Gabby and Alexus Hamilton, secretary of treasury and a member of the president's cabinet. As the secretary of treasury, Hamilton was the principal economic advisor to the president. She played a critical role in domestic and international financial policy. She had been a key advisor to the president for the economic resurgence. Hers was a tough appointment because of her view on tax policy and her outspoken stance on eliminating government debt. But she was one of the foremost experts on banking, and that was the primary reason George had chosen her.

Together, they watched as the German Ambassador explained to the press that Germany had asked for its gold back several years ago. The previous administration had told them it would take over six years to return it. But they had not delivered on their commitments before leaving office. He now implored the current administration to return their gold immediately.

He closed with the statement, "Unless they don't have it."

On another screen, a representative from the International Monetary Fund was demanding the immediate release of gold in payment for debts. He explained that, in recent days, several countries had expressed escalating concerns that the US might not have their gold. He added that, "Even their own states don't have access to their gold." It was an obvious reference to several states who had requested their gold back from the Federal Reserve, to little avail.

As the news conferences came to a close, Hamilton softly said, "We know that, in 2013, Germany asked to have over six hundred tons of gold back from the Federal Reserve. When they didn't receive it, they asked to audit the gold at the Federal Reserve, and were denied. I hadn't thought about it before, but they must have kept it quiet while both countries were under the globalist regime." She was obviously referring to George's predecessor.

Looking at George she said, "Now that you're trying to put more money back into the hands of the middle class, they're counter attacking."

George agreed. "It makes sense, but why now?"

"Maybe they see their time running out. They may be afraid of what you'd do in your second term," Hamilton surmised.

As George hesitated in thought, Hamilton explained, "Remember, the IMF is a group of approximately two hundred countries who are controlled by the world bankers. Their agenda is the one world order. It's a secret organization with no accountability or oversight. If Germany is doing this with IMF backing, you can bet the IMF is thinking something larger."

George interrupted. "Can't we even audit them here in the US?"

"Not at all, sir."

George spoke rhetorically. "Who was stupid enough to do this?"

Hamilton explained. "The International Monetary Fund, or IMF, and the World Bank were created together in New Hampshire and are now based in Washington, DC. The IMF markets itself as an organization that helps countries orchestrate economic growth by issuing loans. They'll loan to just about any country willing to agree to their terms. They enrich themselves off countries who have financial crises, which typically they orchestrate. They currently exert enormous power over approximately sixty countries. The key to uncovering their true desires are hidden in their terms and conditions."

"Let me guess, they demand collateral, like owning the most valuable infrastructure and assets of the countries."

"Of course, Mr. President. You called it… nationalized businesses, natural resources, land, water, you name it." The Secretary waited for other comments but there were none.

George continued his questioning. "Okay, so they get this collateral; then what? It can't be that simple, that's just not the way these people work. Where are the hooks?"

Hamilton's lower lip retracted and she nodded. "That's actually a good choice of words, Mr. President. Remember, the truth be told, these people will capture more natural resources when there's a financial crisis. The country being bailed out is swindled into getting into more debt."

George thought to himself, *so they're going to orchestrate a financial crisis.*

Adam added, "Then, to acquire more IMF resources to keep afloat, one of the terms countries agree to is to allow the IMF to decide how much debtor countries will spend on things like education, health care and environmental protection. To keep the general public unaware, they also control the educational systems."

"We're seeing that here," George commented.

"Absolutely, it's a part of the terms and conditions for money we owe them. They control how much a country can spend on education, and won't allow education about sound financial principles, like the compounding effect of debt on a nation or even an individual." Alexus Hamilton looked around the room and, after a brief pause, continued. "One of their major tactics is to require collateral. Their end game is to get a nation's national resources… anything mined or drilled, including water. By controlling water, they can embed charges into every glass of water the population drinks. People pay for it in their bills, and don't even think about the bill being taxed. They control roads and dams for energy production and tax those as well. All of this is designed to keep people poorer… a poorer middle class… more wealth for them."

"Well, is being strict on environmental regulations one of the things the IMF does well?" Gabby questioned.

Hamilton looked at Gabby and smacked her lips. "They use it as a weapon. You see, they can make the most money in undeveloped countries, where they've purchased large portions of land, because they force the government to keep labor and environmental laws that are cheap for them. Then they impose unreasonably restrictive environmental laws in developed countries to make it more expensive to conduct business. The US is a perfect example. They've paid politicians to increase environmental regulations and taxes, to increase the expense of doing business in the US. Then the businesses moved to undeveloped countries, where they use children and other cheap labor. There, they have few safety regulations, much lower taxes and very relaxed accounting practices. These world bankers make more money in undeveloped countries than they do in countries like the United States."

"Do they really make that much more money in those undeveloped countries? After all, we know the labor is cheaper, but they have to pay for the land, and even build the whole infrastructure system. That's a huge cost."

Alexus Hamilton was patient. "Let me explain. Years ago, these extremely wealthy families purchased large sections of land in these undeveloped countries at virtually no cost." She deliberately hesitated before making her next point. "Then they talked these countries into taking out loans for infrastructure of roads, sewers, utilities... and even built vacant buildings so business would see the possibility and locate there." She paused again. "They didn't tell the countries that they were the ones who owned the very banks they said they had contacts in to get the loans. So, in the end, these super rich families own all this developed land at virtually no cost, while the governments must squeeze the people to pay for the infrastructure for their businesses. Why do you think most of these countries aren't prospering after all of this?" She finished rhetorically.

"OMG." Gabby covered her mouth. "Then they sell the land at a huge profit," she added.

"Sometimes, most times, they lease it. That way they get their ORI forever."

"ORI?" Gabby questioned.

"Ongoing residual income. That's what it's all about. Their hidden agenda is to acquire multiple streams of ongoing residual income from as many people in as many countries as they can. That way, they're always receiving money... from water, oil, utilities, from infrastructure, from rent, from global warming taxes, from you and you and you!" The Secretary pointed at each of them.

Adam was impressed. "That's the best description of the new world order I've ever heard."

Hamilton nodded. "That's what it's all about."

She figured they were ready for more of the truth. "Then they embed their ideology into the culture by mandating decreased benefits, salaries, and even reduced social security benefits to retirees."

George said, "What?" Could what he was hearing actually be happening — and now?

Hamilton was a little sullen. "They did it recently again in Argentina. They reduced retiree income. That's money they can take immediately. Then, when the retirees have less money, they'll have less of an ability to see and influence their grandchildren. All this adds up to the elders having less status and time to impart knowledge to the younger generations. They want the younger generations more susceptible to the globalist influence and brainwashing."

Hamilton hesitated. She wasn't sure she wanted to share this next thought, but if ever there was a time, it was now. "They started this here, with the social security increase in the last administration. Remember, the social security tax went from four percent to six percent. The government pulled in fifty percent more social security taxes from workers. They gave retired people less than inflation, and transferred the money into their coffers through the social security slush fund."

Adam had understood most of this before and this added detail solidified it in his mind. "This cycle gets larger; the problem gets worse and cycles faster as the debt grows. Their model is designed to make the debtor countries fall into more debt, so more resources are transferred to the IMF... and the cycle continues."

Hamilton nodded in agreement. "Have you ever seen a country pay off its debt to the IMF or other countries in the last hundred years?"

That reality hung in the air.

George snapped, "That's what they're doing to us! They're going to try to drive us into taking on more debt."

Hamilton nodded. "Very possibly."

George continued. "We need to audit them and uncover all this."

Hamilton shook her head, and emphasized her previous thought. "Mr. President, we have no authority to do that!"

"Isn't there any way?" George questioned.

Alexus Hamilton explained, "The IMF is accountable only to themselves, just like the Federal Reserve. We have no authority or jurisdiction over them… And it's even worse. They're funded with taxpayer money. They pay off groups in our own government to make policies in the health, education and environmental departments. They're a big part of the deep state." Turning to Adam she added, "That's another means by which they continue their ways for generations to come."

Adam nodded and looked in George's direction.

Hamilton wasn't finished. "Their policies help ensure successful business interests for themselves. For example, countries who are indebted to the IMF are made to give subsidies and tax breaks to other countries, and those countries just happen to be the ones in which the IMF owns large interests."

Alexus Hamilton, a loyal American, wanted to impart enough knowledge so they understood. "Remember, the goal is always to increase a debtor nation's debt until the IMF can take over a controlling interest in the country. During bailouts, these people use every trick in the book to maximize the debt of the nation needing help. They've been known to make countries in Asia assume insolvent debts of private banks in order to maximize the amount of the loan to the country. Then, after they're in, they'll frequently raise interest rates to suck more money out of the indebted country."

Gabby was seeing the picture now. "That's why they go after resource rich countries like the Ukraine, Brazil, Southeast Asia, taking over water resources and taxing it, controlling dams for hydroelectric and all that."

Hamilton could see they were understanding. "Exactly. All of their conditions amount to a loss of the country's authority to govern its own economy!"

* * *

By the time the stock market opened, the news was all over Wall Street. The sell-off came as quickly as the traders could navigate. Fund managers had been given directives to sell prior to the opening bell. Things began to slow down a few hours later when more bad news broke.

The President's Chairman of the Council of Economic Advisors said, "They're saying there's computer problems and no one can pull money out."

Adam had been watching the news. "Cable news is sticking microphones in people's faces as they come out of banks and getting reports that there's a limit put on how much cash they can take out. The customers aren't believing them, and they're making impassioned pleas. They're telling reporters they can't get their money."

George quickly asked, "Is it only this one bank?"

"Yes sir, but it has the second largest public depository," said the Chairman.

"Do we suspect economic terrorism?" George felt he had to ask.

The Chairman was on it. "We're looking into that now, sir. If it hits a second source, that's a definite. In the meantime, we're moving as fast as we can. We've got people investigating."

The speed at which the market hit the automatic shutoff was astonishing.

Shortly after that, a second bank announced that it was experiencing a cyber-attack and would lock all accounts for the day. In an unprecedented move, they said account holders would not have access electronically until they came into their local branch. They needed to reset their passwords after showing their proper identification to authenticate themselves.

The room was silent for a moment. Then Hamilton spoke up. "Mr. President, the dollar is plummeting and, frankly, something else must be going on here."

George had his own suspicions. "Something more than the obvious?"

"Possibly." Hamilton nodded ever so slowly as she gazed into the distance.

George asked, "Market manipulation and possibly currency manipulation?"

Hamilton wasn't fast enough with her answer for George, so he repeated, "Is our currency being attacked?"

"We can't prove it, Mr. President." Hamilton chose her words carefully.

George was getting angry. "What's your best assessment?"

Hamilton gazed at the floor for a second and then looked up. "I can't explain a drop this fast in such a short period of time. It's as if a trigger has been pulled, or…" She hesitated again.

"Or what?"

"Or worse than that… it's an orchestrated attack." Hamilton spoke faster. "We have an undercover agent working in the media. He was given a heads up to be ready… shortly after that, he was dispatched to a bank… we suspect someone knew bank issues were coming."

"If in fact that's what's happening, we need to find out who's behind this," George ordered.

"We'll get right on it, Mr. President." Hamilton knew it was almost impossible to prove, but that answer wouldn't be acceptable.

* * *

Within hours, broadcasts were flooded with news of massive stock selloffs and more countries calling for their gold. The first phone calls came into The White House, asking the United States to pay all of their debt immediately.

By early evening, the gravity of the situation was totally apparent. Hamilton had been by George's side all day fielding calls and making inquiries. With the heavy thinking that went along with the stress of the situation, she was exhausted. But the President somehow appeared to be unphased. He was as bright as he always was. She looked at him and said, "Mr. President, this is the fourth call we've had asking us to pay our debt now."

George retorted, "Well, they can't force us to pay immediately."

"Mr. President, every agreement we have has a clause which basically says the debt is redeemable upon request." Hamilton's tone was grave.

George thought to himself about the people adding all of this debt to the country.

What a bunch of idiots… or worse yet, if they weren't that stupid, they were working for someone else and it was treason.

But that wasn't something to focus on now. He needed to focus on what he could do here and now, not on the fools and traitors who had preceded him and created this situation.

Adam knew what George must be thinking and said, "This couldn't possibly be coincidence."

George nodded his head in agreement. "It's too well orchestrated and too many things are happening simultaneously for it to be coincidence. But who?"

Just then, Gabby came through the door. "I think you should watch this, Mr. President." She picked up a remote and went directly to the channel.

"I thought we got rid of that socialist Malik," George said, scornful of the man he had replaced.

Gabby explained, "He was at a fund raiser here in Washington and you can see the reporters crowded around him."

She turned up the volume to quiet the room. They listened to the former President. "Well, these countries have a right to their gold and the money we owe them."

They didn't hear the question that had preceded his answer.

Former President Malik continued. "The agreements all say they're redeemable upon request. The President will have to find a way to pay them." Malik held up his hand. "I'm sorry, that's all I know about the situation."

Adam turned to George. "He just happened to be at a fund raiser and available to a huge group of media."

The situation room was dead silent.

As the evening went on, everyone had left with the exception of Alexus, Adam and George. They watched as the news replayed the interviews of the day, including one with a member of a major bank. His wording didn't settle well with George. The man warned that if the situation became worse, the US credit rating could be lowered at least two levels. He explained that, since the government wasn't funded for much longer, the US would be paying an escalated interest rate. The damn globalist bankers. George knew these bankers had the country by the short hairs.

Finally, George said to Adam and Alexus, "You'd better get some rest. It'll be a long day tomorrow."

As Adam was on his way out of the White House, Gabby's text came through. "How much longer?"

He responded. "I'm on my way."

CHAPTER 9

Gabby's body tingled as Adam lovingly kissed the back of her neck as he gently but firmly massaged her shoulders and down her back.

When their relationship had begun, Adam had been missing for several days after being kidnapped and held captive by the deep state. She and the President believed they may never see him again. After he had been rescued by a retired ex-CIA spook named Brooks and appeared backstage, they had embraced tightly. Tears had been streaming down her face. But, with the President on stage and only minutes left on the nationally televised address the eve of the election, his priority had been his country.

Adam had gone on stage without any makeup, his face battered and bruised. He'd had a fat lip and a black eye that was almost swollen shut. A punch while he'd been tied up had left a cut on his eyebrow that would leave a scar. He had wiped off the blood that had dripped, but the dried blood was still there. He would need a few stitches to close the cut properly. He stood there for the entire nation to see. It was then that the masses had understood that the globalist bankers and deep state would do anything to stop a resurgence of the United States. It was late that night, when Adam could no longer contain his attraction for Gabby, that they'd fallen into each other's arms.

Gabby hadn't been with him in weeks and she yearned for him, as only he could fill that void. Even though their relationship wasn't serious, they were exclusive to each other. He came over to her place like this from time to time. She had no desire for another man. It wasn't even a consideration.

She knew he could use some support, and that he needed to reduce his stress after what had happened today. So, when they'd had lunch, she'd asked if he could come over. Gabby had been so frightened when she'd met him at his office and had heard of his close call that morning in the basement of the Eisenhower Executive Office Building. Her passion and desire had built all day, which was also fueled by her growing feelings for him. Neither one of them had said they loved each other, but she was on the verge of saying it first.

Adam slowly kissed his way down the back of her neck, rolled her over on her side and then onto her back. Gabby's breasts bounced seductively as Adam's hands slid off. With the combination of the lengthy massage and Adam's slow kissing, he could sense that if he didn't get to it, she was going to grab him by the back of the head in that playful way of hers.

He watched her chest rise as she caught her breath. His hands moved slowly to the small of her arched back.

Now she felt his powerful hands move down her ass and he lifted her torso fully off the bed. She knew what was coming next. As Adam began to satisfy her, she arched until only her shoulder blades, head and arms were touching the mattress. She had never experienced this before with one exception; it was what he had done the first time they'd been together.

A sensation of passion had transferred from Adam to Gabby. He was in total harmony with her needs, and her excitement had built with the softness of his touch. She didn't know or care how he did it. She was unaware that, when Adam lifted her torso off the mattress, he also lifted her lower body off the bed and braced his elbows on the mattress underneath her to hold her up in the air. He could transfer the feeling of his power to her as she was nestled in his palms. She didn't know that he used a significant amount of strength to hold her in that position.

Minutes later Adam saw the lowest portion of her abdomen start to quiver. Then the shudder moved up her mid-section, and another tremor fluttered.

"Don't stop, don't stop."

Then, in an explosion of ecstasy, there was an eruption of tremors. They patterned up and down her mid-section. The speed increased. The tremor moved faster until they were almost a blur. Adam's mouth had become an extension of her needs. Her little woman was firmer. He felt more of her weight transfer to his palms as she shook and convulsed. The smell of her womanhood filled the air.

As she slowed, he followed the signals of her body. He adjusted so he could stay with her, knowing a moment of sensitivity would follow.

He kissed around her inner thighs and lowered her down onto the bed. Slowly kissing his way up, he whispered, "Stay right there. We'll do it again. This time will be a little different."

She whispered something he couldn't hear. It really didn't matter.

He added, "I'll count until we've reached ten. Each time will be a little different."

Her face glowed. Adam had just begun. What a wonderful evening this would be.

CHAPTER 10

Chief scientist Dr. Roy Hemmele opened the door. The motion detectors turned on the lights as he led Krieger and Briggs into the small room at the top of the building.

Dr. Hemmele was the best of the best when it came to EMP technology. His main office was in Area 51, but he was a welcome sight at many other top-secret installations. Because he was pioneer in developing technology to monitor EMPs, the sun lighting and electromagnetic pulses, he had been flown in overnight. He was the inventor of several top-secret devices used by several government agencies, including NASA. He exuded the calmness of a man in his rightful place in life. As his small team headed to their designated workstations, Hemmele sat down and punched the appropriate keys to log in. Then he held his finger to the touchpad, allowing access to the next level. He nodded. His associate followed the same protocol. With the dual person authentication complete, their screens came to life.

Hemmele grinned and turned to Colonel Krieger. "It's working."

The team shared a brief moment of jubilation, which seemed to fade into relief. The incident that had caused the blackout in the city was the first EMP burst of any significance set off in the US outside of a test environment. This location, right here in the blacked-out city, had been set up to record these types of incidents, should they arise. The analysis part of the equipment had just been flown in. They hard wired it to the recording device. It was now up to Hemmele and his team to determine if it could give them any critical information.

Krieger and Briggs's men hovered around the equipment that the experts navigated. They hoped to detect the source of the incident, and identify the whereabouts of the device that had caused the blackout. A new addition to this device might even detect the strength and frequency, perhaps even the direction towards which the device was focused.

Krieger hoped that this new option of tracking the movement of the source would give them an idea of where the perpetrators traveled to after setting off the EMP. Recording equipment like this had recently been mounted in a few major cities without the public's knowledge. Krieger watched as the team worked with a sense of urgency.

Hemmele and his team had designed the recording equipment. The antenna was robust in its design, to maximize its ability to withstand a variety of scenarios. This recording equipment, like the others, was positioned at the top of one of the tallest buildings in the city.

Krieger watched the large screen at the front of the small room come alive. Unique displays appeared. Hemmele was orchestrating his team and the equipment like a composer. Then Krieger noticed Hemmele freeze. After a brief moment, Hemmele smiled.

Hemmele was focused on the screen when he said, "It looks like it lasted approximately four ten thousandths of a second."

Krieger knew the blasts were short, but that seemed too brief. "Are you certain?"

"Yes, they're very quick, short bursts. That's one of the things that makes them dangerous. They occur so quickly that there's no warning, and thus, no time to respond. They're a thousand times quicker than a lightning strike and can be thousands of times more powerful. These EMPs could theoretically even be used to launch a projectile at many times the speed of sound."

From the tone of Hemmele's comment, Krieger felt that perhaps he was working on launching a projectile, but this wasn't the place or the time to ask.

Hemmele added, "Depending on the type of device that caused this... EMP devices that are like a bomb emanate outwardly in a uniform three hundred and sixty-degree radius." He hesitated, taking time to determine whether he wanted to disclose his next thought. He had suspicions because this EMP blast was so small and the effect was localized. He decided he'd better not. Sharing that he had helped develop the technology that could cause the EMP to emanate outwardly irregularly, giving an area of focus, wasn't something relevant to this... or so he thought.

Krieger wanted confirmation of his assessment of what the doctor had just said. "You're implying this equipment can tell us something about the type of device?"

This was Hemmele's first live detection of an actual EMP. "We may be able to, sir; give me a few minutes. We're working on it."

Dr. Hemmele expertly navigated his way through the program as screen shots appeared and then dissolved. Krieger wanted to ask more, but waited as Hemmele asked one of his companions to verify the starting time and central coordinates. When she had verified the coordinates, he began searching through commands in the system. He was looking for the recording at the time of the burst.

A short time later, Hemmele had an overhead view of the area on the eight-foot screen, showing what looked like a high-tech electronic radar signal. The overlaying grid was symmetrical, like a stationary radar.

Krieger finally had to ask, "What are you doing?"

"This is called a radar chart. I wanted to get a visual. This is just a few seconds before the incident began. Watch, and you'll see a red line showing how the EMP burst emanated from the source… Realize that what you're about to see happened in milliseconds."

In slow motion, a red line came to life at the center of the radar chart. It emanated irregularly outward. The lines to the east grew faster and went farther than the lines to the west. They all watched in silence. The lines reached a peak distance from the source and then disappeared.

Hemmele's tone lowered. He was solemn. "That's how it happened. Now, let me take you back to the peak point of the burst."

Krieger and Briggs watched as Hemmele started the visual of the blast over again. This time the screen froze at its peak effect.

"Do you see how the pulse radius is irregular?"

It was obvious. "Yes, but what does that tell us?" Krieger asked as he turned his eyes from the screen to Hemmele.

Speaking a little more carefully now, Hemmele said, "I'll run it through our statistical verification program, but I can tell you that this did not come from a bomb. That's why I didn't use the term blast. We use that term with a bomb that's designed to emit an EMP pulse. Bombs emit blasts that have a relatively symmetrical circumference. Give me a second."

He slid his mouse around until the curser hovered over some drop-down boxes. After making a few choices, the screen came alive with a world of information. Hemmele scrolled up, down, back up and back down.

"There you have it. See this number?" Hemmele pointed to a decimal point followed by three zeros. "That's called a screaming P value. It says the likelihood of this not being a bomb is less than that number... To put it another way, this was not a bomb. It came from a different type of manmade device."

Krieger asked the question Hemmele knew was coming. "What kind of device?"

Hemmele feared that he knew, but wanted to wait until the equipment verified his thoughts, so he said, "We're getting to that. Give us some time."

Krieger watched for a few more moments. Hemmele continued to explain as he worked.

"What most people don't know, is that we've just developed the ability to focus an EMP blast or pulse on a very select place to help our troops go into an area and do what they need to do. When communications are disabled, our troops are able to go in without encountering an organized resistance. It makes it much safer. It also gives us the ability to minimize the fallout to areas we don't want to affect."

Briggs nodded. "Maybe some rogue dictators could learn a lesson the hard way."

"Most people associate an EMP with a total takedown," Hemmele said. "With the most advanced technology on earth, it is possible to have a more localized EMP that has a less dramatic effect."

After a moment of silence, Hemmele continued. "As you know, when you devise something, you begin devising a way to measure it and counter it. So, when others finally get that technology, you can track it and counter it. There are high-power microwave weapons small enough to fit in a suitcase that can disable smaller targets like neighborhoods, banks and stock exchanges. Devices can also be used to cause confusion or to allow someone to infiltrate secure areas by disabling alarm systems. An attacker would simply need to get within a few yards of a target and push a button to unleash the pulse."

Though he'd never seen this process before, Krieger knew that when someone was navigating a complex program using some of the world's most sophisticated technology, it required an extreme amount of concentration to do the right thing so the proper outcome could be realized. So he was patient until, on the eight-foot screen, he saw what looked like the high-tech electronic radar signal chart again. The red line was irregular around the center point.

Hemmele worked at a rapid pace. "I'm matching this pulse distribution against the known devices that can emit this distribution pattern. The statistical part of the program will match the data with known devices. This is similar to a multiple distribution analysis in statistics. Then it'll give us some probabilities, which in your term's sir, amount to a probability of a match. When it comes up, I'll interpret it for you, and we'll see if there are any conclusions to be drawn."

Briggs and Krieger exchanged glances and Krieger nodded. They didn't understand the method, though they knew enough about communications on missions to understand some principles. All they could do was watch and hope.

The computer screen scrolled with data from the bottom up, filling the screen several times. Then it stopped.

Hemmele used his arrow key to scroll up... and down... and back up... and down... thinking... thinking... interpreting. Then he turned to his right with some trepidation. "Lindsey, look at this."

Lindsey, a blond woman who had worked with Hemmele for almost three years, looked. Her eyes lit up and she smiled and then looked down at her screen.

Hemmele turned to Krieger and his eyes were alive. "Sir, we have identified the type of device that was used!" Hemmele turned back to his screen. "See the number to the right of the screen? It's a probability number. It tells us the probability of the pattern of this mapped incident matching each known device and their known patterns. Well, in scientific terms we don't say it that way, but basically we know with somewhere around ninety-seven percent certainty that this pulse was caused by this type of device."

"What type of device is it?" Krieger immediately questioned.

Hemmele's scrolled to the far-left hand side of the screen, and Krieger and Briggs saw his head lower. He highlighted some numbers and letters on the screen and exchanged a look with Lindsey before turning to Krieger. Krieger noticed that the look on Lindsey's face had changed too.

Hemmele didn't answer the question immediately. He chose his words carefully saying, "Sir, this operation is beyond top secret because of the technology. The lack of knowledge about this type of capability... is because it's funded by money that's under many financial approvals that trigger close inspection. What I'm trying to tell you, sir, is that you're about to learn what type of device was used. The perpetrators have no idea there's any way for anyone to know what you are about to know. So, I'd keep this to myself if I were you."

Hemmele looked directly at Krieger.

Krieger was about to ask Hemmele to get to the point when Hemmele finished with an ominous statement. "These numbers reference a device that's only made by the United States Government."

Krieger thought to himself, *I'd better call the vice president.*

CHAPTER 11

That same afternoon…

Outlined against the blue-grey sky, the wolf's hair stood on end. Over six feet long, this male held his head down in a defensive posture.

He must have been separated from his pack for some reason, Brooks mused.

It had been almost a year ago since Brooks had been living back at his cabin in the Alaskan wilderness. Now fully retired, Brooks had spent the last year hunting and fishing. He was a patriot, but a retired patriot. The kind they don't make many of.

After being recruited and then working for the CIA for decades, he became known to a select few in the agency as Griffin. The name was a reference to the invisible man from the 1933 movie. When Brooks went under cover for years, his identity faded, but a new reputation grew. He became known as the CIA's most proficient field operative. Because of his ability for eliminating a target in a manner which made it look like an accident, those within the CIA gave him the name of 'The Shadow.' Almost no one knew who he was. But they knew *of* him.

He retired from the CIA without his identity ever being compromised. After the CIA, he had been doing contract work as a freelance hitman for a group of patriots who were finally beginning to fight back against the deep state. They quietly targeted traitors. It was those connections that had led him to risk exposure to rescue Adam from a remote location where he was being held at the hands of the globalists who kidnapped him.

It had been almost a year ago when, sitting on the back porch of his bush cabin, Brooks had seen the wolf at the edge of the woods for the first time. Eventually, one day, the large animal had come down the path, closer to the cabin, and sat. His silver and white fur had glistened when rays of sunlight peered through the clouds.

Brooks had watched as the wolf looked in his direction and followed his every move in the twilight. That night, Brooks had left a sizeable piece of moose meat on the porch. The next morning the meat was gone. Brooks continued this practice each night. Each morning the scraps were gone.

It wasn't long before the wolf would come and eat the scraps while Brooks watched. Then one time the big gray, now mature, came within ten yards. Brooks backed into the cabin and a few moments later, he threw a slice of freshly carved moose towards the wolf. The canine's black tipped tawny-buff gray hairs on the back of his neck had relaxed. With nostrils flexing in and out, he had approached the meat. With fangs over two inches long, this one could already eat about twenty pounds of meat at a sitting. This piece, slightly over a pound, was just a snack for the big canine.

Brooks tossed another piece of moose and the wolf was more at ease.

In another month, the wolf would come and sit by him on the porch, both predators looking over the open meadow in silence. A bond had developed.

One day, Brooks warily reached out and touched him ever so slightly; the wolf accepted that.

Another month and Brooks had coaxed the lone canine into the cabin. Constantly wary, Brooks had kept his hand on his pistol.

The animal was curious and had sniffed his way around the cabin. As time went by, they both became comfortable sharing the space.

One time, Brooks had walked outside and closed the door behind him with the wolf still in the cabin. The instincts of the wild animal had taken over, and Brooks couldn't get the door opened fast enough as the big gray went wild inside the cabin before he dashed out. It took a while before he was willing to enter the cabin again. From then on, he kept an eye on the open door.

This mutually respectful relationship lasted the whole summer and most of the winter until, when a mission called, Brooks left in the spring. He never saw the wolf again.

* * *

Brooks snapped out of his dream. The incident with the wolf had happened a few years ago. He sat up on the couch. He took a deep breath, still foggy from his nap.

What was that about? he wondered.

He had stayed out of touch with just about everyone since a few weeks after the election.

Wow, that was vivid, just like it had happened. Except for the eyes. They were surreal, different. They were like... not like a wolf's eyes. They seemed to be human eyes.

Strange, was all he could think.

Brooks tried to clear his head. His leathery palms rubbed each side of his face. He had been around long enough to trust his senses, and to pay attention to signs from God, no matter what form his messages took.

Brooks was aging, but the feeling in his stomach was, *I'm being called to serve my country again.*

The Shadow, which was what he had been called many years ago when he had been in the CIA, got up and walked to the bathroom. In there, he took out his pocket knife and scraped grout from around a wall tile. He removed the tile with his knife. He slowly drew it towards him as the fifty-pound braided monofilament fishing line pulled his cache from inside the wall. He reached in and helped his flexible tubular container navigate its way through the hole. In a moment he retrieved a few passports, drivers' licenses and a key to a safety deposit box where he stored gold. He could trade in the gold at a friendly trading shop. He'd get ninety-seven percent of its current value.

Brooks would replace the tile and re-grout in a minute.

First, he pocketed a small plastic bag of SIMs chips and thought, *Maybe it's time to call Ferraro.*

CHAPTER 12

The six-foot-three, two hundred and sixty-pound Sergeant Major Briggs had been getting everything ready all night. It was now two days after the local EMP blast had caused major civil unrest. It had killed several, sending many to hospitals and causing extensive damage to personal property. Hemmele had tracked where the stolen EMP device had been taken that night. Armed with that information, Mauricio, who was the field grade officer spearheading communications for each of Krieger's teams, closed in on the general location. He watched and listened from a distance. It wasn't long before he saw suspicious activity and monitored Arabic conversations centered around an old warehouse.

There was no assurance the device was still there. But the activity indicated that something was definitely going on.

The location fit an ideal extraction point. On the south side of the rundown part of Philadelphia, this warehouse was surrounded by abandoned buildings from a forgotten era when industry fed life into the middle class. With the Delaware river to its back, the ship yard just up river still built ships. But it wasn't what it once was. The location also offered the terrorists easy access to interstate I95, the major highway that ran north and south. The terrorists could move the device on truck or boat. Nestled here, it was removed from the surveillance cameras that panned the busier parts of the city.

Since the national guard had been deployed to some larger cities, Briggs had used the guard convoys to get his people into the city. Then to get closer, Briggs had acquired construction equipment and detour signs. He had men to the north, south and west. Some were on jackhammers; some operated equipment. A few were holding stop signs in case anyone came by.

Krieger had flown up from DC on a small private jet. George and Adam had been adamant that he should not charge in with the entry team, declaring that he was too valuable to be hit in a firefight.

Still, they must succeed, and Krieger was the type of leader who wanted to be there himself. These terrorists were still at large, and now that the handcuffs were off, Krieger could use his fledgling private team to stop this group from striking again.

Krieger had stationed himself about a hundred yards from Briggs, his second in command. But with Krieger focusing so much attention on other matters for the President, this had become Briggs's operation.

Briggs verified final preparations with one of his teams. He waited for a response and adjusted his tactical head gear. He looked at Mauricio, who had set up all of the communications, including the plan of who was covertly speaking with whom. The construction teams in the field had fully covert communication sets with in-ear speakers. Operatives still concealed in trucks had a tactical head gear system which had both tactical command radios and soldier to squad radios. Mauricio asked for final verification from the remote team in a semi-truck. Nothing.

Then from the window of a warehouse they were conducting their overlook from, Mauricio and Briggs saw something drop directly from above. It hit the ground like someone shot a goose out of the sky. They heard the distinct sound of plastic hitting the ground. Mauricio peeked out and caught a glimpse of a few more falling from the sky. Drones.

He looked at Briggs, they both immediately picked up other electronic devices. "Shit, they're all dead."

They had come to the right place. The terrorists had just used the EMP device again.

Suddenly, the window Briggs and Mauricio were conducting overwatch from, was riddled with gunfire. Fragments of the old frame flew and glass shattered. Somehow, the terrorists had trained their weapons on Briggs's location. Not only did the terrorists have the EMP device, as Briggs and Krieger had suspected, they must have other sophisticated equipment allowing them to detect the location of the team to launch a pre-emptive strike.

Briggs raised his modified General Dynamics .338 Morma Magnum machine gun over the window frame and volleyed short bursts from side to side. Then he ducked back behind the security of the wall. After the terrorists returned fire again, Briggs knew they had a bead on the window, so he reached up without exposing himself and unleashed another ten rounds per second from the .338 Morma. He brought the big gun down and put his back to the wall.

"Can you raise Krieger?" he yelled.

"Negative sir, we've got nothing," Mauricio yelled back over the uproar and began searching his pack. "Give me a second."

Briggs shot a few more short bursts. The equipment they had tracked had just been used again on them. With the value of that device, it was likely an HVT (High Value Target) was inside.

Mauricio quickly pulled out his high-tech, hybrid communication device, which used a combination of newly developed miniature vacuum and insulating technology to withstand an EMP burst. At Krieger's request, the good Dr. Hemmele had equipped the team leaders, just in case. The hybrid communication devices didn't have the range of his usual equipment, but luckily, they didn't need that much range.

Inside the building, Mohammed Adair and his men were fighting for their lives, and they were extremely well equipped to do so.

By the time Mauricio called Krieger, Krieger had already thrown down his radio and reached in his pocket for the backup from Hemmele. Once communication with Krieger had been re-established, they agreed and gave the signal.

The back of two unmarked semi-trucks opened and an extra highly trained team of twenty two surged towards the target. With new drones now replacing the fallen ones, Brigg's team, who had been on the ropes, was ready to counter punch.

Mohammed Adair was taken aback. On the screen of the US military device provided by the deep state, he could see the size of the American force. It was surging towards him, forward in an orchestrated offensive from all directions.

Sand sprayed his face. Whatever type of rounds the Americans were using pierced the sand bags stacked against the walls.

He had been directed not to communicate with his superiors until he was out of the area. But this was an emergency. He opened a protective lock box and frantically removed his cell phone. Something was jamming it.

Mohammed's men screamed to communicate over the noise of the firefight. This was a counter-attack he hadn't planned on.

Who were these people? This type force and equipment wasn't supposed to be in cities inside the US.

Briggs's team unleashed tactical sniper fire. Now equipped with the new telecommunications devices, they surged forward in unison. The impact of the tactical hits was magnified by an overwhelming amount of debris filling the air.

A robotic armor protective vehicle led the way. It protected the special operations team that deployed from the trucks.

Drones shot small tactical missiles into the terrorists' stronghold from all sides. Mini-drones flew in through the broken windows. Briggs's tactic was basic: deploy overwhelming force and capture the device before they could either destroy it or communicate with anyone else. He could not underestimate this team. He assumed he was up against highly trained terrorists. They were possibly led by an HVT on site.

Krieger correctly surmised that these terrorists had been told to lay low for a period of time before moving out. With very few signals filling airwaves across the city, any communication would be easy for the US military to isolate. Communications could give them away by allowing the military to pinpoint their location. Since no communication was detected, Krieger was sure the terrorists hadn't communicated with anyone since the EMP attack.

It was a good plan. The terrorists had done what they were told. But they hadn't counted on Hemmele's ability to track their location.

Glass exploded from almost every direction. It rained down on the men inside the warehouse. Flashes of specially designed tracer rounds filled the air. They added to the disorientation of the terrorists. Krieger and Briggs were using every tactic available. The terrorists were overwhelmed. Then a small prototype percussion bomb came through a blown-out window, and exploded inside the warehouse. The impact disabled everyone in the room. Men were sent half way through walls, ribs broken.

These terrorists' ultimate mission had been to overthrow the infidels, to drive the country to Allah, and to allow ambitious globalist men to take control of the resources. Now, that was the last thing on their minds.

Glass exploded outward from the percussion bomb. That was the signal to Briggs's team to take the fight inside.

"Move it!" Briggs yelled. They surged forward.

Krieger followed orders. He wasn't part of the entry team. But he knew his priority was to find these terrorists, eliminate them and, where possible, capture and interrogate them. He had to find out as much as he could.

Krieger waited for Briggs to give the all clear.

* * *

Broken glass crunched beneath Krieger's feet as he walked across the warped wooden floor.

Only three men remained alive in this main room. The percussion blast had taken out those who hadn't succumbed to the onslaught.

Krieger surveyed the contents of the room. It was a textbook stronghold.

Under the debris, Krieger found a US military device. It used a heat signature to detect anyone approaching. It was a recent model. It was one of the best; a US military device.

Krieger picked it up and shook it in the man's face. "Where did you get this?"

The smug jihadist retorted in Arabic. He had no way of knowing that Krieger understood. The jihadist had done his job here, but was disappointed that he wouldn't be able to replicate this in another city. His soul would now escalate to the pinnacle of his religious belief: he would spend the rest of eternity with 72 virgins.

Mohammed Adair looked up at Krieger and wheezed, "Allah Akbar. Now you can make my day. I saw that movie on the internet. We will never talk."

"I saw that movie, too. I have something for you… from the internet also. It's called 27 Bubbas."

The man's terrified look immediately indicated that he understood. Krieger's kill shot ended the discussion.

Krieger turned to the next jihadist, who was limply slumped halfway through the drywall. He had been blown off his feet by the blast. Krieger walked slowly and let his weight crush the bloody glass beneath his feet. It made a crunching sound. It gave the man a few seconds to think. Krieger ejected the clip from his 9mm and caught it in his left hand. Then he showed it to the man draped against the wall. The top round was exposed. Krieger pointed to the hollow point. It was filled with a substance.

"You know what that is? It's an all-natural filler made with pure pork. America's finest pig filling for hollow points."

Krieger did this to remove any doubt that this man's commander had not gone to meet 72 virgins. He had gone to Muslim hell… which Krieger liked to believe was 27 Bubbas, just the opposite of the terrorist's dream.

Krieger put the clip back with one still in the chamber and pointed his Sig at the man's head.

"You want to meet 27 Bubbas, or you want to talk?"

* * *

Brooks sipped on his cooled cup of black coffee as he drove up the side street of the parking lot. He had arrived in town an hour ago. It was the very next morning and he had no idea what had happened the previous day. He turned left and cut slowly across the parking lot. No signs of anyone that didn't fit in.

Only one person knew his vehicle was parked here.

Brooks parked. He was armed. He got out of his vehicle and casually walked up to the old Chevy pickup. He fully expected just to check on the old vehicle and move it.

When he opened the door, a small envelope fell to the ground. He instinctively looked around before picking it up. With the old pickups, you could tuck a small note between the door and the door jamb, and it would be unseen and protected from the elements. This was an untraceable method of communication he and an old friend had chosen to use.

This message could only have come from one man. Brooks got in the old Chevy and opened the envelope. The message was short: they had to meet in person.

A personal meeting meant the gravest of situations. His old steely eyes gazed toward the sky. He had sensed something was up.

Brooks held the note and turned the envelope upside down. A SIM card fell into the palm of his hand. He quickly checked the area again, then he opened the back of one of his phones. He replaced the card with the one he had just received. The authentication text could only come from him. His response was simply a date and time. The location had been pre-determined the last time they had met.

CHAPTER 13

At the same time, Gabby sat across the desk from Adam with her legs crossed. She listened to him intently. Adam's office was their primary meeting place to discuss what they wanted the public to know. Since the globalists had purchased controlling interest in what used to be the media, the administration needed various methods to get their messages out to the public.

To achieve this goal, Gabby, as White House press secretary, had developed an alignment with talk radio and alternative media personalities. They were the only true media left. As Jefferson once said, "An educated citizenry is a vital requisite for our salvation as a free people."

Gabby had established a mutually beneficial relationship with several of the most influential people in these media channels. They would be allowed to break stories on select topics and have the ability to report on topics as directed by her and the administration. These channels could help educate the public by outlining positive impacts of the administrations moves for the American people, while disclosing the globalist's counteractive and divisive talking points ahead of time. This arrangement helped educate the public about the constant false narratives by these globalist marketing organizations. Each person she contacted was elated to be part of the resurgence of the American dream. This arrangement was good for now, although Gabby had a better end game in mind.

These meetings with Adam were structured so Adam and Gabby could agree on items they and George believed to be beneficial to disseminate. Gabby and Adam worked through the logistics of the plans, and Gabby would then call the most influential media personnel to give them pertinent information, so that the public would be less likely to be manipulated by fake news.

Issues were usually extremely time sensitive or strategic. Occasionally Gabby would have some of these personalities fly in for a face to face meeting and brainstorming. These took place in the Eisenhower building, or sometimes somewhere outside of Washington. Gabby mused that no one thought it unusual when a nationally syndicated talk radio host or two was missing for a day, and no one ever asked why.

Last night, after he'd got back to Washington, Krieger had briefed Adam and George. The three thought of a few things they could let the public know about protecting themselves in the unlikely event of an EMP burst. They could use that angle as a springboard to information that the recent outage had been caused by radical Islamic terrorists. They'd even let it out that the terrorists had been funded by the globalists. Using the word globalist was an idea George wanted to cultivate. After all, they knew the globalists were using radical Islam to advance their agenda.

So, Adam outlined the basic information about the EMP burst that they wanted the public to know.

Gabby and Adam had just completed messages to be shared when Adam's phone rang. It was his executive assistant. He pushed the speaker button. "Hi Barb."

"Sorry to disturb you sir, but Congresswoman Madison Dodge is here. She's hoping you have a few minutes."

Adam looked at Gabby. They both nodded; they were finished with the topics on the meeting's agenda.

A moment later Madison walked through the door and warmly greeted Gabby.

Madison looked across the desk at Adam. "You don't mind me stopping by, do you sir?"

"Hi, Madison, actually this is a perfect time. What can I do for you?"

"I just thought I'd let you know that the establishment is at it again. They're trying to see how many votes they can get for an impeachment... again."

Adam wasn't overly surprised. This was one of their tactics. "They'll do anything to keep their marketing channels talking smack to divert attention from what's really happening. Is there anything you need me to do at this point?"

Madison was focused on Adam and shook her head saying, "Not really. I just wanted you to know, because it'll be a story line today or tomorrow."

Adam nodded. "Thank you, Madison, these insights really help and the president and I appreciate it more than you know."

Madison looked down and said, "I do think it would be good to get some talking points out to your contacts as soon as possible."

Gabby perked up even more. "Good idea, we'll do that. This is perfect timing. We just finished reviewing talking points to feed the alternative media this week. We'll add this to the list."

Madison gave Gabby a radiant smile. She was aware of them sharing information with the alternative media. "Wonderful. They'll be able to provide a little buffer." Turning to Adam, she continued, "Well, I've got to go to another meeting. I just wanted to make sure you're ready when the reports come out."

"We appreciate it, Madison," Adam said. He noticed the two women exchange a glance as Madison turned and walked out.

She pulled the office door closed behind her.

George and Adam had made headway compiling illegal activities within the government, exposing members of Congress and causing over fifty mayors to resign. The globalists saw this administration as the most significant risk to their organizations worldwide.

Adam wondered about the next level of establishing communication more directly with the public. "So how are you coming with giving the president direct contact to the people?"

"We're getting close," Gabby explained. "I'm working behind the scenes. The mainstream media will take another shot at the president by escalating complaints about the conditions in the media room again. Several people will complain about the environment and pressure the president to make improvements. But I want to wait a few more weeks. I'll let you know when, so the president will be ready."

Adam loved Gabby's idea. When she launched a full media blitz on the complaints, that would give the president the reason to move the media across the street in order to address their issues. Then Gabby would convert the current White House media room to a world class high-tech media room. From there, the president and key others could communicate directly with the American people, without being censored. It would be the beginning of a revolution to directly inform the public.

Adam smiled. "I love it when a plan comes together. A well-educated public will never vote for globalists or huge government."

Gabby glanced down at her perfectly starched skirt, and asked softly, "Will I see you tonight?"

Adam smiled. "As long as nothing else comes up, I'll see you tonight... right after I talk with Krieger."

CHAPTER 14

That night, Mauricio explained in detail to Adam, Krieger and Briggs what he had learned about the dead terrorists.

"We've tracked the leader back to a group in Chicago," he said. "He was tied to an organization that we believe orchestrated the civil unrest a few nights ago."

"That fits," Krieger agreed.

Mauricio continued. "We're currently monitoring all communications in that location, and we've gone down one layer deeper."

"Good move." Krieger understood that Mauricio was not only monitoring the primary targets of that cell, he was monitoring every communication of every person they were communicating with, and doing it in real time.

"What else have you been able to gather so far?" Adam questioned.

Mauricio looked concerned. "The best we can tell, they're active. They're being extremely cautious in their communication, but all signs lead to them being active. They're being led by someone they call 'The Cleric'. He seems to be calling the shots and supplying money."

Adam looked at Krieger.

Krieger filled in the blanks. "That means we need to deploy a team there and be on high alert. We'll need to be positioned to take them out if they move. In the meantime, do we dare reach out to any local assets?"

Krieger looked at Briggs, who had been personally managing most of the operations in the cities. Briggs shook his head. "We don't dare at this point. Most of these departments have some amount of infiltration by the globalists. Even the patriots that talk to us would tell us they can't do much more than give us information. Their departments are compromised. They can't personally help us without giving us away. Then, with the city commissioner inviting the UN in, they've established themselves to blow the whistle on any operation. You can bet they'll tell the jihadists. We can't risk that happening."

"How about a court order to search the place?" Adam suggested.

Briggs shook his head. "I'm afraid most of the judges have been bought off with election funding. And in most cases, much more… Frankly, sir, if there's a safe judge to go to, I wouldn't know."

Adam understood. "I'll take that as an action item to look into." He looked to Mauricio. "Get me every phone record, text, email, chat, anything you can, to validate why we need a search warrant. We know they'll claim discrimination, so we need the evidence to be crystal clear." Adam switched his gaze to Krieger.

Mauricio answered with, "Affirmative sir. But that's not all." He had their attention. "We've traced a few of the men to cells in two other cities. There has been very little communication in the past month, although their historical records of texts, email and travel confirm the centralization of their efforts."

Krieger wanted a clear message. "What's their activity level?"

"They also appear active, sir," Mauricio answered.

This was the confirmation Krieger had hoped he wouldn't hear.

Krieger and Briggs looked at each other and seemed to agree without talking. Krieger turned to Adam. "We have to garner some support within the Marine special operations. We'll be able to monitor them. Briggs will manage the on-site operations, and I'll have to bounce back and forth. It'll cut us pretty thin."

Krieger looked back to Briggs. "We'd better get going."

CHAPTER 15

"How can we not have their gold?"

It was the very next morning and George wanted answers *now*.

Adam had made this and other government facts a hobby over the years. "Mr. President, this goes back decades. President Reagan, in one of his famous speeches, said the amount we owed exceeded what we had back then. He even said when it all netted out, we don't own an ounce."

Based on the look on his face, George was as concerned as Adam had ever seen him.

Then George stunned his chief economists when he said, "I want to see it."

"What?"

"Now! Let's go, I want to see for myself how much gold we have. Get Air Force One ready."

"Now? Where do you want to go?"

"I want to see it all, Fort Knox in Kentucky, New York," the president said.

Adam was nodding his head, agreeing that it was a good move. He knew that Fort Knox, located on the Army base in Fort Knox, Kentucky, and the borough of Manhattan in New York together *supposedly* housed most of the gold... But Adam knew that wasn't actually the case. It was early morning and the stock market would open soon. It was going to be a volatile day.

George stood to leave immediately, his jaw stern, his demeanor serious. "Adam, we need your presence here at The White House. I'll be back by the end of the day, and we can debrief."

"Sounds good. But Mr. President, there's something else you should know about the gold."

Great, now what?

"We have a lot of gold bars that are actually gold-clad tungsten bars. They're a steely greyish black metal on the inside. We used them as a ruse to give the impression we have more gold than we do."

George frowned. "Who would think of such a thing?" His mind raced to how he was going to fix this mess left to him by generations of presidents.

"When you get back, I'll show you the department of commerce line items for trade show industrial supplies and metals, costing almost two billion dollars a month. That's actually restitution for the Clinton administration sending tungsten bars to Hong Kong bank," Adam explained.

George was becoming more infuriated by the minute. "I'm not going to do any kind of standard official tour bullshit. I just want to see the gold and their current balance on hand. Anyone who shows me tungsten bars is going to be court martialed. Get a hold of Gabby and have her leak reports that I'm going somewhere else, and we'll coordinate another short stop. I don't want the public knowing what I'm doing."

George's choice of words, "get a hold of Gabby", almost made Adam smile, but this was no time for reflecting on last night.

With Adam's agreement, George left the oval office, and Adam stood looking at the first rays of sunlight landing on the Resolute desk.

* * *

In the hours that passed, Adam watched as the stock market's decline continued. Fueled by what they called economic uncertainty, massive selling drove the stock market to another shutoff. The value of the dollar also fell significantly by noon. Stock market and media reports about some branches of banks running out of cash spread across the networks and social media. Signs of panic were beginning as there were record withdrawals from banks and supermarkets were selling out of essentials at an alarming rate.

The news channels began showing empty shelves in stores and kept repeating accounts that Germany had been waiting for their gold for years. Other countries began demanding their gold immediately.

The media pulled out footage, showing how governments in other countries that had faced similar situations had confiscated the contents of their citizens' safety deposit boxes. Some even disallowed their citizens from moving their savings off shore. The globalist-controlled governments had rationed everything from money to energy.

The Dow Jones Industrial Average was now down by about 6,000 points, causing the stock market to close again for the day.

This was a calamity, a drop like Adam had never seen before. Adam recalled October of 2007, when the market had been above 14,000 and had gradually declined to below 6,500, a decline of more than fifty percent. But that had taken over a year. This thirty percent drop had only taken days. It was a massive selloff.

With the market shut down for the day, Gabby and Adam watched cable news. They wanted first-hand accounts of what the media was putting out.

They listened to a report that said, "Citizens are going to their banks and facing the frightening reality that there isn't enough cash. Banks, by law, are allowed to have as little as seven percent of their deposits on hand. That's why they're running out of cash."

The report switched to a video of a huge line of people outside of a bank in New York which had just been shut down. The reporter interviewed a woman who was led out of the bank as the doors were locked behind her.

The reporter asked, "Ma'am, did you get your money?"

"No, they said they were out of cash."

"Did they tell you when they would have your money?"

"No, they told me they didn't have it and I had to leave." With tears streaming down her face, she was still able to articulate her thoughts. With anger building in her tone she said, "When I demanded my money, they had…" Her voice quivered and she composed herself. "The manager said that they are working within the law… he said that legally I don't actually have a claim on the money. Once I deposit the money, I turn over the money to them and in return I own a promissory note."

"He said you don't own your own money?"

She was direct with her answer. "Yes, he said it's a new law from the previous administration. Most people don't own their money once they deposit it in a bank; we only own a promissory note."

The reporter turned back to the camera. "And there you have it. Reporting from New York. Back to you, Rachel."

"Coming up, we'll have a comment from former President Malik."

Those sitting in the situation room were silent with their own thoughts.

Moments later they watched the socialist predecessor speak. As usual, he was eloquent in his delivery. Reading from a teleprompter, he said the US must settle its debt with these countries. He added that the US might have to work together collaboratively with their debtors. He explained that the countries needed to be made whole with what was owed to them, and that America must change with the times. He then said the US must get rid of the extreme debt, to stop burdening its people.

Adam listened to Malik's remaining remarks about either leaving the issue up to Congress or possibly taking it to the people. "What does all that really mean? He added more debt than almost every President in US history combined."

* * *

By early evening George had called Adam and filled him in on the mostly empty vaults where the gold had once resided. "Sure, we had some gold, but when you net out what we have versus what we owe, as Reagan said, we don't own an ounce!"

Adam's thoughts wandered. *I wonder how Krieger and Briggs are doing?*

CHAPTER 16

Across town, Brooks sat down opposite his longtime friend from Langley. "It's been a long time."

Herwig answered, "It has."

"How's Cindi and the kids?"

"They're good. I have four grandchildren now."

"Time flies." Brooks could see concern in his friend's eyes. "I'm guessing you didn't want to see me for a social call."

"I wish it was." Herwig leaned back and waited for the waitress to leave the coffee for his friend. He had ordered it in advance, remembering that Brooks drank it black.

Brooks's eyes watched the waitress sway away and, after he was assured she was out of hearing distance, he leaned forward and shifted back to his friend's immovable gaze.

Herwig got right to it. "Do you remember Sumner?"

Brooks thought for only a split second. "Sumner Davis?"

"Yeah!"

Brooks acknowledged, "He was a good man."

"He was working an undercover assignment and over a month ago now. He didn't check in. It was a professional hit."

Brooks asked, "What was he working on?"

"That's the reason I called you. Officially, he was working undercover as a truck driver. The previous administration hired truck drivers."

Herwig paused because he wanted to take a step back. He explained, "These truck drivers were bringing illegals from Mexico into the country. You know… the worst of the worst… mostly Muslims from radical sects, mostly trained. We all know they were being brought in to change the voting demographics and orchestrate civil unrest when the time was right. I'm sure you're aware of the sleeper cells."

Brooks nodded. "I know, it wasn't much of a secret. I still maintain some contacts. So, did that lead him to something else?"

"Exactly, it was kind of a vetting process," Herwig said, "and those who kept their mouths shut were promoted to transporting concealed trucks with unidentified cargo across the border."

Brooks's brow furrowed and his head tilted back.

Herwig had been squeezed out of his position at Langley and had changed jobs just over a year ago. Although he was ready to retire, he had maintained his contacts in the agency. Herwig knew the deep state operatives were repositioning people and eliminating anyone who aligned with the new president. He was smart enough to pretend to be happy with the move. He even went so far as to ensure that his personal computer, the one they knew about, never searched alternative media sites or anything that would indicate he was anything but a loyal globalist, a deep state hold over. He had played his cards right so he could see what the real deep state operatives were up to.

A moment of tension hung in the air. "He was transporting gold across the border," said Herwig.

Brooks processed the information quickly. He instinctively looked around, then asked, "What kind of gold?"

His worst fear was realized with his friend's response. "They were smuggling gold bullion out of the country across the southern border."

Brooks had his first answer. It wasn't stolen coins, old coins, or even raw mined gold. It was gold bullion. Now for the next piece of the puzzle. Brooks asked, "Bars?"

Herwig nodded affirmatively.

"Were they marked?"

"Yes." Herwig paused again. The old Navy man's tone lowered as he responded with a slow baroque vibration, "With the stamp from our reserves."

Brooks' eyes widened. "They were taking our gold across the border, cleaning out our gold supply from our mints?"

"Yes… and with everything that's happening now, that's why I called you." The comment hung in the air like death.

Herwig continued. "They stopped a few months after the election. Davis didn't know what they were transporting until one of their last shipments. Then, before he could communicate with us again, his team was put on some mundane transports. We were actually thinking about pulling him off the assignment when the entire team was silenced."

Brooks gazed at his friend. The stakes had just escalated exponentially.

Herwig shifted in his seat. "There's someone we need to go see."

CHAPTER 17

The E6 Staff Sergeant Johnson was slumped over the right arm of his maroon La-z-boy recliner. His limp body was still warm. There was a half full glass of protein shake within his reach on the end table, which was splattered with blood. Dressed in sweat pants and a damp t-shirt, he must have just finished working out. The position of his drink and the fact that he was in his chair, indicated that he had either been totally caught by surprise, very unlikely for an ex-field operative of his caliber, or that he knew the assassin.

Brooks and Herwig both had the same instinct: it must have been someone he knew. Since it appeared that the deep state was orchestrating something, the pieces fit.

The killer had executed a perfectly placed shot from very close range. It was most likely from a suppressed weapon. It was obviously a professional hit.

Herwig knew the Director had been expecting him, along with a friend. When they arrived, Herwig rang the doorbell twice. No one answered. They could hear music playing unusually loudly for this time of the morning. They cautiously stepped in through the unlocked door.

Brooks had already unsheathed his Sig P229. It had a stainless-steel slide. Herwig reached to his side and pulled out his preferred Sig 911 max 45 cal. Designed by world speed shooting champion Max Michael Jr, it was personalized for Herwig with a flat trigger, Koening speed hammer, special sliding, and fiber optic front and rear sights. It gave Herwig a small cannon, specifically designed to be a knock down gun at close range. Herwig had gone to this after he'd moved on from his position at the CIA headquarters. He knew the deep state was getting more desperate and, since he'd already had one knee replaced, he was slower than he used to be.

Herwig motioned. They each went in opposite directions to clear the house. Nothing appeared to be out of place.

Johnson had meticulously managed communication for several Special Forces teams. He wasn't a part of the entry teams any more, those days were over. He had decided it was time to let the younger studs have their time. He had transitioned into communications for them. Like a newly retired football coach, he had garnered instant credibility for having played the game at a high level for many years. He knew the business. He knew the good players and many of the bad. He was the main reason his now dead friend, Davis, had infiltrated into the trucking operation.

Now they were both dead, Herwig thought, as he cleared rooms. He walked slowly, quietly, with his weapon held up in ready position.

If the assassin was a deep state operative, he must have received his order from high up. A hit like this would garner an investigation.

If it wasn't a deep state operative, who else could it be and what could be the motive? Could it have been a hit from another case?

Herwig knew of no reason from the recent past. This was the only mission Johnson was working. Whoever it was would have to be an expert to sneak up on a man like this, music or no music. Johnson had just finished working out, he would have been in a heightened state of awareness. All these questions and answers were beginning to substantiate the conclusion Herwig had made in a split second.

Brooks noted the house was neat. There appeared to be a place for everything and everything in its place. This was typical of communications experts. Most items were even placed square to the corner they adjoined. This man was meticulous.

Steadily working their way through every room, the men swept the first floor. They met at the base of the stairs. With the first floor clean, The Shadow motioned for Herwig to follow him up the stairs.

After clearing what appeared to be a guest bedroom and bath, they headed towards the master bedroom.

Nothing appeared out of place in the master or the master closet or bath.

Herwig stood by the shower in the master bath. He motioned for Brooks to come over to cover him.

Brooks walked over and Herwig turned and stepped up on the tile ledge. He pulled out his utility knife. No sooner had Herwig begun scraping grout when Brooks knew how much this young agent must have meant to Johnson.

It was Brooks who had taught Herwig the mantra that the master teaches a few of his favorite techniques to only one person he's mentoring. That person must be his most trusted and valued friend. By teaching each technique to only one person, the master would know who it was, should he ever be compromised. This agent must have been one of Herwig's most trusted friends. Brooks himself had learned the technique from a master who had busted the most notorious Russian spy that had ever compromised the US. The authorities had little evidence on the Russian. It had only been luck that had led them to the hiding place.

Behind a picture was a string that that led down the wall. At the bottom of that string was more intelligence than any five spies had ever gotten put together.

With modern technology being what it was, retrieval devices could be easily detected. That was what the murderer had most likely used when he'd swept Johnson's house. With the hiding place alongside the copper pipes in the wall, anything detected would be suspected to be the water pipe leading to the shower head.

Brooks watched as Herwig removed the tile and carefully pulled on the string. It, too, was a thick monofilament fishing line, although not braided. Slowly, his friend retrieved something.

Herwig put the plastic bag in his coat, then replaced the tile tightly. He replaced as much grout as he could, and wiped it with a towel.

As they walked slowly down the stairs and were heading towards the door, Brooks stopped. There, on the floor by the StairMaster, was a white band. As he drew closer, it looked like a wrist band that had been thrown in the corner. This was out of place.

The Shadow had been careful not to touch anything in the home, but now he picked up the wrist band. On the inside, he found a small folded note.

CHAPTER 18

Krieger and Briggs had flown in the day before from D.C. Now, they sat watching the suspects coming in and out of the large warehouse in Dearborn, Michigan. They were just a short distance from Woodward Avenue where, once a year, people came from around the country to the largest car show in the world. Dearborn was also home of the largest Muslim community in North America.

Back in DC, Mauricio commanded the private communication center supporting Krieger and Briggs over a secure network.

With Adam by his side, Mauricio explained the situation. "The satellite surveillance indicates that the National Distribution Center, or NDC as we call it, is still at full capacity. But the traffic has increased dramatically over the past few days."

"So, the increased traffic could indicate that they're planning something. Am I hearing correctly that there's no indication that we've been compromised?" Krieger's eyes scanned over several screens that broadcast views from each side of the warehouse.

"As far as we can tell, they haven't suspected a thing. And, yes, this increased traffic is definitely unusual and indicative of a heightened sense of alertness and preparation. But large shipments haven't gone out. So, we anticipate that some large shipments are about to be made," Mauricio said.

"How come we know so much about this operation?" Adam asked.

Mauricio explained, "Some people during the previous administration found out that it was the main National Distribution Center for munitions and drugs. But the higher-ups never did anything about it. It was explained to us that at least they knew where it was, and that made it less risky. If anything were to happen, they'd be able to take appropriate action."

"But they never did," Adam commented smartly.

"Yeah, they all knew it was here," Mauricio said with equal disdain. "With the previous administration in obvious alignment with the radical Muslim world, we had reason to believe they gave the clerics in the area a heads-up to be aware that there might not be the same level of tolerance for their drug and munitions running. So, we shut down the surveillance. Then we opened up this operation with our own team. The Colonel put boots on the ground without the deep state knowing we were here. We have sources who've verified that their leaders believe their operations are functioning without being compromised. Since we opened up this operation, we've learned a lot more about theirs."

"Like what?" Adam questioned.

"Like the fact that this small arms and drug NDC supplies most of the Midwest and the east coast. They're more sophisticated than we thought. We've even uncovered the shortest route modeling method they used to choose this location. Let me show you."

Mauricio zoomed in on a large screen showing a map of Michigan, and used an electronic pointer. "Sir, you can see their location here. They take their drugs and go north on I-75, where they take this less traveled route, M15, north to I-69 east. That takes them to Port Huron, where they put their goods on cargo ships to transport to Montreal, Toronto and most of the east coast at much less cost and lower risk than trucking. Then, to supply Chicago, Milwaukee, and most of the other cities in the northern Midwest, they go west on I-69 and go to the shipping ports on the west side of the state. From there, they ship through the Great Lakes."

"So, you're telling me that they did an economic analysis to keep their costs down?" Adam questioned.

Mauricio nodded. "Yes, sir, they sure did."

"Why haven't we seen any terrorism or civil unrest in this area?"

Krieger's voice came through the secure line to address Adam's question. "Good question, sir. When you look at the size of their operations and the span of things going on in this area, there's much more here than this gun and drug running. It's a cultural hub. It's been a haven for radical Islamic traffic. The last thing they want is to bring a level of attention that would compromise their business interests. They need money to survive and thrive. That's why they haven't conducted any attacks here in Michigan. They're the supply line,' Krieger said. "It's actually a well devised and orchestrated tactic."

Krieger felt it important for Adam to know why he wanted him there with Mauricio. "Mr. Vice President, we asked you to be here because social unrest is being orchestrated in the cities, and the chatter indicates that this is just the beginning. We know that these are the drugs and arms that will fuel the violence. Our original intent was to wait until the border was closed to hit this distribution center. But now we believe they'll increase shipments to supply their counterparts in major cities across the north central and northeast."

Krieger let that sink in for a second and added, "Sir, as you're already aware, we picked up two people in Tennessee two days after the Vegas shooting. Well, we also tracked a few back to this location and we believe two flew out of the Detroit airport. It's not only their hub for drugs and guns, it's their safe zone where they feel at home."

Adam knew of the Muslim connection to the Vegas massacre through Saudi Arabia. The President had mandated that the Saudi king purge his empire of the radicals that were involved. Adam thought he understood what Krieger was implying but asked, "So, what's your opinion, Colonel?"

Krieger answered. "My opinion, sir, is that we hit this place before they make their next shipments. We have reason to believe they're preparing to make some large ones. The traffic around the area has increased dramatically. Some medium sized box trucks have been parked in surrounding areas. As soon as they ship, we'll be spread thinner than we already are. We'll have more vehicles to track. The fewer people who are aware of this, the less risk of a leak. At least here we can hit just one location. We'll cut their funding so they can't keep buying off local politicians. On top of that, we'll stop this stockpile of guns from getting into the wrong hands. We want an armed and educated public, not a bunch of terrorists trying to outgun patriots."

Mauricio wanted to clarify for the Vice President. "Sir, we have cut eighty percent of border traffic and, as long as we maintain that, we'll have made a significant impact on reducing ongoing supplies of drugs and guns."

Adam already knew that unrest in cities was being orchestrated by globalists. He knew the deep-seated radical Muslim community, working with the globalists, would continue to escalate unrest until they were either defeated or they carried out an event that tipped the balance of power in their favor.

Thinking this over, Adam reached into his pocket. He pulled out his cell phone, logged in with his password and tapped an app. "Shit," he said out loud.

"Sir?" Krieger questioned over the computer.

"The market's down another four hundred points." Adam scowled. They all felt the connection. *The market is being forced down and we don't have the gold we should have.* That's when it hit Adam. Now he was decisive. "Okay, Colonel, let's take this place out! And after this, I want you to find out anything you can about gold, and I mean everything." Adam checked the stock market app on his cell phone again. "How fast can we move on this?"

"We could move by the end of the day, sir," Krieger answered.

"Good, let's do it! And while you're at it, find out anything you can about the globalists, and any intelligence that will give us an indication of what we're up against and how we got here."

Krieger knew Adam sensed something. "Yes, sir."

"I've got to get back to the White House," Adam said.

Adam turned his attention to his major concerns about the deep state, and the continued stock market decline. He knew the attack on the stock market and these cells being active were related and it was most likely a coordinated attack on the economy to hurt the President's reelection campaign. They couldn't beat him any other way. Right then he decided they needed to purge the country of some bad actors.

As he exited the room, Krieger was planning to handle Adam's request to find information about the gold.

Krieger directed, "Mauricio, I'll need you to hand pick one of your team to send over to the CIA. I want a message delivered in person."

CHAPTER 19

"Wait a minute." Mauricio motioned to Briggs.

The teams were ready to move on the warehouse. Mauricio had just flown in to be there in person. He was looking at a large computer screen, when he saw a magenta colored outline appear around the face as a man who walked out of a building.

"What is it?" Briggs said. He was about to give the go-ahead to the boots on the ground.

"I'm getting a facial recognition of an HVT," Mauricio said.

Immediately, they all understood the importance of the facial recognition technology. The magenta color appeared when the computer authenticated the identification of a high value target. Mauricio filled the sudden silence that followed his comment by saying. "Give me a second."

He took a few seconds for confirmation, then said, "It's Cleric Mohammed Abdullah Akbar. Our voice recognition verified him as the contact for the leader of the terrorists who set off the EMP burst."

Briggs and Krieger now knew that he had been the one who orchestrated the unrest, along with the rapes and violence that had ensued.

Mauricio had more information to offer. "He's also the one we veri-fied coming out of the convenience store in Las Vegas two days before the massacre. We have no records of him traveling by plane. We expect he must have traveled by car… Now he shows up here."

Briggs knew from the NSA database that this cleric was tied to the black-mailing of members of Congress and orchestrating fortunes for deep state employees embedded in the government. He also had ties to Sordid.

Briggs urgently whispered into his microphone, "We need to keep eyes on him."

He and Krieger watched as The Cleric walked around the corner. He was out of sight of the surveillance cameras.

Mauricio confirmed their fears. "We have no cameras up there. If the few men up there start moving, their cover will be compromised. The Cleric has eyes ahead and behind. Don't let his unassuming presence fool us; they're there."

Krieger and Briggs's eyes met. They knew Briggs had planned the details of the operation, and had intimate knowledge of the tactics. He was undoubtedly the best prepared to direct this operation. This sighting of The Cleric was confirmation of sorts. The deep state was making a move. Krieger must take the guns and drugs now.

Krieger knew what had to be done. "Briggs, you take the warehouse. I'm going after the cleric."

With that, Krieger bolted for the back door on the opposite side of the building. He, Briggs and Mauricio knew their cover was about to be blown.

* * *

Krieger hit the street, painfully aware that his attire, size and muscles made him stand out among the regular citizens. He turned left and ran up the alley.

Krieger's headpiece clarified his local support. "Colonel, we have a boot on the ground. He's wearing a black cap and walking out of a local store. Follow him and run by him so you don't blow his cover. He'll walk in the direction that The Cleric goes."

"Roger that." Krieger was moving quickly, but pacing himself.

Mauricio watched his screen as a man on the street answered his cell phone. His head went up. His neck stretched as he looked around. Then, he immediately said something into his cell phone. Their cover was blown.

"We've been compromised," Mauricio said to Krieger. "Two boots on the ground will be around the next corner."

"Roger that," Krieger could keep up this pace for another mile, though he was breathing hard.

In Krieger's ear piece, he heard Mauricio say, "Colonel, Briggs just gave the order. They're going in."

Krieger looked ahead to see two men rounding the corner just up ahead. The one on the left waved him forward. A shot rang out. Just ten yards ahead of him, Krieger saw the man go down. He was hit in the chest. The man rolled slowly towards a car. He was most likely working undercover in the area. Krieger and the second man lunged and took refuge behind the rear quarter panel of a Mercedes.

The young man pointed and said to Krieger, "Colonel, he'll be all right. We have vests on. The shots came from over there."

A split second later, the Mercedes was riddled with small arms fire from a rooftop in that direction.

"Thanks," Krieger simply said. "Where did you guys come from?"

"We work undercover in the area. We received a call an hour ago to stand by. Then, just a few minutes ago we were told to follow an elderly gentleman. I guess he was The Cleric. We were following him from a distance when we must have been made by a spotter, because we saw someone with The Cleric reach for his ear, then they swept him into a side store. The men turned towards our direction. Something set them on high alert. There was no reason for them to make us. That's when we got the call to look for you — and there you were."

As Krieger and the young man hunkered down behind the vehicle, Briggs and Mauricio had their hands full.

* * *

Briggs stormed the warehouse with the SWAT team, and Mauricio watched as seemingly docile members of the community came to life. Briggs suddenly had a small municipality against him. It was supposed to be a straightforward takedown of the warehouse by Briggs and local SWAT teams; instead, Briggs was about to be flanked by a counter offensive he hadn't anticipated.

Mauricio watched in astonishment as men charged towards the warehouse instead of away from it.

Mauricio urgently warned Briggs, "You've got company coming up your six."

Briggs acknowledged. He immediately switched frequencies to warn his team. "We've got company coming in from all directions. Watch your six."

From his overwatch position, Mauricio viewed several screens as his small team communicated with fervor.

* * *

Meanwhile, Krieger and his new counterpart watched as a car slowed and began turning into the parking space in front of them.

Suddenly the nozzle of a gun protruded from a window. Shots were fired as screams came from inside the vehicle.

Krieger turned, and pushed the man by the shoulder saying, "The store, now!"

They lunged towards the front door of the street store. Flying into the storefront, Krieger tucked his right shoulder and rolled onto the floor.

Glass shattered into his hair and shirt. He jumped to his feet and kept moving, rumbling towards the back of the store.

Glancing over his shoulder he saw the panicked face of a young man. He was close behind, running for his life.

As he had anticipated, there was a back door. Krieger hit the horizontal bar hard. The door flung open, bouncing off the cinder block wall on the outside of the building. Running to the left, they were out of sight of the gunman. They ran down the alley, hoping to catch a glimpse of The Cleric or one of his entourage.

Krieger slowed at the intersection of two small streets. The young man came up to his right side. He got a bad feeling when he saw a man catty corner to their right look directly at them, then quickly walk around the corner.

Krieger and his new companion crouched down behind another car as small arms fire erupted. It was coming from a dumpster by a building. Krieger and the young man returned fire. After returning two bursts, the young man moved quickly to the adjoining car to get a better angle. Then he lunged to the next car in line. Thuds sounded as slugs hit the car between them.

Krieger spun and shot... three bursts, three bursts.

The man must have been grazed, because he exposed half of his shoulder from the right side of the dumpster. Then Krieger heard a single shot. His new partner had taken careful aim and eliminated the threat.

It was clear to Krieger that if they stayed there, they'd be pinned down from the other side of the street. It was only a matter of time before someone showed up from behind them. If a local had a rifle, he and his new partner would be in real trouble.

Krieger called for help. "Mauricio, Mauricio, we need support now."

"Negative," Mauricio said. "All assets are directed to the warehouse. Briggs and the men have been flanked. We've redirected all assets there, and we still need one more team to take out a rifle that's creating havoc on the opposite side of Briggs. You're on your own."

CHAPTER 20

Krieger knew the decision had been made for him. Briggs had been flanked. By now, The Cleric was long gone, most likely being transported away from the fray. Krieger could stand and fight, but that wouldn't be smart. It would get him no closer to The Cleric. With Briggs flanked and pinned down, and Mauricio directing men in that direction, Krieger knew that any help Briggs got could save a life. Krieger would never say it, but Briggs was his friend and the closest thing he had to a brother.

Through his mic he told Mauricio, "Tell Briggs to hold on. We're coming!"

"Come again, sir?"

"We're coming. Tell Briggs to hold his ground," Krieger said louder.

Several of Mauricio's communications team abruptly turned their heads in Mauricio's direction when they heard him yell in a high pitch that filled the room. "You're coming? I thought *you* needed help." Mauricio looked back at them and issued a warning. "Tell your teams to watch for the Colonel and keep the lines of communication open."

Friendly fire was a definite concern in a crossfire.

* * *

Krieger turned toward the young face of the plain clothed man who was looking at him for leadership.

"What's your name, son?" he said, realizing he had never asked.

"Bracken, Sergeant Frank Bracken, sir."

"I'm Krieger. Colonel Krieger. Put in a fresh magazine, Bracken. We'll each volley three over there. Then run down this alley and get out of here. We have some men pinned down and we need to counter the assault."

Bracken answered with one nod and said, "Understood sir."

The young Sergeant immediately did as he was directed, but his expression caused Krieger to pause.

With wide eyes, Bracken added, "Sir, this is my first engagement."

Krieger understood what the young man needed. "You're doing great, sergeant. I wouldn't have known." Krieger watched Bracken's eyes closely. They calmed and began to focus. His chest rose with a deep breath. That was a good sign.

"You stay close to me," Krieger added.

"Yes sir, I'm ready on your signal." Bracken now looked ready.

Krieger nodded then glanced to his left. He looked back at Bracken. His voice got louder with every word as he said, "Ready, set, now!"

* * *

Several of Briggs' team had penetrated the warehouse. But not everyone had been able to infiltrate the warehouse at the same time as planned. They had taken out about half of the resistance inside, but there was still some resistance holding their positions. Somehow, when the team advanced, Briggs had been spotted. He was flanked and had been pinned down along the outside wall.

Normally, he would have been able to counter, but shots coming from rifle fire alongside of a building that may have local citizens inside was his main concern. He'd need a clear shot, and he didn't have it.

Two of Briggs's team of four were engaged with the assailants through the window of the old brick warehouse, while he communicated. His other man tried to get a clear shot at the men with the rifles.

Infrared images on his scanner told Briggs that he'd be facing shots from two different locations, outside and inside, if he moved in either direction. His primary responsibility was to minimize the risk to his men. Mauricio was sending help and they should be able to flank the team firing small arms from one direction. Right now, the two men with long range rifles were his greatest risk.

* * *

The Sargent may have been green, but he sure was fast. He matched Krieger's every step, but Krieger knew that he could easily have pulled ahead.

Krieger reached out to Mauricio. "We're coming up on the north side of the building. Where should we position?"

Mauricio was tracking them. "Roger that. Slow down. Take your next right, then look left and you'll see fire about seventy yards ahead."

Krieger heard the high pitched sound of a motorcycle racing towards them, and abruptly turned to see the man had a gun in his left hand. He must have come from the corner of the block on the other side of the street.

"Take cover," he yelled to Bracken, just before jumping over the hood of a car. He thumped to the ground by the front passenger corner.

Bracken bolted for cover behind a small sedan.

Krieger sprang up and rested his 9mm on the hood. He positioned himself to fire. Then he heard screeching tires. He saw a sedan tilting as it rounded the corner behind the motorcycle. They had more company.

Krieger squeezed off one shot and took cover as the motorcycle riddled the car that was his refuge with automatic gunfire. Then it turned left around the corner of the block and sped away. The screaming sound of its high RPMs faded.

Krieger repositioned himself in front of the car's bumper. Men in the approaching car sprayed his vehicle with slugs. He landed several shots in the side of the car as it passed. He had shot out the rear passenger window. The shooter, who was hanging out of the window, was hit and retreated into the front seat. The last shots in Krieger's magazine penetrated the trunk. The car rounded the same corner as the motorcycle and sped away.

Krieger had already seen a man hidden in a brick doorway firing an automatic weapon that was keeping Briggs pinned down. A closer look indicated there must be two shooters.

Krieger got Bracken's attention and motioned towards the doorway. The men didn't have a clear line of sight to Bracken.

Krieger advanced, taking cover wherever possible. When he was in position, Krieger saw that Bracken had closed the distance, and was resting his right shoulder on the corner of a building in the ready position. Sergeant Bracken nodded at Krieger that he was ready.

Krieger shot at the two men who had Briggs trapped. He hit the brick, sending fragments flying. One of the assailants ducked back against the left side of the doorway. He turned to engage Krieger, who had laid down, taking cover. Krieger had done exactly what he would do with a trained partner. He caused one of the assailants to reposition himself, giving this young Sergeant a clean shot. But he hadn't worked with this Sergeant before. Did he really understand?

A split second was all Bracken had before the man with the automatic rifle would be shooting at Krieger.

A split second was all it took. Bracken shot once and hit the man directly in the chest. As the man jolted and began to fall, Krieger saw Bracken take another shot. Krieger raised his head just enough to see Bracken hit the second man. The man fell, motionless. Krieger was impressed. This was a damn good sergeant.

Bracken stepped out and took a few steps towards the downed shooters. Bracken gave him the all clear.

Krieger got up, and spoke into his mic to Mauricio. "Two down… this threat neutralized."

Mauricio's men were engaging the small arms fire about fifty yards away. After one was hit, the rest gave themselves up. Briggs was now clear to advance.

Krieger walked close to the Sergeant and was about to acknowledge the young man when he heard a car racing in their direction. There was also the faint sound of a motorcycle engine in the distance. The car had rounded the block, this time with the motorcycle behind it.

They were coming back to re-engage. They must have had orders from The Cleric to risk coming back.

That thought fueled Krieger's anger.

Bracken sprinted to the refuge of a pickup truck and Krieger positioned himself behind a car to his right.

They focused down the street. This time the assailants knew where Krieger was, and they had automatic weapons. Hiding behind cars wasn't guaranteed safety. One bullet could make it through sheet metal or ricochet off the ground. Krieger knew his odds of not being hit at all weren't good if he stayed put.

His eyes met Bracken's, who had positioned himself to fire from over the hood of a Toyota. Krieger had decided his best chance was to take out the driver.

When Sergeant Bracken saw the oversized Krieger stand up in the street with both hands forward, his pistol in firing position, he knew they were either going to take out the speeding car, or Krieger was going to have a very bad day.

The car quickly closed the distance. Krieger hadn't fired his first shot when Sergeant Bracken saw a man lean out the window. He had an automatic weapon.

Bracken and Krieger both engaged.

Krieger stood his ground. The sound of shots from the side surprised the shooter, causing him to turn his gun towards Bracken, the more immediate threat.

Not knowing Bracken's location, he sprayed three cars around Bracken.

Krieger adjusted his aim after each double shot. He hit the windshield, but the car raced forward.

Things were moving in slow motion; Krieger firing and retraining his sights and Sergeant Bracken shooting in bursts of two and three.

Bracken finally hit his mark with at least one shot. The gunman went limp on the side of the car, dropping his weapon.

Krieger didn't want to weather this storm again. He kept his sights trained on the driver and flexed his knees. His extensive training was second nature. The split second he could save by being ready to jump could save his life.

The vehicle swerved abruptly, away from Krieger at first, then towards him. Krieger's massive thighs twitched. He jumped over the trunk of the parked car to his left and the speeding vehicle passed. It tried to navigate the corner again. The driver must have been hit. He slammed into the side of a parked car.

Seeing movement inside the car, Krieger got up, stepped out and advanced. His brain registered the high-pitched sound of the motorcycle that was trailing the car. He heard slugs streaming past him in a wild spray. The deadly sounds were on both sides of him.

Krieger's head and eyes had turned before his large body could torque and turn. The sound of slugs whizzed all around him. He saw Bracken fly through the air as the sergeant tackled the motorcyclist. The motorcycle skidded past Krieger on its side.

The motorcycle driver was sprawled out on the street, and as Krieger advanced towards him, he saw slight movement. Krieger wasn't taking any more chances. He shot twice to eliminate the threat. Then he ejected his magazine and slapped in a new one. He inhaled deeply. His eyes scanned left and right.

Silence filled the air and Krieger looked over at Bracken and asked, "You all right?"

The sight of Bracken jumping to his feet as only a twenty-something could after an impact like that was what stories were made of.

The sergeant was filled with adrenalin. "Sure! Never felt happier to be alive."

There was no time for revelry. They turned to the sedan. Men were getting out of both sides of the vehicle.

Krieger and Bracken immediately advanced and engaged. Shots filled the air. As Krieger and Bracken hit their marks, they each dropped a magazine and seamlessly slapped in new ones, spraying rounds into and around the vehicle.

Suddenly, in the heat of the fire, they heard an uncharacteristic shot from afar. It was much louder than other shots.

The deep thud sound of a man hitting the sidewalk to Bracken's immediate left startled both men. The body was face down on the sidewalk. His gun bounced off the sidewalk a yard or two away.

Mauricio must have repositioned a sharp shooter as overwatch. Good thing. Even though he couldn't see exactly where the shot came from, Krieger waved in the direction of the friendly fire... With trepidation, Bracken did the same.

A quick look at the men sprawled around the car verified that they were all down.

Krieger released his empty clip and inserted another, slapping it with authority. He was pissed. Now he knew The Cleric he was hunting. These assassins had been sent to take him out as penalty for getting too close. But too close to what? Krieger knew he needed to stop whatever it was before it happened.

* * *

In a safe house near Rochester Hills, Michigan, The Cleric had just gotten some inside information and wondered... *who is this Krieger and how much does he know about our operation?*

CHAPTER 21

Adam slammed his palms on the table. "How could I not have thought of this before?"

"Thought of what, Adam?" John, the Chief Justice of the Supreme Court asked, maintaining his usual polished demeanor.

"The whole damn thing seems obvious to me now. I should have thought of it before."

Adam looked around the room. Krieger and Mauricio had just flown in and briefed him and George on the events in Dearborn the previous day.

Adam explained. "Before we got in office, their plan was to have the country take on enough debt so that the only way the globalist bankers could justify loaning us more money to keep the economy going would be if the country put up major collateral; our utilities, roads, land or our natural resources. It would take that much in exchange for continued financing by the Federal Reserve and their globalist banking friends.

"Of course, that would mean the end of the United States as we know it, and the end of the middle class. Now that we're in office, the deep state insiders can see how we actually plan to start running a surplus. We'll get the country trending in the direction of financial solvency. They don't like it, and they have to do something." Adam was getting louder. "They obviously knew there was no gold… now they're counter attacking. They know that when we can no longer sell our dollar to OPEC, the reduced demand for the dollar will send our currency plummeting. I'll bet they're orchestrating a sell-off in the financial markets, so we have no choice but to take on more debt while putting up our land and resources as collateral."

Adam took a long-needed breath and Madison stepped in with a logical comment. "But no one could predict what amount of debt would trigger the demise of the country and garner enough support to go to one world government."

Adam was brisk with his retort. "That's what they want you to believe. That's the point here. I can't believe I hadn't thought of it before! We can predict it, and they almost had the country to that point."

George looked intently at Adam. Without saying a word, he signaled for Adam to expound on what he had said so far.

Adam had given them enough background, now he needed to explain what he had figured out months ago, but had never told anyone. "Let me give you an example. Let's say you wanted to buy controlling interest in a publicly traded company, how much stock would you have to buy?" This question was a setup.

"Fifty-one percent." Madison answered quickly, without thinking it through.

Adam's tone softened. "Exactly what most people think, but that's not how it actually works. The biggest takeovers in the world aren't orchestrated by someone buying fifty-one percent. You don't need fifty-one percent to control a publicly traded company, and you wouldn't need fifty-one percent ownership of a country to control a country.

"Here's how it actually works. Of the shares you don't buy, what percent of those people do you think will align with you and vote for your suggestions? When a decision is narrowed down to two options, usually one side gets forty percent of the vote and the other gets sixty percent as their best-case scenario.

"Look at the largest victories in any presidential election in history. When it's down to two candidates, you almost never hear of any party winning by over sixty percent and, if you do, they call it a landslide. Reagan had the largest margin of victory in any modern-day presidential election. What people remember is that he took forty-nine states. What they don't think about is, that about sixty percent of the country voted for him. That means that about forty percent either abstained or voted for the tax and spend ideology that would add more debt and send the country one step closer to being taken over by the globalist bankers."

Madison could see where Adam was going. "You're right; in corporate takeovers the purchasers usually shoot to purchase over twenty-five percent of the company they're going to take over."

Adam nodded. "Exactly." Then he told them something they'd remember. "Let's put this principle in terms of how it affects the United States. Once the US total debt reaches twenty-five percent of the total worth of the country, there will be enough people wanting to go to a one world government that it will be done."

John could see it now too. "They'll use the debt of the country as their trigger! They'll say we can't just default on our debts. They'll sell the uneducated masses on the fact that if we go to a one world government and use our land as collateral, they won't have to pay so much of their hard-earned money in interest to the bankers of other countries. They'll sell the entitlement culture that they'll get more. They won't say that the holder of the collateral will be the same families that own Federal Reserve."

George could also see how the globalists would sell it to people. "And they'll never tell them about the new one world taxes, the gradual escalation of taxes, and the plan for the rich to get richer. There'll be virtually no chance for hard working people to ever accumulate wealth or climb up the social economic ladder."

"Exactly." Adam nodded.

George asked, "So, everything that's happening is a means for them to get economic control of the country?" Adam went to the board. "Absolutely. The tipping point to force the United States to go to one world government is somewhere just over thirty-trillion dollars in debt. They're almost there and, now that there's a leak and some of them know how we're going to run surpluses, they want to stop us at any cost. If we show the American people a surplus can be done, it will take them decades to get back to that tipping point. That's why they're forcing the value of the dollar down, and the value of the country with it. They want to change the total debt ratio so they can pull this off *now*."

Gabby gasped out loud. Krieger's nostrils flared. George hadn't thought of that either.

Adam continued. "The countries who we owe money to, have our signed written agreements saying the debt is redeemable upon request. Now, if we assume someone or something is behind all these countries calling in their debt, let me ask you, who would benefit most from this?"

George's eyes got steely. *The families who own the Federal Reserve and their cohorts!* Then he looked at John, who hadn't said a word in a while. "John, what legal process would they use to do this?"

John had been pondering the same question. "It'd have to go through Congress." He paused. "Unless they thought it could get through with a popular vote."

"Could they do that?" George questioned.

"Actually, they could try to maneuver it that way. That's a way they've used in the past to abdicate their responsibility, so the decision can't be used against them later."

John thought out loud. "Most likely the deep state will conduct polls on the use of different language so they know how to sell it and how the vote will go. At the same time, the establishment in Congress will lead the masses in that direction through the media. We all know the elites would promise congress lots if they support it."

Madison could see it happening already. "Bribery! You mean like the comment former President Malik made."

John confirmed with a nod before looking down. The room fell silent.

Madison put her thought out there. "With the recent developments and the amount of debt we have right now, and with the values of the land and businesses driven down, we've got to be close to that tipping point!"

George remembered, "Come to think about it, didn't Malik suggest a popular vote just a day or two ago? That can't be a coincidence. Even before this attack on the dollar, all they actually needed to do was reach the breaking point of somewhere over twenty-five percent of the value of the country to force their agenda through."

"I never thought of it that way." Madison was stunned and wanted to make sure she was understanding what Adam had said. "They're forcing a recession and the value of the land and businesses have gone down, so they may be able to force this play with the debt we currently have."

Adam said, "Absolutely."

John agreed. "I'm sorry to say, it looks that way."

George had listened intently and finally said, "I don't see us being in a situation where we'd allow a popular vote. We should have the votes to stop it, don't you think?"

Madison said, "Sir, we all know they're trying to get you out of office. On top of that, if civil unrest makes them feel insecure, that could play a significant part. Also, let's keep an eye down the road. What about the next president? If they force a vote at any time in the near future, these other countries — or their banks — could claim part ownership of our country."

George immediately turned to John. "Could they do that?"

"The constitution gives no foreign entity or body power over any part of the United States. However, the answer to the question gets complicated. With the power given to the UN by Obama, there is already international legal precedent to show they have legal rights if we recognize those globalist agreements as law. You see, the globalists have tried to move away from countries having sovereign authority. It's all a lie, but that's a legal weapon they'll use."

"But we haven't," George retorted.

John had the floor. "I'm afraid they could make a strong argument with these precedents in their globalist circles. Now, there's no legal one world government, but the way these other countries are banding together, you can see how they'd try to make a case for it."

George had another realization. "Malik said something about eliminating the burden on the taxpayers. That could be their angle."

John agreed. "It could be a major selling point to garner public support."

"You can bet on that," Madison declared. "It would be naive to believe that a significant number of people wouldn't want to go to a one world government. Part of the globalists' control is that they've taken over our education system in exchange for us taking more debt. Schools have been indoctrinating our children with this for decades. Plenty of people would pressure their senators and congressmen to vote for a one world government, thinking that it would somehow be better. Even when the Founding Fathers were fighting to gain our independence from England, about a third of the country stayed loyal to England and King George. They called them Tories."

Now George chimed in. "You're right. Today, a strong third of the country would be loyal to Malik and the socialist one world government agenda. They call it progressive, to signify the progression away from the Constitution and the middle class's ability to retain the wealth it earns. Their followers are the modern-day Tories. Only about a third would be loyal to us and fight to reduce the excessive taxation that's causing them and their children yet unborn to be indentured servants to the wealthy."

Madison added, "The rest of the country resides somewhere in the middle."

"We're in real trouble." Adam turned his head and took a drink of water.

George had heard enough on that subject. "We need to start a list of everyone in congress who would vote for globalization." Looking at Adam, George continued. "You know... something like we did at the mountain house before the election."

"Sure." Adam looked towards Madison. "Madison, can you help me with that?"

"Absolutely. I'm here all day. We can start right after this meeting."

George had one more thing on his mind. "Madison, can you look into the Federal Reserve and give me everything you know about them."

Madison was eager; it was right up her alley. "I'll be happy to, Mr. President." She hesitated slightly. "There are some things I already know, though there are some things I've always wondered about. These things will require access to sensitive information. Could I borrow Colonel Krieger, if he would be so kind as to offer his assistance?"

Standing stoic like an oak by the door, Krieger's jaw instantly protruded out even farther when Madison said, "Colonel Krieger, would you be so kind as to assist me?"

"Absolutely, Senator. It's probably a good idea to get some real background at this point. We can discuss some and I'll get things rolling; then I have one thing I need to attend to. I should be back tonight, so we can reconvene then."

* * *

After touching base with Madison, Krieger was double-timing it down the hall.

Mauricio stepped out and grabbed him by the arm and said, "I know you have to go, but we need to talk, it'll only take two minutes."

"That's all I've got," Krieger responded.

Mauricio nodded for Krieger to follow him into the room. Once inside, Mauricio closed the door and the men stood facing each other.

"Colonel, there's something I believe you and the president should know." Mauricio was wide eyed. "I'm able to go into the NSA database and map traitorous activities. I can find money laundering and all kinds of governmental corruption. These secrets inside the database haven't been processed. We can provide enough documentation to allow the president to uncover every agent of foreign power. We can uncover how members of foreign governments are bribing and blackmailing more than half of Congress. Colonel, we'll even uncover how members of the CIA, FBI and NSA are bribing and blackmailing Congress to protect and build their budgets. The president will have enough evidence to indict a thousand people, and take thousands more out of their positions for working with the globalists to undermine the country." Mauricio was deadly serious.

Krieger's wheels were turning. He had known for several years that Mauricio had access to this information. "So, you're telling me you can put together chronological emails, texts, actual cellular audio recordings and so forth, and in sequence, so they can be taken to a judge to indict the deep-staters?"

Mauricio smiled at this positive reception from Krieger. "Exactly. The evidence we can attain would be irrefutable. I just need the authority, and a small team we can trust. We must do this without anyone knowing. These globalists will only fall when the special ops and military refuse to protect them. Believe me, there are others like us who are ready. We finally see our opportunity with this President… it could be the only opportunity we ever have, and we know it."

Krieger liked the idea. "Do you have anyone in mind?"

"I do, sir."

"Good. I also have a person or two in mind who should be able to help," Krieger responded. He wanted Mauricio to start immediately. "We'll set up interviews. We won't tell them exactly what the assignment is until they accept, and when we do, we'll monitor every move they make and restrict their travel. They'll work in a totally secure location. I'll arrange that. This will be above top secret."

Mauricio smiled, but in his heart, he had a deep sense of hope. "Understood, sir."

Krieger nodded and turned towards the door. Then, grabbing the handle, he slowly turned back with a genuine smile and said, "Mauricio… thanks."

With that, Krieger abruptly turned, opened the door and went down the hall. He had a plane to catch.

CHAPTER 22

The sound of Gabby's clicking heels echoed down the marble hallway of the White House as she and Madison walked swiftly towards the situation room. Madison, who was dressed in a very professional, though fitted, navy-blue suit with a white blouse, noticed a guard's eyes tracking Gabby's bouncing breasts. She thought, even in times of crisis men will be men.

Gabby kept her eyes fixed straight ahead as she said, "Thanks for coming back, Madison."

"I was only across town. If you hadn't called me, I would have called you," Madison replied.

It had been two days since either of them had seen Krieger.

Gabby explained, "The president will be here in a few minutes. Colonel Krieger just flew in and has the files that confirm what you were told."

* * *

George had spent the day talking with other heads of state and with his economic advisors. When he walked into the room, greetings of, "Mr. President," resonated around.

George obviously did not display his usual uplifting demeanor.

He walked to his seat, and briefly looked down with a furrowed brow before looking up and saying, "Let's dispense with the formalities. Gabby told me there was something you thought I should know about tonight."

Madison sensed his tension; she nodded and began. "Yes, Mr. President. Colonel Krieger and I have been able to uncover information that we believe you need to know about." She glanced at Krieger and back to the President. "Mr. President, Colonel Krieger insisted that you have this information tonight."

George's eyes narrowed slightly. His lips pressed together. He glanced at Krieger, who wasn't one to overstate the criticality of a situation.

Madison continued. "We'll give you some history about the Federal Reserve to show you what we're up against and how we got to where we are today."

George had a passing thought about his day and asked, "How could this happen?"

Madison responded. "This situation has been building for a long time."

George cut her short in mid thought, "I don't mean that, I meant …" Suddenly recognizing that he had cut her off abruptly, and had used a tone he reserved for those less loyal, George lowered his shoulders ever so slightly and cocked his head. He softened his tone and said, "I'm sorry, Madison. I had my mind on other things. You're right, we should understand the background to know what we're dealing with… please."

His manner and open palmed gesture settled Madison. Her cautious expression faded, and her normal poised delivery returned. "As I said, this goes back even further than I was aware of. We found documentation in the Presidential archives before 1900. Actually, let me read what I found. It takes us back to 1895 and uh, this was an attack on the United States, organized by London and by Morgan. The goal was to force the US off the gold standard by buying up all the gold that was in the banking, the backing of the US dollar. At the height of the crisis there was a meeting between Grover Cleveland and Morgan.[6] It's a matter of record that Morgan clearly said, 'London and I demand to control the US public debt. If you do that, we'll stop attacking the dollar, but if you don't, we'll wreck the dollar and we'll cause a depression and that will be the end of you.'"[7]

Madison addressed George. "To put this into context, John Pierpont Morgan was best known as JP Morgan, and was a banker who dominated corporate finance consolidation. His biggest coup was the banking consolidation."

Gabby questioned, "So, the economy was entering a recession, when the President found out that several extremely wealthy families were purposely attacking the United States economy?"

Madison affirmed. "Absolutely. In the interest of time we won't get into the details here, but what is notable is that these families threatened the President, saying that if he didn't take their money and pay what, at the time, was an exorbitant interest rate, they would force the country into a depression. By the way, it had become clear that interest rates to these extremely wealthy families were a method to extort money and funnel it to themselves! Well, the president finally gave in and they paid these families with tax money from our middle class."

George looked around the table. "I wasn't aware of anything going back that far."

Madison hadn't been either, until today. "It does, and there's more."

She paused for a moment and briefly looked at eyes around the room before fixing on Gabby and then Adam, saying, "Remember when we were in 'The Old Place' on the estate in Pennsylvania, and I told you about the sinister way the Federal Reserve was put together?"

Adam nodded and Gabby joined and said emphatically, "I remember."

"Well, let me tell you what led up to that point… why Morgan was so desperate."

Now it was Adam who looked around the room, intrigued, before refocusing on Madison.

Madison, who hadn't sat down, began to pace as she spoke. "Did you know that JP Morgan of the JP Morgan Chase bank was the financial tycoon who financed the Titanic?"

"What?" George probed.

"It's true," Madison said and then thought to herself, *wait until he hears this*. "Morgan not only financed the Titanic… but because of the magnitude of the money involved and the significance of the venture, he was very hands-on with all phases of the project. During the design and construction of the Titanic, he aggressively cut costs in order to maximize his personal profits. It was well documented that he continuously disregarded the advice of experts on the number of life boats the ship required. In addition to this, against the advice of the best engineers, he used iron instead of steel. He totally disregarded the explanations that iron becomes brittle when it gets cold." She paused. "In the frigid waters of the North Atlantic, the warnings of those engineers came to fruition. As we all know, the Titanic sank at 2:20am on April 15, 1912."

Those around the table were all leaning forward, spellbound. This was like something out of a movie, but a movie that they'd never heard of.

Madison continued. "As the months passed, Morgan was not only reeling from the loss of the ship, he was besieged by law suits, many of which submitted into evidence written warnings from engineers about the brittleness of the ship in the cold seas of the North Atlantic. With copies of these letters being used as evidence, along with written notes from meetings before and during construction, Morgan was caught." Madison stopped, faced George. "He used every trick in the book to get out of paying everything due, including his usual huge bribes. When that failed, he pretended to be an advocate for stricter maritime laws. After it was all over, he had taken a devastating financial hit. He was looking for a way to pay these people off and recoup his money, but he needed something big, and he had learned his lesson. According to family records, he was panicked and desperate about the possibility of losing his wealth, so he wanted something without risk."

Madison got an unusually cold look in her eyes. She stopped walking and turned, putting her hands on the table. "Desperate men take desperate measures. It's said that, out of necessity, creativity is born... some say evil is born! It was from this incident that Morgan devised the idea of getting the government to enforce paying him with tax money from the people of the country. He thought the most constant thing in life was taxes, and every government needed taxes and the US government had military might. He planned to use the US government's military as the enforcer, so he could stay removed from any direct collections."

John linked things together. "That's why the IRS and the first 1040 Income tax form appeared in 1913!"

Madison confirmed with a nod. "Absolutely, and that's why the IRS is armed and enforces taking money with their guns. As far as we know, Wilson and Morgan were talking as early as early 1913, and there are indications that it was most likely earlier."

George looked at Adam. "They moved quickly."

Madison again nodded in affirmation. "There's even a letter from Morgan to the president, stating that the war could be a tremendous opportunity."

"Opportunity?" Gabby cried out.

Madison wanted to keep the story moving. "These aren't choir boys we're talking about. They tried to get the idea of a central bank through Congress and to get public support, but the country wasn't having any of it. Wilson tried different titles a few times, but still no one wanted a central bank. People weren't that gullible. So, in desperation, Wilson and his cohorts changed the name to the Federal Reserve. The name 'Federal' was key. As we all know, it's not Federal, and it's sure not a reserve.

"Then, just as Congress was leaving for Christmas, Wilson and Morgan sent secret messages to a few loyalists, telling them to stay in Washington. In exchange, these men were allegedly paid handsomely in advance for what they were about to do. On December 23, 1913, after most of the senators had left town, only the bribed senators remained. The huge sums that were paid made those families wealthy for generations to come."

"Where'd they get the money to pay them off?" Adam asked.

Madison took a deep breath. "Wilson was put into the White House by a consortium of bankers and robber barons, including Warburgs, Rockefellers, Morgans, Schiffs, Kahns, Harrimands and Europe's Rothchilds, who wanted private control of America's money supply. Together, these families had plenty of money. This is why we need campaign refinancing laws, but that's a story for another day.

"In return, Morgan would have his Bank or Federal Reserve bank bill passed, which would not only save his fortune, it would set his family up as one of the most financially powerful aristocratic families for generations, actually centuries, to come. The mountain of corruption around the bill would lie undiscovered.

"Today these same men own the banks that now, in addition to having a steady flow of tax money at virtually no risk to them, use the IRS, financing systems, taxes and marketing as a means to take people's hard-earned money away from them. Behind the scenes, they support tax increases on the middle class and don't want a flat tax, even on those who make over a million dollars a year, because they'd have to pay their fair share instead of using loopholes designed for themselves. Many of us are aware that some of their trusts are tax exempt."

John commented, "I seem to remember some facts about how few taxes these people pay, but the exact numbers escape me."

"We're trying to get some examples," Madison said. "But it's a lot harder now that wealthy globalists control the media. Before they owned the media, some of that was exposed. You won't find that reported anywhere today. For example, in a newspaper article somewhere around 1970, it was disclosed that, the Rockefellers pay practically no income taxes despite their vast wealth. The article reveals that one of the Rockefellers paid the grand total of $685 personal income tax."[8]

Gabby proclaimed, "I can see why they took over control of the media."

Heads nodded around the room. Most of them knew these families owned controlling interests in the entire US media and controlled the information war with fake news, which had helped them control much of the voting for decades.

Madison's lips tightened and she continued. "Today, the dollar is worth about ninety-six percent less than when the Federal Reserve started!"

* * *

After some brief conversation surrounding this figure, Madison looked at Krieger as if to ask if he was ready.

Krieger nodded once.

Madison, speaking a little louder to silence the murmuring around the room, said, "Mr. President, I think you need to see what Colonel Krieger has."

Krieger, who was seated at the far end of the table, stood as Madison took her seat. He walked up and put his heavy hand on the empty chair at the opposite end of the table from George. Krieger's commanding presence needed no punctuation.

"Mr. President, what you're about to see is a compilation of top-secret information and interviews conducted by local news channels, most of which were immediately confiscated and never made national news. What I'm about to show you is a top-secret documentary, compiled in the aftermath of the Kennedy assassination."

CHAPTER 23

Meanwhile, The Cleric sipped his tea to lessen the chill of the slightly damp basement of the estate. Being underground with the concrete walls and small windows sound proofed was safer. With their electronic devices in the secure insulated metal lock-box, they felt free to talk.

The Cleric was pleased with the situation. "The operations are performing quite admirably. We're flooding the US border, and there's practically no way they can do any screening."

The senator acknowledged the cleric. "You've done a great job."

Morgenthau, one of the descendants of the famed banking family called the house of Morgan, simply listened. He knew this cleric was getting much of his money and direction from a fellow banking family patriarch, Rothmayer.

The Cleric refused the praise. "I am just a humble servant. It's Mr. Sordid and his friends who deserve most of the credit."

Morgenthau understood the money funneled from Rothmayer to Sordid, who gave it to The Cleric.

The Senator understood the power structure and the players. The Senator was the minority leader and had been in politics for almost fifty years. He also made his money from the globalists who rewarded him for his role in funneling money to them, and that typically meant spending more, which increased the money they made on interest. In return, it was the Senator who was instrumental in initiating the now customary five percent kickback that politicians received. It was a win-win for them.

The senator asked, "Are you seeing any resistance once they're here, or is everything still flowing?" He was obviously referring to the new administration trying to do everything it could to stop giving money to illegal aliens. If this was happening, the senator would get some of his legal people involved and bring it to a halt.

The Cleric was soft spoken, as usual. "Everything is working as it should. We're setting them up in cities and we get them on the government's payroll, so we don't have to fund them. We mail them voter registration cards and absentee ballots and tell them who to vote for. You can relax; it's all still working as it should."

Then The Cleric asked, "Your plans with our mutual supporters are proceeding well, my friend?" He was referring to the senator having just got back from meeting with Sordid in London. The question obviously referred to the attack on the currency and the economy that they were orchestrating, to force the administration directly into their hands. This was important, because The Cleric's main role and responsibility was to stir civil unrest and insecurity, so the public clamored for help and relief.

The senator nodded. "Yes, the business is proceeding as planned." Knowing they had moved faster than they had anticipated on creating financial havoc, he added, "Are we moving a little quickly? The stock market is going down, and we understand we're applying more pressure than we had hoped we'd need to."

The Cleric nodded and said, "I understand. This President isn't easily persuaded. He's making it difficult. But we are ready when you need us."

Neither Sordid nor the senator were happy with the state of the uncloaking that the President had managed to make public. They had spoken about it when the senator was over in London.

The senator explained. "There's no other choice. At this point we have to keep taking the economy down until the president capitulates." Emphasizing with a little more clarity in his tone, he added, "He's compiling information on many of our middle level people. We need to keep the momentum going before they begin to implicate some of our close allies. The more people he moves on, and the more he declassifies, the more the public will be on his side — and the greater our risk becomes."

They both knew that taking down the stock market and the value of the dollar was the last resort. The senator had confirmed for the cleric that they were going to continue the takedown until the president succumbed. If they didn't, they would be exposed and they both knew that hundreds and, most likely, a few thousand deep state loyalists within the government would be unmasked by those who didn't want to go to jail. They both knew that the president had started offering plea deals to those willing to cooperate.

Morgenthau spoke up. "Do you really believe the president can run a surplus that fast?"

The Senator appeared confident. "Until now, he could never get it through Congress. But don't underestimate him. If the next election doesn't go our way, and we give him time to use information from the NSA database against others in Congress, they'll have no choice but to vote with him. We've seen it with one or two already. But to answer your question, our people inside the White House say he can run a surplus the first year of his re-election."

The senator spread his hands on the table in front of him and continued. "He's already aware that we're funding the caravans through the UN, so he can easily cut four hundred billion there. That government waste group that we've never had to worry about before, outlined another four hundred billion in waste. His people also uncovered the research budgeting line items that allow us to spend up to one hundred percent of our budget without over-sight. If he makes that public, he'll get support to make cuts. Then, with the balance of trade and even a slightly fairer trading, he'll be at a surplus, and if these things drive the economy to its potential, the surplus will be sizeable."

The silence was palpable.

Turning to The Cleric and changing the subject, the senator adjusted his tone to match the calm demeanor of the one he was addressing. "I heard you had a close call in Dearborn. I'm glad to see you're okay."

The Cleric appeared calm. "Alas, the circumstances were unfortunate. We were not prepared for such a disruption of our plans. It was a setback."

The Senator knew he needed to ask a tougher question. He had other people to answer to. "What about ammunition and arms?"

"Ahhh, that is another matter. We have other supplies, although as you know the incident was an unexpected complication." He was referring to Krieger and Briggs taking down their munition's distribution center.

The senator was empathetic. "We understand. We've had similar setbacks at his hands."

The Cleric nodded and took a sip of his tea. He was aware that Krieger had retrieved the EMP device.

The senator wanted to know how the arms supply was going to be recouped. "What about the supply to the northeast?"

The Cleric simply said, "We're working on that."

CHAPTER 24

Krieger addressed the group. "President Kennedy had uncovered the reason behind the massive amounts of money disappearing and the unexplainable cost of the government." He had their undivided attention. "In 1962, Kennedy proposed across-the-board tax cuts for corporations and all individual tax brackets." Looking at George he said, "Similar to what you did, sir."

Krieger picked up the remote and turned on the large television screen. It lit up with a larger than life still shot of Kennedy.

Krieger said, "I've put together a series of pictures and video to substantiate everything I'm about to explain. I'll switch between the video and pictures and I'll fill in the blanks."

George briefly looked at Adam and back to Krieger. "Okay Colonel, let's see what you have."

Krieger began. "On June 4, 1963, President John F. Kennedy signed executive order 11110, which authorized the US treasury to start printing a new form of the silver certificate, called the United States Note.

"John F. Kennedy issued four billion dollars' worth of this new cash money free of debt, free of interest, and it was enough money to allow the nation to conduct its business without needing to involve the private Federal Reserve Bank. Only five months later, John F. Kennedy was shot by the crazed lone nut, Lee Harvey Oswald.[9]

"At least the government and others want us to *believe* that he was shot by a lone nut. What most people don't know is," Krieger took a breath, "as soon as Kennedy was buried, the United States notes were pulled out of circulation and destroyed."[10]

Eyes around the room widened and no one spoke a word as Krieger continued.

Krieger's tone was extremely serious. "If there was no link to these notes, why was John J. McCloy, former president of the World Bank, former president of Chase Manhattan Bank, appointed to the Warren Commission? For those of you who don't know, the Warren Commission was the group put together to give the official report of the Kennedy assassination."

Krieger advanced the recording on the television and stopped it, showing a picture of McCloy.

"McCloy was also a former trustee of the Rockefeller foundation. Why would a financial person be on a presidential murder investigation, allegedly committed by one lone shooter?

"In 1976, the US House of Representatives Select Committee on assassinations was established. They determined a shot was fired from the grassy knoll and, in summary believed, I quote, 'on the basis of evidence available, President Kennedy was probably assassinated as a result of a conspiracy. The committee is unable to ID the other gunman or extent of the conspiracy.'"[11]

Krieger advanced the screen and showed the picture of an aging man. "Right before his death in prison, a man named James Files, a known organized crime hit man, confessed on video tape to shooting Kennedy, and later passed a lie detector test. He went on to say that organized crime was contracted to do the hit, though no one knows who contracted them. The man was interviewed twice, the last time being in 2003, when this picture was taken.

"A guy named Joe West was doing an investigation and wanted to exhume Kennedy's body to look for traces of mercury, because Files claimed that Kennedy had been shot in the head by a special round made with mercury. Since the traces of mercury would still be there, it could be detected in an autopsy."[12]

The room maintained absolute silence as Krieger continued. "The court had accepted the case."

Krieger paused and then showed a small screen shot of an obituary. "Shortly after the court accepted his case, Joe West passed away after accidentally being given the wrong medication."[13]

Krieger turned back to the television. "This part of the video is a compilation of clips from a top-secret report on the Kennedy Assassination."

Before the sound began, Krieger teed up what they were about to see and explained that a woman named Beverly Oliver (known as the babushka lady) said she'd seen the man who had shot Kennedy, and had actually filmed him with a brand-new high-quality movie camera. She had filmed Kennedy from the street light, at an angle, with the grassy knoll perfectly in the background. He asked them to listen to what she said. Krieger pushed the button on the remote again.

The screen showed the woman being interviewed at the scene. "I had Kennedy right in my zoom lens when I first heard a noise. I was not aware that that was a shot being fired, and maybe, perhaps that's why I continued to film because I thought it was a backfire or a firecracker. I mean, I wasn't used to being around guns. I did not realize those were shots until I saw in the frame of my camera, President Kennedy's head come off, the back of his head, then I realized that that was a shot. Uh, I don't know how many I heard, I know that where I thought the shots came from (she was pointing to the grassy knoll), uh, the picket fence area in that... around that large tree, somewhere on the other side of those steps, but in the picket fence area. There was a figure there and there was smoke there. I will always believe that the man that shot President Kennedy was standing somewhere in the picket fence area and no one will ever convince me any differently."[14]

"After the assassination, Beverly was contacted at work by FBI agents, who took her undeveloped film and promised to return it within ten days. She has not seen it since."[15]

Krieger looked around the room. Everyone was listening intently, wondering where he was headed with this.

The video continued. "Fortunately, a few feet to Beverly's left, Mary Anne Moorman, in the dark coat, took her picture a split second after the President had been fatally struck in the head. In that picture, there is convincing evidence of a gunman up on the knoll."[16]

What the picture revealed was a man who was probably wearing a police uniform or some type of uniform that was close enough to what the Dallas police were wearing so that he could pass as a police officer.[17]

Krieger froze the screen and added, "You can see this photo isn't too clear because the area of the photo had to be enlarged so much, but you can undoubtedly see what the secret service dubbed as 'badge man', referring to the man in the uniform pointing the gun from the grassy knoll."

Krieger pushed play again. "Behind the picket fence there is a car park, and in 1963, Gordon Arnold was a twenty-two-year-old service man, just out of training camp and on route to a posting in Alaska. He was filming the motorcade from the grassy knoll, and at approximately seven minutes and forty-five seconds into the film he said, "A shot came right past my left ear, and that meant it would have to come from this direction."[18]

The man in the video was standing on the grassy knoll, reenacting what happened and pointed to the same tree that Beverly had pointed out.

He said he instinctively went down and added, "to me it seemed like a second shot was fired over my head.[19] While I was laying on the ground, it seemed like a gentleman came from this particular direction and I thought it was a police officer because he had a uniform of a police officer, but he didn't wear a hat and he had dirty hands... Literally what the man did was kicked..." The man on the screen was trying to compose himself, "kicked me and asked me if I was taking a picture. I told him that I was, and when I looked at the weapon, it was about (holding up his hands) that big around and I decided I'd go ahead and let him have the film. I gave it to him and then he went back off in this direction."[20] The man was pointing behind him to the parking lot.

Krieger paused the film. "To corroborate Gordon Arnold's story, you can see the Moorman photo shows Arnold on the grassy knoll with his movie camera."

Gabby gasped. "Oh yes... I see him."

Krieger moderated again. "Further verification of Gordon Arnold's presence came from a Senator... Senator Yarborough." Krieger pushed play, letting the others see and hear for themselves the Senator's own words.

"During that shooting, my eye was attracted to a movement, and I saw a man just jump about ten feet. I thought to myself, there's an infantryman who's been shot at in combat, or he's been trained... trained thoroughly. The minute you hear fire you get under cover."[21]

"By the way, the Senator retired a very, very wealthy man," Krieger added before he paused the video. "Are you ready for the next piece of the puzzle? In the same photograph, you can see another image standing directly behind the badge man. This appears to be a person in a hard hat. Because the photo was blurry and they didn't have the technology we have today to rebuild a photo, it was important to those not skilled in photography to have corroboration from other sources."

Looks were exchanged around the room as Krieger pushed play again and showed the digitally enhanced photo, which made the images unquestionably clear. Krieger heard a gasp and continued. "There was a railroad signal man named Lee Bowers who testified to the Warren Commission that, when Kennedy appeared in Daley Plaza, there were two men behind the fence.[22]

"Two years later, a reporter following leads met with Bowers and was set to interview him for a piece he was putting together with local witnesses that day." Krieger pushed play and then stopped the screen with a blown-up FBI report. "Lee Bowers died in a mysterious car accident, two and a half years after the assassination."[23] Krieger let that resonate for a moment, then added, "Bowers' story was confirmed by a man named E.F. Hoffman."[24]

Krieger pushed play, to show Hoffman at the scene being interviewed and explaining that he'd seen two men who looked suspicious, over in the car park.[25]

The classified CIA documentary video started, and the man walked to the fence where he had stood during the assassination, and reenacted the incident. "I saw a man standing here wearing a black hat and a blue jacket. I saw a puff of smoke and I thought it was a cigarette, but it wasn't. He had a gun and he walked towards the railroad. He tossed the gun to the second man, then he turned and straightened his jacket, adjusted his hat and walked casually away.[26] The man with the railroad shirt walked over to the electrical box with the gun. He took the gun apart. He put it in a toolbox. He then walked slowly away in the direction of the railroad track.[27] I went to the FBI to tell them what I had seen. They didn't want me to say anything. They offered me money to keep quiet."[28]

Krieger confirmed, "The FBI has over fifty reports saying the shot came from that area." Krieger let the moderator in the video continue.

"The FBI started the investigation right away, and they had all these reports, over fifty reports from eye witnesses, saying at least one of the shots came from that area and here all of a sudden they've got a photograph that shows the precise area within a sixth of a second of when the President's head exploded… They knew the evening of the assassination that there was a second gunman up on the grassy knoll.[29] That means the medical evidence has been altered.[30] The question then is, who was involved?"[31]

Krieger paused the video. "There was a French man named Christian David Ire Anavied, who was an intelligence agent for a number of intelligence agencies in Europe, turned drug smuggler, who was also in Leavenworth Penitentiary. He says while he was over in Marcay, France, he was offered the contract to kill Kennedy. He went on to say that there were three men involved and the contract was managed by European mafia. These men came across the border in Brownsville, Texas, and were picked up by a member of the Mafia and taken to a safe house.

"These men spent several days taking photos of Daley plaza, studied the photos and arranged a crossfire. This man, without ever seeing evidence of the photograph, described how the hit men wore uniforms. Ten days later the men flew out of the country to Montreal." As the video continued, Krieger added, "This is Colonel Fletcher."

The Colonel explained that the assailants had used an explosive bullet known as a frangible bullet, which is designed to fragment into dozens of pieces upon impact. He explained that during that time, only the CIA and a few others knew of this technique. He further explained that the assassins were paid with a substantial amount of heroin.

"Colonel Fletcher Prouty believes even more powerful forces were responsible. They needed sufficient money to undertake the mission, then they needed sufficient ongoing capital and influence to keep it covered up for years."

The video continued with Colonel Fletcher saying, "You're dealing with a very high echelon of power. It doesn't necessarily reside in any government." Then he posed the question of who would have the power to put together the Warren Commission, get the police and judges in Dallas to go along with the cover up and control the media. "All the media, not just one or two newspapers, but *none of them* will print the story other than Oswald killed the President with three bullets, something that's absolutely untrue."[32]

Krieger turned the television off and looked at George. "Mr. President, Kennedy bucked the Federal Reserve and paid for it with his life. That is without question. We wanted you to see this before you undertake what's most likely a war with the most powerful, ruthless and well financed presence on the planet."

President Carnegie addressed Krieger. "Let me get this straight. Kennedy was taking the power of making money away from the Federal Reserve, by having the country print its own money and by doing so it was eliminating the interest — or profit — the families who own the FED charge the US taxpayer. In addition to that, by the simple fact that the FED prints the money, there are countless documented times when billions have gone missing. Simply put, they take truckloads and just keep it."

Krieger affirmed his summation. "Yes sir, and you're obviously talking about the reoccurring examples, like the $9,000,000,000,000 (trillion) missing from the Federal Reserve during just one incident towards the end of your predecessor's reign."

George nodded in agreement. "Yes, and it's more than $50,000 per person paying federal taxes, and we believe it's over eleven trillion."

"I remember being part of that investigation," Madison said. "Rep. Alan Grayson questioned the FED inspector General about where $9 Trillion dollars went.[33] He already knew, he said, 'Inspector General Elizabeth Coleman hasn't a clue.'[34] He also knew that when they were giving testimony under the previous administration, they said, they have no jurisdiction to investigate the FED![35]

George was pointed. "So, you believe that the people in charge of the Federal Reserve had Kennedy killed… a sitting president!"

Krieger didn't just believe it, he knew it. "Yes sir, and he's not the only president to meet his fate at the hands of these men. As I was told, it's the drive for power on the part of men in high places to use any means to bring about their desired aim – Global Conquest.[36]

Krieger punctuated his point by naming other presidents who had met similar fates. "Jaime Roldos, president of Ecuador, and Omar Torrijos, president of Panama… Their deaths were not accidental. They were assassinated because they opposed that fraternity of corporate, government, and banking heads, whose goal is global empire."[37]

Madison added, "This goes way back, sir. It's well documented that Lincoln was having disagreements with the international bankers who eventually became the Federal Reserve. The disagreements were over the excessive interest they wanted to charge to finance the Civil War. The details are a story for another day, though the principle is the same."

Madison paused and wanted to punctuate a point Krieger had made. "They're getting even more brazen. They're just printing money."

Gabby was still processing it all. She sighed and added, "This is a little much. Aren't these banking families rich enough?"

Adam put his answer on an emotional level. "It's human nature to always want to progress. That's why kings long ago went to war to conquer foreign lands. Think about the greatest battles in history, Genghis Kahn, Napoleon, Tso; how do you think we got Hawaii?"

Gabby gasped. "What?"

Adam explained. "We acquired Hawaii because a banking group led the overthrow of the ruling monarchy with the plan to let the United States come to the rescue and take over. Of course, the US was using the Federal Reserve at that time, and the bankers knew the country would turn to the Federal Reserve Bank for a loan, which of course would lead to the owners of the FED getting richer. Remember the strategy Morgan began the FED on? He wanted to use the military might of the United States government to increase his wealth at virtually no risk to himself and his friends. He wanted a pipeline of money from the American taxpayers to himself."

Krieger eyed the president. "They tapped into the most lucrative pipeline of money in history, sir. To save the country you'll have to go up against these people. They have the most untraceable cash in the world. We'll be outgunned, out financed, and they'll stop at nothing to destroy the country and basically keep our people as indentured servants. They want every person in the country working for them, and they're ruthless. Are you sure you want to go up against them?"

George looked around the room, tightened his lips for a moment and then spoke. "The real question is, how many of you are with me?"

CHAPTER 25

Brooks arrived at his town house that night, just before dusk. He pressed his personalized access codes into the keypad and put his thumb in place. Then he took out his Sig, opened the door, and stepped in cautiously. He walked softly. It had been almost a year since he'd been here. He never stayed long, though having a place within driving distance of DC gave him access to the city. It also allowed his one acquaintance the ability to drop things off, or in this case, arrive.

Smelling coffee, he slowly entered the kitchen. He saw his friend and neither said a word as Brooks took out his phone and removed the SIM card and battery. He walked to the wall, slid the picture to one side, opened the safe and placed the disassembled phone pieces inside, next to his friend's. Protocol was protocol and was strictly followed.

"Black as usual," came the greeting from Ferraro with a smirk. He looked down at the cup of coffee he had just poured and placed across from him at the kitchen table.

"You're early," Brooks said as he holstered his weapon and pulled out the chair to sit down.

"Nobody's ever on time. You're either early or late."

Brooks had heard Ferraro say that many times.

"Did you make the sweep?" Brooks asked, questioning to ensure Ferraro had the place scanned for any type of surveillance devices.

"Sure did, we're clean," Ferraro said. "Had the surrounding buildings checked too. They're good."

Ferraro was a unique individual in this day and age. He was a Don in the Mafia who had worked his way up through the ranks. Ferraro knew more than most the influences that the Russian Mafia and the mid-eastern terrorists had gained in Washington. He had watched these types come into the country with significant financial backing. This financial backing granted them favor with the political elites. Together, what they were doing to the country and the middle class wasn't good. Ferraro knew first hand the plight of middle-class families. Most of his legitimate businesses dealt with middle-class people on a daily basis, and he was sympathetic to their plight. They had gone over twenty-five years with raises less than inflation. Ferraro knew what corrupt forces in Washington had done and were planning to do. That was why he'd hired Brooks, the ex-CIA operative, to begin to take out the worst threats to the sovereignty of the country. When Ferraro and the Shadow had seen a man running for President who wasn't part of the deep state, they stepped in to save the candidates who eventually became the current president and vice president.

Ferraro watched The Shadow turn on the jamming device for assurance.

Comfortable that he could talk freely, Ferraro got right to the topic of the meeting. "I've watched the video you sent, and showed it to our friend, and he agrees."

Ferraro looked at Brooks and nodded, keeping eye contact.

Ferraro made their intentions clear. "We've already made the transfer." He was referring to a transfer of funds from Ferraro to Brooks before a job.

"All three?"

"Affirmative."

The Shadow looked at Ferraro, who added, "That should send a message."

They had become aware of the deep state plans to overthrow the will of the people and assassinate the president. If the deep state couldn't orchestrate the assassination, they planned to drive the country into financial turmoil in order to take over again. The scary thing was, the globalist empire was working diligently on both fronts.

Ferraro's method of dealing with these traitors was unconventional. He wasn't a politician, but he realized that, with the power of the deep state, justice wouldn't reach those who were connected. He could, however, take a small step towards delaying the threat, causing other traitors within the government to pause. He needed to slow them down. He needed to buy time, which had become a precious commodity.

Brooks asked, "He doesn't think we can prosecute?"

"Wishes we could. He says you have the evidence. The issue is that the president has a few positions filled by people he thought were loyal, but they're compromised, too. Not to the extent of the others, but they've taken money in the past just the same. The deep state is blackmailing them. As long as they're in place, we won't get the prosecutions we should. If the president moves these people out, that's another story, but we sure can't contact him. Until then, we either sit by and watch them commit treason or we take action."

The look on Brooks' face begged for more clarification. He always wanted to ensure that his methods were a last option. Ferraro knew and respected that about The Shadow.

Ferraro explained how the attorney general would have to appoint a special council. Even though hard evidence showed these people plotting to kill the president and create financial turmoil, both separate treasonous activities, it would never see the light of day in Congressional hearings, the media, or a court room. He explained how attorneys could discount it on the grounds of how it had been obtained. Then the traitors would simply carry out their plans using alternative methods.

Brooks knew the legal advice from Ferraro's source was as good as it gets. "I understand… I guess he's right. So, the video is worthless?"

"Not at all. Actually, it's extremely valuable. After they're assassinated, we can release it on the Internet. We've set up several transmission points for just this type of thing. We'll send it from a few locations at the same time and, even though they'll be able to track where it came from, they'll have no way to trace it back to any individual, just locations that we'll never use again. So it won't get them anything. Our people will be long gone."

Brooks felt better about being able to use the information. "Sounds like a plan."

The assassination of three corrupt politicians would send a message. These three had one thing in common: in their time in politics, each had sold out the country to foreign entities for personal benefit. One was a second-generation senator and this message would resonate with others of this kind in Washington. The time had come when traitors were being eliminated by patriots who weren't part of the government… people who understood that the best way to kill a snake is to cut the head off. Hydras like this needed many heads cut off. It would soon be obvious that the country would either become part of a one world government with the sovereignty of the United States and its middle class lost forever, or the takeover would be thwarted.

A political war of the highest stakes was under way. In this chess match, the one world government elite were making their move, not anticipating a counter offensive of this magnitude. The message would be sent that some patriots would not go quietly into the night.

The Shadow had his next assignment. As he was about to stand up to freshen his coffee, Ferraro said, "After that, there's someone in the government who needs your help."

CHAPTER 26

Madison had just walked into the Cabinet Room that adjoined the Oval Office. It was early the next morning and several of the president's staff and a few politicians were discussing the growing civil unrest. Senator Madison Dodge hadn't planned to stay for the whole meeting. She only had a short period of time before her meeting with the president.

The national security advisor had worked the back channels before the meeting to garner support for his viewpoint, though he couldn't get through to the minority members. They just wouldn't do anything reasonable for this president.

He explained it to Madison. "After consulting with many people, we believe the magnitude of the current civil unrest is unprecedented, and most of it is being spurred by social issues. In incidents like this, one approach is to send people into the city having the problem. We investigate, define the issues, look for local leaders, talk to them, and find common areas to use as a platform for resolution."

The house majority lead shook her head. "Unfortunately, this is beyond our capacity to manage."

Madison cut the house majority lead's usual long windedness short. "What are you suggesting?"

"It's been suggested that we bring in a small number of UN troops to help alleviate the burden and help move us towards healing."

Madison's eyes got bigger.

"They'll be viewed as impartial and will bring a calming presence," the corrupt majority lead added.

Madison glanced out the window at the Rose Garden and then at the busts of George Washington and Benjamin Franklin that were positioned at the sides of the fireplace. *What would those two think about bringing in a foreign military presence?*

She glanced above the mantle at the picture depicting the signing of the Declaration of Independence, then at the empty chair of the president, two inches taller than the rest of the chairs. She wondered how long that tradition had been in place. *I wonder if it signified that the president must stand taller than the rest in times of uncertainty?*

Madison had thought it through enough. She looked at the house majority leader. "To suggest that the escalation or even explosion of unrest is above and beyond what local law enforcement can handle is simply not the case at this point. Yes, we've had some initial losses, but the cities are adjusting and from my reports, things are beginning to stabilize. The president has told law enforcement to ensure that they keep control and not let these incidents get out of hand. Frankly, if you're asking me to support you bringing foreign troops into this country, troops who we both know won't be under the control of the US military, I just don't think that's what the country is all about."

The woman, who had been taking kickbacks for decades, responded by saying, "Senator Dodge, you're thinking about where we're at this morning and, frankly, relying on some optimistic points of view from local officials. What if it gets worse? What happens when it escalates? These troops are a safeguard. They're trained for this type of thing and we can bring in troops who have experience in European situations."

"I don't see the need. In fact, to me, the risk exceeds the reward. Frankly Ms. Speaker, I don't know how but I believe the people that fund you are creating this unrest." Madison closed her tablet. This meeting was scheduled to last a few more minutes, but she had heard enough. She knew how UN troops came under the disguise of being impartial, though they were a globalist entity controlled by the same people who were funneling hundreds of thousands of illegals to the southern border. These same people controlled the FED.

Senator Madison Dodge wanted to put an end to the thought that there was any possibility that this group of compromised individuals would ever get her support. "Congresswoman, you know me; I keep an open mind. It's my opinion that bringing in foreign troops is a step in the direction of globalism, and that's everything we stand against. It's what the president ran against.

Besides that, it's not the civil unrest that's causing this. If you and your group will support items to jump start the economy, most of this civil unrest will dwindle away, and you know it." *You bitch.*

Madison knew this congresswoman was a member of the establishment. What she didn't know was that the senator she was with knew about the preparations for munitions to be supplied to cities across the Northeast. She was just giving it one more try to see if Madison would support the UN troops. That would give them plausible deniability. The way this whole thing was shaking out, it was going to be messy. But still, when her friends took back control of the FBI, CIA and White House, none of this would ever be investigated.

CHAPTER 27

The significant losses triggered the stock market to be shut down again. Several other countries were experiencing economic slowdowns and had demanded that the United States pay its debts immediately. The dollar was no longer being accepted as payment to these countries, so US owned companies were scrambling to purchase currencies and commodities like gold, silver and copper as mediums of exchange to make payments on imported goods. COD, or cash on delivery, had been imposed by other industrial countries on all goods and services. US-owned companies worked at a frantic pace to keep their supply chains and revenue flowing.

Although retail purchases across the country had almost halted, food was flying off the shelves as fast as it was stocked. Processing businesses for meats, poultry and grains began reporting that local contractors had dramatically increased prices or stopped supplying, most likely to secure their own positions. This, and the recent decline in the stock market, was driving up food prices.

In an unprecedented move, George had closed the Stock Market for the last two days of the week. He had fielded enough calls from heads of states and the head of the Federal Reserve to know things were about to get worse, much worse.

George, Adam, Madison and Gabby were scheduled to meet with Lord Rothmayer, who was the largest stock holder of the Federal Reserve. The good Lord had called George yesterday and requested an early morning meeting. He'd said he could help.

* * *

Lord Rothmayer sat confidently, with an air of royalty. He was a Lord, an endowed title from his English heritage, although his roots went back to other places.

After cordial greetings were exchanged, the Lord began by recounting the good working relationship he and his partners had enjoyed with the United States over the years. He spoke of the tight spots they had been in going back to the 1890s when his family had lent the country much needed money to avert a recession. He spoke about the creation of the Federal Reserve to help finance the country, which had led to eventual victory in the First World War. He spoke of the undying support they had offered to help the country out of the 2008 recession. All of it was a lie.

With both hands on the table and virtually no other mannerisms whatsoever, the Lord continued. "This may be the worst situation we've been in. As you know, countries are demanding payment in terms other than the dollar. We've been holding the value of the dollar as high as we can. But we don't have much time left. We can only hold it another two to four weeks at the most."

George was intently listening, and stoically quiet.

Rothmayer's chin was lifted, causing his eyes to have to look downwardly. He spoke slowly. "You have very little gold and the other countries know it. The United States has gotten herself into a position where now, with the confidence in the dollar being eroded, countries want to ensure that you're not just going to print more dollars to pay them back with a currency that's devaluing by the day."

Rothmayer hesitated; his years of training in negotiations had taught him not to make things personal. So, he said, "Mr. President, you didn't cause this. Even as far back as Reagan, the country was over leveraged on its gold reserves. The sad part is that your country's politicians did it to themselves. For example, years ago, when some of your predecessors wanted to prop up other countries, they knew they just couldn't give them gold, so they increased what they called foreign aid, then they let those countries buy your gold with your own money at a fraction of its true worth. Reagan even knew this when he said, "In the last six years, 52 nations have bought... billion dollars of our gold, and all 52 are receiving foreign aid from this country."

George's eyebrows raised. He knew politicians had been blackmailed and bribed for decades, to go along with these Federal Reserve antics.

The Lord continued. "In recent years, most of the remainder of the gold has disappeared. Your vaults are practically empty. When Germany asked for its gold, they were told that it would take many years to get it back. Now it's public knowledge, and you have countries lining up to retrieve their gold and you don't have it."

The banker looked down at his hands, which were still both palms down on the table. With seamless ease, he turned his hands so that his palms and wrists appeared. "The only thing that kept your economy afloat was the value of the dollar, and that value didn't come from intrinsic value, it came from confidence, and that confidence is gone." He waved his right hand as if to indicate that it didn't matter what George and the others would say next. His word was what was important.

Rothmayer looked at the others around the table, then focused back on George. "But we can help you restore it and save your economy! There are ways," he stated. "You'll need collateral. Just like any other loan, you need to put up some kind of security. Since you have practically no gold, we need something else."

"What about the gold we do have?" asked Madison.

"You have a little, but that still leaves you with a substantial shortfall that you need to fill with something of intrinsic value."

George's steely eyes narrowed.

Madison's eyes got bigger. "You're not talking about our land and natural resources?!"

"What else do you have?" Lord Rothmayer had expertly drawn out this exchange so they were the ones to say it, not him. He was smooth.

In seconds, Madison, Adam and George had the same thought: what other collateral is there? The president and Adam were in their first term. They hadn't been the cause of eliminating the gold and selling signed promissory notes to the Federal Reserve and other countries, but those notes were all now coming home to roost. This was obviously an orchestrated attack — one that had been played rather well.

Sensing that his adversaries were silent because he knew they had no other options; the banker twisted the knife. He sat back in his chair, folded hid hands over his ample belly and held eye contact long enough to make his victim shift uneasily. He smiled condescendingly. "As we see it," he said, "your only options to satisfy your commitments are to put up the collateral. With the right amount of collateral, we can help. We can convince the other countries that this would stabilize the world's economy and put them all on a more level playing field."

Rothmayer hesitated and looked over his glasses, then sat back in his chair with his chin up. "Of course, they'll demand some show of good faith and want to guarantee payments. This could be handled with a moderate tax of just a few percent. We suggest that you make it a gradual implementation."

"You mean a global or world tax, like that damn carbon tax?" Adam said with a tone fraught with anger.

The banking patriarch shrugged. "You have to pay them back somehow."

Adam wasn't about to say what he was really thinking. He knew the carbon and global warming taxes were actually slated to go to private entities owned by these people. That was why he and George had got out of them.

In what was obviously a rehearsed and polished delivery, Rothmayer went on to explain rather eloquently how this could all work together for what he called 'the good of the world'. George and Adam knew it was another lie. They understood it was the globalist banker's way of getting a constant flow of money from the middle class.

"Your only other option would be to default on your promises." He looked directly at George before adding, "We wouldn't be able to support you under those circumstances."

They all knew what that meant.

Rothmayer continued. "Your currency would collapse. We would have to let the other countries know the gravity of your financial situation, and no one else would accept your dollar. They'd start demanding to be paid in a more globally acceptable IMF currency or gold. As soon as your supplies of imported goods are used up, your economy will come to a full halt and your corporate tax revenue will virtually disappear. Then massive layoffs would lead to a drop in your personal tax revenue." His tone lowered. "That would be the end of the United States of America."

He stopped speaking; his position was clear. Crystal clear.

George was the only person in the room whose face lacked emotion. But Adam watched George's white knuckles clasp his pen, mentally strangling the man's throat.

Satisfied that Rothmayer had said all he wanted to before opening it up to an exchange, George surprised the banker by saying, "We appreciate you coming here and offering us your support. I know we don't have much time, but this is a big country with many political dynamics. It'll take us some time to get everything prepared. I'd only ask that you give us as much support as you can, and give us a month."

The man nodded. George immediately stood and held out his hand. The men shook hands and George said, "I'll have another meeting scheduled to discuss our next steps."

As the men walked out of the room, George thought, *Krieger's team is our only chance.*

CHAPTER 28

George settled in next to his wife. She stirred.

"Did I wake you?" he asked softly.

She rolled over. "No, I couldn't sleep. I've been tossing and turning. Do you want to talk about it?"

George usually told his wife what was on his mind and, even though this was a little complicated and he was still sorting it out, he chose to share.

"There's a huge risk in going up against these people," he said. "They'll stop at nothing. Even George Washington had an army. These days it would be easy for one gunman to take me out. They've infiltrated so much of the government. They shot Reagan. They shot Kennedy right after he had the country drop the Federal Reserve and print its own money again."

George's wife, Renee, didn't know what to say to comfort him, though she knew her husband well enough to know that he was a light sleeper. With both of them rolling around all night, George wouldn't get much sleep. So, she stood up, grabbed her two pillows and said, "I'll sleep in the other room so you can get your rest."

Early in their marriage he would have been reluctant to let her go. But in the past few years, he realized that when he needed to perform at his best, he was better after a good night's sleep. He simply said, "Okay hun, you get a good rest, too."

With that, she bent over and they exchanged a quick kiss and she left for the other room.

George laid there with the thoughts of the day circulating in his head. He began to pray silently. *Archangel Michael, give me a sign tonight so that I know and understand what to do. I know you communicate through dreams. If you send me a sign through a dream, I'll understand that the message is from you. Please send me a sign that's vivid enough for me to understand.*

The last thing George saw as he fell into a deep sleep was a beautiful, vivid, royal blue. Divine Providence was about to show him an exact account of what happened to the leader of the country centuries ago.

* * *

George dreamed that one day after the new year dawned, *on January 2, 1777, Lord Cornwallis marched on Trenton. He brought five thousand men from Princeton.*[38]

It was dusk when the British saw the distant campfires of the Americans. As the British moved in, Cornwallis could see that Washington was as good as trapped.[39]

Washington could see that in front of him was the enemy; to his rear was the icy Delaware. It was a bad spot.[40]

As the evening sky grew even darker, Washington called his highest officers around him in a tense council of war.[41] It was at this group meeting that Washington decided to counter attack, and slip away in the night, to take Princeton out from under the British.

The next day, two miles outside of Princeton, Washington was within a few hundred yards of Stony Brook Bridge when his advanced guard began taking heavy fire at the bridge. Within moments, they were overrun. When their commander fell dead, the guard retreated towards Washington.

As Washington sat atop his mount among a group of his closest supporters, he saw his men scurrying in a panic from the direction of the bridge. Washington immediately knew the whole plan was in jeopardy and, if they let this opportunity slip away, the fledgling country might be lost.

Without taking time to utter a word, Washington *perceived what was happening, and he spurred his magnificent white horse into a fast gallop, waving his hat and calling his men forward. As Washington raced heedlessly toward the enemy, the astonished Red Coats lifted their muskets, pointed at the man on the horse, and fired.*[42]

Washington's advanced guards watched in horror as he had raced between them and the enemy. When Washington got to the base of the short bridge, he paused, and his stallion reared. Washington was directly in front of them on the birth of the bridge. All accounts estimated that hundreds of Red Coats had clear shots from the concealment of the far bank.

They fired almost simultaneously. Washington was so close to them that musket smoke filled the air, and neither side could see what had become of the General.[43]

More than one account recorded that, as the gray white smoke filled the air and engulfed him, the last thing they saw was the General disappear into a blaze of swirling royal blue and faints of red. Then the smoke lifted, miraculously, and Washington still sat astride his great horse, urgently calling his men to battle.[44]

Several British soldiers later recounted that, at that exact moment when the smoke was clearing, the heavens let out the loudest thunder they had ever heard in their entire lives. One was quoted saying it was deafening and came with a percussion that hit their chests and almost knocked them over as "it shook the very ground we stood on."[45]

Immediately, the spirits of the patriots rose as one and they charged forward.

The entire British army was overwhelmed by the sight of this man who, it was said, could never be killed in battle, and by the accompanying thunder from the heavens above. The British soldier continued saying, "The spirit of fear overtook us, and we ran."

Washington muscled his horse around. "After them, my boys," General Washington called. "It's a fine fox chase."[46]

Five hundred British were killed, wounded, or captured in the engagement. The Americans lost fewer than fifty.[47]

Later that day, several accounts stated that British captives said that when they saw the General, wearing royal blue with a red blazer and white satchel, was still sitting high atop his great pale white stallion after hundreds of British marksmen had shot at him from a distance slightly longer than the short bridge, and then the heavens sounded off like never before, they knew Washington had been protected. Fear made them incapable of attacking. Thus, their superior forces were routed.

Bartholomew Dandridge seemed to echo the feelings of many when one patriot wrote: "It is plain (that) Providence designed you as the favorite instrument in working out the salvation of America.[48]

* * *

George woke dripping in sweat. He gasped for air and looked around. There was total silence. He blinked hard to see the clock more clearly. It was 3:33am.

The message was clear. *I know what I must do.*

CHAPTER 29

President Carnegie's tone was confident. He moved about as if presenting to a sizeable group, though only Krieger, Gabby, Adam, Madison and John were sitting in the Oval Office. After his dream the night before, George felt inspired. He had renewed energy. It was a new day.

"This is a complex problem that needs to be addressed on a variety of fronts," the president said. "We need to be creative with our actions, and we don't have much time. The vision I want you to have this morning is that we will fix the country and set it up for another two hundred years of prosperity. In the process, we'll address some of the things that have brought us to this point. We need to brainstorm possible solutions to get us out of this mess. What we need is a mastermind group, a brain trust, a team of people that will create a way to fix the country. I think getting the right people here is our first priority," George directed. "I want you to find the best and the brightest minds and get them here tomorrow if you can. Their job will be to figure out how stop the country from being taken over!"

George's mind was racing. "We'll need some of the best in state government. People who have turned their states around. We'll need some of the best in a variety of business sectors like technology, manufacturing, social media, and whatever else you can think of. We need people who think outside of the box."

"What do we tell them?" Madison asked.

"Good question," George said. "We tell them we're putting together a mastermind group to save the country with the goal of putting the country financially on the right track in the next ten days."

"Ten days?"

George nodded. "In our meeting with the Federal Reserve, I told them to give us some time. I told them we needed a month. But the bastard nodded and didn't respond. I don't know how long we have, but I do know they're thinking about days and not a month or more. Our goal is to save the country in the next ten days. John, I'll need to work hand in hand with you to pull out all the stops."

John was on board. "I'll be here every morning, unless you want me somewhere else."

George nodded and gave him a solemn look of thanks.

George directed, "Adam, why don't you and Madison take the rest of the day and develop a list. Then contact them."

"Sounds like a plan," Adam said.

Madison agreed, saying, "We'll get right on it."

George thought for a second and his speech slowed. He had another thought.

Heads were nodding as he looked towards Adam. "I want your group to work here, right here in the White House, to address fixing the economic issues. I want them to work in secrecy. Whatever area you choose, make sure they're not monitored by anyone other than those we personally vet."

Adam nodded and, as he saw George immerse himself deeper into thought, Adam asked, "Mr. President, what are you thinking?"

George responded, "I'm thinking we're going to need two groups. We'll need a separate group, a group of military experts, to work out of a secure location."

Turning to Krieger, the President said, "Colonel, I'll leave the location up to you."

"Yes sir, Mr. President."

Adam, accepting his role, said, "Understood. A few states have made dramatic changes. I was just reading a book on how government can work. It has an example of one state that has taken their state tax code down to one page. We can pull in a few of those people." He looked down and jotted down a few notes.

Madison chimed in, "There are a few senators and one congressman I can think of that we can trust."

George became more demanding in his tone; the executive presence of a leader reaching a higher level. He was dealing with a crisis. He reaffirmed.

"Get them all here tomorrow morning. And find some business people that are doing things outside of the box."

"Good idea!" Adam understood. He looked down at his pen gliding silently over the paper.

George turned back to Krieger. "We also need to put together a loyal team from the military, and I mean loyal to this country." Maintaining eye contact with Krieger, the president continued. "First, I need a high-ranking general who's loyal to the country and what it once was… make that two. But no politically correct pussies. You may want to think of who's still available among the Generals who were forced into retirement by my predecessor. Find the ones who are fiercely loyal and bring them back."

Krieger showed a trace of a smile.

George made a sweeping hand gesture. "We'll need people who can put a mission together within days."

"What kind of mission sir?" Krieger asked.

"One to save the country, that's what kind," the president responded.

George thought for a second. He hesitated to say too much in front of the others. He had a thought, and the fewer people who knew, the better. He did, however, want them to know that he would be tied up with other world leaders and working closely with Krieger and his group.

Looking back at Krieger, he said, "Get our best Special Forces operatives from around the world, and put them on our fastest jets and get them to the location you designate within forty-eight hours."

"Yes sir!" Krieger's large lips were now perfectly horizontal.

George wanted to be clear. "I don't want any of these people coming to Washington. We'll talk after this meeting, but for now, think about a place for our military group to fly into and work out of. We'll need a large area that's equipped to immediately prepare the group."

"Affirmative, sir." Krieger already had a location in mind, and he'd have them fly directly there.

Keeping eye contact with Krieger, George continued. "Colonel, I want whatever location you choose to be at totally gutted of any non-loyal people immediately, and by immediately, I mean at least twenty-four hours before any of the others arrive. Put together a robust plan to ensure that only patriots are there. And immediately stop all traffic in and out, unless it's part of this mission."

Madison questioned, "What are you going to do, sir?"

"We're going to save this country. Washington won independence by playing defense, and dodging attacks from the enemy. Then when they least expected it, he struck," George snapped.

He turned directly to Adam, then to Krieger. "We're going to attack. They declared war... we know their play. Now it's our turn to play the only cards in our hand."

The president turned back to Adam. "Who was that guy who helped save you when you were kidnapped? You said he was the one we saw in Pennsylvania at the other side of the river. After the shootout, he waved, then he disappeared into the shadows."

CHAPTER 30

Gabby looked out over the diverse group that would soon become their economic mastermind. It had taken two days to get everyone here, but now, the room was filled with business entrepreneurs, an economist, an actuarial, an efficiency expert and a few patriotic politicians.

At the far side of the room, an actuarial economist named Haley stood speaking with a senator. A governor spoke with another person. The eccentric billionaire Szegda, known for his unfiltered remarks, hosted three spellbound female listeners to the right.

When the announcement was made that the vice president was about to address the group, everyone took seats. The room fell silent.

After his introduction, Adam began. "Ladies and gentlemen, thank you for coming. The very existence of the United States of America is being threatened. You were brought here to form a mastermind group to save the country economically. Each of you was chosen for your unique traits in a specific area of expertise. Your mission, should you choose to accept it, is to, within one week, create an economic plan to save the country."

Adam let that sink in. He watched heads look from left to right. Then he said, "Our process will be as follows. Should you agree to join us, you will not be allowed to leave until the actions we take are being announced and/or implemented, which we anticipate will be within a month. In a few moments, you'll individually be led into rooms and given a lie detector test. For those of you who pass, we will have assistants at your disposal to help you take care of arrangements such as family matters and business needs. Anyone not interested in undertaking this mission can enjoy a great brunch down the hall, after which you will be released. Those of you who are willing to take on the challenge, please stand by one of the men or women along the side of the room where you see your name. They will take care of you and address your questions.

"When this process is complete, we'll reconvene, and the president will address the group. Thank you for coming. When you make your decision, your personal assistant will take you to the proper location."

Adam abruptly turned and left the room.

* * *

Meanwhile, Herwig drove the public road. There was no traffic. He and Brooks paid little attention to the signs that warned people not to get out of their vehicles. They were approaching the designated dropoff location. Every foot of this public road that cut through the massive military base was monitored with cameras. Signs instructed civilians that, if you experienced any vehicle malfunction, to stay in one's vehicle and someone would help shortly. There were barricaded crossroads and signs on creek beds. They all warned people not to stop.

Herwig took his foot off the gas. The vehicle rolled to a stop at the designated bridge. Looking over the side, he saw a small dry creek bed. Brooks got out and looked down the desolate road in both directions. He opened the rear door, reached in the back seat and pulled out his duffel bag. He drew down the brim of his Filson hat and closed the rear door.

Leaning through the still open front door, he looked at Herwig one more time and extended his hand. He fully realized he might never see his old friend again.

There wasn't much to be said. They both knew the gravity of the situation.

Herwig, possibly his friend from the CIA said, "Good luck."

Brooks nodded and said, "Take care and thanks."

Then they exchanged one last look as Brooks closed the door.

As soon as the door shut, Herwig pushed the gas pedal and drove away.

Brooks turned and stepped into the woods. He side stepped down the embankment and into the dry gulley, turned to his left and looked under the small bridge. There was a large, hulking silhouette.

Brooks walked forward and stepped under the bridge.

He extended his hand and said, "Colonel."

Krieger reciprocated with a warm greeting of respect and thanksgiving. "Thank you for coming. Every precaution is being taken to protect your identity."

Brooks nodded. Without another word, they disappeared.

CHAPTER 31

George greeted John warmly. John's legal advice as the chief justice of the Supreme Court would be crucial. George had Madison attend the meeting also. He wanted to get the perspective of someone from Congress. She sat next to Adam.

Ten minutes later, John explained that he would need to put together a small team of seasoned lawyers to write executive orders that could be signed within days. The orders would be released to the media so people could see some immediate wins.

John said, "Executive orders can come out daily as they're drafted and signed. We'll do everything legally in our power."

George nodded. "I want an executive order to say that because of the threat of foreign takeover, no politician can spend more money than the government is taking in."

John nodded. "We can do that. The threat of foreign takeover gives you the angle, and we can use precedence."

"What precedence is there?" Madison asked.

"Cities all over the country have emergency managers in place who control finances and ensure that elected officials run surpluses. That sets legal precedence to a degree. No one has tried it with the federal government though." The chief justice looked at the president, and said, "No one before you ever had the balls. They'll fight it for sure. But we have a friend who will file a law suit in a state where we know that constitutional judges will support you."

George was appreciative. John always gave great advice. "That'll buy us enough time."

George stood and walked. "They've slowed the economy to a crawl and I just find it hard to believe most of the gold is gone. I wonder where it went?"

Madison had even more inside knowledge of corruption. "Mr. President, I don't know where all of the gold went, but I do have some insight about some of it."

George looked at her and raised his eyebrow, indicating that she should continue.

"Between the years 2000 to 2002, gold prices went down. There was speculation on why and how these prices dropped to a twenty-year low. The president sold over 400 tons of gold to the UK. What's unexplainable is that he sold it at an average price of under three hundred dollars an ounce! At that point, those of us on a certain committee were privy to know that the UK was in dire financial straits. We learned that he cut a deal with bankers and basically gave them what amounted to doubling their country's gold supply at this low price. It was an attempt to bail them out. We don't have time to go into it here, but the politicians in the UK kept spending too much money. Now the people have lost control of their own country. They're mostly controlled by the globalist bankers. That's why most of the average middle-class workers in the UK will never own a home in their lifetimes, and they're being taxed out of their wealth. That's why they voted to leave the EU."

Adam slapped the mahogany table violently with his open palms and stood. "That's it! Why haven't I thought about it before?" Before anyone could say a word, he continued. "That's their scheme! Germany asked England for their gold and learned that England didn't have as much as they were supposed to have, so the bankers drove England broke by bribing their politicians to support massive spending. They knew England would either be under their control or choose their only other option… to get our gold. The dirty bankers could then go after both of us. They win either way. This must have been planned for a long time."

George was putting it together. "So, that's why the public never heard of us selling massive amounts of gold to the UK. They didn't go public. They secretly sold it or took it."

Adam expounded. "The gold scams are everywhere. Comex gold supplies have decreased by about eighty percent! They're selling about 80 ounces of paper contracts for every ounce of real gold, so they're selling 80 times the value we actually say we have in gold."

Madison further explained. "When Roosevelt called in the gold in 1934, they revalued it from $20.67/ounce to $35/ounce. Washington insiders made seventy percent overnight, while the working class got screwed. The working people had paper money, while the Washington establishment kept their gold. When the Roosevelt called in the gold, if you had a hundred dollars of gold and turned it in, you got a hundred dollars. If you had saved that one hundred dollars, today the purchasing power would be under ten dollars. If you had kept the gold, that amount of gold would be worth almost ten thousand dollars. That's why Allen Greenspan said, we can guarantee cash benefits as far out, in whatever size you like, but we cannot guarantee their purchasing power."

John nodded. "Money is only as good as the assets supporting the liabilities. When governments can't raise enough money, they go after the free money sitting in retirement and checking accounts."

Madison agreed. "These poor people who buy gold and silver from companies have no idea that the law allows them to sell many times more gold and silver than they have. This is designed to keep prices down, so truly wealthy people can purchase the real thing. Then when the poor middle class tries to cash in their piece of paper if the market goes down, they'll find out the hard way that they've been taken again!"

Adam commented, "All of this makes me think something is going on. JP Morgan is declaring that its gold is being 'removed'. The question is, removed by whom? They, and most other banks, are steadily writing down the amount of actual gold and silver on their books. They even declared that, in ninety days alone during the previous administration, 1.8 billion dollars of gold was removed from their vaults. This is a trend that's hitting almost all of the major banks, and certainly all of them that are owned by a select few families. They're taking the gold somewhere and for something."

With the meeting time about to end, the president stood. "I'm sorry, that's all the time we have. I've got to catch a plane."

CHAPTER 32

A few hours later, at the military base in Georgia, Krieger and Adam walked into the small conference room. Adam sat at the first chair to the right, while Krieger walked to the head of the oval walnut conference table.

Krieger began. "Good morning. First, I'd like to say that the reason you were each given a lie detector test last night and again this morning is because of what we're about to undertake. Lie detector tests give optimal results up to about six or seven questions. Due to the gravity of the situation, we needed assurance in the areas you were questioned. I hope you understand."

The men nodded. They were keenly aware of what was happening with the country, although they had no idea what their role could be.

Krieger continued. "I want to thank you for coming on such short notice. The reason you're here is because you're deemed to be the most loyal and, frankly, the most brilliant military minds in our country today. You were asked here to join a cross functional team brought together to stop the progression to a one world government. Gentlemen, you're here today to save the United States as we know it.

"Before we get started, I want to make perfectly clear that the president wants to reiterate that this is an optional assignment, and that whatever happens here today and hereafter regarding this assignment will never be documented or disclosed. We've even turned off all recordings in the room. If you have any reservations, now is the time to air them, or bow out."

Krieger paused and looked at steely eyes peering back at him. General Abrams had commanded Krieger years ago. With that relationship in mind, he spoke first to Krieger. "Don, we've each been watching the demise of the country and our way of life. Frankly, none of us ever thought anything would be done about it in our lifetimes. You and the president can be assured I'll do whatever I can — and that means whatever it takes."

"The same goes for me, Colonel," the second general affirmed.

In seconds, every individual in the room had affirmed, with the exception of The Shadow, who only nodded.

Krieger knew he was on board. "Okay, that's all we need to know."

Krieger looked at Adam, who got up and stepped out of the meeting. Krieger stepped to the side. The president was in the next room over with Madison, listening for the affirmation that they were all on board.

A moment later, the door opened. Adam walked back into the room, followed by Madison and President George Carnegie.

Krieger said, "Gentlemen, let me introduce the president of the United States."

Then Krieger moved aside and let the president take his place at the head of the table.

George looked around the room at the faces that were eager to understand the gravity of the situation. He saw Adam, Krieger, the generals, a few other military experts, and The Shadow, who didn't sit at the table, was in a chair with his back against the wall.

He cleared his throat. "We just had a meeting at the White House with another group of individuals. Their mission is to fix our economy and turn it back over to the people for another hundred years… Your mission is different, and I want to be clear that their group has no knowledge of this undertaking. Both groups must succeed to save this country."

George went on to explain the magnitude of the country's predicament. He informed them about the missing gold and the threats from world bankers. He finished his short briefing with, "Gentlemen, we have less than two weeks to save the country before they use their media, working with foreign governments and the politicians they control, to take us down. They'll crash the stock market further in their next orchestrated attack. Internal and external forces will demand that we turn over the nation's land, natural resources and infrastructure. It will be the same control that the Trans-Pacific Partnership would have started. In short, we'd be forced into turning over the sovereignty of the nation."

George handed the meeting off to Adam, who debriefed them similarly to how he had informed the group in Washington. When he got to the comment about the sovereignty of the country, this group had a much deeper under-standing of what that meant. He had their undivided attention and he had stirred their emotions. They were angry.

Now, Adam thought, for the part he *hadn't* told the mastermind group in Washington. For this, Adam turned it over to Krieger, whose credibility among the group had been established long before this administration took office.

Krieger reiterated, as George had confirmed, that the gold was missing and then filled them in on the information that much of the remaining gold had been trucked over the border and then shipped overseas. The room was spellbound.

Krieger finished with a synopsis of what he had uncovered about pres-sures on presidents in the past, including the assassination of Kennedy, after Kennedy had cut out the Federal Reserve.

Krieger opened the floor to their comments by saying, "Gentlemen, it's up to us to come up with a plan and execute that plan."

General Abrams looked to the head of the table. "Mr. President, how far do you want to go?"

All eyes were on George. He wanted to be crystal clear. "The constitution tells us that, when faced with a life endangering threat, it is our duty to defend this country and eliminate that threat. From what I've seen, we need to eliminate this threat permanently, or it'll just come back to attack the next generation."

That was all they needed to hear.

The Shadow made eye contact with one of the Generals for the first time.

George continued. "I've asked the Federal Reserve for a month. We already know they're planning to escalate their attack in two weeks. You were brought here to put together a plan, create the team to orchestrate that plan, train them, embark on and complete the mission within about two weeks."

George let that sink in for a minute. Then his tone lowered, and he said slowly, "That's all the time we've got."

George stepped away from the head of the table, and an eerie silence overtook the room.

General Elder looked at Adam, then quickly at Krieger. Besides many other things, the General was an extremely educated, well-read man.

"There's no time to waste. We need to act swiftly and show the country substantial progress."

Turning his focus towards George, General Elder continued. "Kotter says that it's all about creating a sense of urgency - and that's the first step in a series of actions needed to succeed in a changing world."[49] Everyone was now focused on General Elder. He continued. "Kotter describes four tactics. The first is to *bring outside reality into groups that are too inwardly focused*. You've done that. The second is to *behave with a true urgency... every day*.[50] You're behaving with a true sense of urgency, although I think you need to show the nation the sense of urgency and some wins immediately. Since this group is the most secretive and we don't yet have a defined mission, the other group must show the country some wins — now!"

"Great idea," George said. "I'll take that one as my action item. That makes sense. I've read that we remember the things that happen first, and the things that happen last. In times of crisis, people need our reassurance by our first actions. We'll give them some first wins."

Several heads in the room now nodded in affirmation. This was a brain trust at work.

Elder continued saying, "the third is to *look for upside possibilities in crises, and the fourth is to confront the problem... do not put up with people who relentlessly create experiences that kill urgency*.[51]

"That leaves us with number three, looking for upside possibilities in crises. Does anyone have any ideas?" George said as he looked around the room for input. He sure hoped they would come up with something.

"Mr. President," General Abrams said.

George looked at General Abrams and aligned with his formality by saying, "General."

The General stood. "As Sun Tzu says in the Art of War, when the enemy leaves a door open, you must rush in. As the challenge escalates, the need for teamwork elevates."

Everyone in the room knew that the General was headed some-where, but where?

"When you think back in history," the General said, "great moments have synergies that sometimes show up opposite each other. The universe works in mysterious ways! We all remember 9/11. What many people don't realize is, that on 11/9, years before that, the Berlin wall came down."

General Abrams wanted to acknowledge that what he was about to say was not meant to replace General Elder's statements. "The groups working on legal and economic matters need to show the people something tangible almost immediately. That's important. But that's not our role. Our role, as I see it, is different. We need to stop the fall of the country and take our country back from the world bankers — and I see only one way." The General looked around the room. Then his nose flared and his voice rasped, "Where the hell is our gold?"

His seemingly rhetorical question, which he believed would need some discovery, hung in the air.

A second later, the General was the most surprised person in the room when a voice resonated through them all.

"I know where it is." The response came from the only person not sitting at the table.

The room fell silent as all eyes landed on Brooks.

"There's some gold from Fort Knox in Indonesia," Brooks said. "We can get that quietly with a few small teams. Then there's more that's very well hidden and guarded. And there's even more that's funding the deep state."

Who was this man? The Generals did not know Brooks, the man known decades ago as The Shadow, although his presence at this meeting and the message he had just conveyed immediately established his stature.

Brooks looked to Abrams. "General, if you want to retrieve the gold and want to stop the deep state funding, you'll need every person you've got, and I mean everyone. If you're willing to counter this threat, I'd be more than willing to offer a dose of retribution."

CHAPTER 33

Brooks explained a small portion of what he knew. "The deep state took some of our gold reserves for themselves. Now it's part of what's called 'black gold'. The term 'black gold,' as most of you know, is used to describe gold that's in private hands and not traceable by any government."

Krieger was gruff with his question. "How could they do this right under our noses?"

General Elder looked at Krieger. "First, Colonel, realize who put almost every president in power."

Krieger nodded with understanding, and eased back into his seat.

The General continued. "Also realize that, years ago, the shadow government turned Fort Knox and other gold retaining facilities over to the Federal Reserve. Most people don't know that Fort Knox is controlled by the owners of the FED. They lease that land on the military base."

"What?"

The General elaborated. *"The notion that all this gold somehow belongs to the American people is a carefully cultivated myth. Most people think Ft. Knox is a government vault but, while it is built on government land, it's managed by the FED. Since the creation of the Federal Reserve System, all the gold vaults of the FED have been guarded by America's largest domestic private security organizations like Diebold, Inc., an Ohio-based security firm established in 1859. In each vault, gold is kept in numbered chambers, and its actual ownership is known to only a handful of FED officials. The largest of these rectangular lockers are 10 feet by 10 feet by 18 feet, so each locker is big enough to hold $17.1 billion worth of bullion, given a market rate of $400 per ounce,*[52] at the last count."

Madison said, "So that's currently over fifty billion."

The Shadow wanted to get back to what's happening now. "Correct Senator… What's happened over the years is, gold that was once the people's gold, has been secretly moved into private holdings. Most of this gold is now in the hands of banking families that we know as the globalists. Some black gold is still within sects of the CIA and other governmental organizations, though the gold was never put on the books, so this allows them to fund things by using this black gold that can't be traced."

Brooks wanted to keep them focused on what he was about to say, so he stood. "Many people know of the storied Nazi treasure. There have even been movies about it. But the globalists have successfully stopped movie producers from outlining key facts about what the Nazis really did with the gold they captured, and there are virtually no movies about gold not getting back to its original owners. *To eliminate any trace of original ownership, the Nazis had it melted down, and recast it as ingots hallmarked with the swastika and black eagle of the Reighbank. There were other reasons why the gold was difficult to trace. Many of the original owners had died, and pre-war governments had ceased to exist.*[53] Washington's 'official' (public) figure for recovered Nazi gold still is only 550 metric tons. A reliable *source said he was taken to the courtyard of a convent in Europe where 11,200 metric tons of Nazi looted bullion had been collected.*[54] That's an example of how Nazi gold fell off the radar. What we're talking about here dwarfs that."

George asked, "What do you mean?"

Brooks felt that George threw him a softball to keep the floor. With that, Brooks nodded and began to slowly walk back and forth on the far side of the table.

"What no one talks about," he said, "is the much larger amount of Japanese gold that the US captured in the Philippines from Japan. So much was added to the Nazi gold that the combination of these two is why there's a massive set of funds called the Black Eagle Trust."

George already knew about some of the black gold funding the deep state and insurrection in the country, but he wanted the rest to hear it and he wanted them to hear it from The Shadow. "And much of this isn't part of official governments records, so it's open to either good use without oversight or it's been taken over by the deep state?"

"Exactly, Mr. President," Brooks confirmed.

George wanted to keep Brooks talking, "What's the magnitude of what we're up against? How big is it?"

Brooks turned at the end of the far side of the table and walked back. "Well, let me put it this way. Prior to attacking Pearl Harbor, Japan had spent years conquering other countries in Asia, and had systematically taken gold, platinum, jewelry and all kinds of priceless arts from every country it conquered. *The treasure – gold, platinum and barrels of loose gems – was combined with Axis loot recovered in Europe to create a worldwide covert political action fund to fight communism. This is 'black gold'. It might have been a wise decision at the time, but it had had tragic consequences in the longer term.*[55] Remember, this trust was their solution to be able to stop the spread of the Nazis and their kind."

Brooks turned again and cocked his head as if thinking back. "In retrospect," he said, "recovering Golden Lily treasure vaults and setting up the Black Eagle Trust were the easy parts, done for patriotic reasons and a noble cause. Making intelligent use of so much underground money and keeping it in patriotic hands was not an easy task, and has been something that has failed the American people. One of the problems was that the Trust was discussed with some of America's allies, which are interested in their own benefit, not that of the United States."

"What do you mean by 'Golden Lily'?" Adam questioned.

"That's what the Japanese called their operation," Brooks answered. "This *total secrecy enabled corrupt people to abuse the resulting slush funds, and these abuses have multiplied like a cancer, ever since. A global network of corruption has grown around the slush funds. Bureaucrats, politicians, spooks, and generals, have become addicted to black money.*[56]

Adam looked at George. "I guess that's why they hate us. We're a risk to their slush funds."

George finally smiled. "Yeah, and we're about to become much more of a risk." Turning back to Brooks he said, "Please continue."

Brooks continued, saying, "According to official figures, there have been less than 200,000 tons of gold ever mined. However, this isn't true, because the official figures never accounted for the gold in Russia, India, China and all of Southeastern Asia. They've been mining gold for centuries and have mined more gold than the rest of the world."

General Elder clarified that. "Mr. President, there are some of us who know the US took possession of large quantities of gold after WWII and kept it from the American people. It was off the books."

Brooks sat back down in the same chair.

Elder continued. "Frankly, Mr. President, we just don't know enough about the history of these funds or their whereabouts, besides they're massive and spread around the world like an octopus with tentacles everywhere. The globalists are extremely secretive and, if anyone in their organizations begins to have a change of heart, they're usually found dead. The only way we'd ever find out more would be if you could find an elder CIA agent who was around in that area. But frankly by now they'd likely be dead at the hands of the globalists, unless they went underground or ceased to exist. By now they'd be fairly up in age and if there was one left, it would only be one. What are our chances of finding him? Some form of providence would have to deliver him right to us."

Krieger's eyes raised from where the spot on the table where he had been staring. For some reason everyone looked at Krieger, who still hadn't said a word. A presence filled the room as Krieger turned his head. He and Brooks made eye contact.

CHAPTER 34

Krieger's phone vibrated. The text read, "Your friend The Cleric is here." The message was from Briggs, who was with Mauricio and a team in Chicago at that very moment. Mauricio had set up a network of surveillance equipment that uncloaked most electronic devices that well-connected deep state operatives and politicians were using. Most of these people were either on the take, or the few who resisted were being blackmailed.

Through information his team had extracted from the NSA database, Mauricio knew who was working with the deep state. Now Mauricio knew the players where he was at in Chicago. He had set up a small room at a black house, where he and his team were listening into emails, texts, voice and radio traffic.

The Cleric was now in Chicago, so they knew something was up. Briggs just didn't know how big it was and when they were going to strike.

Mauricio and Briggs were setting up satellite listening stations in safe houses in several major cities. No one had ever gotten evidence that the deep state was paying politicians or police chiefs, but the teams hoped to get some from their surveillance.

Mauricio directed Melissa, the head of his surveillance team in the city. "Get that location. I want to see every available camera within two blocks. Then track his movement."

As a Special Forces Communications Staff Sergeant, Melissa's skills were above her rank. That was why, by the end of the day, Mauricio would inform her of her new rank. He had been working on her promotion through the NSA chain of command, with Krieger's blessing. Melissa was an expert at communication techniques of unconventional warfare and surveillance. She already acted as Mauricio's detachment commander in all communications matters. She not only was an expert at installation, operations and utilization of any kind of equipment he had ever given her, she was an outstanding trainer. It was a skill not always commensurate with being an excellent tactician.

With long straight black hair, Melissa either had native American Indian descent or something else Mauricio couldn't put a finger on. The way her hair was so straight sometimes made Mauricio wondered if she ironed it. Still, in her mid-thirties, she was as fit as any women he'd ever seen. She dressed in a sharp, edgy style, and her clothes were always well-tailored. The tone of her voice usually didn't fit her looks. It was feminine, but when the action started, her tough, fiery persona took over. With the handle of extreme freak, those who knew her realized she liked to live life on the edge and get every bit of excitement out of it.

Mauricio knew why she'd chosen communications as a specialty. It was the action and the fact that, just before she turned thirty, she'd realized she needed to transition out of active Special Operations. She'd successfully managed her evolution into communications with the NSA. That way she could stay in the game longer. After watching her, Mauricio believed she had found her calling within the special operations communication field she now directed. He was glad she was on their side.

Mauricio added to his comment to Melissa, "He's a cleric, we need a visual."

"Yes sir," was all she said as she navigated equipment and directed others.

A moment later, she asked, "Is this him, sir?"

"Affirmative, send it out to the team," he said, referencing the people watching and navigating the surveillance cameras.

Melissa had one of her men send the picture. A moment later it appeared in the bottom corner of their screens along with the message, "HVT. Track him, and I want the secondaries to track everyone he talks to." Secondaries referred to the team who would track whomever the primary targets spoke to. Mauricio had the operation set up to track followers like an organizational chart. Some people on his team were designated to track the top level, which were usually HVTs. Others were ready to track the next level down, and so on. Mauricio was taking no chances that any communication would fall through the cracks. That was one reason why he was the best at what he did, and why Krieger had chosen him.

Several minutes later, Melissa said, "Sir, I have a visual. He just met up with someone. We're recording."

CHAPTER 35

Brooks stood and slowly looked around the small room as he thought.

Based on the fact that they had all been hand chosen and given a lie detector test, The Shadow knew these men were vetted. They needed to know… He suspected at least one of the Generals knew some of it, though Adam, George and Krieger needed to know.

"When I first worked at the CIA," Brooks said, "I was set up to work with an aging man called Santy. He wanted me to help his family after he passed."

The whole room sat in silence as they prepared themselves to listen intently about this black gold that had no governmental oversight.

Brooks continued. *"In the closing months of World War II in the Philippines, several of Japan's highest-ranking imperial princes, were busy hiding tons of looted gold bullion and other stolen treasure in nearby caves and tunnels, to be recovered later.*[57] *This was property of twelve Asian countries, accumulated over thousands of years.*[58] Overseen by the princes, 175 'imperial' treasure vaults were constructed throughout the islands.*[59] *Several were 220 feet underground,*[60] while others were deeper and, as time ran out, Japanese General Yamashita was forced to conceal the last of Japan's loot in a few shallower sites."

Brooks wanted to be clear. "The Black Eagle Trust is only one of many trusts this black gold currently resides in. In fact, unlike the Nazi gold, the gold Japan looted from Asia wasn't recast, leaving an issue of traceability for the Japanese and eventually those who found the gold, the Japanese."

The Shadow looked across the table at General Abrams. *"It was code-named 'kin no Yuri' (Golden Lily), the title of one of the emperor's poems.*[61]

The General nodded and looked at Krieger with a look of thanks for somehow, some way, having Brooks (The Shadow) present to explain this.

Brooks paced as he talked. "For our purposes, there were two major players. One was the original individual who found the location of the gold. He *was a Filipino-American intelligence officer named Severino Garcia Diaz Santa*

Romana, a man of many names and personalities, whose friends called him 'Santy'.[62] Some of you may have heard of the name of the agent who was Supervising Santy, *Captain Edward G. Lansdale.*"[63]

Brooks thought to himself, *they'll love this.* "It's not coincidental that the CIA was formed on September 18, 1947. What's been kept secret is, that in 1945, the OSS was officially shut down after the war, though the heads of the organization never lost a paycheck and were tasked with setting up the CIA. They had an official and an unofficial black gold budget. Of course, the two-year gap is a political way to show there is no affiliation. In reality, this time was used to recover, conceal, ship and secure the black gold from the Philippines into many different places around the globe to reduce the risk of exposure and the risk that one source could be compromised."

"Thus, the octopus, or hydra," George said.

"Exactly," affirmed Brooks. "The CIA began with this black gold, so it started with an official governmental budget and a black ops budget that was beyond Congressional oversight. It's important to realize that the CIA only got *some* of the gold from Germany and Japan. The Japanese gold reserves were so huge that *MacArthur strolled down row after row of gold bars stacked two meters tall,*[64] for more than a half an hour. *According to Roy Cline and others, between 1945 and 1947 the gold bullion recovered by Santy and Lansdale was discreetly moved by ship to 176 accounts at banks in 42 countries.*[65] Remember, gold at that time was worth $35 an ounce, and we're talking about tons of gold and platinum that were deposited in the world's biggest banks, including Union Banque Suisse and other Swiss banks, which became major repositories of the Black Eagle Trust. Some of the names of these banks have changed and documents have been burned to stop any possibility of legal action and traceability. But the players are the same. *Sandy used his aliases in behalf of the CIA and the treasury department.*[66]

Brooks looked at Adam. "Over a period of decades, some of the world's biggest banks became addicted to playing with the black gold in their vaults. Now they will do whatever is necessary to keep the gold."

Adam asked again, "So there were real ancient gold artifacts mixed in with all the rest of the treasures?"

Brooks nodded. "Absolutely, *Rogelio Roxas, a Filipino locksmith, found a one-ton solid gold Buddha and thousands of small gold bars hidden in a tunnel behind a hospital in the mountain resort of Baguio, which had served as a headquarters for General Yamashita.*[67] Roxas," Brooks explained, "was eventually taken prisoner by President Marcos. He was tortured and killed and Marcos took much of the gold, which there was a lot of. *A hospital employee estimated that ten boxes each day were loaded into the trucks over a period of one year, which would come to approximately 3,600 boxes, or 10,800 bars weighing 75 kilos each. In 1996, a US court in the state of Hawaii awarded his heirs a judgement of $43-billion against the Marcos estate, the largest civil award in history.*[68] That was only a small percent of the value of the money in that one tunnel."

Brooks' thoughts came back to the current day and the crashing stock market. There was a question he wanted an answer to. But first he wanted to frame it. "These people have plenty of money. Heck, the M fund alone is worth over a trillion, and they have tens of trillions in untraceable gold. For them to have done what they've done and be taking such drastic actions against the stock market and fostering the current civil unrest, they must view you as a major threat. I know you've gotten a few trillion dollars of their black gold. My guess is that for the past year or two, when the globalist bankers ordered their people to navigate selloffs in the stock market, you have a group of your own people buying up the stocks to pump the market back up. My sources say you've been doing this for a while as your way to pump up the stock market to give it back to the people… Until recently, and now they're taking drastic actions because of the upcoming election."

Brooks looked at the president, who just stared at Brooks, not acknowledging or denying what Brooks had said. The room was dead silent with the pause. Krieger and Adam knew about confiscating some of that gold. Heck, they'd been involved in the process. The gold they had already confiscated had been used to prop up the stock market which had almost doubled since the president had taken office and begun to capture some of the deep state gold.

Brooks concluded with his question. "What else, may I ask, have you done - or are you about to do - made them pull the trigger now?"

It was a legitimate question. Adam and George had thought about it and had come up with a most likely scenario. Adam looked to George for approval to explain.

With a nod from George, Adam began to share. "We're certain we can run a significant surplus in the first year of George's second term, without cutting anything going to American citizens. The other thing this budgeting method would do is drastically reduce money going to the deep state and others who siphon money out of the middle class for their personal wealth building. You see, almost every department uses a line item of what amounts to miscellaneous expenses. Well, this expense has no oversight, and thus doesn't really go to the people. It keeps the politicians in office, and it's a virtual slush fund for corruption. Politicians funnel money to those who find legal ways to funnel some of that money back to them."

General Elder said, "Some of us are aware of it. It's how the average person in Congress is worth millions of dollars, and that's excluding their shell corporations that don't count to their direct net worth."

Brooks said, "So both the swamp and those who benefit from the swamp could have their funds dried up overnight?"

"Absolutely," Adam nodded. "And, with our plan, we'd be paying off the national debt exponentially, starting with a trillion in the first year and..."

Adam looked to George, who affirmed with another nod.

Adam said, "we could eliminate the entire national debt by the end of our second term."

Brooks' eyes darkened. "You've got a problem. They'll stop at nothing to prevent you from achieving this."

George asked, "What would you suggest?"

Brooks tilted his head to one side and regarded the President. "It depends on how far you are willing to go."

"The survival of the country is at stake. If we don't do something to eliminate the deep state and their funding, we may win the battle and a series of battles, though they'll eventually win, even if it's after my terms."

Brooks knew George was correct.

George came back with another question. "If we wanted to do everything in our power, with all of the might at our disposal, what could we accomplish?"

Brooks looked at Krieger. "Colonel, you requested that we come here to plan to keep the country secure."

Krieger confirmed with a nod.

"What if we took all of the resources at our disposal and could accomplish three main things: first, we get the Federal Reserve to give us back the twelve trillion dollars that are missing, and pay off half of the national debt. Second, we get enough of our gold back and pay off the rest of the national debt with that. Third, we purge the country of some of these bad actors, I'll call it a deep state takedown and we engineer a reset for the country to set it on course for true prosperity like they've never seen."

Turning to Adam, Brooks continued. "Then that surplus you'd be running could be used to build a strong depository that'll secure the safety of the country for centuries to come. Think about it. The interest the average middle-class person pays on the national debt will be gone. As the repository builds, the interest will pay some of the country's expenses. Heck, if somehow, we could come up with some of this gold quickly, we could bailout companies and take stock at extremely low prices in return. Their dividends could also fund the government, so the people wouldn't have to."

Adam almost jumped out of his chair. "That would immediately give hundreds of dollars, almost a thousand a month to the average family, without us cutting any services for the people."

"Exactly."

George again asked, "How much gold is there and where's it at?"

CHAPTER 36

Krieger read the text. "Mayor and Police Chiefs recorded giving stand down orders for upcoming civil unrest."

Krieger smiled. This was huge. Briggs and Mauricio had been hoping to capture evidence of these types of things. There was no question about it standing up in court. John had ensured any evidence they captured would be admissible.

Krieger focused on Brooks. He knew his team of Briggs, Mauricio and the rest were capturing some great information in Chicago.

* * *

Mauricio had other questions he wanted to have answers to, including the level of involvement of the Mayor and Police Chief. The surveillance of these key individuals and the people they spoke with could be crucial intelligence to help understand their plans.

The further down the chain the surveillance went, the less hands-on Mauricio could be and the more he'd rely on his team to pick up the critical pieces of information and escalate them to the proper level. The team was crucial. He and Briggs knew it. They would be there for a few days and then move on to set up another listening station, leaving the new leader — Melissa — behind as the leader.

As the team continued their work, Mauricio pulled Melissa into a small area to break the good news to her. Melissa had proven to be a reliable leader, and Briggs shared Mauricio's confidence in her abilities. She not only commanded well, somehow, she did it while maintaining the respect of those around her.

When Mauricio and Melissa came out of the room, he made the announcement to the team. The news was met by an enthusiastic applause and hoots from the small group. Melissa being promoted to a Deputy Director of

Intelligence sent a message that Krieger's team was expanding and strengthening. This would increase their sense of urgency and importance. It was a huge promotion. With its announcement, the team members knew something was up that was beyond their understanding. Even if they couldn't possibly comprehend the magnitude, they were proud to be part of doing anything to save the country. It was them that needed to ensure public safety and reduce the damage the deep state could inflict.

Until Krieger, Adam, George and their group had their counter strike figured out and in place, Mauricio and Briggs knew their primary role was to find out what the deep state was up to civilly. They knew the civil unrest would be parlayed into a call for U.N. support. That would be another step towards the end of the United States, and that wouldn't happen under this administration, no matter what it took.

CHAPTER 37

Brooks began to walk slowly around the table as he reminisced. "This is going to take a minute, but it's important to understand in order to save the country.

"Before the US got into the war, Japan took gold from at least twelve countries, including Korea and China, all of which had accumulated gold, platinum and precious jewels for thousands of years. The Japanese imperial family had much of it shipped back to Japan, where it still lies in private reserves. What we're focusing on is only what they stashed in the Philippines."

Brooks went on to explain that a group called the Kempeitai were the Japanese secret military police unit that specialized in gathering gold from China. *"At least 6,000 metric tons of gold are reported to have been amassed by the Kempeitai during this first pass through one section of China. Historical research into looting shows that what is officially reported typically is only a tiny fraction of what is actually stolen.*[69] *Great quantities of loose diamonds were kept in oil drums*[70] *and, according to journalist Robert Whiting, some 800,000 karats of diamonds were later transferred from the Bank of Japan to the custody of MacArthur's command, and these diamonds were never seen again.*[71]

"Santy, Santa Romana and Lansdale only recovered a portion of the treasure from 1945 to 1947. A decade passed before other significant recoveries occurred, and those were again only a portion. More gold has been found over the past twenty years, and there's no reason to believe it's all been found. Some of it was buried over three hundred feet deep in caverns that were well below the water table with booby traps, boulders and other natural obstructions put in place."

Brooks continued pacing. "There were so many discoveries over the years that were kept from public knowledge. Heck, *in July 1942, a gold Buddha over 15 feet tall arrived at Manila's Pier 15. Decades later the gold Buddha was rediscovered by accident, when a housing development was built on Marikina Field.*[72] Realize," Brooks said as he paused his slow walk around the table, "a twelve-inch cube of gold weighs 1,200 pounds."

Heads were turning in the room; Brooks had them mesmerized. Never before had they heard such a detailed and knowledgeable account.

Brooks continued. "Several other vaults were put beneath the San Augustine Church and the monastery next door because there were cata-combs already there which held remains of priests, nobles, and wealthy commoners. Since the hill was solid rock, there was no need for shoring, and they disguised the entrances to these vaults. *Golden Lily employed Japanese ceramics experts, who were able to produce concrete to extraordinary hardness. By molding a cement plug to resemble a normal section of tunnel wall, and tinting the composite with pigments and local soil, the entrances blended perfectly with their surroundings. Nobody would ever guess that an entrance to a branch tunnel existed.*[73] This is how much of the gold lay hidden for over fifty years, and some is still there today."

Brooks explained how the church paid a heavy price. "When priests and others naively commented about how the rooms in the catacombs had changed, *the Kempeitai was given the job of killing the priests and church laborers.*[74]

"These weren't the only casualties of hiding this vast amount of treasure," Brooks said. "*Without exception, eyewitnesses told us that each time a treasure vault was filled and sealed, the POWs and slave laborers were buried alive inside, to guarantee their silence. One measure of Japan's total plunder is that all these treasure vaults being created in Manila, plus the tunnels at Corregidor, were not enough. Other vaults were being dug in Mindanao, in Mindoro, and other islands in the Archipelago. And in the mountains north of Manila, another imperial prince was hard at work enlarging natural caverns to create the biggest treasure vaults of the war outside Japan.*[75] *There were 175 imperial sites specially built for treasure belonging exclusively to Emperor Hirohito and the imperial family.*"[76]

Brooks paused to let that sink in.

"That's a lot of sites," Adam said.

Brooks nodded. "*Yamashita had more than 275,000 men on Luzon.*[77] *There were trucks and freight cars bringing gold bullion and other treasures.*"

General Elder said, "I heard that *America had realized for some time that Japan was hiding plundered treasure in the Philippines, although the details were not shared with Britain or other Allies.*"[78]

Brooks nodded in agreement. "Exactly. President Truman decided to keep the discovery secret. Without counting the black gold, Federal statistics show that at the end of the war the United States held 60 percent of the world's official gold reserves.[79] With the black gold, that number was grossly understated. There were many mistakes with the gold. For example, in the late sixties, *US Air Force made emergency airlifts of gold from Fort Knox to London to keep the bank of England afloat.*"[80]

Brooks explained another twist. "If you want to know how Japan recovered so quickly after the war, well, it was more than their efficient manufacturing. You see, the US let Japan keep large amounts of gold, platinum, diamonds and other precious items to stay anti-communist. They used underworld bosses and let them amass thirteen billion in gold, and that was when gold was worth thirty-five dollars an ounce. Let's also remember that the People's Republic of China came into being at the end of 1949, so the circumstances surrounding that upheaval hindered their efforts to make claims for their stolen gold."

"Who else helped set up these trusts?" Krieger asked.

"*Britain's biggest financiers participated in setting up the Black Eagle Trust.*[81] *Gold was moved from Clark Air Base on US aircraft*[82] to banks in Hong Kong, Zurich, Buenos Aires, London, Wells Fargo and Citibank's all over the world," Brooks said.

Brooks wasn't going to tell them that, when he was a very young man, Santy had befriended him and they'd remained close until Santy's death. Brooks did however want them to know the vast amounts of untraceable gold the deep state had at its disposal. "*By the start of 1970, when gold was under forty dollars an ounce, the accounts closely linked to Santy, and considered by some sources to belong to him, were modestly estimated to total well over $50 billion.*[83] He was by far the world's richest man, dwarfing the top ten put together today."

General Elder asked, "It seems like this guy must have known people would be after his gold."

Again, Books only wanted to disclose a certain amount. He surely wasn't going to say anything about his involvement here. "He did. But he was working day and night securing the treasure. By the time he got around to protecting himself, setting up shell companies, some in the CIA were on to him."

Brooks explained how, after Santy died, the deep state CIA took some of Santy's big accounts, notably one listing Santy as the holder of record at UBS Geneva, said to contain 20,000 metric tons of gold, and they were changed to list Major General Lansdale as the holder of record.

Krieger frowned. "What about the traceability for that gold?"

Brooks looked at Krieger. "President Marcos set up refineries to re-melt gold bars to alter the chemical composition. He also changed the hallmarks to Philippine official numbers and stamps."

"So that's how Marcos became so rich," General Abrams said.

Brooks nodded. "Yeah, at least temporarily. Another huge stash was found in 1975. That's when word leaked out to the Federal Reserve and Bank of England. They threatened Marcos, and he knew damn well what they'd do. So, he gave *the Birch society exclusive rights to market up to $20 billion worth of any gold recovered.*[84] That's how the Federal Reserve families got much of the gold."

Krieger was inquisitive. "Was Marcos working with the Mafia and the CIA?"

"*Marco had connections beyond the CIA to a shadowy network called The Enterprise, a cluster of private intelligence organizations (PIOs) and private military firms (PMFs). These were staffed by former CIA and Pentagon officers*[85] who got their start when Nixon cut a bunch of them. *Over a thousand CIA agents were cut or obliged to take retirement,*"[86] Brooks affirmed.

George was putting it all together. "So, billions in gold have been moved to Suisse, German and Chinese banks, and the interest it generates is available but isn't on the government books, so it's not disclosed to our government?"

Brooks confirmed. "Absolutely sir. By 1981 the Showa Trust was generating over one billion dollars of interest annually. It's generating over $10 billion annually today from that trust alone. There are over 170 caves. In 1983, *the first trench alone was for 716,045 bars, at a sale price of $124 billion.*"[87]

Adam quickly calculated. "That's half a trillion dollars in one cave today."

Brooks emphasized, "Absolutely. You have to understand that thirty-two countries claimed to have been looted of thousands of metric tons of gold. Remember, this was gold they had acquired over centuries. Japan took a large section of the world's total accumulated wealth in gold, jewels… and stored it in Japan and the Philippines."

General Abrams now understood more of the why. "The Japanese always planned to maintain control of the Philippines, that's why they stashed it there."

Brooks liked the way the General put the pieces together. "You've got it, General. Marcos had in his possession — and sold — $1.63 trillion worth of gold bullion at a huge discount, when gold was selling for somewhere in the $300 an ounce range at that time. That's why the price of gold dropped during those years. Marcos had what amounts to, let's say, nine trillion in gold, not to mention the diamonds, platinum and other precious metals."

Adam questioned, "What percent of the total did Marcos find?"

"Not much, less than ten percent."

"What ever happened to the gold Buddha?" Madison asked.

Brooks looked at her and explained. "An influential law firm in LA filed a law suit. The gold Buddha trial was finally set for May 25,1993. As the trial date approached, the firm arranged for body guards to escort Roxas from Manila to Honolulu. On May 24, the head of that law firm called Roxas and told him to catch a plane to Hawaii immediately. Unfortunately, the law firm had been bugged, and an hour and a half later, Roxas was dead. After that, there was a mysterious movement of gold bullion from Santy's accounts at Citibank Manila to Citibank New York. Citibank held 4,700 metric tons of gold bullion belonging to Santy's estate."

Adam asked Brooks, "How did they launder all of this gold? I understand that they just kept massive amounts off the books, but some must have been put into circulation?"

Brooks nodded. "You bet. There was so much, Santy had moved billions into 176 bank accounts in forty-two countries. *Two thousand dummy corporations were set up in Delaware to funnel money for nearly a decade.*"[88]

Brooks paused, looked at the president and said, "The Senator at that time was Joe Biden. Does knowing all of this now give you a better understanding of how he became vice president?"

"You're not going to find all of this money," Brooks said. "That's beyond our scope at this point. What we need to do is focus in on which funds the deep state has control over, and which ones are large enough so we can at least pay off the entire national debt and go get that gold."

George wanted to know about the past presidents, since the past few had all been globalists. "What about the Bush and Clinton families? Do you have any insight on their knowledge of or involvement in all this?"

"Absolutely, Mr. President," Brooks answered. The rest of the room could see the sourness in his expression. "First, let me state that the reason they've kept as much of this from you as possible, is because you're the first president to not be put into office and controlled by the globalist banking empire."

George and Adam nodded and exchanged a look.

Brooks followed up with some information on recent past presidents. "Remember, President George H. W. Bush was the 11th Director of the CIA, so it's no coincidence that, in March 2001, only weeks into the new Bush Administration, two US Navy ships arrived in the Philippines carrying teams of SEAL commandos. According to a source at the US Embassy, they were sent to the Philippines to recover gold as part of a plan to enlarge America's reserves."[89]

The President saw something in Brooks' eyes. "And?"

Brooks responded, "Well, let's just say that some of that gold was rumored to have fallen into the Bush's private holdings. It may have been the standard kickback of five percent, or it may have been more."

George nodded. "What about Clinton?"

Brooks continued. "It's known in some circles that Clinton somehow lent thousands of tons of gold bullion to speculators and bullion banks, notably Citibank and J.P Morgan Chase."

George snarled, "The Globalists."

Brooks nodded. "Of course."

Madison, who had been quiet for most of the meeting, suddenly said, "Oh my goodness, could there be a connection…?"

They all looked at her, including Brooks as she said, "I remember an amendment to an appropriations bill that made it illegal for the State and

Justice departments to spend any of their 2002 budget *to file a motion in any court opposing a civil action against any Japanese person or corporation for compensation or reparations in which the plaintiff alleges that, as an American prisoner of war during World War II, he or she was used as slave or forced labor. This amendment was passed with overwhelming bi-partisan support one day before the World Trade Center Attack.*"[90]

Brooks nodded, turned and helped explain to the others. "Slave labor was used to dig tunnels for the gold and some of them had started bringing law suits."

"What I don't understand," Madison said, "is why Japan was about to collapse economically if they have that much gold."

Brooks filled in the gap. "The royal families kept most of it for themselves, and have it in their personal wealth possessions. They own the largest Japanese companies, which are so sizeable, they could buy ten fortune 100 companies and not even flinch... It's the same here in the US; the people never benefitted from the gold."

Madison understood now. "The globalist families will stop at nothing to keep their gold. I've heard people say they won't even redeem any sizeable certificates for gold. A Senator once told me, *"It has now reached a point where you can go into one of the big banks in New York, London, or Zurich, give them half a metric ton in return for a certificate of ownership, walk around the block for ten minutes, re-enter the same bank, and they'll deny ever seeing you before and have you arrested for presenting them with a counterfeit certificate."*"[91]

Krieger forcefully asked, "Could we go into the Federal Reserve banks and find that gold that's rightfully ours and confiscate it?"

Brooks shook his head. "Good thought, Colonel. But, *in 1986, the Federal Reserve decided to recast all the gold bars in its vaults, changing bars from traditional rectangular ingots into trapezoidal-shape. It allowed the Fed to change the hallmarks, serial numbers, and all other identification, which included re-papering and earmarking, effectively erasing all record of ownership of many thousands of tons of gold in its different vaults.*[92] The Fed then declared massive amounts of gold notes and bonds as counterfeit."

"How convenient," Adam quipped angrily.

"In September 2001," Brooks explained, "a case came to trial at the US District Court for the Northern District of Chicago. An expert witness, economist Dr. Martin A. Larson, stated 18,000 metric tons of gold were placed into the Federal Reserve vaults of Ft. Knox."

Adam offered, "Let me guess. Now there's no proof of who rightfully owns it."

"None at all," Brooks said.

"So, what happened, did the Federal Reserve get to keep the gold?"

"Pretty much," Brooks confirmed.

"Thieves." Adam shook his head.

"Of the highest order," Brooks emphasized. "It's an octopus. Anyone who worked against them ended up dead, *including Frank Nugen, journalist Danny Casolaro, and former CIA Director William Colby legal counsel to the black banks, whose body was found floating in the Potomac River estuary in 1996.*"[93]

"Imagine if that happened today," Madison said.

George knew firsthand what would happen. "Nothing would change, because the major media outlets are owned by these same people. If anyone in the media reported it, they'd be fired. That's how they control the narrative."

Brooks looked at the president. "It's no use going on with this. Now you understand where the deep state is getting a lot of its money, and where the globalist bankers got a lot of theirs and what their agendas are. But the main point is, there's a hundred trillion dollars in black gold that belongs to the American people at this point. What are we going to do about it?"

The room fell silent and eyes widened; everyone sat up a little straighter.

"What if we could align with these other countries so the globalists had to fight a financial war on multiple fronts," George said. "What if we could bring back the gold backed dollar as the currency of the United States? What if we could do that, eliminate the Federal Reserve, kick them the hell out of the country and pay off the national debt all at the same time before they could complete their stock crash?"

All eyes were on George. "There's well over ten trillion dollars missing from the Federal Reserve, could be twenty. We can't audit them as it stands right now. What if we went in, forced them to transfer the missing money to every country we owe and then shut them down and took over all of the Federal Reserve locations? That would mean we have control of our remaining gold and the locations. Then, we take back some of the gold they transferred to their vaults overseas and put it back in our vaults, controlled by our military."

Adam said, "We could give the middle class a permanent tax cut of ten percent just by eliminating the interest charges on the national debt. The rest of the economic impact would double that. It'd ensure your re-election, sir."

General Abrams said, "Mr. President, you're talking about attacking on two fronts. It'd have to be done simultaneously to pull it off."

Krieger looked up, "Three!"

The General abruptly turned and looked at him.

Krieger said, "General, during this meeting, I've received texts from a team that I have monitoring pending civil unrest. We've uncovered a multi-faceted assault of civil disruption being orchestrated by the deep state."

The General nodded and scowled. He was aware of their years of prepa-ration, and could see this was the time for the deep state to make its move. He turned to George and said, "Mr. President, this means a complicated orches-trated counter coup on three major fronts."

George offered up one of the sayings he was known for. "The questions we ask ourselves lead us to the answers to those questions. So, the only question I'm going to ask is, how can it be done?"

CHAPTER 38

The bodies were too heavy for The Shadow to lift. Luckily, he had plenty of help.

After the meeting in Georgia two days ago, plans were underway to save the country. Brooks had left the base to take care of a few things to prepare. This gave him the time he needed to contact Ferraro and take care of those several treasonous politicians and deep state officials he hadn't gotten to yet. And for this, Brooks needed help, so he reached back out to Ferraro.

Ferraro had spoken with the one man from whom he took advice: a high-ranking person within a branch of the government. They had chosen two men to assist Brooks. Two men who hadn't known each other and would never have a chance to run into each other in the future.

The one was the middle-aged CIA man who had been in hiding for over a year now. Going against the deep state wasn't good for a CIA man. He had testified in front of a committee about the Uranium sample he'd seen delivered in a brief case. He testified that the man who delivered it had taken an active role in trying to get the president removed. He had also exposed other payoffs from Ukrainian oil companies. The payoffs of tens of millions of dollars went to a few of the most established politicians in Washington – and their families. Because of him, evidence of these payoffs was now being circulated on social media. These politicians knew it was him who had leaked it. Luckily for him, they didn't know where he was. The new administration had hidden him

The money he was being paid for these hits would set him up with a good living for the rest of his life. He may need it. If these people weren't prosecuted, he'd have to remain under cover for the rest of his life anyway, so having enough money from this job allowed him the ability to disappear forever. He'd have to get his face changed, but with this money he could do that now.

Brooks pointed to the corpse the man had just laid on the grass and said, "Don't leave her arms crossed."

He didn't want this congresswoman's or anyone's arms crossed. In Brooks's mind, he wanted these seven traitors to look less like they were put to rest and more like what a body looks like when it's hung. Arms limp by their sides.

The other help Brooks had was a hit man Ferraro had chosen. Ferraro had used this man before, and knew he really wanted to retire. Ferraro made him a good deal. The job paid over a million dollars. After this, the man could retire in peace.

These men placed the bodies as Brooks directed. Brooks wanted the bodies laid out in a semicircle fashion, facing the eternal flame that lit Kennedy's grave. The hill overlooking Kennedy's grave provided the perfect backdrop. When photos of these traitors were taken, Kennedy's grave would be in front of them and the Arlington House monument would be in the background.

Arlington was guarded at night, but it was nothing compared to many other places in the area. Brooks had simply put the guards to sleep. They'd awake around dawn, then they'd discover the bodies.

Brooks chose this location because of the symbolic nature for the president who was trying to take down the Federal Reserve.

* * *

The President heard the pounding of a fist on his door. "Mr. President, wake up. There's been a development!" It was Krieger's voice. There were a few more thumps of his palm on the bedroom door.

George lifted his head. He was used to being woken up now from time to time, but the tone of Krieger's voice was different. It was more urgent.

The president took a deep breath. He sat up and took another one to project his voice. "I'll be right there."

George pulled on his Orvis khakis and slipped his bare feet into his shearling lined slippers. He pulled a T shirt on and then a blue shirt that he buttoned up.

"Seven people were found dead at the Arlington National Cemetery," Adam stated when the president walked out of his room.

"Murdered?" George asked.

"Apparently so," Adam said. "They had hoods over their faces. But they are a few representatives, at least two senators and a few other appointed officials. The identifications are coming in now. But they won't be released to the media until family members have been notified."

Krieger had just taken a phone call. When he hung up, Adam looked at him and asked, "Any new developments?"

"The security were put to sleep by gas or something. When they woke up, they discovered the bodies lined up on the hill overlooking the eternal flame at Kennedy's grave. The grave wasn't disturbed. But the big news is, it's either a copycat or the same group as before." Krieger hesitated and then said, "There were notes on them and they found a flash drive... It has a video on it."

"Notes like before?" the president questioned.

"Yes, sir," Krieger said. "Notes on the corpses. They were personalized like before, alleging that they had been engaged in selling out their country for their own benefit. Each note accused that person of treason, and gave specific allegations. The notes had one thing in common. They each ended with the phrase, 'Corrupt politicians will no longer be tolerated!'"

Adam asked, "Is that the same phrase that was used last time?"

Krieger's forehead rose. "I can't be sure, but it sure sounds like it. We'll check."

"What do you make of it, Colonel?" the president asked.

"Sir," Krieger said, "I can only speculate at this point. But if I had to guess, I'd say whoever did this believe the AG and the rest of them aren't going to prosecute these people. They don't believe anything will happen, so they're taking justice into their own hands. If I had to guess, I'd say whoever did this is a patriot. The reason I say that is because every one of these people either is trying hard to get you out of office, they and their families have taken bribes and huge payoffs and they're working with the globalists. Every damn one of them is a traitor. Whether you agree with their tactics or not, I'd say they're trying to help the country, sir."

"Well," the president said, turning to Adam, "have Gabby stay on top of it and get out some sort of condolences, nothing more... We've all got places to go, so let's not let this get in the way of our purpose for today."

CHAPTER 39

George knew getting the gold would only do good if they could keep it away from the politicians and the deep state.

Wicked behavior by ruthless rulers and cunning bankers was why America's Founding Fathers had tried to do things differently. From the moment the United States became independent of Britain, it was liberated from British currency and taxation. Money was to be backed by gold and silver and kept under the control of the central government, on behalf of its citizens. But the federalist clique of Alexander Hamilton, which had strong financial and emotional ties to Old Europe, began lobbying to put US currency in private hands. US presidents Jefferson, Madison, Adams and others had fought this, and the early attempts to set up a pseudo 'United States Bank', that was actually in private hands, were reversed. That was why in 1816, President Jefferson had warned that, "*Private banking establishments are more dangerous than standing armies; and the principle of spending money to be paid by posterity, under the name of funding is but swindling posterity.*"[94]

George understood that he was a once in a lifetime president. He was a real estate billionaire, so he couldn't be bought off. But that wouldn't be the case with others. His predecessor was now worth over one hundred and fifty million dollars after only two years out of office, and he didn't own a business. That meant before taxes he made a quarter of a billion dollars in two years without a business.

George knew he needed to put money into the country, but still do something to stop the globalists from paying off politicians in the future. He also knew there was a high likelihood that the gold in the Philippines could one day be used to start a gold backed currency.

The only option to save the United States and the power of its currency in the long term was to kick out the Federal Reserve and exile them from the country, while at the same time rolling out a United States dollar that was backed and redeemable in gold. He had to replace the Federal Reserve note.

The only way to do that was to get back some of the missing money and gold that rightfully belonged to the people of the United States.

Brooks verbalized the same thing the president was thinking when he said, "Mr. President, the way I see it is, if we get enough gold and money to pay off the entire national debt, can you pass a constitutional amendment stating any politician who even brings up privatizing the monetary system again as a possibility, immediately advocates their position in office along with their entire pension and all ongoing benefits?"

The president shook his head. "That's a nice thought, but we'd never get it through."

The Shadow looked at the president. "NSA electronic surveillance records which you have access to will give them no choice."

The look he gave Krieger made Krieger wonder how much Brooks knew.

Brooks added, "We can take evidence of their nefarious and illegal activities, and have a team visit some of these people personally. I can help choose a team. We'll make them an offer they can't refuse… It'll go through."

For the first time all day, George had a gleam in his eyes.

Adam thought it was time to get to the point. "So where is the gold we can get, or I guess I should say, with all the tentacles of the octopus, where's our best target rich environment?"

Brooks hesitated, then answered. "Most gold and other precious metal goes into underground vaults deep in the Alps. The caves are also strongholds of the Swiss Army, as security against nuclear war."

General Abrams asked, "How big of an operation is this?"

"General, we'll need every loyal Special Forces soldier you've got," Brooks said.

Krieger added, "Sir, understand, this will be the first time in history since the start of the country that the United States has moved against the central bankers and their deep state."

The president looked at Krieger. "Understood, Colonel. That's why we've got to strike on multiple fronts with precision. We must strike with devastating blows. They can't see it coming.

"We finish this now."

CHAPTER 40

In the dark of the night, Ahmed Mohammed Al-Habib stood outside and called Abdul Khalid Ahmed in Chicago.

"Sir, we have live audio," the corporal announced to Mauricio.

The corporal put the call on the speaker so everyone could hear.

Abdul Khalid Ahmed answered on a phone that had been purchased for him with cash. Thinking the line was secure, Ahmed spoke freely. He needed to gain more understanding of timing to ensure his moves were orchestrated with others across several cities.

Mauricio, Briggs and their team listened as the voice came out of the speakers. "The fires will burn in the belly of the beast, and Allah will rejoice."

Ahmed was a trained mercenary who traveled across Europe. He had never been directly tied to any of the terrorist operations over there. But he was known to have traveled to several of the cities before terrorist operations were carried out. He had been in Paris and London just a week or two before the terrorists struck, but he was always out of the country before the event.

Ahmed being in the country made sense. He wasn't here on a sightseeing expedition. Mauricio drew air in to speak, but before he could say anything, Melissa pointed and directed a tier two team to find and follow that lead. It became apparent; the growing network within the US was planning unrest across multiple cities and she wanted to follow every lead.

Melissa felt eyes on her, and in the heat of the action looked at Mauricio. He smiled and nodded his approval. It was because of her that they were hearing this. She had put all of the pieces together and found this connection. This further proved her promotion was deserved.

As much as they could decode, fires would burn as more paid protesters whipped up the local youth. As they listened, it became obvious that whatever they were planning was coming close to fruition and these people were in it for the long run.

Meanwhile, Briggs's mind raced. *Who was organizing this unrest and what was their ultimate goal?* So many questions… For now, Briggs was keeping all of this in mind, though his training kept his focus on what his next best move would be. Briggs knew he had to fill Krieger in and request reinforcements.

Little did Briggs know that Krieger was about to tell him and Mauricio he was pulling them out of this operation for another, much riskier one.

CHAPTER 41

"Colonel," Ferraro offered his hand. "I never expected to be meeting you like this."

Krieger shook Ferraro's hand, looked at Brooks and said, "You came highly recommended for the job."

Brooks had found out from Krieger at their meeting two days ago that large amounts of civil unrest were being planned in several cities. The civil unrest would work simultaneously with the attack on the stock market. With few other options, Brooks had suggested bringing in Ferraro and the families.

Krieger was going to need every loyal Special Forces operative he could find to pull off the mission to save the country. This meant taking Briggs and Mauricio with him, leaving the recently promoted Melissa to run surveillance operations stateside. That would leave the cities vulnerable to the globalists.

Ferraro, in his six-thousand-dollar Brioni suit and custom handmade wing-tip shoes, responded with a smile. "What job could an honest businessman like me possibly do for you, or should I say for the government?"

Krieger set the stage by saying, "I recently learned something from history… and let's say I'm not really a fan of history repeating itself, although in this case it may be our best option."

Ferraro waited for Krieger to elaborate.

Krieger wasn't about to tell Ferraro that almost his entire team was being sent on another group of missions to orchestrate the largest counter coup against the globalists in history. Krieger had contemplated using the militia. That was a topic of some heated conversation that led to this decision.

Brooks, or as Krieger and Ferraro knew him, The Shadow, had pointed out that although the militia could keep the peace, the long-term effects of using them would be that the terrorists would live to fight another day. They would do a better job of hiding after learning their lesson and crawl deeper underground to multiply and resurface at another time when the country was weak; maybe with this President, or worse yet, maybe with the next, who may not have the balls to do what it would take to hold the country together.

No, Brooks had another idea. He had explained to Krieger that the Japanese had used a similar technique, as had Hitler and others throughout history. When faced with multiple fronts that would dilute their strength to a compromising degree, history is riddled with governments who have turned to the Mafia to do the dirty work.

Brooks had made the contact, then Krieger had had Ferraro brought to the base where they could talk in absolute secrecy with all recording devices turned off and with the best sound proofing and jamming devices surrounding them. This would be the only time they would talk directly. If Ferraro chose to accept this opportunity, future communications would be made by pre-determined signals that could not be traced back to anyone in the government.

Ferraro's amenable smile didn't fool Krieger for a minute. This was a tactful, very calculating man.

Krieger said, "Anything we discuss from here on will never be documented and will never be confirmed. This conversation never existed. In fact, we have technology showing you having a very nice dinner right at this very moment."

"I don't doubt it," Ferraro said, maintaining his smile while thinking, *he's not messing around, and he's not taking any chances.*

Krieger didn't want to be too rough, although he wanted to establish himself as meaning business and this was as serious as it got.

Krieger's Adam's apple fluxed. "Over the past several days we've uncovered evidence that several cities are about to come under siege in what's actually an orchestrated movement of unrest. We're gradually learning that at least one mayor, and we believe there to be more, are taking money from a communist named Sordid. The mayor of Chicago has already directed the chief of police to have his department stand down during the upcoming incident. Evidence across multiple cities show similar actions are being planned. All of these cities are tied to sources who have put extremist politicians in place. We've tracked the finances of several of these mayors, and we've been able to identify millions flowing directly to them."

"I wondered how all those mayors were always millionaires," Ferraro commented, as a way to indicate he was listening. He knew firsthand some of the illegal means the politicians used to get rich.

Krieger continued. "We know that, in the past, one mayor funneled peaceful patriotic protesters into a narrow-restricted area, where they were attacked viciously by paid weaponized protesters as the police watched. Countless people were sent to the hospital."

Ferraro was sympathetic. "I saw that. Several alternative news media documented the incidents although the mainstream globalist marketing arm, as I call them, but told a mostly fake news story by leaving out the details that led to the atrocities. Usually, all they showed were the parts where a large clean-cut person was whipping someone's ass."

"Exactly," Krieger agreed. "And now they're planning something across multiple cities and we're afraid that they're going to make the past incidents look like child's play. They're bringing in heavy hitters across the country, and there's a distinct possibility that a significant series of orchestrated events could be happening simultaneously."

Ferraro knew what this pointed to. "So, I'm guessing you're thinking they're planning this to work hand in hand with them attacking the stock market."

"You must have some good connections, Mr. Ferraro," Krieger said.

"It doesn't take a genius to see what's happening to the stock market. They're planning something significant, and if they can pull off some kind of extreme civil unrest in multiple locations, it'd make sense that they'd do it."

"You're right on track," said Krieger. "Let me explain some of what we know. You remember the blackout a few days ago?"

"Absolutely, I lost a good amount of money in that blackout. I have business interests in many cities," Ferraro said, maintaining his smile.

Krieger wished Ferraro would dispense with the politically correct bullshit, but he let him play it coy for now. He'd probably be doing the same thing. Krieger said, "That blackout stemmed from a piece of equipment that came from the US government. We believe their technique is to create civil unrest to divide and conquer. With New York, Philadelphia, Chicago and LA in riots, they would create a call for help from within the populace."

Ferraro was intrigued by the conversation and the tactics. "But why are you telling me about this?"

Krieger maintained eye contact with Ferraro. "We need your help on two fronts."

As Ferraro listened closely, Krieger went on to explain that everyone knew the media was owned and controlled by the globalists, so they were escalating the emotional unrest by amplifying the impact of the attacks. When Krieger had arrested known terrorists, who had started the riots in Philadelphia, the media didn't report.

Krieger explained that he had nabbed the other terrorist cell with the EMP equipment. Now he feared that terrorists in other cities would be activated simultaneously to light the emotional fuse of a citizenry who was full of anxiety. It needed to be stopped, or the citizens would most likely clamor for help and invite in the UN trojan horse.

Krieger needed a presence that knew the landscape in these major cities, who knew the players and the foreign agents. A presence who had no sympathy for knocking off competitive elements who would take over more of their territory. Krieger needed undercover Mafioso to work on the country's behalf.

Krieger had taken out another terrorist cell while in LA. With little time to waste, Krieger had had his people interrogate the man. Not wanting to die with the pigs, the man had finally squealed.

Krieger couldn't control the media and he didn't have the resources to take down the elements of the Islamic deep state that had been let into the cities.

The globalist media were a unified front. It was a great example of a spread-out power source acting in the same manner. There were some good people in the media. These good people who had families to provide for, knew they had to be complicit with the message, or be terminated.

Krieger ended this part of his explanation with, "We're thinking about letting your people handle it."

Ferraro maintained his composure. "My people?"

"We think we can work together for our mutual benefit," Krieger said, ignoring his polite faux-ignorance.

"How so?" Ferraro asked.

"We understand how the segments of various foreign cultures have infiltrated your territory. In most major cities, you're sharing territories with a variety of foreign crime syndicates from Asia or the Middle east." Krieger paused. "What if I told you that, in exchange for you taking out some specific targets for us, we'd be willing to let you take out some competitive threats of your own which have infringed on your territory?" Krieger enticed.

Ferraro immediately went to what was in it for Krieger. "We'd be tasked with taking out select targets of your choosing."

"Of course," Krieger said, nodding.

"Why can't you take them out, and why now?" Ferraro questioned.

Krieger saw a look in Ferraro's eyes that indicated he wasn't going with it. Krieger changed his mind right there and thought he'd better disclose a reason why.

"Let me lay my cards on the table," Krieger said. "The country's in dire shape. The globalists are attacking us on multiple fronts. To fight them, I'll need every resource I've got. If we hold these people in check, we realize that the threat will be there for years to come unless it's eliminated."

Ferraro thought about that for a moment.

Krieger continued. "Think about it, if we let the cities handle it the way they're planning, they'll stand down. We'll give you a few days of freedom to eliminate some HVTs for us, and then let you clean up some, shall we say, *issues* of your own. We can give you surveillance, and with the plans of the deep state, your operations can fly under the radar as part of the collateral damage started by them. We'll provide that cover."

"You're talking about multiple cities," Ferraro said. "This is a nationwide undertaking. With an operation of this size, I'll need help to orchestrate an effort like this. I'll help with everything I've got, but why would the families do this?"

Krieger nodded. "Good question. I understand, and I'd feel the same way. So, here's why the families will align together. First, they'll have the freedom to take out their competition across the country. These Muslim and Chinese mafia are simply extensions of the globalists. The Red Mafia is embedded, and they've also taken over a significant amount of your action, cutting into your profits. With the borders closing soon, the ability to get drugs across the border will be drastically reduced, putting a squeeze on business. This operation we're talking about will allow your groups to increase your power and influence for decades to come."

Krieger let that sink in as Ferraro pondered, and then he raised his left eyebrow. "Frankly, I just don't think they'll do it." Ferraro went on to explain *why* he couldn't do it, and Krieger listened and didn't say a word.

Then the door began to slowly open. Ferraro stopped talking.

Adam walked in. He had been watching the exchange from a screen in the other room. He, George, Krieger and a few others had talked through what actions to take and what to say if Ferraro didn't want to do it.

Adam wasn't messing around. He looked at Krieger and nodded, then he walked to the opposite side of the table from Ferraro.

Adam started by saying, "Mr. Ferraro, we appreciate you being here, we really do." He then put both knuckles on the table and leaned forward and said, "You'll do it. The families will do it, and here's why." Adam spoke through his teeth. "You can tell the families if they don't, we'll take control of the gold in two of the Mafia's main stockpiles, the gold in the bank of Italy and," ... Adam hesitated for a split second to let the impact of what he was going to say next build, then Adam said, "your gold in the Vatican."

Ferraro's stomach lurched, though his face remained impassive. *They wouldn't touch the Vatican gold... would they? How do these guys even know about it?*

Ferraro knew the Mafia had first became involved after the war when a lot of Santy's gold had been moved to banks in Italy, including the Vatican bank, as part of the CIA effort to keep the Italian Communist Party from coming to power. The interest this gold generated as the price of gold went up from its thirty-five dollars an ounce level, gave the Mafia its century long power. Ferraro understood why Adam was so confidant, and Adam knew he had Ferraro by the short hairs.

Ferraro knew the Mafia counted on this money as the backbone that fortified their other streams of income. Over the decades, the Mafia had done anything to keep this money a secret and it would do just about anything to keep this money, period.

Krieger watched, and was encouraged by Ferraro's questioning. He had been around long enough to know that tough questions didn't mean no. Ferraro was asking questions to understand what he would tell the families. How would this all work. The Dons would have questions, and would want answers on the spot.

Ferraro was thinking on the fly, trying to figure out the best way for it to work. His series of questioning continued as he began to visualize a plan in his mind. For this operation he would want to be there in person with his hand-picked team to take out the designated HVTs. He'd need real hit men, real seasoned professionals. The best didn't travel in packs and didn't work in groups, so this would be different. Without question, the best were within his grasp, although they came with a high price tag.

Krieger was adamant as he jumped back into the conversation and explained to Ferraro, "The only thing you can tell each group of local people is that you know there's been a stand down ordered by local law enforcement higher ups, and you have sources telling you the local competition is going to hit them before the feds come in. You can assure them, and you can give them a day or two advanced notice to take out the competition."

Brooks added, "If they believe this is a rivalry that's no different than any other rival trying to infiltrate their territory, they'll want to protect their power and they'll keep quiet."

"Mr. Ferraro," Adam said. "We'll do everything in our power to protect you. Think about it from your perspective: the benefits to the family will last for decades to come. Be assured that we need this to succeed, so we need you to succeed. I've got to go. The Colonel will work through the details with you."

With that, Adam left the room.

Ferraro thought about that for a minute. He had an idea. "Is there any way we can create chatter that appears to come from these organizations saying they're planning on taking over the inner-city crime organizations? If the family members think they're being set up to be taken down, it would provide the impetus we're looking for."

Krieger smiled. "We can arrange some chatter that your men will pick up."

"Great. If our men get wind of this, they'll be the first to uncover what's going down against them. If it's not coming from me, they'll be coming *to* me," Ferraro thought out loud, looking at Krieger. "And if the chatter's picked up nationally, let's say in several cities, it'll create a pull and it'll align the families."

Krieger nodded in agreement. "Now we're getting somewhere." A plan was formulating. "So, you'll garner support from multiple families. Then you'll have to orchestrate their attacks."

"Absolutely. First, I'll need to talk to the heads of the six major families. Without their support, this won't happen." Ferraro also wanted to clarify. "I understand this meeting never occurred. I'll disclose what we spoke about, but I'll never mention who I met with, and they won't ask."

"You sure about that?" Krieger questioned.

"Absolutely. I'll make them understand it'll be safer for them not to know." Ferraro's comment lingered in the air with the seriousness it deserved. "The hard part will be the HVTs you're talking about. I don't want to leave those to locals. There would be too many people involved that could lead to too many unanswerable questions."

"So you want to bring in professionals for the HVTs?"

Ferraro nodded. "I'm thinking we'll need a team that lives under cover. People who make their living by being quiet. We don't need to tell them much, but they're not dumb either. We could keep the numbers down if we moved them from place to place. We'd need secure transportation, and we need to make it worth their while."

"We understand," Krieger said. "We'll have it taken care of. We'll pay half in advance, then we'll arrange the remainder after the operation."

"These types get paid up front."

"Okay, three quarters in advance," Krieger said. "We need assurance that the job's done, and done right."

Ferraro could see in Krieger's eyes that this wasn't a negotiable item. Krieger had had these things thought out before the meeting; the threat of taking the gold from the Mafia, the plausible deniability… the mutual bene-fits… the incentive to the families and the payment terms.

Ferraro knew that was about all the information he was going to get at this point. He held out his hand to Krieger and said, "I'll see what I can do."

Krieger stood. He had one more thing. "After this meeting, we need to cut all communications to each other, to ensure the security of the operation." Reaching into his suit coat pocket, he pulled out a few cell phones in a plastic bag, opened the bag and let the phones slide onto the table. Ferraro picked up the phones.

Krieger continued. "Here's how we'll give you the dates and times for each city. We'll only use one phone at a time and when we transition to the next phone, immediately discard the used phone appropriately. Remember, twelve midnight of the last day for each city is your shut down time. My people will pull in at 6am sharp the morning after, to give us a few hours buffer. From that point on, you need to have all of your people pulled back, so they don't get caught in any crossfire."

Ferraro confirmed with a nod.

"After you get the information, we'll send a courier to arrange ongoing communications with our field operation."

Ferraro smiled. *They're thinking of everything.* "Understood."

Krieger had one more thing. "We will give you the information of our contact in the field. They'll be the ones in communication with you from here."

CHAPTER 42

Krieger pushed his men harder than ever. This time was different though. He'd handpicked these men and women for their T&T as he called it, which meant talent and tenacity. Krieger had fully disclosed the situation the country was in, and the mission ahead. The individuals that had been chosen knew there were no hidden agendas, and knew they were the only chance for the United States to remain a sovereign nation.

The foe trying to take down the country had the best technology money could buy. They had inside information. They had paid people off in legal positions, the FBI and CIA, and deep state allegiances in Washington.

Krieger had divided the groups into two large teams with many smaller sub teams. Two separate missions would have to infiltrate distinct locations simultaneously to achieve the overall objective. Then there were the SEAL teams. Some would help each of the two operations, while others had individual targets to immobilize the same day. It was the only way to buy enough time for the getaways. Because as soon as the word got out, the heads of the hydra would engage. They would immediately take whatever actions necessary to stop the patriots, while other globalist segments would begin to cover their assets. Others would most likely go into hiding. Two teams working on two different assignments, with satellite Special Forces teams working in harmony, must all succeed to save the country. They all knew it.

There wasn't time to waste. Krieger put together a master TIP (Tactical Implementation Plan). It was choreographed so that as soon as one of the Glass Houses (mock-up of the target) was constructed, the construction crews would be moved to work on another Glass House and Krieger's men would move in to get acclimated to what they were going to encounter. Krieger even had his teams work with the construction crews. Familiarity was something Krieger wanted to instill from the beginning.

After long days of physical training, Krieger's teams were educated on as much intelligence as they could absorb, including how they'd get in, the possible places they'd be watched, and how to react when, not if, something went wrong. Krieger understood that much of the success of the mission depended on planning and how agile the teams could be under adverse conditions.

Everyone knowing about this mission was isolated to the base, with the exception of Adam, the President, Mauricio and Krieger himself. Once on the base, the only outside contact for anyone was by secure communications provided to them at a designated location. Krieger not only provided the best technology, he implemented a preventive monitoring system where any person going into the room to communicate with the outside world was partnered with a person designated to monitor them, side by side.

Every electronic device had been confiscated from every contractor and military personnel alike. Once construction crews arrived on base, they were quarantined from outside contact. Krieger had moved every military team directly into the base. Even communication with spouses was monitored. They couldn't afford to have anything slip out. Krieger wasn't taking any chances; he would stop it before it even had a chance to happen. This was a communication lockdown.

Fueled by the protocols and the sense of urgency on the base, along with the knowledge of what was happening around the country, the construction crews displayed a focus and drive beyond what anyone had ever seen. They had no idea what they were building. Though they were government contractors, and they had never seen anything like this before. Krieger had held a mass meeting with them. Knowing they had a mundane work life and most of them knew deep down that they'd never effect any meaningful change in the world, Krieger had told them this was one time in their life where they could make a difference. After they'd finished, they could tell their families and friends they'd played a vital part in the most important mission since World War II.

The workers sensed it was the most important thing they would ever build in their lifetime. They were inspired. No corners were cut. To a person, they followed every dimension on every blueprint and they worked tirelessly.

Building, preparation and training were at a war level pitch that no one of this generation had ever experienced.

Krieger had a similar group meeting with the entire military. With two Generals standing by his side, Krieger had told the group the same thing he'd told the contractors and more. He had conveyed that it was going to be up to them to save the country from this global threat. He told them that unless they succeeded, their entire families would be devastated. That, the reason there was a communication blackout was because they couldn't trust congress and even many branches of the military had been infiltrated by the deep state who would use any and all resources at their disposal to stop them. Krieger was the operations commander, and everyone knew it.

Rumors and sightings of Adam helped the energy. With everything moving at lightning speed, Krieger had to step away and think. He didn't like the fact that Adam was going to have to go into the lion's den. Krieger wouldn't be there to protect him. He had to think; who could he send with Adam, and how could they get clearance to get in?

He needed to talk to Brooks.

CHAPTER 43

Brooks had to look twice to recognize the disguised technical expert. Sasha was a man who needed to keep away from any facial recognition technology while meeting with Brooks. Among other things, to conceal his appearance this morning, Sasha's hair was almost black, and his shoes allowed him to appear slightly taller than normal.

Being from a Ukrainian father, it was his German mother's side of the family that had given Sasha his start with the CIA. After seeing what the globalists had done to Germany and seeing how the Russians had successfully dealt with the world bankers, Sasha had been helping Brooks for two decades and he was one of the few people on earth that knew Brooks' former identity as The Shadow.

Being the chief designer for advanced prototype equipment used by the world's deadliest people, he not only had access to some of the best field equipment available, he benchmarked the best mechanisms foreign agents had at their disposal and had an extremely lucrative budget to work with. In addition, every time a foreign agent went down across the globe, the cleanup crews quarantined the body and every article in their possession was sent to Sasha and his team.

Sasha also knew the deepest secrets of the most elite undercover operatives the US had.

Decades ago, Reagan, who had globalists in his own midst, was saddled with Bush as a prerequisite for receiving the RNC funding to support his campaign. A nationalist to the core, Reagan knew Bush's family oil business was aligned with Saudi globalist interests. As an ex director of the CIA, Bush had deep state contacts which would last for decades to come. So just before he left office, Reagan secretly set up a small private organization under the cover of a small medical device organization. In reality, it specialized in providing small high-tech apparatus to the loyalists in the CIA and other privately held organizations that secured the country.

A decade after the organization started, the top person wanted some young talent and Sasha was chosen. Sasha had moved out of his government job with the CIA advanced equipment team to lead the R&D side of the private organization. Thus, he was impervious to the restraints of governmental overreach by the deep state that had infiltrated the CIA, FBI, NSA and of course, congress.

But only one person left alive knew that Reagan had had a loyal CIA operative orchestrate the recapturing one of the gold reserves stolen from Santy. That gold would provide uninterrupted and untraceable funding to this private group of patriots. The man who had pulled it off was a very young Brooks. He was known to Reagan only as The Shadow. He was forevermore held dear by Reagan who, in return, had rewarded him by letting him keep a truck load of gold for himself so he would have the financial freedom to do the nation's work. Today, Brooks was much older, though he was about to embark on a mission as important as any the country had ever needed.

When Brooks retook the gold trust that the deep state stole, even Sasha didn't know where the funding for his private organization came from. Reagan, who Sasha met once just before his passing, and who could barely speak at the time, had whispered to him to always support The Shadow.

Sasha would always remember that warm sunny day in May when he'd first met The Shadow. Although they were both young men working for the CIA, even at that time, no one knew The Shadow's real name. Brooks had been credited with several kills and had begun to make a reputation for himself in the CIA and NSA. After working with Sasha and utilizing some of Sasha's devices, the legend of The Shadow began to grow.

When Brooks went deeper under cover, he left behind interaction with almost everyone from his past. Sasha was one of those exceptions. Sasha and he had developed a unique and trusted friendship. Neither could afford anyone to know of their relationship. No one knew who The Shadow really was, and very few knew of Sasha and the work he truly did. While he provided top secret devices to a very few select CIA undercover operatives, Sasha provided the most unique and advanced items to The Shadow alone.

Sasha moved to his new position. As threats grew across the globe, so did Sasha's budget and span of influence. He never wanted to do anything else, he wanted to be his own boss, and to be creative. He also wanted to be extremely well compensated for it, and he was.

Today, the traditional rivalry of Russia and the United States was simply fake news to Sasha and Brooks. Both countries were watching each other closely, and each country was pulling its own shenanigans. At one point in time, both men actually helped the globalists, but that was before Sasha and The Shadow realized the depth of the globalists' deceit and desire.

Over the years, Sasha and The Shadow, regrettably, helped carry out some infamous missions. The operations typically went something like this: polished men would go into an undeveloped or struggling country and buy up large plots of land for the globalists, who were comprised of the same families who owned the central banks. These men would orchestrate this without anyone knowing who was buying the land, which was usually purchased at mere dollars per acre. They would buy as much as they could. Usually it was tens of thousands of acres. Then, these operatives would develop relationships with local politicians. This would lead to them working their way up the political ladder, to the tops of the countries. From that vantage point, they'd offer financial assistance for elections and more. The next step would be under the ruse of getting them help to develop their country. They would let the naïve country's leaders know that they might have contacts who could help finance their development.

Then, bankers would fly in to make arrangements for loans. All the while the country would never suspect that all of these people were the globalist banking families, and it was a setup.

The country would be deceived into taking out loans to build infrastructure, and that infrastructure would inevitably be built on the very land originally purchased by the globalists

Sasha and The Shadow realized that the people who the globalists said they were helping, were being taken advantage of by making them pay for the interest rates on the loans to build the roads, utilities, sewers and other infrastructure on the very land the globalist families still owned. In addition, family farms and land had often been taken by force. Locals were paid very little and, with the globalists developing a monopoly of mass housing, the quality of living for locals usually went down and whole cultures were transformed from a peaceful rural existence, to living to drug infested, crime ridden metropolitan centers that siphoned money from the people to the globalists.

Millions of people in countries across the globe had been saddled with payments to the globalists in the form of interest payments. Then, when timing was right, as had been seen recently, the globalists would gradually raise the interest rate, until it became impossible for the countries to make the payments. And when the country was on the verge of collapse, the globalists would offer to bail them out. Of course, the country would need to put up collateral. The country usually increased regulations on utilities and then nationalized them so they could turn them over to the globalists. Highways, water rights and other sources of ORI (ongoing residual income) were usually targeted. As one globalist once told The Shadow, "We're much smarter now than we were two hundred years ago. We don't call people slaves. We tell them that they're free so they can go to our stores, make payments on our cars and live in our homes. All the while they think they're free and we've got our system down to the point where ninety percent of them don't actually own a thing. They make payments to us and we actually own their homes, cars and almost everything else — including half of the clothes on their backs."

When other country leaders realized what was happening, some resisted. In the early days, Sasha and The Shadow were personally responsible for the deaths of several country leaders. For example, President Roldos of Ecuador gave a speech at the Olympic stadium in Quito, outlining to his country and for all others to see, the globalists' agenda and tactics. It was apparent he would not cave into the globalists' demands that would eventually lead to them owning Ecuador.

After that speech, Roldos had died suddenly at the hands of an assassin.

The globalists were taking charge, and they wanted everyone who might consider keeping their nationals interests first to know it.

Panama's President Torrijos was next to rebut the globalist agenda. Armed with the evidence from Roldos, Torrijos was equipped and ready. He was in a much more secure position. Panama was much more predominant. Being the leader of Panama, the entire United States was familiar with the Panama Canal, and any ill-dealings would be hard to keep out of the US media.

Unbeknownst to Torrijos, the globalists were in the process of quietly buying up controlling interests in the US mainstream media and actually putting the media under their marketing departments, so the networks could be used as a tool to control the facts and manipulate public opinion. The globalists approached Torrijos with a vision for the future for the next hundred years. With international trade booming, they forecasted the unprecedented wealth Panama could achieve. The only thing was, to attain this wealth, Panama would need to update the Panama Canal and, while they were at it, update the surrounding infrastructure to make it the undisputed world class mecca of trade.

Torrijos read the fine print and saw through the ruse. The deal would eventually put enough debt on Panama that the default clauses would kick in, and the globalists, not Panama, would own the Panama Canal.

Torrijos mirrored the President of Ecuador's sentiments and findings in a television broadcast to his country. He would not cave into the globalist demands and outlined his plan to self-finance the initiative, and use Japanese companies to upgrade the canal, agreeing to keep trade with the United States and all other countries open. The only thing that was changing, was he and his country would finance it themselves and pay Japanese companies as they went, so eventually Panama would be among one of the richest and freest countries in the world. This move not only allowed Panama to be independently wealthy, it didn't allow the globalist bankers to make money on interest or eventually own Panama, and they wouldn't even make money through the construction through their huge company Bechtel, who they proposed would do all of the construction work.

Torrijos had his first inkling that something was wrong when the United States media did not broadcast even a suggestion of his television broadcast. He immediately increased his security.

Two months later, on July 31, 1981, Omar Torrijos died in a plane crash caused by a similar device that had been used in Ecuador.

The globalists struck again in South America, where they took down a jet carrying another leader who had defied the globalist takeover of his country.

Then, in 1989, on December 20th, when most people in the United States were on Christmas vacation and focused on family, the globalists had their man Bush in place, and the United States attacked Panama with the largest airborne assault on a single city in fifty years, coinciding with special forces on the ground taking out any resistance that was left in a government that would not bow to globalist financial demands. The deep state CIA military even kept the red cross and all medical relief out of the city for three days while bulldozers driven by globalist-controlled UN personnel from other countries buried bodies and other evidence. By that time, the US media was taking their talking points directly from their globalist bosses as they began filtering out facts. The narratives were false and the few who questioned the stories on air soon learned there were new rules to play by; either follow the rules or lose your job. It was the dawn of a new age of using the media as a weapon to aid in economic warfare.

About a year later, President Bush launched five hundred thousand US troops against Saddam, who made the mistake of invading oil-rich Kuwait. Little did the US public realize that Saddam had followed the same mistakes as the other leaders in South America. Leading up to the US invasion, the globalists had been working with Saddam to undertake a massive developmental project on the Tigris and Euphrates rivers that flowed through Iraq. There was little knowledge of the long-term plan to develop these rivers, but the plan encompassed massive economic trade, power companies and privatizing the valuable waterways and water supply for the entire region. It would represent a vast windfall of money. Expansive economic plans showed infrastructure being developed throughout Iraqi. Trade barriers were being developed to be put into place in the US so the businesses would flood to their privately-owned land with infrastructure financed by the globalists. The transfer of more businesses from the US to Iraq would happen in droves. That was the plan.

Saddam listened for a few years and then, when the deal was finally drafted, he read the fine print. It was a financial trap. He decided he would not sell out his country to eventual ownership by the globalists.

If he hadn't invaded Kuwait, Bush would have had to come up with another excuse to take him out.

As for their part, The Shadow had quietly eliminated several proponents to globalist agendas, each of which the US media portrayed as being assassinated at the hands of Saddam.

After the removal of Saddam, the Bush administration awarded the infrastructure rebuilding to the globalist-controlled company of the Bechtel Group out of liberal San Francisco, as well as Halliburton, of which Vice President Cheney was once the CEO. They were awarded billions for infrastructure rebuilding.

The Shadow was not surprised when Obama and Clinton let ISIS take over Iraq again and destroy much of this infrastructure. It was then rebuilt by the same globalist-controlled groups again, at the expense of the American taxpayer.

The Shadow and Sasha began to realize that these globalists were in the process of doing the same thing to the United States from within. It was then that they joined forces to fight the globalists.

After Brooks retired, he and Sasha had their way of doing business. When they needed someone to orchestrate their missions, someone with wealth, power and influence, someone separated from the government though someone who also realized what was happening to the middle class and who wanted the middle class of America to survive, there was one likely choice. A choice from The Shadow's past he could trust. Ferraro was that wild card.

* * *

Sasha watched Brooks, who looked around and paid close attention to every detail of everything around Sasha. The utensils and condiments were placed in exactly the proper spots. That was their authentication. Sasha's body position, feet, elbows and the slight pitch to his head gave final verification that the coast was clear. They were free to talk.

After a long conversation, Brooks was assured he'd get everything he needed. Except one thing that he wanted to ask Sasha about.

"There's one more thing I need," Brooks added.

Sasha smiled and his left brow rose. "I thought there might be."

"I need to get through security at a globalist stronghold, and I'll be in a position where I'll have to go in with others, so I need to walk right in through their scanners. I need access technology. Can you get me an identification badge?"

Sasha's shaking head wasn't a welcome response. "Even we can't get you that kind of identification. They use combined technologies. It's information strips embedded into an extremely high-tech screen-printing technology with a variety of ultra violet inks and coatings over a portion that's a three-dimensional lenticular technology. We don't have that kind of equipment."

"Who does?" Brooks asked.

"The only place that does is hidden in a small industrial complex here on the east coast."

"I'm guessing it's privately owned?" Brooks questioned.

"Affirmative," Sasha said. "It's foreign owned, French and another company, I forget who. They transferred ownership a few years ago. I don't keep up with that stuff. They make all of the identification for the highest-ranking people in our government… and I mean the highest. They make the identification badges for generals, for anyone receiving access to the White House, Langley, you name it, they make it."

"It figures. They're a globalist-controlled company?"

"Of course. The only way you're going to get in wherever you're going is by getting one of those badges. I'm afraid that the protocols and security in that building are almost impenetrable. You'd never get the clearance and, if you did, there'd be a leak." Sasha let that sink in and added, "Unless you had the highest authority, you'll never get authorized and even if you did, it wouldn't be completed in time."

"Why's that? Brooks asked."

"It takes days to make badges from start to finish," Sasha said.

The comment Sasha made about the highest authority resonated with Brooks. If it took the highest authority, then that's what he'd get. After all, that was who he was going to be there to protect.

CHAPTER 44

"Where are we going?" Mauricio asked.

"The President wants to see you," Krieger said as they briskly strode down the marbled hall of the White House.

Mauricio stopped in his tracks. Just yesterday Krieger had told him about this new assignment. They were in Washington for less than a day, now the president wanted to see him.

"Don't worry, it's good," Krieger said, then he nodded a 'let's go' as he regained the pace. "We've got a small window of time, and that's all."

Moments later, Mauricio nervously entered the Oval Office. The president approached.

George extended his hand and said, "I wanted to personally thank you for showing us how to tap into the NSA database and uncover all the electronic information on the deep state."

Mauricio calmed as the president firmly shook his hand.

The president continued. "We're taking the evidence to the compromised members of Congress and giving them the option to either retire or be prosecuted. My opinion is that we'll see record numbers of retirees this year."

Mauricio was aware of some recent retirees. Most had announced that they were going to retire to spend time with their families. Now he understood the real reason.

The always eloquent and well-spoken Mauricio was gracious. "Thank you, Mr. President. I'm only doing my part. The team is uncovering the information."

The president knew Mauricio still had his hands on the team and added, "Well, your part made this all possible." The president smiled broadly at Mauricio, thinking to himself, *Son if you only knew how important it is to get some of these people out now.* "It was the crucial piece we needed to get the ball rolling … Speaking of getting the ball rolling, I know you two have a few huge endeavors to undertake. I wanted to take this opportunity to say that your country is counting on you to be successful on all accounts. All of this needs to work together for us to be successful."

"Thank you, sir," Mauricio said, and he could read the president's body posture. Their window was closing, it was time to go.

Walking down the hall, Mauricio got a call from Melissa.

She said, "Sir, it's The Cleric again, he's here."

Mauricio knew what he was about to say would irritate Krieger. "Your friend's back," Mauricio said.

"The Cleric?" Krieger scowled.

Mauricio nodded, then he listened to Melissa. "We've picked up one of the cell phones we know he's using, and he contacted Sordid." Mauricio slowed his walk.

Melissa continued. "They agreed to start insurrection here in Boston during the demonstration… Your hunch was correct, sir."

Mauricio was relieved that, although he had crews watching several cities, he had chosen Boston as the place for Melissa to be stationed. At the same time, he was anxious.

Krieger felt a surge of adrenalin go through his body when he heard Mauricio tell Melissa, "You know who to contact. Tell him game on."

Mauricio and Melissa both knew he was talking about Ferraro.

They all knew that Ferraro had his team assembled and was ready waiting for the call.

After filling the Dons in on Adam's ultimatum, the Mafia families knew Krieger had them by the short hairs. It was risky, though the reward outweighed the risk. The benefits Krieger had pointed out could drastically enhance their territory, which had been taken by well-funded and connected foreigners over the past two decades.

The private plane was waiting for Ferraro and his team. The only thing they needed was a destination, and now Melissa would provide that. Ferraro would fly to Boston while he alerted the Dons to be ready in the other cities.

* * *

An hour later, across the street at Krieger's office, he and Mauricio sat at the conference table with Dr. Roy Hemmele, the expert on EMPs and a myriad of other similar technologies.

Hemmele sat forward, his hands clasped. "There isn't really anything else I can do right now," he said, "so I'll just stay available, unless there's something else you need me to do."

Krieger looked at Mauricio, and said, "We appreciate it, Doctor. No there's nothing else... Unless you know how to fool state of the art radar."

Something inside Krieger made him say it out loud. He and Mauricio were planning their mission and knew there was a high likelihood of a few of the ships being tracked. He took a long shot, not expecting the doctor to be able to help.

Hemmele looked up across the desk at Krieger. "How crucial is this... whatever you're doing?"

Krieger wasn't going to let Hemmele leave Washington anyway, so Krieger said, "The country falling into globalist hands is at stake."

That was all Hemmele needed to know. The scientist was a patriot at heart. He looked directly at Krieger. "There is a device that may be able to do that. It's not meant for that, but its basic technology makes it plausible."

Krieger enthusiastically slapped his desk in a rare show of emotion. He said to Dr. Hemmele, "Let's go get it."

Hemmele laughed. "You don't go get it. You have to go to it."

CHAPTER 45

Two groups of patriots had each worked tirelessly for two weeks. They were independent of each other. Both groups needed to succeed in order for the country to be of-by-and-for the people again.

One was a large multi-faceted group, comprised of all branches of the military. They were working at a large military base, building, training, rehearsing, and making modifications to equipment and vehicles. Even a submarine was being given some last-minute enhancement for the mission.

The other team was the economic team working in Washington. They had been quarantined to a secure floor of a hotel. They met, ate and even slept there. No one left. Their communications with the outside world were monitored closely. They didn't mind, that's what they'd volunteered for. Sound scrambling technology made it impossible for the deep state or anyone else to listen in on them. They had been focusing on economic issues of the country.

The team decided that their first step would be to diagram the current state of the economy. With input from key team members, they had quickly agreed that the solution to most of the problems in the country was the ability for the working middle class to gain and accumulate wealth. There were many reasons for it.

They had diagramed the key inputs to a prosperous middle class. When members of the group categorized the effect of all the inputs, the facts were undeniable. The exercise helped align the entire team on a common purpose. The analysis had shown them that the monetary policies, taxes and banking were taking the majority of the hard-earned wealth of the average American. Add these to artificial trade barriers and other things that made doing business in the US more expensive, and those were the real problems.

After they completed their current state analysis, they briefed the president and vice president. This briefing wasn't to outline solutions, that would come later. George had requested it as a check in point. The agenda was to let him and Adam know what the team believed they needed to work on, and why. George and Adam also thought that if the team wasn't going to focus on an area that they believed it needed to focus on, they would take that opportunity to add that area of focus to their efforts.

The economic team had voted for Haley, an owner of an actuarial firm, and Szegda, an eccentric millionaire, to make the two-hour briefing to the president, vice president and Madison.

After outlining the weaponizing of the government, banking, monetary and legal system as primary drivers of the middle class's inability to work for and build wealth, they told the three of them why they believed that and went into some of the history.

They explained that it all led back to the fact that the country had vast resources which belonged to the people. Those resources could easily be the assets behind the financial systems that could be and should be owned by the citizens of the country. That was the founder's intent.

Instead, private families, most notably the Rothschilds, Rockefellers, Goldman Sachs, Lehmans and Kuhn Loebs, Warburgs of Germany, Lazards of France and Israel Moses Serifs, had monopolized banking in the United States and across the globe. They had infiltrated governments, and recently militaries, to ensure more control. The banking business had turned into one where it printed and distributed paper to sell as currency, while banking families were secretly taking all of the real money, the gold, silver and other precious metals for themselves, setting them up as the ruling class forever.

Then when it came to getting into the details, Haley did most of the talking. Presenting facts in an easily understandable way was his forte. He had started with a simple pareto bar chart of who held the wealth; the diagram showed that the people's wealth had somehow been taken from them and transferred to the elites.

Haley made Madison, the president and Adam realize that these families, not the United States of America, were the wealthiest and most powerful entity on the planet. He laid out several of their shell companies and trusts which showed that the *Rothchild's are worth over 100 trillion dollars*[95] and the information was over ten years old, so that number would be much higher today.

Haley pointed to a few posters taped on the walls with printing too small to read from their seats and explained that the top four families in banking were called the four horsemen, and *the four horsemen of banking were among the top 10 stockholders of virtually every Fortune 500 Corporation,*[3] in addition to owning the Federal Reserve and other central banks around the globe. With this knowledge, the president and Adam understood why large corporations often sided with the globalist agenda.

Luckily, this team in Washington was diversified. A few knew how the central banking cartel was made up of about fifteen or sixteen banks. They included the Royal Bank of Scotland, HSBC, which was the Old Hong Kong Shanghai bank, Lloyds Bank, the Bank of America, Citicorp, JP Morgan Chase of course, UPS, Crediscris, Deutschbank, the Royal Bank of Canada, and a few others. He outlined how they pretended they were are all competing entities, though many had the same owners and, in recent times, had more closely aligned as one, acting as an oligopoly.

Then the team put a pile of consolidated income statements in front of the president.

Haley said, "The Rockefeller bench control 25% of all assets of the 50 largest US commercial banks, and 30% of all assets of the 50 largest insurance companies."

That was when Madison quipped, "Sounds like we need insurance reform."

Haley went on to mathematically show the impact on the working people of the country and the retired people for a half hour.

To wrap up his presentation he said, "In his epic book, Tragedy and Hope, historian Carol Quimby wrote that the Bank for International Settlements was part of a plan '*to create a world system of financial control in private hands able to dominate the political system of each country and the economy of the world as a whole … to be controlled in a feudalistic fission by the central banks of the world acting in concert by secret agreements… in order to enslave the planet.'*[96]

The president understood these corrupt people wanted to make money off everyone in the world and take the largest percentage of other people's efforts. He knew this was a criminal conspiracy, and it would never be anything else.

Madison had previously explained to him that the Federal Reserve had positioned itself to obtain assets like utilities, shipping ports and highways, which they'd toll even more. These bankers owned well over a trillion in housing stock and were behind the mortgage industry housing bubble; their intent was to make it burst again by artificially driving up prices by giving loans to people who statistics showed would default. They were doing this by paying off politicians to put in government policies, so when the housing industry expanded then burst again, the bankers could come in and say they were going to rescue the industry. Of course, the term rescue actually meant that they'd take ownership of the deeds, which meant they'd take owner-ship of the land. But luckily the president getting elected had put an end to that, for now.

George knew some of this. That was why, in his commencement address to the nation, he'd said, "We will no longer surrender this country of its people to the false song of globalism. The nation state remains the true foun-dation for happiness and harmony. I am skeptical of international unions that tie us up and bring American down! And under my administration, we will never enter America into any agreement that reduces our ability to control our own affairs!"

Shortly after that, Steinmeier, German's foreign minister, said in retort to the president's statements, "The world has changed; no American president can get around this change. America first is no answer to that."

When the presentation hit the two-hour point, the president, vice presi-dent and Madison stayed for another half hour. With that, the team under-stood how important their task was.

The group would now begin to work on the future state, or as they called it, the Ideal Future Result (IFR). It would take them days to decide what had to be accomplished to give the country back to the people economically. They knew that, after that, everything else would fall into place. Then, they'd present their suggestions to the president. From there he'd make the final decisions of what to do and how to get support for immediate implementation. Then he'd announce its implementation to the country.

George had commended them on their great work. He reaffirmed that they were on the right path. Then he left them and confirmed that he would be back to hear their suggestions. He challenged them to suggest economic systems that would set the country up for another century of prosperity.

After George, Madison and Adam had left the room, the team felt there was something more going on. Something huge. Nobody told them there was, they just knew it. They could *feel* it. They sensed that something else huge going on and it would determine if their work was even viable. It would determine the fate of the nation. They knew it and they were bound and determined to be ready.

How right they were, but that was in the hands of Krieger and his men.

CHAPTER 46

Adam had to fly out for the New World Order financial hub in London without Brooks. Adam was about to put himself at a far greater risk than any modern-day VP ever had. If Brooks couldn't catch up with the vice president before the meeting, that would leave Adam with his personal detail and they were excellent, but they weren't Brooks.

Over the past two weeks, all sorts of plans and contingency plans had been made. Everything major had been agreed upon two weeks ago, with the exception of what Adam was about to do and how he was going to do it.

It was during some last-minute planning sessions that it became apparent that the best option for the good of the country was for Adam to undertake this mission. Because of the risk, it was determined that someone with either Special Forces or CIA training needed to be part of the diplomatic envoy in case the vice president was threatened, but it needed to be someone that could blend in with the rest of them. Someone who didn't look like a threat. Someone who, if things went south, could improvise and possibly secure the vice president. Brooks volunteered to be that someone.

Anyone going in with Adam had to be pre-approved in advance. That was the easy part, though they all needed the proper identification badge to get through security — and Brooks didn't have one.

Posing as a noted economist, Brooks looked similar enough to the actual man to pull it off, but could he get there in time?

Adam had a loyal patriot secretly make the contact for the badge. Why these badges weren't made by an American company was obviously another way the deep state kept its people in strategic parts of the government. With a foreign organization making these credentials, almost anything could be compromised. Adam would deal with that after the mission.

Krieger and Brooks had driven up to the small industrial park where the badges were produced. From the outside, it looked like a small to medium sized business. Nothing indicated what it was. They pulled up to the gate and had to give their names to be let in. Once inside, there were a series of security protocols, starting with a badge swipe and a fingerprint scan. Then, the further you went into the location, the thicker the vaults got. They looked like bank vaults. When getting close to where the most secure identification badges were made and stored, there were retina scans and the door to the vault looked to be five feet thick. When the badge was finished, Brooks and Krieger immediately headed out. Krieger had arranged the only way left for Brooks, The Shadow, to arrive in time for the meeting with Adam.

* * *

At Dover Air Force base, Krieger had arranged for a secured hanger. Pulling in, a lone fighter jet waited. When they got out of the Hummer, Krieger looked up and saw a gregarious bald man approaching.

Krieger shook his head with a smile and said to Brooks, "I'd like to say you'll be in good hands but with this one, you never know."

In his usual exuberant fashion, Tim returned the sparring comment. "It's good to see you too, Colonel. It's always nice to be appreciated."

Krieger softened his tone. "How've you been, Tim?"

"Pretty good." Tim immediately let go of Krieger's hand and reached for Brooks. "It's good to see you again too."

When Adam had been held captive by globalist forces in a remote cabin in the Idaho wilderness, it was The Shadow who had burst in and rescued him the night before the election. It was Tim who had flown the helicopter that had dropped Brooks and Krieger off in the woods. Then it was Tim who had flown Adam and Krieger in a prototype supersonic jet that made no sonic boom to the last nationally televised event George was making before the election. That sequence had led to the country realizing what length the globalists would go to in order to keep an independent patriotic billionaire they couldn't control out of the White House. Tim was now retired, which made him a good choice for this mission, because he could fly off the record and, with his history of being a Top Gun, teaching at Annapolis and the Naval War college, and having over two thousand safe carrier landings, he was one of a kind.

Tim didn't want to waste any time. After shaking hands with Brooks, he said, "You'd better get dressed, we don't have much time."

* * *

Meanwhile, Gabby nervously sat with the vice president on Air Force Two. She made a call to leak the news that Adam was flying to London to meet with world bankers to acquire financial relief.

She knew some of the media would immediately send representatives over. The plan was in motion.

* * *

With The Shadow in the sky, Krieger headed towards his own flight. He, Briggs and Mauricio had their own mission they could now focus on... or so they thought.

* * *

The president looked across the Resolute desk in the Oval Office at Madison. She had a look of trepidation in her eyes. It was just the two of them. They were keeping tabs on various parts of the multi-faceted mission that was underway: the mission to save the country.

The Shadow, Brooks, was finally in the air.

Madison looked at the time. "It'll be close, but he'll make it."

The president looked tense. "Krieger, Mauricio and Briggs are on their way to New York. After that, they'll join their task force. Then they'll be on a communications blackout."

Madison didn't know if it was for the President or for herself that she said, "Everything'll be okay, sir. You've done everything you could."

He gave a tight-lipped smile. "And so have you, Senator... I really appreciate everything you've done. The country will appreciate it too."

The President and Madison sat in silence for a moment. They'd just wait until it was time for them to fly west for their part of the mission.

They never expected the phone call that was about to come through.

CHAPTER 47

The phone call took the president by surprise. Adam was still in the air, and Krieger was in route to his next destination, so the president thought he wouldn't hear much for a few hours.

He looked at Madison and said, "It's Colonel Krieger."

He pushed the button on the phone to put it on speaker.

"Mr. President, arms are on the move," Krieger said as soon as he was patched through.

Madison was also the Chair of an Intelligence committee. She asked, "From where?"

"Port Canaveral," Krieger said. "Mauricio has a team monitoring the port. A massive number of trucks are leaving. Our scanners have picked up munitions.

"Mr. President, as you know, Mauricio and I will be out of contact for a while. We'd like to do a three-way call, so the person filling in for Mauricio domestically can brief you, then Madison can contact her if need be."

The president looked across the desk at Madison. She quickly nodded her approval.

The president said, "Go ahead Colonel, put her through."

With the three-way call set up and a quick introduction out of the way, Melissa started by saying, "They got the munitions in through *Florida's Port Canaveral cargo container terminal. Unfortunately, this port of entry gives the deep state ...unfettered access to the entire United States."*[97] She hesitated ever so briefly then continued. "In a secret operation known as Project Pelican, Barack Hussein Obama and his deep state administration awarded communist and Islamic extremist countries a thirty-five-year container terminal lease through a secret operation known as Project Pelican."

Krieger jumped in. "How did this get by congress?"

Madison knew something about the project. "Colonel, I'm afraid to say they bypassed the national security reviews by doing a private lease. Actually, it was a company called Gulftainer who got this lease, without all of the required national security reviews. We tried to stop it, but back then the deep state was everywhere, and they were brazenly flexing their muscles."

Krieger was fuming. "I should have known. Who helped orchestrate this?"

On the other end of the phone in Washington, Madison's head sank for a brief moment before her gaze lifted off the desk. She looked at the president in anticipation of Krieger's response to what she was about to tell him. "Colonel, you might want to be sitting down."

Krieger wasn't about to sit down. Through a tight jaw he said, "Congresswoman, go ahead."

Madison explained how it was orchestrated. "The Committee on Foreign Investment in the United States (CFIUS) bypassed the mandated thirty and forty-five day national security reviews of the Gulftainer, Port Canaveral transaction. In the end, they got total access to our port. Much of this was orchestrated by an immigration attorney, who made a living representing people from the middle east seeking asylum in the United States. He's a Pakistani immigrant, and member of the Muslim Brotherhood, who had no apparent national security experience."

Krieger's voice got louder as it came through the speaker. "Well how the hell did he get in a position to orchestrate this? Who was pulling the strings?"

Madison looked at the president, wishing there was someone else there to tell him. She stood up to the plate and looked directly at the president. "That Pakistani attorney and Robert Muller were partners in the same law firm."

"What?" the president bellowed.

Krieger said, "Okay, great. Those sleaze ball attorneys using our own laws against us."

Melissa wanted to alert them of something else. "Mauricio."

"Yes?"

"We linked Baghdad-born Dr. Jafar to Gulftainer. Jafar and Gulftainer own one hundred percent of the shares of the club K system and..."

Mauricio cut her off. "Dr. Jafar's collaboration with North Korea with weapons delivery systems? We're talking ships filled with containers that can be loaded directly on to flatbed semi-trucks and rail cars. Jafar, or his cohorts, could bring in one of those newly advanced delivery systems that would fit right on a semi and look like any other container."

Madison stepped into the conversation. "Mr. President, there's something else you should know. Gulftainer is owned by the United Arab immigrants and Hammed Jafar and Sheik Sultan Al Kisan, ruler of Sharqiyah Saudi Arabia. They use shell corporations to mask the fact that the company is actually owned by a foreign government, because that would make this deal illegal."

Krieger said to Mauricio, "The advent of a new advanced delivery system and the involvement of those who lease port Canaveral sure smells like it's a high-risk situation."

Madison chimed in again, saying, "You may also be interested in the fact that, not surprisingly, it was one of Hillary's confidants working with James Clapper that masterminded this and Arabs of Dubai purchasing thirteen ports along the east coast."

The president added, "That must have been one of the things in their playbook. I recently became aware that similar shenanigans were used so the Uranium one deal didn't go through the CFIUS."

Melissa said, "You can't make this stuff up."

George understood there was nothing Krieger could do from where he was at. "Okay, is there anything else we should know?"

"That's all from this end sir," Melissa said.

Krieger looked at Mauricio, who nodded. "That's it from here, Mr. President. I'm sorry to dump this on you but, as you understand, we have to go."

"Understood," George said. "We'll take it from here Colonel. Thank you and good luck."

Krieger hung up and looked at Mauricio, who'd just been handed a note.

The Shadow had arrived on time.

* * *

The vice president looked around from the top of the gangplank of Air Force Two. Gabby stood just behind him. In the background, a navy fighter jet had just touched down with its one-man cargo.

Adam took his time as the detail of vehicles were already lined up.

By the time Adam got into the limo, The Shadow, posing as an economist, was seated beside Gabby.

The meeting would be attended by families of the Federal Reserve and the Bank of London.

The drive from Lakenheath RAF (Royal Air Force) base was a short one. As the largest European Air Force-operated base in England, and the hub F-15 fighter wing of all US Air Forces in Europe, they were equipped for the heightened security the vice president commanded during these trying times.

As the motorcade drove slowly south towards London, Adam pulled up the stock market report. The globalists had sold off substantial shares of American stocks, driving the markets down even further. George would counter with some of the money they'd already confiscated from the globalists, but it was now a battle of the president against the globalists.

The globalist bankers had forced George's hand. With a very short window after the initial attack on the market, they had given George an ultimatum of negotiating for another series of massive loans, backed by substantial assets of US infrastructure and rights to resources, or the next series of economic warfare would spiral the country into an economic collapse. It would be the equivalent of a modern-day Great Depression. But this one would be worse, because this time the globalists had people planted in cities that would mount insurrection.

George, Adam and their advisors knew that the consequences of an economic collapse of that magnitude would be much graver. It would most likely end in the deaths of tens of thousands of innocent people, and possibly more.

For Adam to pull off what they were about to do, they needed enough of the key globalist players in one location to make the authorizations. Krieger was vehement that allowing George to go wasn't an option. He didn't like it when Adam volunteered, but Adam showing up personally was the only way to ensure the highest-ranking members of the banking families would be there.

Adam saw a new alert. "Insurrection in Chicago fuels fights in other cities."

Could it be a coincidence that this had happened as he was on his way? Adam didn't think so. Without saying a word, he thought to himself, *is Ferraro up to the task?*

CHAPTER 48

"They've got armed overwatch on top of the buildings," Ferraro heard Melissa say in his ear piece.

As Ferraro walked down the city street towards the mosque, he turned to his right, pretending to address his partner. "That's good, that means we've come to the right place."

Melissa was orchestrating the command and control from a private high-rise apartment. The height of the building offered uninterrupted communication. The clear view from the penthouse gave her oversight over the entire area. This was one of six communication centers she was monitoring. With Mauricio on another mission, these operations were all hers to command. She understood that she and Krieger were kicking off the first parts of the complicated mission. These two things would appear unrelated, but it was all part of the plan. That's all she knew about what Krieger was up to. She was told that much, so when news broke, she wasn't surprised. She would know that it was all part of the plan and she needed to stay concentrated on her part. She had no knowledge if the president or even the vice president knew. She had no way of knowing the president was currently at the White House watching and listening to the many moving parts. He had kicked off the largest single operation since D-day.

Melissa's lead relayed information from each field command post (CP). The decentralized command centers could each make decisions and adjust to circumstances as things developed. This structure allowed Melissa to best accomplish the main mission of providing overwatch and offering good information to Ferraro. Collecting and relaying information was all she was authorized to do. The dirty work was up to Ferraro and his people.

Melissa and her teams had been monitoring increased activity for days. Armed locals had been moving through alleyways and gathering in small groups at several locations in the vicinity. Most of the communication was being directed from the mosque, and those who had ties to the mosque. Ordinarily, this wouldn't happen. It was almost impossible to get approval for legal surveillance in cities any more.

Melissa's team had picked up reports about the plans to escalate the civil unrest during the upcoming demonstrations, when local police would stand down.

Ferraro's teams were in place, and they all had their assignments. These men were professionals. They didn't know anything about the operation, besides what Ferraro had told them. They believed the efforts of the foreign globalist backed insurgents were to overthrow them. That part was true. The radical arm of the Muslim nation had a goal of total domination, and they hated the Christian side of the Mafioso culture. Those working with Ferraro knew this pre-emptive strike was needed to ensure their livelihood for generations to come. They also understood they had a window of time to make their hits and get out. This was their only chance to beat back the competition.

Now, Melissa's team listened in silence. Even though they had secure scrambled lines, they were letting Ferraro handle this. Mosques these days had lookouts for police and federal agents, and Ferraro knew it. If a lookout detected a risk, they would radio the inside of the mosque, then those in charge would take the appropriate actions.

Usually mosques had a lead imam who almost always had enough money to pay off informants or someone in government, so they knew when the authorities were coming. However, unexpected infiltration would be met with the highest sense of urgency. This mosque not only had the usual safe room, it had an extra room in between, which offered those inside added security. It also bought them time in case they were infiltrated.

Two of Ferraro's team worked from a distance so as not to be identified. No one except Ferraro and Melissa knew who was behind the drones.

At Ferraro's confirmation signal, four small drones took off for the four corners of the mosque and one flew to the center. Being less than ten inches across, they were quiet and could remain unnoticed unless someone happened to glance directly at one.

Ferraro's man, a well-paid retired military woman of Italian ancestry, watched the monitors. After she was satisfied it was all clear for Ferraro to move in, a woman walked out of a door up ahead. She brushed the back of her skirt and then stopped and examined the heel of her shoe as if to look for something. This was the all-clear signal. Ferraro was a go.

This would be his first hit. After Ferraro eliminated the HVTs, Melissa and her teams would immediately leave town. For the remainder of the day, Ferraro and his team would be allowed to handle their own business before pulling out.

After accomplishing the purging, Ferraro would move to another city via a secure private plane provided by someone in the family. This travel wouldn't show up on any budget and thus was as secure as it could be.

Though brutal, this was a way for the only free country left in the world to turn back the tide of economic overthrow by wealthy banking families aided by Islamic terrorists. It had to be done, because they all knew, when the deep state gave the signal, the Islamist extremists would strike a series of fatal blows to unsuspecting masses across the country. Ferraro had to complete his purge before theirs began.

Ferraro had another twist he planned to add to his methods; when the Islamic recruits saw this, few Islamic terrorists would want to come to the United States, and many of those who were still here would flee of their own accord.

As soon as Ferraro and his companion crossed the street, the jamming device over the center of the mosque actuated. It would effectively interrupt the communications from the mosque and a small surrounding area.

Ferraro walked directly up to one of the sentries at the front corner of the building. Ferraro was obviously Italian, and the man figured he was a local small time Mafioso who wanted something. He never paid attention to what was coming from behind. No sooner had he been shot in the head with a suppressed weapon, when a small van pulled up and two men dragged him inside. One of Ferraro's men inside the van grabbed his ear piece and pistol and took his place. That sequence went seamlessly one more time.

The driver parked the old van they'd stolen the previous day in the alley by the dumpster. He locked the doors, threw the keys away, and put his thin rubber gloves in his pocket.

Ferraro was accompanied by an elderly middle eastern man who had long ago changed his name. Sam Perra had been born and raised in Iraq, and he'd witnessed his eldest brother taken away by the guard and forced into Saddam's army. Sam's mother, knowing Saddam's guard would come back again in a few years and take her other two sons, trained them throughout the summer and the following winter. Then, in the spring, she sent them over the mountains to escape. Both had made their way to the United States. Sam's elder brother had started up a small restaurant, while Sam earned his red belt in Karate and eventually made his way into security work. Then, through a series of incidents, Sam ended up going back to Iran and other countries in the middle east as a contractor working for US intelligence. He had searched, but never saw his mother again.

When his second contract was up, he went back to the US where, fueled by his anger of stories about his mother's disappearance, he had gotten into a conflict with some men. After holding his own with two, a third had knocked him silly from behind. They were Mafia, and it had been Sam's unlikely introduction to his new way of life.

Sam had seen what evil men had done to his family and friends when he was a boy. He knew evil was here, trying to take away the way of life he now cherished with his American family.

With Sam obviously being of mid-eastern descent and Ferraro a half step behind him, they were paid little attention. Once inside, they went straight to the men's room to give the team some time, while they pretended to clean themselves.

They could hear the hustle of men and their fast-speaking middle eastern dialogue. Sam understood they were upset about the loss of communication. He nodded to Ferraro, ever careful in case they were being watched or listened to.

They walked casually down the hall where the back rooms were for the most important men in the mosque. Money flowed from the middle east to leaders in mosques across America. The well-connected Muslims had infringed on traditional Mafia businesses for decades.

Even though it was well known that this imam was responsible for training and supplying individuals conducting terrorist activities, they had so many people paid off, their nefarious activities were allowed to continue. That was all about to end today.

Ferraro checked his watch as he followed Sam down the hall. It had been less than twenty seconds since entering the area they weren't supposed to be in.

A man with a heavy mid-eastern accent asked, "May I help you?"

Sam Perra, still walking in front of Ferraro to buy them the few seconds they needed, responded fluently in his native tongue. "I'm sorry." Reaching into his jacket pocket he continued, "Maybe you can help us find…" Sam pulled out his suppressed 45 and shot the man square in the chest before saying, "…Jesus."

Knowing the suppressed sound was loud enough to be identified in the next room, Sam moved quickly and burst through the door. Ferraro followed.

As shots were fired throughout the room, Ferraro's handpicked men busted through two other entrances of the mosque and came in shooting. They didn't wait until they'd identified every person. With the mosque closed, everyone they saw was male and of mid-eastern decent and thus connected. This was a hit, an extermination of an element that would no longer be tolerated in the country.

With one man down in the first room, Perra moved quickly. He threw open the next door, staying behind the wall. It was a good call that he had learned while helping the military clear houses in his homeland, because he watched as rounds riddled across the door and wall. Reaching around the doorframe with his 45, Perra emptied his magazine.

He quickly slapped in another magazine, looked at Ferraro, took a few more shots and they both lunged into the room firing.

Only the imam was inside. The .45 had hit him with such power it had thrown the gun out of the imam's hand. Perra thought, *That's the advantage of using a .45 at close range.*

Ferraro looked at the HVT with disdain, knowing he was responsible for countless deaths of innocent children, knowing what they did to women. These were both things his traditional Italian culture despised.

Ferraro said to the man, "Your day has come. Today begins the purge of your kind."

The imam coughed up blood and, through a pained look on his face he grinned and said something in his native tongue.

Ferraro looked at Perra. Perra shot through the imam again, finishing him.

Reaching into his pocket, Perra had come prepared with a message he'd acquired from a family member on the south side of town where the slaughter house was. Pulling out the heavy plastic bag, he carefully opened it and spread the pig blood and parts on and around the man. These Muslims had died with the pigs and whoever found them would know it. The message was Ferraro and Perra's alone, neither Melissa or anyone else had any knowledge of it. By the time Ferraro and his team were through, the message that was being delivered there and in several other locations would be received by the entire Muslim community throughout the nation.

"What'd he say?" Ferraro asked.

Perra turned to Ferraro. "He said, no, soon the time begins to purge the great beast."

Ferraro looked back at him, knowing they had accomplished their mission here by eliminating this HVT. "Let's get out of here." *Something big is up. I hope whatever the military is doing works.*

* * *

Hours later, after taking care of numerous foreign criminal elements, Ferraro and Perra were safely at the airport. Ferraro pulled out another secure phone and made a call to the only number in it.

A familiar voice simply said, "Hello?"

Ferraro confirmed he was all clear by a pre-determined code phrase, saying, "Is this the florist?"

With the authentication that Ferraro was safely out of the area, the voice simply said, "Nice day to send flowers," and hung up.

Ferraro was on to the next destination.

*　*　*

Their next stop started off rather unusually. One of Ferraro's assassins pulled out his gun, carefully aimed, and squeezed the trigger. He barely grazed the mid-section of the officer with a perfectly placed round about two inches above the belt.

The shooter immediately concealed his weapon and walked casually around the corner with his head down, and got into a car. The officer fell to the ground, screaming in pain.

Drapes opened in the building across the street. The officer screamed for them to come out with their hands up. After a short delay he was met with a hailstorm of bullets.

Over his radio, the officer called in, "Officer down, I repeat, officer down. I've got multiple armed assailants. Need backup."

The officer knew two things: first, his brothers in uniform would react without mercy to these foreign infiltrators who were packed into the building just across the street. Second, he would be compensated very well by his Italian family for taking that grazing shot.

As Ferraro left town, several tips led local police to the other staging grounds where terrorists were held up, preparing to unleash terror on the unsuspecting public. At each of these locations, somehow shots were fired at police, who vented their pent-up anger. Ferraro was a brilliant man, using every tactic at his disposal. This way he could purge much more.

*　*　*

A few hours later, the plane took off for its next destination. In the back of his head, Ferraro knew Adam, Krieger and others were up to something much bigger than he was undertaking. He had no idea what it was, although something in his gut told him it was only a matter of time before the lid blew off this thing and all hell broke loose.

* * *

The motorcade carrying the vice president pulled up to the New World Order headquarters. Adam's face gave no indication of the sense of relief he felt when he glanced back over his shoulder to see that The Shadow had made it through security.

They entered through the front door and walked down the ornate marbled hallway of the globalist banking stronghold. They went up the elevator. As they headed towards the conference room, Adam knew he was about to set in motion a sequence of events that were the only hope of saving the country. To do so, this meeting was going to rock the world banks.

* * *

"Gentlemen, let me get started," Adam said. His opening silenced the room immediately after introductions. He had their undivided attention.

George had told the bankers that Adam would show up personally to negotiate the terms of the United States putting up collateral in exchange for their ongoing financial support of another huge loan to keep the country from collapsing. With little negotiating leverage, George's only demand was that the heads of each of the families that owned the Federal Reserve attended the meeting personally. Present were: heads of *Goldman Sachs, Rockefellers, Lehmans and Kuhn Loebs of New York; the Rothmayers of Paris and London; the Warburgs of Hamburg; the Lazards of Paris; and the Israel Moses Serifs of Rome.*[98] George had made it clear that a roll call would be taken, and if all families weren't present to negotiate in person, Adam would leave.

From the bankers' perspective, the globalist families were overjoyed that they'd finally, personally, witness the transference of a significant amount of the assets of the United States of America over to them. Along with the terms came ongoing economic control George had taken out of their grasp when he'd backed out of the TPP agreement. They already knew approximately how many miles of infrastructure and the magnitude of the natural resources that would become theirs.

Everything the globalists did was with the intention of enriching themselves. Slogans and movements like save the environment, political correctness, humanitarian issues were all a lie to get more money out of people while the globalist bankers kept the lion's share and gradually increased their control over working people everywhere. Adam couldn't think of one agenda ever that reduced taxes, let people keep more of their own money, or let people have more control of their own lives… not even one!

George hadn't wanted Adam to be a part of this, but there was no other way. The globalists would only agree to having their top people there if Adam represented the United States. With all these players, at this location, they could orchestrate the transfer of any amount of money and communicate directly with any branch they had around the world. Direction from this headquarters was the supreme authority and, per the agreement, George had these bankers prepared to make what was to be the largest financial transfers in the history of mankind.

Each reigning globalist family member knew huge transfers were coming. They'd had paperwork drawn up, teams were standing by, and other bank headquarters around the world had been notified and pre-authorized to immediately make huge transfers of whatever amounts were agreed upon during the meeting. They only awaited the account numbers and amounts.

The United States needed these funds to avert an imminent collapse — within days.

These men expected to receive the United States subservience. They were at ease. They were surrounded by their own private military, and the most capable protection of any civilians in the world.

Though it would never be publicized this way, the globalists expected Adam to set the stage for the final economic surrender of the United States as a viable entity and sovereign nation.

With everyone accounted for and the door closed, Adam stood. He took a breath and, before continuing, thought to himself, *if things go as planned, this is going to be anything but what these bastards expect.*

Adam began. "Gentlemen, our first order of business must be to address the proper allocation of missing funds from the Federal Reserve. As I'm sure you know, over eleven trillion dollars were printed and taken out of the control of the United States. We've tracked these funds and found they were transferred to your coffers. You will immediately transfer those funds to accounts of our choosing."

"What is this?" One of the bankers leapt to his feet.

Adam's demeanor was like nothing these aristocrats had expected. He met the man's eyes and abruptly said, "Sit down and shut up." He looked over the room. "We tracked every form of communication in preparation for this moment. We know you have your people here ready and pre-authorized to make any huge transfers you direct. We also know that you told your banks around the globe you're going to be making the largest transfers in history, and these banks are awaiting the amounts and the routing numbers."

Seconds into the meeting where the banking families had convinced themselves they were about to finalize the financial takeover of the United States of America, Adam's comments were shocking the globalist patriarchs to their core.

"Eleven trillion dollars?" Rothmayer bellowed.

"Absolutely," Adam agreed, "and you're going to transfer it while I'm here, and no one is leaving this room until we have verification from the recipients that the money has been received."

Adam explained, in more detail than they had ever expected him to know, how the money had been taken away from the American people and where that money had been transferred to. They knew it was true, but that didn't faze them. They believed it was their right for global conquest and rule. They believed they had the right to take anything, and no one was entitled to question them.

Briefly glancing his way, Adam noticed Brooks trying to take down notes on a piece of paper. Brooks scribbled aggressively, but his pen wasn't working. Adam hadn't thought Brooks to be a note taker and didn't know what notes were applicable, but maybe he was taking note of which bankers showed the most defiance.

Adam extended his arm and handed Brooks a pen.

Brooks slowly accepted and nodded.

Continuing his message, Adam emphatically said, "W*e questioned the FED inspector General as to where nine trillion dollars went.*"[28] Adam had their undivided attention. "With the access to our NSA database, we've been able to trace the funds right back to your empires. The money actually appears to be well *over* eleven trillion, possibly twenty trillion, though there wasn't enough time to track it all down, so for now, we're going to have you transfer eleven trillion. It's over $50,000 per federal tax paying American, and we want it back."

Adam reached into his left suit jacket pocket and pulled out a flash drive. He held it up. "Here is a list of accounts and the quantities we want trans-ferred to each of our creditors. The money is to be transferred immediately, and then we'll continue."

Adam then held up a folded piece of paper. "I have a duplicate list of the accounts here. As the transfers are received, I'll cross them off the list. When all of the money has been received, we'll begin the next phase of our negotiations."

"This is ridiculous," one of the bankers said.

Adam cut the banker's sentence short. "Then, when our audit is complete, you'll transfer the remainder of the missing funds."

"You're in no position to negotiate... and you have no authority to audit us." The defiant voice came from an elderly white male at the other end of the conference table.

"We're in a perfect position to negotiate," retorted Adam.

Right at the designated time, the speaker phone on the table came alive with a heavily accented voice of the executive assistant. "Sir, I'm sorry to disturb you but there's an urgent call for the vice president from the president of the United States."

Adam immediately said, "Yes, put it through."

"He's not on the line, sir. He just left a message that the communication issue has been taken care of."

Adam said, "Thank you."

Knowing communications had been cut to all federal reserve gold repositories in the United States, Adam realized the second phase of the plan was under way. Only he and Brooks knew what the message meant. None of the transactions they were about to orchestrate needed any communications with any Federal Reserve repositories back in the US, but the important point was that those locations couldn't contact them; that would be imperative as soon as Krieger set off on the next phase of the mission.

Breaking into the brief moment of silence, another member of one of the Federal Reserve families interceded saying defiantly, "And what makes you think you can get away with this?"

The man's sentence was interrupted by the slamming sound of the globalist's head hitting the conference table. Suddenly, bodies jolted with an impulse that sent shivers through the room.

Right before he killed the man, Brooks thought, *you started this.*

Brooks had had enough. He knew these men needed a sense of urgency, or they were just going to keep talking. He had grabbed the man's hair at the back of his head and smashed his face directly into the thick, ornate, teak table. By the time their eyes registered what had just happened, Brooks had yanked the man's head back so his face was pointed towards the ceiling, exposing his throat. They all saw the man fight to take a breath, and then Brooks threw him to the floor.

Brooks had disassembled the pen Sasha had given him and reassembled it in a T shaped position. He thrust the pointy end into the man's trachea. The top of the T end of the pen supported the pressure on Brooks' palm, and he instantaneously suppressed the top of the pen. The suppression shot a miniscule amount of mist into the man's windpipe, through his trachea. When the globalist banker instinctively tried to take a breath, he inhaled the poisonous mist. A CIA special. The man's gasping was a horrific sight. Brooks and Sasha had talked about it in advance. They had decided that if Brooks needed to use it, that most likely meant he would also need to make an impression. He got the effect he desired as the man clutched at his throat and his face turned from red to magenta to purple. The man then began shaking uncontrollably.

Initially, Adam didn't know why Brooks did it; he had no idea that the man was reaching for something under the table while all eyes were directed towards Adam.

The spectacle of the dying man gave Brooks a moment to reach under the table for the gun the banker was reaching for, then Brooks shot the man closest to the door. He knew that man was security for the globalists. Adam didn't know whether Brooks saw him doing something or just wanted to eliminate the risk. But Adam did know Brooks got the gun before the globalist could turn it on him.

Brooks then peered down the table at the insolent man who had asked the question about why Adam thought he could get away with this. "If you don't transfer every penny of the money, we'll kill you all."

As that sunk in, Brooks thought about the conversations he and Krieger had had. They'd agreed it was best if Adam didn't know every contingency. So, although Adam didn't know everything, he did know that Krieger, Brooks, George and their teams had plans in place for his safety and ultimately the successful completion of the mission — and Brooks had just taken one of those actions.

Brooks realized it was better to address it right now before these globalist bastards tried to negotiate. "And even if you don't value yourself, think about your families." Brooks looked directly into Rothmayer's eyes. The implication was clear; their families were in peril if the money wasn't transferred.

Brooks waved the gun from left to right. As he looked around the table he said, "That includes every one of you."

Adam didn't want to waste any time. He had been debriefed enough to know that if things escalated, it was only a matter of time before others outside the room knew something was wrong. Then he, Gabby and their team would be the target of the internal military team. Every second counted.

Adam held up the flash drive. "Start the transfers."

CHAPTER 49

Krieger entered with a much larger and better armed contingency than the banker's security had expected. The meeting had been set up in advance and, with Adam currently meeting with the world banking heads in London, no one had thought twice about the streets being blocked off or the overwhelming force Krieger showed up with at the Federal Reserve bank of New York. This building took up an entire city block and held more gold than any other Federal Reserve entity across the country.

Officially, the vault contained over ten percent of the world's gold reserves. Unofficially, the amount was twice that, because numerous depositors had been swindled out of their gold over the years and those amounts remained in different books controlled by the globalist central banks and IMF owners.

Krieger addressed the commander of the dignitary protection team that expected to help guard the president. "Commander, the president will not be coming today. Instead we have…"

Krieger was interrupted by a plain clothed man stepping forward. He was shocked to see Krieger's men flooding in the door in quantities greater than he'd expected. "What's this?"

"This is an audit and immediate confiscation of our gold and the proper disposition of other gold you've swindled people out of."

Krieger's men were fully armed with live ammunition and went directly to their designated positions. They knew the officers of the Federal Reserve bank were private and were certified to carry a variety of weapons, including assault rifles and machine guns, in addition to the usual shotguns, tasers and other standard police-issued equipment.

Krieger addressed the commander. "You and all of your employees are being relieved. We're taking over from here until our audit is complete and the gold is transferred to one of our secure facilities."

"What's this all about?" the commander demanded.

"It's about your company and all of its affiliates across the country being relieved immediately. The United States Marines are taking over control of every one of our stockpiles of gold from here to Fort Knox, to every other entity that before," Krieger looked at his watch, "before three minutes ago was being controlled by the Federal Reserve and your IMF cronies."

Krieger had been in communication with other teams at Fort Knox and every facility holding US gold in the country. He already knew they were prepared and knew they had also gone in under the auspices of a variety of feasible reasons.

The commander asked, "On whose authority?"

Krieger was getting irritated. "On the authority of the president of the United States, and enforced by the US Marines."

Seeing the man hesitate, Krieger decided he didn't want a blood bath. "Let me make myself clear: my men have been directed that this is a military takeover, and to engage as such. Any of your men who don't lay down their weapons will be killed." Krieger let that sink in. "Including you."

Two marines behind Krieger had drawn their ARs and pointed them. Reaching out his hand, Krieger said, "Now hand over your weapon."

The officer reluctantly handed over his 9mm pistol and said, "We'll see about this." Turning to his second in command he said, "Get me Washington."

Krieger knew their headquarters was in Washington DC. He also knew that Mauricio had made sure they couldn't communicate with anyone outside of this building.

* * *

A short while later, after Krieger and his team had secured the building, Krieger took off on a flight destined for Europe, where the perilous next phase of the mission would be carried out.

* * *

While Krieger, Briggs and Mauricio were in flight, Adam and his team received verification that the last transfer had been received and had arrived in the designated account. The total of these transfers paid off about half of the national debt. With the last of the eleven trillion dollars transferred to the creditors, Adam knew that was only one phase of the retribution.

Tension in the room had escalated with every transfer and were reaching a boiling point. Adam had been warned about this by Krieger, who had directed him to get out of there as soon as the last transfer had been received. These men would stop at nothing to keep their conquest of the United States of America within their grasp.

Adam put a check in the last box, stood up and said, "Now, gentlemen, let me tell you the rest of the story."

He knew, even with the communications blackout Mauricio had put in place at each Federal Reserve location, that it would only delay the knowledge of what was happening at the Federal Reserve repositories for a short period. The globalist bankers would find out what he was about to tell them anyway as soon as he left.

But Adam wanted to see their faces when they found out. "During this time, we've taken control of every major gold repository in the United States. We know you melted down all of your gold bullion and re-branded it in your name to mask your theft. We also know you hired one of the most renowned smelting firms in the world to help you do this, while melting gold together from several sources, so metallurgical tests couldn't verify the rightful owners of the gold."

Adam folded his paper back up, and put it in his top left inside suit jacket pocket. He didn't want to disclose much more, though he explained, "After this, the United States will be solvent and, effective Monday, we are discontinuing the Federal Reserve. All of your partners and foreign agents of any type will be directed to leave the United States by the end of the day."

Infuriated, Rothmayer shook as he said, "You'll never leave here alive."

Little did Adam know that a worker just down the hall had made a phone call to Sordid.

What was happening had just leaked.

CHAPTER 50

Blood oozed out of the High Value Target (HVT) Ferraro had just disposed of. Ferraro pried the cell phone out of the man's clenched hand. A text had just come in.

It read, "Operation go-cart is a go immediately."

He handed it to Perra who looked at the message. Seeing the look on Ferraro's face, Sam Perra asked, "What are you thinking?"

Ferraro stared straight back at him and said, "I'm thinking that either there was a leak, or something has gone wrong with another operation. Let's move."

* * *

Simultaneously, Melissa was interrupted by the Senior Communications Lead. He said, "Sir, the HVT devices we're tracking all received an incoming message. It must have been sent to a distribution list to the HVTs."

"What does it say?" Melissa asked.

"Operation go-cart is a go immediately."

Melissa took a minute to decipher. *What does it mean? 'Go' is self-explanatory, something is starting, but what does cart mean? It could mean cartel, or califate, or... it doesn't matter. They must be triggering something.*

"Where did the message originate from?" Melissa asked.

"Give me a minute, sir."

A moment later, Melissa's senior communication expert gave her an answer she hadn't expected. He said, "It originated from just north of London, in the globalist banking headquarters."

Melissa knew where Adam was. Somehow his mission must have been compromised. She reached for a secure phone to call Ferraro.

With her voice encrypted, the urgency still resonated as she said, "We're a go nationwide. Repeat, nationwide immediately."

Ferraro was startled, because he had been just about to contact her. He confirmed his receipt of the directive. He immediately picked up another secure phone and gave the code for the pre-determined go-ahead.

The purge of radical foreign influence was on, nationwide.

* * *

As the phone on the other end closed, leathery, creased hands pulled out his pliers, took out the SIM card and melted it with a small hand-held cigar lighter.

The older man looked at his son. "Go to the designated location and contact all the major families. Use the plan we have set up and nothing else. Tell them we're on nationwide immediately. The cells have all been activated."

CHAPTER 51

Adam looked at Gabby. "Time to go."

A message had just come through the ear piece of Lieutenant Goodman, the special agent in charge (SAC) of the Presidential Protective Division (PPD). He was out in the hallway.

He immediately opened the door to the room. "Sir, we have reports of armed security moving into several positions." He felt he should explain further. "There's significant private security here under the control of the banking organization."

Brooks understood that members of the PPD team occupied the floors directly above and below their current location. He also knew they had PPD down the hall, around the elevator and on the main floor and the main door. Remembering that the elder statesman had told him they'd never leave here alive, Brooks said, "Well then, we'll need some insurance."

Brooks pointed his commandeered 9mm at the same man who'd said they'd never leave there alive. "You're coming with us."

The banker crossed his arms defiantly. "I'm doing no such thing."

Brooks immediately shot the man through his chest, and then the man next to him, sending a clear message. "Anyone else feeling difficult?"

One of the agents in the hallway, hearing the suppressed gunfire go off, opened the door part way and looked at his Lieutenant. Brooks looked at Lieutenant Goodman and said, "Time to go."

Brooks had no sooner said that when a voice came from the hallway. "Sir, there are more men coming in from both ends of the hall. It's a stand down. We need to get out of here *now*."

"Affirmative," Lieutenant Goodman, the agent in charge said as he drew his .357 Sig.

Goodman look at Gabby and Adam. "You four come with us. No matter what happens, everyone stay close." He received nods all around. "Our tactic will be what we call cover and move. That means, the guys in the hallway will cover us and engage any threats as we leapfrog them. Then we'll take cover and engage any attackers, while they move and leapfrog us. We'll move this way through the building until we get the vice president outside and into the limo, understood?"

With confirmations from everyone, the ex-Seal turned PPD looked at Brooks and, referring to the cowering bankers who were coming with them, said, "We need to position them."

Waving his 9mm at the first two men, Brooks directed. "You two, come here and stand by the door."

Seeing the trepidation in their movement, Brooks waved his gun back and forth and barked, "Move it!"

As they moved towards the door, Brooks said to the agent, "Let's sandwich the vice president and Gabby between them, and we'll move in unison."

"Affirmative sir."

Brooks pointed to the rest of the people in the room and directed them to follow them out into the hallway and stay behind the vice president and Gabby. "You make so much as one wrong move and I won't hesitate."

These elites understood what he meant. They had never been spoken to in such a manner. Brooks had already established himself as a man of immediate action and the look in his eyes cut right through them. The thinning ranks lined into place as directed.

The Lieutenant moved the group swiftly into the hallway. The banker's private military were coming into each end of the hallway, carrying automatic weapons. The vice president's security team had already commanded them to stay at bay and not advance, and the PPD all had their guns at the ready with safeties off. It was a tense situation.

Adam's PPD team kept imploring the private security to, "Stand down, stand down." They didn't want the vice president to be caught in a cross-fire, and they didn't want a blood bath.

Gabby and Adam stayed crouched down on the heels of the men in front of them with their heads positioned directly behind the heads of the bankers, as directed. The rest of the suits followed. They provided a barrier from behind.

Half way down the hall, those who could packed into an elevator. The remaining bankers were left there as the elevator doors closed.

In the close confines, Adam felt the disgust these bankers had for him for taking back the money that rightfully belonged to the American people. Their disdain was so strong he said, "I'll bet Kennedy wished he'd taken the fight to you bastards rather than just let you kill him when he cut out the Federal Reserve the first time."

The elevator went down to the first floor. When the doors opened to the large main hallway, Lieutenant Goodman carefully peered out and looked in both directions.

He sent two men and a woman out ahead. They positioned themselves behind the closest pillars and were at the ready. Goodman then received confirmation that a small team had reached the entrance doorway and would also provide cover.

Anxieties were high. They all moved quickly out into the ornate marble hallway. No sooner had they gotten into the center of the hallway and started towards the front door when a female agent behind Brooks said, "Gun, behind us, down the hall."

Bringing up the rear, Brooks, who had been keeping the globalists in front of him in line to protect Adam, glanced back and saw a man with a rifle getting down.

Brooks yelled, "Snipers!"

Goodman immediately began to push the vice president and Gabby around the corner of an adjoining hallway, urging them to move quickly, then peered back around the corner. Seeing the man was just getting into position he said, "We're lucky, he wasn't set up yet."

Brooks grabbed one of the bankers in front of him by the collar of his six-thousand-dollar suit and positioned him to protect his back. The question he had now was, would the one elite globalist who wasn't in the meeting going to sacrifice his fellow banking family heads to get Adam, or would they wait for a clear shot?

* * *

On a plane, Mauricio and Krieger watched the video of what was happening with the vice president that was being livestreamed through body cams. Sitting by Krieger's side in the plane, Mauricio was getting communication feeds. Then Mauricio heard something in his ear piece that Krieger needed to know.

"Colonel, we just intercepted a communication from inside the facility that directed the mercenaries to kill everyone except the vice president. They want him alive... They'll use him as leverage to get the money back."

Krieger squeezed the screen he was holding. "Can you get me a direct contact with the Special Agent in Charge with the vice president?"

"Sure, stealth's is out the door right now anyway. I'll have him in a second," Mauricio said.

Mauricio gave some directions to his communications commanders and, in a moment, the connection was made.

Mauricio told Goodman, "Lieutenant, they've just given the directive to engage you. Take cover stat. We've got your six and more on the way."

Hearing Mauricio through his ear piece, the Lieutenant commanded his team, "You've got help ahead, but the private security force has just got orders to engage and not let the vice president out of the building. Stay covered down."

Suddenly, a volley of gunfire came from up the hall.

A small team of the vice president's protective detail that was stationed outside burst into the building and engaged soldiers coming out of an adjoining hallway up ahead before the globalists' private security firm could ambush Adam, Gabby and the team.

In the initial volley, two of the globalist bankers in front were killed by their own security detail. As the head of another Federal Reserve family was shot behind Brooks, the banker in front of him ran towards a pillar.

Brooks had his answer. The wealthiest globalist of them all, who Brooks knew wasn't at the meeting, had given the directive to get Adam at any cost. They would even kill their own.

Now, in the fury of a gunfire, the Lieutenant had everyone in temporary seclusion in the last adjoining hallway to their right where two of the globalists' private security now lay dead.

Adam took an AK47 and a pistol from the one downed soldier and Gabby grabbed the other soldier's rifle. She swung around, leaned around the corner of the hall, and shot a burst. Then she pulled back in the alcove just before a shot hit the marble.

Her eyes widened with the reality of the situation. "That was close."

"Affirmative, he's got a bead on us now," said an agent who was behind Brooks.

Goodman had his back flat against the wall.

* * *

Goodman remained calm even in the fierce firefight. He responded to Mauricio, "Charlie Foxtrot, but the vice president is okay... we're all okay, thanks to you, but we're pinned in this hallway."

Gabby heard the comment and asked Adam, "What does he mean by 'Charlie Foxtrot'?"

Adam's edges of his mouth turned up for a split second and over the noise he said, "Think of the first letters of the words. It stands for Cluster F..."

"Oh."

Through his ear piece, Goodman heard Krieger direct, "Stay there until the front doorway's cleared, and when they give you the signal, cover like hell and get the vice president out of there, understood?"

"Affirmative Lima Charlie." Goodman said. His response was military terms for yes, loud and clear.

Goodman filled Krieger in. "We still have that sniper behind us to contend with. I can tell you that I've thrown the ROE out the window in the past sixty seconds."

Krieger heard and understood; the ROE were the rules of engagement Goodman and his team had been given prior to the mission. Krieger also needed Goodman to understand he agreed.

"Affirmative, use any and all means necessary to keep the vice president alive. It's yours from here." Krieger also understood that the last thing the PPD teams needed was to be micro-managed from afar. He would just help with other resources and leave the mission up to the teams that were there.

As Krieger and Goodman had discussed the plan, Brooks noticed the patriarch of the Vanderbilt family assessing the situation from the security of the pillar at the other side of the wide main hallway. Brooks knew the man was getting ready to dart down the side hallway behind the pillar, but he didn't have a clean shot. He also knew who this man was, and that his family had several separate stashes of black gold they'd got from the American people. It was stolen, untraceable gold he and his family were using and would continue to use for the destruction of the American dream and the American culture.

Brooks nudged Goodman. "I need to get to that banker across the hall before he gets away, and we need to do something about that sniper."

Adam said, "We need to draw him out so someone can get a clean shot at him."

Goodman shook his head. "Negative. He won't come out from his position to give us a clear shot. He's trained to stay concealed and only reveal enough of himself to take a clean shot."

Hearing other globalist reinforcements scurrying in their direction and Goodman talking to Krieger, Adam thought to himself, *this decision needs to be made now.*

He leaned over to Brooks and, in his ear, whispered, "I'll run over to the other end of the hallway with you and give him something to shoot at."

Brooks shook his head. "You'll be trapped there... that's if he doesn't hit you."

Gabby said, "I can cover you."

With globalist reinforcements coming into adjoining halls, they were about to be outnumbered and possibly overrun. Brooks had heard the Lieutenant making plans with Krieger to position their own sniper to engage the globalist sniper, but their man was still at the front door.

Looking at another PPD soldier in a suit, Brooks asked, "Sergeant, how good of a shot are you?"

"I took first place in my training class, but I'm not a sniper."

Brooks and Adam looked at each other. Brooks told the young soldier go get ready and the young soldier readied his FN P-90.

Brooks put his pistol in a banker's chest and looked at Adam. "We'll take him with us as a shield. We'll run towards the pillar. The sniper can get a glimpse of you. Then run back to this position."

Brooks directed the young sergeant with the FN P-90. "When we take off for the other side of the hall, you slide out a few feet into the hallway in flat position and get ready. You'll only get one shot at him, and it'll probably be when the vice president is on the way back."

The sergeant checked his load and looked through the scope. "Understood, sir."

Brooks looked around at the agents ahead of them, who were engaged with those from up the hallway. Things were getting ugly, fast. "We ready?"

With affirmations of "ready" from everyone except the banker, Brooks pushed his pistol into the man's side. He said, "If you don't run for your life and shield the vice president, I'll shoot you myself, do we understand ourselves?"

"You're a brute," the banker said.

"Yeah, and don't forget it. Get up."

They all got to one knee and on Brooks' count they ran for the seclusion of the large pillar on the other side of the hallway.

Goodman looked up just in time to see what was happening. His ear piece exploded with expletives from Krieger who watched on his screen.

To the far left was the globalist banker, shielding Adam, who was hugged tight on his right side. Brooks was to Adam's right watching every stride of the globalist, while shielding Adam from any fire they'd draw from the other end of the hallway.

Gabby lunged to the ground in the middle of the hallway while the Sergeant rolled partially out, flat on his belly, feet spread and out of sight of the sniper's angle. He steadied his breathing.

Goodman bellowed. "Cover them, cover them!"

The hallway erupted in fury.

Right before Adam made it to the pillar, the single shot that jolted him was accompanied by the immediate boom of the sniper rifle echoing through the hallway. The shot had hit the banker with such force that the banker's lower chest had exploded out the other side, sending the pulse of pressurized air and tissue into Adam's side. Adam realized what had happened as the banker suddenly became limp. He was heavy. Adam pulled up as hard as he could but it was no use. He let go of his grip on the banker and lunged behind the pillar. Brooks was on his right.

Before he could fire, Brooks saw Vanderbilt run down the far hallway and take an immediate right.

Adam looked at Brooks. "Go get him."

This was all-out war: the globalist bankers against the sovereignty of the United States of America — which was the only place left on the planet for people to be free from oppression. The mission was clear: eliminate the threat now, or the threat would remain.

Brooks nodded and took off down the hallway.

Adam saw Gabby had positioned herself right in the middle of the hallway with the FN P-90 she had. There wasn't any time to waste. Gunfire was exploding from the area up by the front door. Gabby wasn't in an optimal position, but it was about the only position where she could cover Adam. His eyes met hers and they both knew. Gabby shot in the direction of the sniper, sending marble flying while Adam started his short run back across the hall.

As Adam ran across the wide hallway, Gabby emptied her magazine. She got up on a knee and lunged for the wall.

Hearing the magazine empty, the sniper peered around the corner of the hallway. He took aim. An instant later he briefly saw Adam in mid run through the lens of his scope. He started to squeeze.

Suddenly, his eye was no longer in the scope. The impact of the Sergeant's round shattered his shoulder blade. He was hit. Another split second later he lay flat on the cool marble floor.

At that moment, Goodman heard the directive in his earpiece he'd been waiting for. His fellow PPD teams had cleared a path to the presidential Limo.

He looked at Adam and loudly said, "Sir, we've got to go now… this way."

Adam pulled Gabby in by the waist, looked her directly in the eyes and kissed her with passion. "Stay close."

She lit up and came right back with, "You stay close."

They both smiled and looked at the Lieutenant. Adam nodded. "Let's go."

Adam turned right into the main hallway with Gabby's hand clutched tightly in his. He could see the car through the glass door.

He heard in the background, "Keep moving."

They both knew it was the Lieutenant telling them the team was covering them and it was their turn to leap frog all the way to the limo.

CHAPTER 52

At that moment, George looked across his desk in the Oval office at John, the Chief Justice of the Supreme Court. It was a good thing George had asked him to remain with a block or two of the White House just in case he needed him. It only took the Chief Justice fifteen minutes to show up at the president's door.

"We've got to surround those ports and search them."

The Chief Justice nodded slowly. "I've spoken with a judge and she's ready." A judge was waiting for John to tell her to issue the paperwork. She had been provided with substantial evidence that warranted the search. She wasn't compromised by the deep state.

* * *

"Okay, make the call, have her issue the warrants."

John could tell George's concern had heightened. "What's wrong, Mr. President?"

"When we issue the order for the naval blockade, it'll be news almost immediately."

"Frankly, Mr. President, this going public is the least of our concerns," the Chief Justice said. "And actually, it may be a benefit to us. Blocking off Project Pelican at Port Canaveral will let the globalists know we're going to seize anything they have; arms, weapons, money, gold, anything. On top of that, it'll get them trying to cover their tracks. They'll have to align quickly, and people working hurriedly make mistakes. You'll be able to uncover communications that you may not have been able to uncover otherwise. You can draw out more of the rats."

The Chief Justice made some good points. George knew that, with this move and what Adam had just orchestrated, the deep state would do anything within its power to counter-attack and stay in power.

John could see it in his eyes, so he asked the president, "You're going to purge the deep state, aren't you?"

"It appears the time has come."

George had decided to make his move to do just that, and if it wasn't evident yet, this would let the globalists know he meant business. The evidence Mauricio and his team had come up with was undisputable. There was a group of over a thousand people in the US government, the deep state, who had committed treason and were going to pay the price. Working with John as a confidant to steer matters to judges who would actually follow the law, attorneys had prepared paperwork to indict more than a thousand of them. Within a day or two, he was purging the NSA of twenty percent of its workforce and the CIA of about a third of its workforce. When the axe fell, the FBI would also be reeling from losing over a third of their people. In addition, over the following days, almost five thousand others would be given the option to quit, retire, be indicted or align with the nationalist movement and become superior performers for the wellbeing of their country.

George got up and offered his hand to John. "Thanks for all your help. I've got to go."

When George opened the door of the Oval Office, he saw the nervous Dr. Roy Hemmele sitting there with Senator Madison.

They were taking Air Force One to a secluded place out west.

CHAPTER 53

Adam and Gabby ran out the front door of the globalist's headquarters. A group of marines laid down covering fire, holding back the globalists' private security forces. The private security had no authorization to get in the proximity of the vice president. Their intentions were clear. They were to stop the Vice President from getting away.

As the globalists private security poured out from multiple locations, the Marines and the vice president's personal protective secret service met them with the hellfire of men and women who were fighting for someone they believed in.

Adam and Gabby ran with their heads down. Men to their right and left fell.

"Keep moving," someone behind them yelled.

They lunged into the open door of the presidential Limo. Just then, an apache helicopter came over an adjacent building, and began firing off tracer rounds at lightning speed.

Krieger's directive from the plane had been clear: "Get them all," referring to anyone outside of the building who was shooting at the vice president, "and then return to base immediately."

When the door slammed behind them, the Limo took off, leaving the fight to the others.

The back of the trailing suburban opened up. A tripod machine gun unloaded fifty caliber rounds. Troops poured out of what appeared to be concealed tunnels. They filled the lawn firing. Adam and Gabby had reached the Limo just in time.

Tires screeched as the huge vehicle abruptly turned and slid. Steel pillars had begun to emerge from the street level. The vehicle wouldn't have gotten through. The gate was blocked.

The driver swung around and slowed.

Adam's personal security agent listened to his ear piece, then looked at Adam. "Sir, we're trapped, we've got to get you out of the Limo. Driver, slow and turn sharp over by that doorway, we're getting out."

As the Limo slowed, the agent opened the door. "Follow me." He, Adam and Gabby rolled out.

Leading them to an open door, the agent said, "Quickly down the stairs. U.N. troops are gathering at the gate."

Adam immediately realized the globalist bankers controlled the U.N. troops. They weren't loyal to him. They reported to the globalists.

As the door closed, the agent hoped the blueprints he'd studied during his preparations were up to date.

* * *

Brooks drove the banker's knee into the marble floor hard with his right shoulder as he tackled him from behind. Brooks elbow hit the floor. He grimaced in pain, then pulled out a 9mm pistol. Both elderly men sat facing each other on the floor, breathing heavily.

The man in the six-thousand-dollar suit hadn't ran in years. After a few more deep breaths, he said, "I never thought your country had it in you."

It was an admittance of guilt, along with an admiration that Brooks hadn't expected.

The banker shook his head. "But it won't be enough."

Brooks eyed his pistol and said, "It's a beginning. Now most of our country is awake to the fact that you've bribed and blackmailed most of Congress. You could have all lived like kings, but you kept taking. Now your days are through."

Brooks pointed the pistol. He was about to pull the trigger. But he had an idea. "Do you want to live?" Brooks asked.

The banker looked at him. He was listening. He had no choice.

"I think we can come up with a mutually beneficial agreement," Brooks said.

"What kind of agreement?"

"I'll let you live," Brooks said, "and you disclose a few more locations of black gold that was taken from US gold repositories. Gold that's now being used to fund the deep state and insurrection in our country."

"I don't even know where it all is," the banker said. "It's in several very secure locations. Even if I knew I'll do no such thing,"

Brooks remained confident, "I believe you will and here's why."

The man interrupted. "I know how this is going to work. You need me as a hostage to get out of here, so you need me alive."

"No, I'll be leaving in a moment and I'll leave you here, dead. Or, you give me two locations of black gold and I'll tell you what… in return for your cooperation, you don't even have to give up your own gold. You just give us someone else's gold."

Brooks could see this was something that resonated in the eyes of the man.

"Just realize," Brooks said, "if the locations are phony, we'll come and find you and we'll make it a slow process… very slow."

A minute later, Brooks got up, walked behind the man and opened the door to the hallway. He heard footsteps. He had to move quickly. He turned around, grabbed the man by the back of the suit jacket and pulled him out through the hallway and into the adjoining staircase. "Remember what I told you. I'll find you, and there's nowhere for you to hide."

The man thought to himself, *not if you're dead.*

"Now, I'm going to do you a favor," Brooks said.

Without warning, Brooks shot the banker.

The banker fell down reeling in pain and howled, "What did you do that for?"

"You can't just tell them we sat here and had this chat now, can you?" Brooks said. "Don't worry, you'll live. It's only a flesh wound."

Brooks grabbed the banker and dragged him down several steps, leaving a nice smearing blood trail. "There, you even have a nice trail of blood, like you crawled here."

It was time for Brooks to try to make his own escape.

* * *

Meanwhile, back in Washington, the president's messengers began making their rounds to members of Congress. These men and women were hand chosen patriots who had been quietly helping the president and patriots fight against the deep state from within the middle ranks of the FBI and CIA.

From the moment these individuals were chosen, they were detained and secluded from any contact from the outside world. They were paired up in twos. Each team of two was comprised of one man and one woman. They were fitted with tailored suits, fitted to a T. They were taught mannerisms and other behavioral techniques, including how to walk together. The purpose was to exhibit the utmost aura of power and confidence.

They had also been waiting for the president's directive to begin. Now, deploying across the city in pairs, they were the next piece of the plan. They too were told that they played a pivotal role in saving the country. Although their role wasn't on the battle field, their role was in the part of Washington that had been compromised: Congress.

Their appointments had been scheduled in advance in offices of more than half of all members of Congress. The teams had a message to deliver. Each team would disclose evidence of the felonious activities of the politician they were speaking with, then the member of Congress would be offered a Presidential Pardon. The Pardon was conditional on their willingness to immediately debrief the team on who was blackmailing them, and then they must vote for the surplus amendment to the Constitution, repealing the sixteenth amendment and any other bills the president offered in the next ninety days to save the country.

The choice would be theirs. They could go along with it and go down in history as a political hero who helped save the country, or they could go down in history as a traitor, in which case they'd be financially ruined and thrown in a military prison.

The teams left the offices of each politician with three main thoughts. The great negotiating president wasn't going to negotiate on this. They also told the politicians that all of their communications and movements would be monitored and recorded from here on out, and they'd also be used against them in a court of law. The president was also doing something else they would learn about shortly that would eradicate the globalist bankers from the power structure in Washington.

The president kicked off this phase of the plan and hung up the phone, then looked at Madison. "This should be interesting. I've never been to Area 51 before."

CHAPTER 54

Standing atop the oil rig miles off shore, Krieger took a deep breath and had an unusual thought that the sunset looked more like a sunrise. It's a sign of hope.

Sergeant Major Briggs walked up and stood alongside Krieger. "Everything's ready, sir."

Krieger slowly nodded. For a moment, they stood side by side in silence.

Krieger had had the oil rig shut down by a friend of his in the CIA. Now the rig was a staging platform for the operation. Every one of the men and women walking around was US military. The crew had all been vetted by either Krieger, Briggs or Mauricio, and had been trained at the base for this operation. During that time, Krieger wanted them to know why they must succeed. He had shown them videos, copies of actual contracts, and had even had people flown in to give personal testimony on how the IMF and Federal Reserve bankers and their accomplices had siphoned tons of gold out of the United States, other countries and a few private very wealthy citizens.

Disclosing this to the soldiers made every man and women on the mission realize the globalists' intended conquest of the United States by taking it over financially, rather than militarily. As Krieger summed up their reaction when George asked him how they'd taken it, he said it 'gave them resolve'.

Dusk had turned into night. The reflections of the stars began to twinkle off the waves and individual commanders finished the final debriefs for their teams.

The teams then assembled. Now it was time for Krieger, as the overall commander, to make a few brief remarks. He reminded the entire team of their purpose and gave them the pertinent information about how, just within the hour, Adam had gotten trillions in stolen money back from the globalist bankers. These men and women all knew they were fighting for the way of life for themselves, their families, and tens of millions of others across the country.

After Krieger made his impassioned remarks, he allowed the teams some time to reflect in the silence of their own thoughts. Finally, it was time to embark on the mission.

Krieger boarded the most highly classified small frigate in the navy's arsenal. Invisible to enemy radar, it had a top speed of eighty miles per hour in perfect conditions. Its unique stealth design allowed the vessel to evade submarine sonar. This was to be the crown jewel for special operation of the navy of the future. Designed for long range with the ability to careen through low water levels, it was the perfect vessel for this mission.

The captain took off from the oil rig and they skimmed over the water at fifty miles per hour.

When the engines slowed, Mauricio got up and looked over the female navigator's shoulder. They were right on time as they approached the mouth of the river.

Months prior, the US had agreed to partner with the group of countries in a joint U.N. military drill. These joint U.N. operations had become more prevalent during the previous administration.

George knew these joint operations were to prepare for the end of English sovereignty. When the final days of sovereignty were at their precipice, the globalist-controlled government knew they'd have malcontents, who would not submit to globalist control. Those were the people who would have to be dealt with. When London was controlled, the rest of the country would follow. That was why this location had been chosen by the U.N. That was why the plan was to have U.N. sanctioned troops from other countries do the dirty work for the globalists.

This drill was supposed to test logistics and joint coordination in and around the city.

This exercise was the perfect cover for Krieger's teams. They could stage equipment without suspicion.

As the boat slowed, Krieger stood, looked at Mauricio and said, "Give the orders."

With that, Mauricio made the secure communication with a simple predetermined phrase to commanders: "Retribution for the republic is revered."

In unison, activity quietly initiated from multiple locations.

To their northeast, a hanger opened up by the sea and a helicopter unfolded in the darkness. Panels lifted from underneath to buffer the wind. The bird was the stealthiest ever designed.

Somewhere upstream, 'the sea shadow', a prototype to this point, left its concealed dock and headed towards its destination. Invisible to radar and sonar with masking to model the light of surrounding water, it was virtually invisible at a glance. It would navigate the river with a four-man SEAL team, ghosting along under bridges where locals would only hear a wisp of a breeze coming from the water and see nothing but the remnants of a small wave reaching the shoreline, if they saw anything at all.

The Ghost Stealth III was the most advanced prototype the US navy had. It would be seeing its second live mission that night. It would follow the Sea Shadow to carry the precious cargo to the mouth of the river.

Simultaneously, trucks began to roll out of several locations just north of the city. Some trucks carried specialized equipment, while others were fitted with extra suspension and fortified for the extremely heavy cargo they'd carry.

The trucks had designated semi-autonomous teams that would take various routes to several extraction points. Should any one team be compromised or run into complications, the team commander would make their best decision for the ultimate success of the mission, which wouldn't depend on an individual caravan of trucks. It would depend on the group's overall ability to accomplish their mission.

Simultaneously two SEAL teams deployed for their rendezvous at their appointed target.

CHAPTER 55

Krieger and Mauricio scanned the area through the green glow of their night-vision goggles. Krieger always visually verified what the intelligence photos had showed. Sometimes distances and angles could differ enough from the photos to make a difference in an operation.

They heard the faint rumble in the distance. It was the far away sound of diesel engines, and they were getting closer. To the people around London and here on the grounds of the castle, they expected the vehicles were for the joint training operation the next day. That wasn't their purpose.

Security here at the old castle grounds was at a normal level. With everything that transpired with the vice president today and him still being missing, this is what they'd hoped for.

One of the first actions was for a SEAL team to take out the guard posts and maintain communication at the main entrance while Krieger and his team got inside the vaulted cavern.

The SEAL task unit commander had his small joint squadron of Navy SEALs and Green Beret ready to dismount the vehicle whenever Mauricio gave them the go-ahead.

Briggs had convinced Krieger that, although the commander was young, he should bring him along as the squadron commander. Based on what Krieger had observed from the young man in the grueling mission preparation, he'd made the right decisions. The young commander engaged his team, communicated well and delegated autonomy to others he could trust. But this wasn't training.

Mauricio received stage gate signals from six different teams. This was the first call that indicated the teams had completed specific steps of their operation. Besides that, the teams were somewhat autonomous and only needed to communicate with Mauricio if there was a major decision needing to be made.

The mission was to knock out communication, move in quietly, and then load up as much black gold as possible for transport back to the states.

Krieger, Mauricio and Briggs disembarked from their stealth craft and quietly moved into the brushes.

Krieger and Briggs looked over Mauricio's shoulder at his screen. The countdown began.

To reduce any chance of a communication breach, each of the commanders would simply send Mauricio a number depicting the seconds of delay, if there was one. As the countdown headed towards zero, no such messages came through. Everyone was in position. At the appointed time, Mauricio blocked all communication.

Suddenly, teams moved forward from air, land and sea.

When the communications went down, the SEAL commander and his team sprang into action, captured the front gate, and retracted the barricades into the concrete. Now the trucks could drive freely in and out of the grounds. This and two other service locations had been cleared in a similar fashion.

From the rear of the castle, Krieger advanced. Another joint special forces team took out the primary guard house at the rear of the castle.

Mauricio received verification from each team as they accomplished their portions of the overall mission.

With confirmation that the outside locations were secure, Krieger and his team were a full go to engage. There was no time to waste.

While Krieger surprised the private security inside the lower level of the compound at the rear of the castle, Briggs took charge of the other joint task forces as they cleared and secured the rest of the castle.

Mauricio had set up encrypted communications.

He continued communicating with each commander as Krieger pushed forward towards the main vault.

Less than an hour later, Krieger jumped in the first truck. It had been loaded with over fifty tons of black gold. As they pulled out of the lower level of the castle, Krieger looked up at the majestic structure and thought *this must double as a delivery entrance.*

With approximately fifty tons in each truck, they'd be slightly over the maximum weight regulations allowed. Krieger wasn't worried about the regulations; he was worried about the roads holding up. But they kept the weight close enough that it shouldn't be an issue. Most trucks had been refurbished with enhanced suspension and siding, designed to blend in with local trucks. They didn't look weighted down.

The castle had been a busy tourist attraction, but it had been shut down for renovations over ten years ago for what had been described as 'upgrades' to the tourist site. The renovations were a perfect disguise. The real reason for the upgrades was for the castle to be fitted with a vault in the lower level. The vault would house over two thousand tons of untraced black gold. This was one of the places the globalist central bankers secretly held gold that had been taken from US vaults.

Krieger rode in the back of the truck to the river while the next truck was being loaded. Logistics teams had developed the plan. Most of the gold would leave by boat. Forty trucks would need to make it clear to get the gold from this private globalist stronghold. Getting forty trucks through the London area wasn't a viable option. However, in addition to the gold being transported by waterway, a number of trucks would go out the main and service entrances of the castle and disperse in all directions. Each truck had a rendezvous point to get the gold out of the country. This strategy would reduce the risk of a total mission failure.

When the truck Krieger was in made it to the designated spot under the shade of a large black stealth tent at the edge of River Thames, Krieger jumped out. He didn't have to say a word. The team already had the back of the truck opened and were unloading. The engineers had equipment to grab the gold and place it on the gate of the amphibious landing craft. From there, the electric winch system on the craft pulled it into position.

They were finished within minutes. Krieger climbed back in. From the back of the empty truck, Krieger watched the craft skim over the water and disappear quietly into the darkness. He couldn't even hear the next stealth vessel pull into place.

Over the next few hours, the teams unloaded most of the gold. It was apparent this portion of the operation was under control. Krieger, Briggs and Mauricio let the rest of the team shut down operations, then they rode with the final load to the river. By the time the last craft was loaded, the tent covering was dismantled and the three got into the helicopter. As they lifted off, they watched another truck leave the rear entrance. In another hour the last truck would be out of there, and there were still a few hours until daybreak. They were ahead of schedule.

When they flew out to sea to meet their next transport, Krieger pointed. Mauricio and Briggs smiled as they watched one of the vessels full of gold drive into the underbelly of an oil tanker.

Krieger did feel some comfort for a moment, then, ever driven to complete the entire mission, he remembered they had one more place to infiltrate.

He turned to the others. "We'd better get some shut-eye. This next one won't be as easy."

CHAPTER 56

Intensifying sounds of first responder sirens blared. Gabby tensed. The vehicles came right down the street. Her emotions waned a moment later when the sirens faded as the vehicles passed. They were heading towards the globalists' Central Banking headquarters.

Lead Agent Francisco Gonzalez put both palms on the table. He leaned in towards Adam and said, "Sir, we need to get you out of here."

Part of the CIA Special Activities Division, Gonzalez ran this and several other safe houses in the London area.

"By when?" Adam questioned, sensing Gonzalez's urgency.

Gonzalez stood straight up. "Early tonight, or even sooner."

"Why's that?" Adam's question was intended to make Gonzalez realize that he and Gabby had just escaped with their lives and could use some down time.

Gonzalez had been running this safe house for two years. Posing as a successful small business man from California, Gonzalez used his passion for refurbishing old houses to serve as his cover. He'd had the CIA purchase some older homes, which were expensive for their size. Gonzalez slowly refurbished them. He sold a few and gained a reputation locally for his creative ability to maintain a home's charm, while embedding every modern convenience and offering the homes at a fair price. This strategy allowed the agency to maintain several such safe locations throughout the city.

Gonzalez's mother had migrated from the mountainous Jalisco state of central Mexico. Coming across the US border at Mexicali town on the northern tip of the Baja illegally, she was a migrant worker. She had moved to Pomona, a suburb of LA, California, and started her family. Gonzalez was only about five foot six, but he was always gifted at anything he did. Even the gait of his walk was fluid. With his complexion and full head of dark hair, he was a man who could blend in anywhere. With this upbringing,

Gonzalez knew all about hiding out, and he knew Adam and Gabby didn't have much time.

"Sir, this is a top-secret safe house and it's very secure. We blend right in. But, pretty soon, the local authorities are going to do what they've been trained to do. They're going to draw circles out from the last location you were seen, and methodically clear houses. If they know you left the banking headquarters, they'll search their cameras. They could possibly identify you on one of the cameras about a block and a half away from here... and that's the best-case scenario." Gonzalez's expression revealed another concern. "Worse than that is the possibility that there are several people in the CIA who would have access to this location."

Gonzalez hesitated, letting Adam realize for himself what he was about to say. "If just one deep state CIA agent has access to safe house locations in this area, they'll be searching for addresses. If they find this address, they'll contact the relevant people locally, who will come directly here."

Adam already had his own impression of what he was about to ask, but he wanted to hear what Gonzalez said. "What are the odds?" Adam asked.

"I'd say about fifty-fifty, sir."

Gabby's blue eyes met Adam's. They both turned to Gonzalez.

"How long do we have?" Adam asked.

"I'm afraid they're most likely starting the process now," Gonzalez said. "I would be."

"Do you have a back way out?" Adam asked.

"Of course, we have a few," Gonzalez said. "But they won't help. Whichever way you take, you'll need to walk out on the streets. You'll be exposed among the public. You need to get out of here before they quarantine the entire area."

Gabby looked at Adam and, holding out her open palms, indicating their attire would help identify them, she said, "How are we going to do that?"

"You'll have to blend in," Gonzalez said. "I have everyone looking for some clothes to help you fit in."

Adam looked at Gabby's face and, in a brief moment, realized his efforts to save the country had allowed him to orchestrate the transfer of enough stolen money to pay off more than half of the national debt. And, if Krieger was successful, the entire national debt would be paid off. Adam was satisfied. If it was only him, and he died getting away, he would feel his life had been complete.

His eyes moved from Gabby's eyes to the smooth skin surrounding what he playfully called her perfect nose. The strong presence she still maintained reminded him how she had managed to talk him into letting her come along on this assignment. Her logic had convinced him, George, Madison, and even Krieger. With Gabby along on the visit of what the globalists assumed would be the economic surrender of the United States, they would be disarmed. And they were, because they had been told she wanted first-hand knowledge of the transactions to convey to the public. It sounded logical; they all knew Gabby was well respected in the media and among the masses. They believed that, with her advocating to the world how this was a good move for all, it would settle down the unsuspecting masses and especially the President's most loyal supporters. Those nationalists were the globalists' biggest threat. It was the perfect plan.

But now, Gabby and Adam were trapped. Their escape had been compromised and, after barely making it out of the NWO compound, they were about to be closed in on.

Adam and Gabby's relationship had been kept a secret because of the potential political fallout. Adam now questioned if keeping the perception of him being the most eligible bachelor in the country was shallow. Gabby deserved better. She deserved everyone to know. And here she stood, unwavering in her commitment to the country and to him. He admired her loyalty, her acceptance for who he was, her uncompromising devotion to her profession, while at the same time her total understanding and support of his calling. It all flashed before his eyes at that moment.

Now he and Gabby were getting more comfortable with eluding those they worked with and the press. They were rendezvousing in remote places where they wouldn't be detected. He was feeling at peace with all of it. But she deserved better, and it had taken this for him to realize it.

Even after becoming the vice president and being reasonably secure, some of his actions had still been haunted by the financial devastation he hadn't emotionally gotten over.

He scanned her upper cheeks and then back to her eyes, which he immediately remembered thinking would still be beautiful when she was eighty years old.

It was lucky he and Gabby had even made it here. This safe house had been their primary backup plan, but the route they'd planned to get here hadn't worked out. Instead, they'd had to scurry down stairs and into an alternate escape route designed to facilitate the bankers' escape. Now with the city being squeezed tighter than a garter belt, the sand in their hour glass was running out.

Adam focused on the extraction plan. "Where's our backup transportation?"

"Compromised," said Gonzalez. Seeing the concern on Adam's face he added, "We're exploring other options."

Adam felt an immediate escalation of concern for Gabby. At that moment, the door began to open and he watched the right hand of Gonzalez deliberately reach for and grip his Glock. That movement alone reaffirmed the seriousness of the situation.

Then three agents walked in the room. The first agent in the door had a piece of paper in his hand. He walked directly up to Adam and said, "Mr. Vice President, sir," as he handed Adam the note.

Adam looked up at the agent and took the paper. Before he read it, his eyes focused on the blue eyes watching his every movement. For a brief second he took in her beautiful eyes and simply smiled.

She returned the smile and watched for his reaction. The coded message from Mauricio told him that the first extraction of black gold was complete. He saw Gabby looking at him. She could read him by now and, though she didn't know the details, she asked, "Everything's going as planned so far?"

A broad grin came across his face. "It is."

Then she asked, "What about The Shadow?"

He hadn't heard about Brooks and wasn't sure if anyone knew Brooks was on his own.

Adam's expression changed to one of concern. He knew the team was still in the air, so this would be a good time to make contact.

Adam looked at Gonzalez. "I need to talk to Colonel Krieger. See if you can track him down."

* * *

When Adam hung up the phone, he looked at Gonzalez, who looked over at the other two agents who had entered the room a moment ago. The female agent stepped closer to Gonzalez.

"Sir, we did the best we could. We have viable options for the vice president, but," turning to Gabby, the female agent held up a duffel bag Gonzalez immediately recognized. The agent said, "I'm the only woman here and my clothes won't fit you, so Commander Gonzalez had something in his car. Let's see if they fit."

Then the female agent placed the duffel on the table for Gabby and handed Adam some clothes. "I'm sorry Mr. Vice President, we have several outfits we could give you, but since you'll be traveling together," she looked at Gabby, "we need you to match."

Adam held up some jeans and the accompanying T shirt and a button-down shirt.

The female agent explained to Adam. "Put on the T shirt and then the other shirt on top is to wear untucked and unbuttoned."

Gabby felt something uncomfortable was coming. "So, what are we dressing as?"

The middle-aged female agent turned, unzipped the duffel bag and reached in. She pulled out a top and held it up. It was a tightly fitting skimpy tube top. The agent's other hand pulled out black spandex type bottoms. Gabby's eyes got big.

The agent explained. "Our only option is for you to go as a cute chick, maybe just out of college. I'm sorry… This is all we have." The agent's tone and expression were sincere.

Adam tried to break the ice. "Well," he said, "we can't go like this," referring to their current attire. Then, to keep things moving, he started taking off his suit.

Gabby walked to the far end of the room and turned her back. She took a deep breath and began to take off her jacket and top. When the male agent started to gawk, the woman jabbed him with her elbow. "Can you give her some privacy…?"

The male agent nodded. His shoulders sunk and, with a reluctant look on his face, he turned and went out the door.

When Gabby turned back around, Adam's eyes widened. He swallowed.

Gabby made another adjustment to the top.

Gabby tried to be light hearted. "Couldn't you get something a little tighter?"

Adam didn't think that would be possible.

Gonzalez finally said, "Sorry ma'am, it's my daughter's. That's all we have."

Gabby tried to make light of it by joking, "Teenager?"

She hadn't really expected the Gonzalez's affirmative response, "Yes ma'am."

Gabby looked at Adam. *Well, that explains it.* "When Gonzalez said we were going to be exposed in public, I never thought he meant this type of exposed."

Gonzalez shook his head. "Next time we'll have a few more fitting options… no pun intended."

The female agent looked over Gabby. "We need to do something with your hair. How about pulling it back or putting it up? It needs to match your look."

Gabby nodded and took some barrettes out of her hair, letting the rest of it down. She asked the agent, "Do you have a tie?"

The women spread open the duffel bag and, after searching the bottom said, "We have two."

A moment later, Gabby had her hair pulled back and looked young enough to be just a few years out of college. She bopped towards Adam. Her pony tail wasn't the only thing bouncing. She stopped in front of him and said, "How's this?"

The one man left in the room besides Gonzales immediately refocused away from Gabby's bouncing breasts.

"That'll work," Adam said with a nod.

"What's wrong?" she asked Adam. She knew he was fighting back saying something.

He shrugged. "Well, no one will be looking at your face, so I guess we're good."

Gonzalez looked at the female agent and knew he needed to take control of the conversation and get them focused.

"Well," Gonzalez said, "maybe this will work in our favor. Here's what we're going to do."

CHAPTER 57

"Son of a bitch, I told you I'm too big to parachute," Krieger bellowed as it took two SEALS to pull him into the vessel. It was only a few hours later. This was the route Mauricio had chosen to get them to the next phase of the mission.

Dripping wet, Krieger stood and turned to watch Mauricio, who got pulled aboard with one arm. Krieger continued his poke at Mauricio. "Parachuter's are like gymnasts, the smaller they are, the easier they tumble and land. You don't see many two hundred-and fifty-pound gymnasts, do you?"

Mauricio quickly looked back at Krieger after almost getting caught making eye contact with the SEALs.

Mauricio offered some banter of his own. "Well sir, it was standard procedure in case the plane was being tracked. Besides that, you did great. You got to the water faster than the rest of us and may I say you made the biggest splash with that entry."

The SEALS enjoyed the moment. While they knew of Krieger, they didn't know him well enough, so they thought they'd better leave the banter between Mauricio and Krieger. One of the SEALs helped Mauricio pull in the pack that was attached to his strap. The pack had some of his special communications equipment in it.

The captain approached Krieger. He said, "Colonel, I've got an urgent communication for you from London."

Krieger looked at Mauricio. They weren't expecting a call from anyone. They both knew something had gone wrong.

Krieger went down below and took the call.

After a brief discussion where Adam explained that they'd left Brooks in the globalist banker's headquarters and he was most likely in grave danger, Krieger asked, "Are we free to engage?"

"Colonel, he saved our ass and, if you're successful, possibly the country."

"Understood sir," Krieger said. "I'll get someone on it."

"Colonel."

"Yes sir?"

Adam said, "And let the QRF know that. I want them to know why they're going back into the teeth of the globalist stronghold for him."

"Yes sir." Krieger actually smiled and looked at Mauricio. He knew that the men needed to know why they were going back. With that knowledge, they would take on the fight, no holds barred.

Krieger disconnected from speaking with the vice president. Now, he'd make the call to send a small extraction team after Brooks.

* * *

The frigate sped off, cutting through the water like no other. Krieger and Mauricio quickly got into dry gear. Conditions were almost perfect. The Captain continued to increase speed up to over seventy miles per hour. This stealth vessel was like nothing else on the ocean, and was being used on its first mission. With a cargo load capacity designed for the weight they'd be transporting, it was the perfect vessel for the application.

* * *

Krieger said to Mauricio, "Get me the Independence."

This operation required a surprise and extraction from multiple vessels, but none was more important than the LCS2 Independence out of San Diego. This vessel had been chosen because of its formidable jamming technology and vast array of capabilities. At over four hundred feet long, it had the capabilities of a small assault transport, including a flight deck and hangar for housing two SH-60 or MH-60 helicopters, a stern ramp for operating small boats and cargo volume and payload to deliver a small assault force with fighting vehicles in a roll-on/roll-off port facility.

The man who was instrumental in designing the Independence was called in to consult on the capabilities and design modifications for this mission. The General working with him learned that the vision for this vessel had come to him in a dream, in which his dream told him the vessel was going to be needed to save the country. At that point, the General knew that providence had awakened.

Not only had the vehicles on the ship been swapped out for local transport trucks with reinforced suspension to carry the gold, the Independence was also equipped with autonomous air, surface and underwater vehicles. These capabilities allowed Special Forces teams to launch by air, land and on and under the sea.

* * *

It took a few hours but Krieger, Briggs and Mauricio joined the combined special forces team in position overlooking their final target, with daylight a few short hours away.

This area of the Swiss Alps boasted eight of the highest mountains in the range. Dramatic hillside landscapes gave way to sheer walls of limestone cliffs which jettisoned skyward. Their makeup and the topography made this area of the world the ideal terrain to drill caverns and conceal their entrances.

What had started as a necessity after World War II, Switzerland now had countless mountain bunkers. In fact, Switzerland had once disclosed to its people that they had enough bunker space for every Swiss citizen. What many people didn't know was that countless fake rocks would move or split in half to open up, revealing tunnels or missile defenses. One such rock was to the right of the tunnel openings Krieger was eyeing through large binoculars.

The US had had a few troops stationed here during the previous administration. But they'd been pulled out right after George's unexpected win in the election. It was The Shadow who had let the president in on the dirty secret of why.

This particular Air Force Base held over twenty aircraft in the main cavern. Just beyond the main door was an S shaped tunnel, making it almost impossible to blow the hermetically sealed second door from the outside without a significant blast that could be felt and heard for a hundred miles. That was something Krieger didn't want.

The facility was CBRN protected (Chemical, Biological, Radioactive and Nuclear) with concrete reinforced steel and other advanced military compounds and, as long as those doors were closed, they were almost impenetrable. Inside the caverns, there was a crane system on rails, capable of lifting and transporting planes deep inside the mountain.

Krieger had another idea for that crane system on rails.

This particular cavern was fully equipped with its own power generating system and was complete with personnel quarters, food and water storage, a full mess hall, a command and communication center and several briefing rooms. In short, it was self-sustainable for months.

Looking through his binoculars, he was focused on the door that intelligence indicated led to the cavern containing the gold the Federal Reserve had melted down and re-branded as their own.

CHAPTER 58

The Commander of SEAL team Bravo had taken the call. Part of the Quick Reaction Force (QRF), their storied history included being the team that had captured the hostages in Ramadi. They were the most experienced Special Forces urban combat group. Their order from Krieger was clear: go back into the teeth of the globalists' city and find the man who was responsible for the information that had led to the mission to save the country.

"Commander, tell your team he was a snake eater," Krieger had added.

With reverence, the Commander responded, "Affirmative, sir."

Krieger added the term 'snake eater' to let the commander know that this man was once a member of the Special Forces... one of their own. Krieger had relayed enough information to the commander so the team would understand the man they had to save was responsible for the series of missions that were currently underway.

* * *

Brooks was in a tight spot. He had made it out of the building just before the city had exploded with activity from all directions. Now he was scanning the area, seeking cover in alleyways. He kept moving.

He was alone in a city that was hunting anyone they could vent their anger on. Local and military law enforcement would never be told the truth. They would be told they were hunting a killer, and they'd be fed a variety of fictional stories. The Shadow understood that if he was captured, he'd never see the light of day again.

He moved quickly. Police sirens were everywhere. Helicopters were flying low towards the New World Order headquarters, still only a block away. He instinctively wanted to put space between himself and the center of all the activity. They'd be blocking off the area soon. When they did, he needed to be on the other side of the quarantine area.

Business people were walking with a purpose. Tourists sauntered about. Brooks slipped down a narrower street. He unbuttoned his suit jacket and tie. He folded the tie and put it in his jacket pocket. Authorities would obviously be watching cameras for anyone out of place. In this expensive suit, he'd be someone they'd take a second look at.

In the busy thoroughfare ahead, he saw several police and a military vehicle speeding in the opposite direction. He knew he had to keep moving. The fastest way to put distance between himself and the location was also the riskiest. As the last vehicle passed, he stepped out of the shadows. He turned left and cut across the street. He matched the pace of others on the sidewalk. He used a unique landmark in the distance to keep his bearings.

Most people were gawking at the speeding vehicles. Brooks kept his head down. By the time he made it to the end of the block, he had a feeling he was being followed. His training had taught him to notice unique movements in groups of people. The flow of pedestrians had a natural rhythm. He looked around.

He kept his pace casual but deliberate, moving by slower pedestrians when he could. When he passed a group of business women, he positioned himself in front of the taller one and quickly glanced at a window across the street. He looked for potential tails in the reflection. Everyone looked preoccupied, except there was one abstracted head he couldn't see.

Refocusing forward, he checked both sides of the street. He didn't see anyone closing in on him from up ahead. It was then that his instinct told him to pick up his pace.

A minute later, through the reflection in a window, he caught a glimpse of a head. Someone was closing the distance on him. Brooks reached into his pocket with his right hand and undid the cap on another pen Sasha had made for him.

Hand to hand combat with a trained assailant wasn't practical at his age. If it came to that, his only chance would be for him to get the first strike in.

Another several seconds passed before Brooks saw the man's head again. The man kept his head down but, based on his shoulders being above the rest of the crowd, this man was definitely out of place and still closing the distance.

Brooks kept pace with the other people. He worked his way another block. His phone pinged as a text came through. He reached into his pocket.

It read, "Turn right at the corner."

Brooks had to decide. The encrypted message left no identifiable number. There was no way of telling who this was. But only three people had this number. He put the cell phone back in his pocket and freed his hands.

He turned right at the corner.

Ping came the sound from his phone again. With his left hand, he reached in his pocket. It read, "pick up pace and cut diagonally across the street NOW."

The capital letters sent a sense of urgency surging through his body. Brooks glanced both ways and bounded across the street.

Suddenly, he saw a large man cutting diagonally across the street. The man had cut half of the distance between them.

Brooks gripped the pen tight. He may only get one shot at this. This guy was formidable.

Brooks moved towards the left side of the sidewalk. He wanted to put the man on his right side, giving himself the best chance. He needed every advantage he could get.

Just then he noticed a large man coming right at him on the sidewalk.

If the person texting him was friendly, where the hell was he now, or had he set him up?

Brooks could feel his senses heighten. This guy was getting close, coming towards him and positioning himself to walk about a foot or two off his right shoulder. It was a perfect place to make a move from his blind side as they passed. The man looked past Brooks then down at the sidewalk.

Brooks calculated every step. He changed the length of his gait so his feet could be in the optimal position when the man attacked.

But the man passed Brooks, just about four feet away. He never made a move.

Suddenly, he heard the distinct sound of a military silencer. It was almost drowned out by a sudden blast of music. Brooks jolted instinctively.

Brooks glanced at the window to his left. He kept walking, waiting to feel something he hadn't felt in years: the sensation of being shot.

With his feet still underneath him, he caught a glimpse of the large man who had just passed. The large figure was hugging another man. Brooks watched as the large man set the other man down around the corner of a building.

His phone dinged. "Turn left."

As Brooks turned left. A glimpse over his shoulder was all it took for him to realize that the man being leaned against the building was dead. That meant the man now walking towards him wasn't after him, he had been sent to take out the assailant coming in behind him. Brooks had help.

It also meant he'd been spotted. Most likely by the cameras on street corners. He needed to get out of there — now.

The large man that passed wasted no time catching up to Brooks.

"Sir, we need to get you back to the base," he said.

Brooks kept his eyes forward. As they walked in unison, he said, "Nice work back there."

The large SEAL shrugged. "You must have some very powerful friends."

Brooks didn't answer.

The SEAL added, "Whatever it was that you did, we appreciate it."

The SEAL knew he'd struck a chord when Brooks responded, "Thank you. There's a lot that needs to happen to save the republic. I just did my part."

"Take a left at this corner."

In a few yards, they both turned left. Brooks was happy to put more ground behind him and the N.W.O. headquarters.

"Do you have overwatch?" Brooks asked.

"Affirmative."

"How's it looking?"

"Not good. They're everywhere and they're closing in. We're going to have to get you out of here fast."

Brooks kept pace with the big man. "How do you expect to do that?"

"We're going to cut across the street and turn down that alley."

They kept a pedestrian pace as they walked across the street. Just before entering the alley, Brooks looked both ways to ensure they weren't being followed. Part way down the alley, the SEAL stepped into a small alcove to his right and stopped in front of a brown metal door. They were obscured from view. A harness descended from the rooftop.

The large SEAL helped Brooks strap in and shook Brook's whole body as he checked the connection of the clasps.

"This will take you up to one of our overwatch stations," the SEAL said. "They'll fly you out... This is where we say goodbye."

The SEAL signaled. Brooks was immediately lifted to the rooftop where another SEAL greeted him. The man, rather gruffly, began putting additional apparatus on Brooks. The SEAL had just finished latching additional straps to the vest when he looked with concern over Brooks's shoulder. After clasping the last latch, he smacked the vest and pulled a ripcord. A balloon unleashed.

Brooks looked up to see a stealth helicopter coming in low. A word was coming out of his mouth when air was forced out of his lungs as he was lifted in the air. He gasped for a breath.

Brooks was reeled into the helicopter.

"Sir," a woman said. "We have orders to get you to the airport where a jet is waiting. We need to get you out of this harness and into a flight suit."

Brooks knew who had pulled this together, and he was grateful.

"Affirmative," Brooks said, "things were getting a little heated down there."

"It was Sordid," she said. "He was the one calling the shots back at the headquarters. We picked up his frequency and sent a team after him, but we're spread thin and he had plenty of help."

That verified for Brooks that Sordid was the one who wanted the vice president killed.

Brooks knew better than to ask her about their mission, though his questioning eyes were enough for her to add, "He just took off in his plane with two fully loaded escorts." She shook her head. "He'll live to fight another day."

Brooks scowled and looked out the window.

CHAPTER 59

The President, Madison and Hemmele landed at Area 51., This was where they were going to conduct their part of the operation from. With little fanfare, the president stood momentarily at the top of the stairs and looked over some of the Marines and the advanced security detail who were already positioned.

Area 51 is part of the Nellis Military Operations Area. Over twenty by twenty-five miles, this massive area is one of the most secure places on the planet.

As everyone deplaned and several Special Forces contingencies took their positions, Dr. Hemmele greeted a friend, Dr. Hina Owen.

Hemmele turned and introduced Dr. Owen to the president.

The president said, "Dr. Owen, why don't you ride with us?"

She was delighted at the offer and her, Hemmele, the president and Madison climbed in.

Owen could detect something was afoot and, as soon as the presidential Limo turned left, she asked, "Roy, where are we going? The facilities are the other way."

It was now time to let her in on what they were doing there. Hemmele looked at her and said, "We're not going to the main facilities. We're going to the GD."

Owens's eyes bulged and her mouth hung open.

* * *

Mauricio looked at Krieger and said, "affirmative sir." This confirmed everyone was in position. Briggs was on the other side of the base with a Chief Petty Officer, while Master Sergeant Tasker and his special operations team had worked their way into the compound.

Simultaneously, Mauricio and Krieger checked the time. It was shift change. At this normal level of security, men and women came casually in and out through the tunnel as they had for decades. Security was there, though since none of these installations had ever had any attempted infiltration, overall security was relatively lax.

The entire platoon was working by their mechanical watches now. They had already placed their communications equipment in the protective shields embedded in their backpacks.

Mauricio and Krieger remained glued to their watches as they counted down to the appointed time. Their eyes met, and Mauricio hit the switch. The small EMP burst went off.

Mauricio had been trained by Dr. Roy Hemmele himself. He had learned as much as he possibly could from the master. Ever since Krieger had captured the EMP equipment from the terrorists, Hemmele had spent tireless days and nights redesigning the apparatus for this mission. He had tested it, but how much of it would penetrate the caverns was undetermined.

Hemmele was confident, however, that the effect behind them would be less than what they experienced on the radar chart, but by what degree, again Hemmele couldn't test in his small laboratory. Without time to take it to a secure location, he could only give Mauricio an estimate.

As soon as Mauricio actuated the burst, the peaceful military base was besieged by Krieger's men from all sides.

The Marines and the 2nd battalion came from the west. The team leads all pulled their communications devices from their backpacks. Mauricio, Briggs and Krieger did the same.

Relief was an emotion Krieger rarely felt. But that's exactly what he felt the moment when, after his device came to life and he said, "testing," he saw Mauricio smile and heard him say through his earpiece, "they're working." Hemmele had allowed them to capitalize on the element of surprise.

Mauricio gave the order to let the drones fly. The roof opened on a parked semi about a mile away. It was specially insulated from the EMP burst by Hemmele's team. Mauricio held his breath until the first group flew out the top of the open roof of the truck. He had each unmanned drone pre-programmed with their desired location.

When they were free and clear, three much larger drones took off from another truck. These three each had one marine in them.

Krieger charged ahead with one platoon towards the main opening of the cavern that housed the gold. Brigg secured the other tunnel entrance.

The battle to take back the stolen gold was exploding.

* * *

"Move out," Krieger bellowed to the driver. The first full truck pulled out. Gold was coming out of the tunnels quickly. Krieger turned to observe the team loading the helicopter and spoke through his earpiece to the Sr. Chief Petty Officer. "How much longer?"

"One more and she's full," the man responded. The next helicopter had landed. "Keep them coming."

As Krieger stood surveying the activity, Briggs walked up and said, "The other tunnel is secure sir. We're right on schedule."

"How's it going inside?" Krieger asked. He was talking about the extraction team in charge of getting the gold out of the tunnel. The team had infiltrated the main tunnel with the vaults and had used the rail system to transport the gold out of the tunnel. Krieger watched as multiple trucks, helicopters and the C4 planes were loaded simultaneously.

The extraction was a complicated endeavor which called for trucks to leave the compound and rendezvous with other trucks that were disguised to blend in with local traffic. The two small cargo planes had been taken out of another tunnel and were being loaded. The first helicopter that landed had come in full of large parachutes designed to allow the planes to drop their cargo so the gold could be dropped from the sky to teams waiting on the ground.

Helicopters were bouncing back and forth to designated locations along the river. Some of the gold would be extracted on the waterways.

Krieger asked, "What's the casualty count?" Krieger knew Briggs' team had run into a PKC Russian belt fired machine gun.

"Four KIA, another two expectant (not going to make it) and five wounded. They're all evac'd," Briggs said, confirming they were all off the base.

Krieger nodded. Briggs turned to take care of his tasks at hand.

Krieger watched all the activity and thought to himself, *as long as most of this gold makes it stateside, we'll be good.*

Krieger wasn't aware of the details of how they came up with the exact points to extract the gold, but he knew Adam had been intimately involved in the planning with a special team that used scientific techniques such as shortest route models and multiple comparisons simulation tools specifically designed for military operations. They simulated the possible locations the enemy could respond from, and conducted what was called a multiple factorial response optimization technique to choose the optimal routes and handoff locations to maximize the chances of the most gold getting out of the country the fastest ways possible. But Krieger didn't need to know that. He needed to get the gold on its routes where the field commanders would follow their individual plans, and he needed to hold the communications blackout as long as he could.

Krieger had each extraction team briefed on alternate routes to take so they could adjust their course if circumstances dictated. George and Adam wholeheartedly agreed. They understood that with a mission of this size, some of the teams would be faced with unforeseen circumstances, and would have to operate in silence. There was a high likelihood that some would most likely be either in a chase, or get caught and not make it through.

A few minutes later, Krieger watched as the small transport plane took off with a full load of gold.

CHAPTER 60

Brooks climbed into the newest naval fighter jet and took his position behind Tim, whose radio check was met with, "Check, now let's get the hell out of here."

Brooks had barely escaped with his life. When he got back to the base, Tim was there waiting to take him stateside.

With a sudden burst, Tim took off. As soon as he was over the open ocean, he took her down to under a thousand feet ceiling.

Wanting to get out of range, Tim said, "Hold on."

He took it past Mach 2 and continued to increase speed. Knowing the pressure exerted at this speed, Tim asked, "You doing alright back there?"

"I'm fine," Brooks said. "I'd be better if I'd gotten that globalist bastard Sordid."

"Affirmative, he'll turn up somewhere," Tim responded from the front.

"Yeah, he'll turn up on your radar flying the other way," Brooks said smartly.

"What?"

"The bastard got away, and is most likely flying in the direction of Brussels right now. He may even have The Cleric with him," Brooks said from the rear seat.

"What?"

"He just took off on his private jet, escorted by two fast movers. He put the hit on the vice president. Luckily the vice president got away."

Tim immediately processed what he just heard.

The next thing The Shadow heard was Tim breaking radio silence. "I need an air pocket to the east and patch me through to Mauricio." The air pocket was the term used to detect and track enemy aerial movement.

Tim wanted approval before creating an international incident.

"Sir?" the person on the other end of the radio questioned.

"You heard me. Get me Mauricio."

The connection went through quickly and Tim was patched through to Mauricio.

Tim asked, "You with Krieger?"

"Affirmative, but we're kind of busy right now."

Tim could hear all the commotion in the back ground.

"Tell him we have positive confirmation of the financier of the assassination attempt on the vice president, and he's getting away. The source says that The Cleric — who attempted to put the Colonel in an early grave back home — is with him."

The next voice Tim heard was Krieger's. After Tim reiterated what he had just told Mauricio, Krieger asked, "He's flying where?"

"He's going east sir."

"How do you know The Cleric's with him.?"

"Our communications team verified they got together about the same time the vice president landed. We can't be sure if The Cleric is still with him but we believe he is. It could be a two-fer."

That was it, Krieger put it all together. If the Cleric was there before the Vice President landed and the communications team verified that he was with Sordid, he had cause to pursue.

"What's your ten?" Krieger asked Tim.

"I'm heading west. I can turn east."

It sounded good but Krieger needed approval for any further escalation, which they both knew would most likely be needed. He wasn't going to make this call on his own. Since the vice president was on the run, he would need to call someone with authority.

Tim heard the hesitation and pressed, "Do I pursue?"

"Affirmative, pursue," Krieger said. "Demand they land at a nearby base but do not engage. Repeat, do not engage."

Krieger knew Sordid could be flying to Brussels, but he could also be flying to Turkey or Hungary, where he'd been born. There wasn't time for him or Mauricio to get any more involved in the details. He knew Tim was once the best pilot in the navy and was flying a state-of-the-art fighter jet with a titanium composite frame and a turbofan engine which would allow Tim to close the distance quickly. In addition, the radar evading technology should buy him some time and allow Tim to be undetected for a few minutes until Krieger could get back to him and give him an answer. If Tim encountered another fighter jet, his abilities, along with the superior maneuverability of his fighter, would give him an advantage.

Krieger turned to Mauricio. "Get me Senator Madison Dodge."

Tim said, "Hold on." He banked a sharp turn and headed towards his target. The one thing he hadn't told Krieger was that Sordid was being escorted by two fighter jets.

CHAPTER 61

Madison's looked at the encrypted number on the screen of her cell phone as she and the president got out of the vehicle. She looked at the president and said, "I've got to take this."

She stepped several feet away so no one could hear and in a moment her eye contact was all George needed to understand it was part of the ongoing mission. The military team had put together secondary protocol for emergency communications.

Mauricio and his team had taken every precaution possible to ensure no communication could ever be tracked. Still, just in case somehow there was traceability, they wanted to keep George free and clear, so nothing could ever be traced back to him.

So as a secondary protocol, in case Adam's cell phone was cut off or compromised, they had his calls for this mission forwarded to Madison, knowing she would secretly be with the president. In the unlikely scenario where something was traced back to Madison, she could be pardoned by the president.

George, Hemmele and the others stood there waiting for Madison to go into the building. When Madison's concerned eyes met George's and she motioned for him to come over to where they could talk. George knew it wasn't good.

Madison pushed her mute button and said, "It's Krieger, he…"

"Secondary protocol?" George said.

Her lips flattened and she nodded slowly.

"That means…" George said. He already knew what it meant.

"I'm afraid so sir."

Both of them knew something had happened to Adam and most likely Gabby too, and whoever else was with them. They both knew this call wasn't about that, it was that Krieger needed something and it must be important and beyond the scope of the mission planning for him to call.

"What is it?" George asked.

"He has recorded evidence that Sordid ordered an attempt on the vice president's life," Madison said. "And he's getting away. He's flying east and there's a strong likelihood that he's traveling with The Cleric, who we know flew out of New York yesterday. This is the man we believe to have funded terrorist activity domestically and... Krieger has ordered pursuit on his plane and wants to know if..."

"Active pursuit of an international terrorist?" George asked, using wording he wanted alignment on from Madison.

"Affirmative sir. Active pursuit of a terrorist suspected of just orchestrating an attempt on the vice president's life." Madison also chose her words carefully so they had agreement on the reason they'd give the international community.

George knew Krieger wasn't calling for diplomatic suggestions. He was calling because he suspected force would be needed, and wanted authorization before committing an international incident.

Smart man, I'd do the same thing.

George knew Sordid would go underground and be hidden away for years. He also understood that the globalist families had furnished him with enough black gold of his own to fund continued deep state operations and terrorism for years to come. George also had seen evidence that he was the one who'd funded the assault on them at the Mountain House when George's family had almost been killed. This chance wasn't going to come along again any time soon. With the recordings they now had tying Sordid to the attempted assassination on the vice president, that was enough reason to continue pursuit.

"Where are they at?" George asked.

"Still over international waters," Madison said, "but not for long."

George nodded. He would leave it up to Krieger. If it could be handled without force than good, if not, then so be it. He wasn't going to let this opportunity slip through his hands.

Madison took her phone off mute and relayed a go-ahead to Krieger. Then she disconnected. Out of hearing distance from the others, George and Madison hoped they'd get some good news from Adam and Gabby soon.

Then, as Madison gazed off into the flat desert, her eyes were inquisitively drawn to some kind of equipment in the distance. This apparatus wasn't like any satellite communications network she'd ever seen.

* * *

Madison and George turned and walked towards the small group waiting for them.

Hemmele, moving with a purpose, led the way into the building. In mission planning, Dr. Hemmele had filled Krieger, Adam and George in on this technology. This particular building and what it did was so top secret that every person had above top-secret clearance, and some presidents never even knew it existed. The team inside had just been debriefed on the president visiting them. They were told they were going to have an opportunity to play a pivotal role in a mission that was underway to save the country. This small group was all given an option to stay, or they could leave and not be involved. To a person, every single one of them wanted to do anything they could do to save the country. They would soon understand what that would be.

When Hemmele, Madison, George and the others entered the control room, a hush interrupted their surge of activity. Dr. Hemmele took a familiar place at a control center. He made a quick announcement and began giving directives. This was where he was in his element.

Madison asked, "What does GD stand for?"

Hemmele was focused and didn't even look up at her when he answered, "It stands for gravity detector."

"It's a gravity detector?" She said it loud enough that a few heads in the room turned momentarily towards her.

Hemmele gave a few more directions to staff members. Then he answered, "Yes. It's designed to look out into space and detect gravity."

George glanced at Hemmele. He let Madison continue with her questioning. He'd been debriefed at a high level, so he understood top secret gravity detection technology was in existence, though he wanted to know more.

He listened as she asked, "What are you looking for?"

"Well if a planet explodes, or a large meteor collides with something, there's usually a change in a gravitational field, and we can detect those changes," Hemmele explained. "Without this device, those types of things could never be detected. This technology has been a huge benefit to us because, as you can imagine, we can't monitor every star and planet in the sky."

Hemmele also knew about the fields of black holes and other such phenomenon that the team studied, but he wasn't going to get into that.

Madison nodded. "I understand, it makes sense, but I've never heard of a gravity detector."

Madison saw Hemmele and Dr. Owen exchange a glance. This made her even more curious. "Doctor, why is this device here in Area 51?"

Hemmele looked at Owen who smiled and said, "You started this," as if to say he had dug his own hole and it was up to him to dig his way out.

Hemmele looked at the president before addressing Madison's question. The president gave no indication of wanting to stifle the conversation.

Hemmele said, "Well, you see, *theoretically*, UFOs could be using some kind of device that warps gravity to allow them to accelerate to such great speeds. We also believe they could use this same technology to mask themselves from our technology, so we can't detect their whereabouts."

"UFOs have mastered gravitational fields?" Madison asked.

Hemmele cleared his throat. "Theoretically."

George looked around to see heads within hearing distance turn while others stared straight ahead at their computer screens.

Madison was quick with another question. "And we're learning to manipulate gravity?"

Hemmele almost scoffed and thought to himself. *It's not like we can pick and place items in exact locations*

After that brief thought, Hemmele said, "Hardly. All we've been able to do so far is to monitor gravitational fields and to do this, that device you looked at outside," Hemmele had evidently noticed Gabby looking, "goes on for over a mile just to do that."

"This thing is a mile long?" George asked. "Is this the only one of its kind?"

"Actually, no," Hemmele said. "We needed to be able to look out into space from every direction across the planet. We had to strategically position a few around the globe to give us the three hundred and sixty degree view we desired."

Hemmele quickly began asking some of the other scientists and technicians about settings and readings. It was apparent to Madison that he didn't want to explain any more, so she let it go.

Hemmele's mind focused to the reason for them being here. Krieger had told him how the physical stockpiles of gold in the US had gone from over twenty thousand tons down to its current level of approximately eight thousand tons. In the process, the deep state had taken control of thousands of tons and that was where they'd got some of their untraceable funding. In addition, there was much more gold than that, that never made its rightful way to the vaults after World War II. Hemmele knew the deep state and globalist bankers would continue to drive the country into submission unless those funds were taken back.

Hemmele was half talking to himself and half to the others when he added, "This will be the first time we try to warp any gravitational fields for military purposes here on the earth."

He kept working, looking at settings, while he added, "And for the sake of the country, this had better work."

CHAPTER 62

One fighter jet engaging two trained fighter jets was never a good idea.

Tim had closed the distance on Sordid who now, along with his two escorts, was on the radar and within communication distance. It was the moment of reckoning.

Tim broke radio silence by identifying himself. "We have reason to believe there is an international terrorist on board who orchestrated an attempt on the vice president of the United States. We are going to redirect you to the nearest US military base. This intercept will follow you. Turn north and our ground communications will talk you in."

There was silence.

Tim and Brooks watched their radar screens. The two jets peeled off. It was a classic move to position themselves to engage. This confirmed their intentions.

Tim repeated his directive carefully, knowing everything he said was being recorded.

Sordid's large jet throttled up. A voice came into Tim's helmet. It said, "Go to hell. You Americans are so arrogant…"

Tim spoke to Brooks. "Get ready for a fight, they're positioning themselves to engage."

"Roger that."

"We've got a score to settle."

Tim had won the Top Gun, and taught at the Naval War college and Annapolis, though that had been over a decade ago. He hadn't been in a real dogfight for twenty years.

Brooks hadn't been in a fighter jet for decades before the trip over, and he had never been in a real dog fight. This wasn't good.

Originally trained as the person who sat in the back seat while the pilot flew the jet, the position of RIO, or Radar Intercept Officer, was crucial. The

RIO watches for targets and serves as another set of eyes for the pilot. Fighter jet teams usually train and stay together for years because, just like great team sports, it takes time to develop the chemistry to make sure the gaps for ACM (Air Combat Maneuvering) are minimized.

Watching the screen, Brooks tracked the positions of the two approaching fighter jets. He began reading them out to Tim. They'd be in range momentarily.

* * *

The gold was en route, but the globalists had been notified immediately after Krieger and his team left the base.

Now, it was the highest stakes chase of the century.

Krieger stood alongside the captain at the helm of the frigate. They sped across the open seas at nearly eighty miles per hour. Riding on pontoons, this frigate not only evaded radar detection, the technology allowed the vessel to even evade submarine sonar. Designed for long range with the ability to careen through low water levels, it was the perfect vessel for this mission. Krieger had chosen this vessel partly because, of all the stealth vessels, this was the largest.

Krieger would rendezvous with the LCS7 littoral combat ship. Its almost four hundred feet in length would allow it to carry the heaviest cargo of gold while it would only draw 13 feet. Her water jet propulsion allowed her to reach significant speeds on the open water.

Mauricio loudly interrupted Krieger. "Colonel, they're removing the barricades from the highways. I'm putting out the BOLO word to the commanders."

Krieger knew many highways in Switzerland that adjoined military air bases were designed to double as extra runways by removing the medians between the lanes so planes could take off. Krieger also knew several of the military bases in Switzerland were actually run by their own version of globalist elites, who had infiltrated almost every country in Europe. Flying supersonic was prohibited in most of Switzerland because of the risk of avalanches and the number of tourists so high up in altitude. Krieger hoped they didn't break that rule. Every second counted.

Krieger looked over the captain's shoulder. They were already at full speed. Mauricio was watching the screens. One by one, his team was identifying each major gold transport. This ship had been retrofitted to act as the mobile TOC (Tactical Operations Center) for this mission. Equipped with the latest BFT, a cool little gizmo that allowed them to link up with a satellite and give the locations of friendly and enemy units, maps, and routes.

Krieger asked Mauricio, "How are you coming?"

"We've got most," Mauricio responded.

Krieger let Mauricio focus to work with his team identifying the others. There were several ships of various sorts and a few planes.

Some of the other smaller amounts of gold were still being transported by delivery trucks, retrofitted cement mixers and rail car. A few large turbines on rail cars were actually hollow and filled with gold. Trucks were given multiple check points with people stationed to watch for tails. If any one vehicle believed they were compromised and being followed, they had a dummy extraction point to go to so they didn't compromise the loads in the other vehicles. If they believed they were free and clear, they would go to their designated location.

C-5M, Super Galaxy is the US Air Force's (USAF) largest transport plane and could take off with in excess of 350 tons. The General had suggested this one because it allowed for quick loading from the front and rear simultaneously. This was Krieger's biggest concern. He was focusing on the largest payloads first.

It wasn't far to the Geneva airport, which could accommodate the goliath plane. Once that gold took off, it would be safe. Krieger would then turn most of his attention to the other loads.

He asked Mauricio, "Have they taken off yet?"

Mauricio's lips were uncharacteristically tight. "Not yet, but it won't be long."

"What about the rivers and the other vehicles?" Krieger asked. "What's the chatter?"

Mauricio was listening intently to the communications flooding in. Usually succinct and clear with his communications, the only way to explain it to Krieger was by saying, "It's flooding in so fast we can't keep up with it."

Krieger knew he couldn't do much about it. The mission was in the hands of the commanders now, who were given options, depending on the situation. He wasn't about to communicate with most of them.

It was time for Krieger to check on the status of the next key component of their getaway plan. Krieger nodded to Mauricio. "Affirmative. Get me Hemmele."

CHAPTER 63

"Put him on the speaker," Dr. Hemmele said. "Colonel, we're almost ready. We've got your location and the others, and we're preparing. We should be ready in minutes."

Hemmele and his team were a little ahead of schedule in preparing for their role.

Krieger asked, "So how's our pilot doing with his end of the mission?"

Suddenly George and Madison realized no one had checked in on Tim and Brooks. The last they'd heard, they were heading east after Sordid. There was no one else to check on them.

"Tim's after Sordid, the last we heard from him," said Madison.

The president said to Hemmele, "Can you pull him up on the screen?"

"Affirmative sir," Hemmele said. "Mauricio, can you give me the identification on his jet?"

Mauricio relayed the information.

Hemmele gave them to Owen and said, "Get him up on screen number four."

Everyone in the room watched until the screen switched over to show a small dot. Owen took over directing the operator. "Zoom in on them," She said, "and establish communications."

"Affirmative sir," the middle-aged man responded. He started to zoom and said, "Communications will take a minute."

Owen watched as the man zoomed in so they could all clearly see. What they saw wasn't good. Tim's aircraft was being flanked by two fighter jets and they were closing in on him fast, about at the distance to engage.

Owen responded, "Make it quick."

George looked around the room and processed the complex situation quickly. Just like the special forces teams who embarked on their missions, this group of people needed to know.

George's deep voice projected with resonating baritone, "I want everyone to listen to this and understand what we're looking at. The friendly pilot in this plane is one of the most decorated fighter pilots alive. He's a top gun award winner and has flown one of the most top-secret missions of any pilot alive. His copilot is the man who gave us the intelligence to have a chance to save our country. At this very moment, they're after that aircraft out front who's carrying one of the most notorious terrorists of our time. His name is Sordid. He is responsible for an assassination attempt on myself and my family at our mountain house, and he just tried to have the vice president killed." George took a breath. "Do whatever you can to save these men."

George glanced at Hemmele, who simply nodded with affirmation. He appreciated the president setting the stage.

In the meantime, they all watched it unfold on the screen.

* * *

Brooks compressed into his seat as Tim banked hard.

Brooks relayed, "They're almost in distance."

"Affirmative," replied Tim, knowing that, today, pilots must rely more than ever on their highly sophisticated radar. Many times, enemies only come into sight in the final moments of battle.

Brooks was watching the screen and the horizon. "Bogie number one at 120 degrees at 78 miles."

"Affirmative," Tim replied.

"Bogie closing bearing 110." Scanning the horizon, Brooks caught his first glimpse. "Second bogie maneuvering bearing 360 at 72 miles... Speed 570, just over fifty miles now. Bogies heading directly at us, at 40 miles now and closing."

His communication was almost non-stop. "Bogies starboard 210 at 30 miles and eleven thousand feet. Bogies inside twenty miles... Sixteen miles."

"Roger that," Tim affirmed. They were in distance to engage.

The first bogie was positioning for a shot. Brooks had no sooner said, "Bank right," when Tim banked it right, hard. He'd had the same thought, and didn't want to get flushed out to the second plane.

"Bogie still maneuvering bearing."

"Got him." Tim banked a hard right and then, as soon as he saw the first pilot react, he banked left as sharp as the jet could handle.

* * *

Back in Area 51, George and Madison stood side by side watching the screen.

George asked, "What's the closest location of help?"

Owen replied, "I'm in contact with one of our carriers, but it'll take fifteen minutes for them to get air support there."

George shook his head. "This thing will be over in less than three."

George knew they wouldn't be there in time, but fighters en route would deter any other adversaries from deciding to join in.

Madison and George exchanged a glance, and watched the dogfight.

* * *

Brooks said what Tim already knew. "We're heading right towards bogie number two."

"I'm coming down hard."

Without another word, Brooks understood that Tim had positioned them so both jets were in front of him. The first jet was maneuvering away from them and the second was coming in fast from the horizon.

Tim knew he had to take out one of the jets before they sandwiched him.

Tim banked right, then left, then right again to stay on the tail of the fighter in front of him. He had closed in, but was running out of distance between him and the second fighter. He had to get a lock.

"Lock him up, lock him up."

"Affirmative. Almost, almost… got it, fire."

The missile went away.

Tim held tight. Then, in an instant, the orangish yellow ball of fire accompanied by the explosion verified success.

"Splash one," Brooks said.

An instant later, Brooks was surprised to see that Tim had kept his trajectory. He was headed right towards bogie number two.

They hadn't been able to get a lock yet when suddenly Brooks called, "He's got a lock."

Instantaneously, the beep sounded and Brooks alerted, "Missile away, he's fired." With the missile coming at them, Tim immediately lowered the left aileron and raised the right aileron, banked right and released the flares.

The aerial infrared countermeasures were the best the navy had. The new design with strontium nitrate, potassium perchlorate and magnesium burned with a powerful oxidation mix. They gave off extremely bright orange reddish flames.

The explosion came quicker than Brooks had expected. "That was close."

"Affirmative."

Brooks was getting used to Tim's short remarks. He was beginning to realize Tim was in the moment, concentrating on everything and taking everything in. Brooks knew his job was to feed Tim information. Looking behind them, Brooks saw the bogie bank. "He's banking left, don't let him get behind us, bank right."

Tim banked right hard. The pressure from the Gs on Brooks was significant as they passed by his adversary.

Brooks looked behind. Before he could see the bogie turn, Tim banked left hard.

"Hold on, stay with me," Tim said. He was pulling as many Gs as he could, and hoping Brooks didn't black out.

It only lasted a few seconds, and Tim heard Brooks take a few deep breaths and say, "I'm here… barely."

When the bogie banked, Tim had his side and was closing fast.

"Now let's finish this," Tim said.

Following left and right and left, the bogie went skyward and then banked right. Diving down to his right, Tim throttled up as much as he could. "Get it, get it" he urged.

"Locked, fire."

The ball of fire served notice in the sky that the navy still had the best fighter pilots alive.

Tim's voice was distinctly less stressed. "Now let's get that Sordid."

They both knew Sordid wasn't in a fighter jet. They'd now close the distance and either force him down, or bring him down.

* * *

Back in Area 51, Brook's voice came through the speaker. "Splash two."

Jubilation filled the room.

Madison and George looked at each other. She hadn't seen George so happy in weeks.

Then, Madison noticed Dr. Owen had slowly stood up.

Madison had followed Owen's gaze up to the screen. She wasn't sure what she was looking at. "What's that?"

Owen's tone was panic stricken. "Those are fighter jets heading towards Tim."

Hemmele leaned forward. "And he can't see them yet," he said. "He's being led right into a trap. He's heading for Sordid and fighter jets are headed right for him... Six of them."

CHAPTER 64

Madison's executive assistant, Alexus, had come along as part of a supporting detail. She had kept her distance from the action. But as she listened to a message coming through her ear piece, she gasped. She pulled out her large notepad and scanned through several developing stories. The uniformity of the wording in the headlines and suddenness of their appearance confirmed this was another orchestrated narrative from the globalist media.

Her feeling of anxiety intensified as she scrolled.

Alexus had learned about Adam's history from Gabby. There was no question that Adam had known the risks. Even after brainstorming other options with the entire team, they couldn't think of any other way to have the world bankers transfer back the money they'd stolen from the United States.

Alexus saw Madison looking over her shoulder. Alexus pointed to her screen, indicating there was something Madison needed to see, and Madison motioned for her to approach.

Madison noticed Alexus's eyes had filled with tears. Alexus slowly extended her hand and passed the device to Madison. After a few scrolls across the headlines, Madison's mouth hung open. She looked up and made eye contact with Alexus. They froze for a moment.

Then, turning to her left, Madison said, "Mr. President, you need to see this."

She handed the large pad to George. He quickly began scrolling.

"Mr. President, all of these stories just broke," Alexus said. "Notice the similar wording. They're reporting a terrorist strike at the World Banking Headquarters in London, and they're saying the vice president is inside and the UN troops are en route to contain it… and protect the vice president."

George locked eyes with her, then turned to Madison and said, "More like kill him."

Madison stiffened.

George asked, "Have we heard from the vice president yet?"

"No sir," Alexus said, "not a word."

Madison recollected, "The last contact we had was when Adam had just gotten in the presidential Limousine, but he never got to the base."

Alexus added, "Now the media is reporting that the base is blocked off by UN troops as a precautionary measure."

George's eyes widened as he looked at Alexus, and then turned to Madison. "Precautionary measure, or *preventive* measure to ensure he didn't get to the base?"

George thought for a moment. "So he got into the Limo and never got to the base, that means he's somewhere in between, or…" George stopped speaking.

"Or what?" Madison had to ask.

George looked at her. "Or, heaven forbid… they have him."

George's eyes went back to the large screens and focused on Tim and The Shadow as they flew right towards almost certain death.

George's bellow filled the room in a tone Madison hadn't ever heard. "Hemmele, do something! With all of this technology, there's got to be something you can do!"

After a brief moment of thought, Hemmele had an idea. As they watched six fighter jets close on Tim and The Shadow, Hemmele said, "Sir, we could take all the jets down by disabling their electronics. All of their electrical systems will go dead and they'll drop like rocks out of the sky."

"Do it!" George commanded.

Hemmele was already barking out orders. The room had to refocus on other equipment to do this.

"We've reestablished communications," Owen said.

Madison quickly set the stage. Speaking to Tim she said, "Captain, you've got six bogies headed directly towards you. You should see them on your radar in a moment. We need you to bang a hard-U turn and get the hell out of there now."

"We're almost in range," Tim said. "How much time do we have?"

"Not enough, get out of there."

In the rear seat, Brooks had the aircraft's radar in search mode. It began to sweep a radio beam back and forth across the sky. He was watching a square white box. It indicated Sordid's plane still wasn't within range. He didn't see any other bogeys yet. Brooks confirmed the target's angle, heading, air speed and their closure rate.

Brooks said, "Switching to SAM."

Tim agreed, "Affirmative."

The SAM feature allowed the radar to combine both tracking and scanning, so a pilot could track incoming bogies to see the big picture, while keeping sight of the main target.

Brooks checked closing speed. "Thirty seconds."

Madison interrupted. "Negative, you don't have enough time. Abort, I repeat, abort the mission."

Suddenly, Brooks saw white squares appear on the top of the screen.

"We've got two bogies... make that three."

"Tim, abort, we'll be able to take them down from here," Madison urged.

Tim knew of the technology that allowed the government to disable the electromechanics of a plane. He knew it had been used before. "Will they be able to eject out of their planes?"

Madison and George looked at Hemmele.

He shrugged his shoulders, indicating he wasn't sure. Pressed by their looks he said, "Possibly."

"Unacceptable," Tim said.

Hemmele looked up at Madison and said urgently, "Captain you've got to divert now, or you'll be in the fallout." His tone escalated. "Get out of there."

"Tim, this is an order, you are to turn around now," Madison said.

"Captain, remember mission protocol. It's your call," they all heard Brooks say to Tim.

Mission protocol established that the commander in the field had full autonomy to make calls to alter their plans in order to complete the scope of the mission. Those protocols were for every scenario.

After a brief second of silence Tim replied, "Negative, evoking mission protocol, proceeding to target. I'm going after Sordid."

Tim was almost at full throttle and now pushed it to the limit.

"Tim, Tim…" Madison went silent, knowing Tim had made his decision and needed to concentrate. She knew that Tim and Brooks realized if Sordid could parachute out, he'd live to fight another day. Madison looked at George. They both knew that Tim and Brooks wanted to see firsthand that Sordid was dead.

* * *

Towards the bottom of Brooks' screen, the square identifying Sordid's plane turned yellow, indicating it was in range. The other squares were still white, but closing fast. Brooks called out, "Bogie bearing 120, bogie bearing 140, four more bogies on the screen. That makes six."

Tim glanced down to see the big picture. "Just give me the closest ones."

"Bogies bearing in at… shit, they're firing. Missile away, break left."

Suddenly Tim banked left and shot out a batch of flares, then he banked back to his right to get back on course. He paid little attention as the missile exploded into the ignited flares.

Tim's headset was equipped to give him a low slow beep as aircraft approached, and that pitch would go up when the enemy radar went into lock guidance mode. That shot had been taken before the jet had acquired radar lock.

No sooner had that thought crossed his mind, when the pitch in his headset increased. One of the incoming bogeys turned yellow on their screen, indicating the pending danger of the enemy's capability to lock their aircraft.

Brooks's tone was telling. "He's got a lock… he's firing."

Tim banked hard, releasing another set of flares. The missile went through, and he had no choice but to deploy another set.

A flash of light and an explosive sound that followed. Tim re-focused on Sordid's plane.

A moment later, the yellow square on the radar screen identifying Sordid's plane had a square around it.

Brooks said, "Got a lock, fire one."

"Fox three," Tim said, indicating the type of missile that was fired.

Even though he knew the radar in track mode would focus more energy on its target, Tim still said, "Fire two." He didn't want to take any chances. He wasn't going to have enough missiles to fight six fighters anyway, so he wanted to make damned sure he killed Sordid.

Sordid was the main figure the globalist bankers gave money to so he would do their dirty work. He drew attention to himself so the globalist bankers could keep themselves off the radar. With this money Sordid funded all kinds of insurrection and troubles. He funded The Cleric he was traveling with and many others. He and his associates had bought off members of congress and, the ones who he couldn't buy off, he orchestrated situations by drugging them and then taking photos of them with young women or girls while they were incoherent. It was an effective blackmailing technique that had been going on in Washington for decades. Now, Tim and Brooks were out on a limb. There was a protocol that they commanded their own mission. But it was a fine line whether they were covered or if they had just disobeyed the orders of Madison or even the president. The least they'd done was manipulate the rules.

The president and Madison stared at the screen. With fists clenched, knuckles white, his neck stretched forward and his mouth open, the president realized that these two men had just put their lives on the line. He saw no way for them to get out alive. Even if they did, he realized both men knew he could create an issue out of them disobeying his order, even with the mission protocol, but he would never do that. He realized why Tom and Brooks had made their decision to sacrifice themselves to shoot down Sordid.

The missiles' momentary drop from underneath Tim's jet was undetectable. A fraction of a second later, hot flames ignited. A trail of white smoke traced the path of the missiles.

The new AIM Air-to-Air missile was a long-range missile with the ability to defeat electronic warfare jamming. With its new radar guidance system, it had the advantage of being a weapon the pilot could fire and immediately direct his attention and his plane to the next priority. The seven-inch diameter missile screamed towards the target at Mach 4, over 3,000 mph.

The explosion had a bright white center. It turned yellow, orange and magenta as it emanated outwardly and spat across the sky.

Brooks', "Splash…" was interrupted.

"I've got two inbound bogeys heading 170, closing at under 1,000 knots at a speed of 900."

"We've got two bogies coming in from the left. Two more from the right," Brooks confirmed. "That makes six bogies."

* * *

Back at Area 51, Madison gasped when she heard Tim say, "That was our last set of flares."

Now Madison and the rest heard, "Bank right," from the back seat.

"They're surrounded," Madison realized. She looked at George. "He turned right into them."

Suddenly, Tim's voice came across the speakers. "Hemmele, are you ready?"

"What?" Madison questioned.

Tim was in no mood for questions. "Damn it, Hemmele, are you ready?"

Madison and George looked to Hemmele, who said, "We're ready, but we can't deploy, it'll take all of you out."

"Tim, did you hear that?" Madison questioned.

"Affirmative," Tim said and he banked hard left, right and left. He was doing the best he could. "We're not going to make it out of here… On my zero, you take us all down?"

"What?" Hemmele demanded.

"Take us all down exactly on my zero!"

As the fighters converged, it was obvious on the screen that Tim and Brooks were going to be in range any second.

Then the inevitable happened. Brooks said, "He's got a lock."

George looked at Hemmele, who stood at the ready. Hemmele swallowed hard and immediately responded, "Affirmative."

Just then Brooks said, "Missile away."

Tim glanced at his screen to see the missile heading towards them.

Tim screamed, "Hemmele, three, two, one, zero."

There wasn't any time for debate; Hemmele deployed the device, knocking out all of their electronics.

George and Madison watched as the images on their screens stopped advancing. Then disappeared.

"What happened?" Madison asked.

Owens looked back at her and answered, "They're splashed. They're all down."

The room fell silent.

CHAPTER 65

"We have confirmation that fighters have taken off from multiple locations," Mauricio told Krieger. "They'll be over the Mediterranean in a minute."

Krieger knew they'd be coming. "Is Hemmele ready?"

Mauricio was already contacting Hemmele for confirmation.

When Mauricio's face dropped, Krieger froze.

Mauricio put Hemmele on the speaker. Hemmele said, "We're still getting set, it'll take a minute."

Krieger and Mauricio locked eyes. They both had the feeling that something had happened.

"How long?" Krieger questioned.

There was a hesitation. Hemmele and his team were scrambling with the settings as quickly as they could. "Approximately five minutes."

Krieger looked at Mauricio, who was tracking the jets headed their way. Mauricio nodded.

"It'll be close," Krieger said. "We won't have any longer than that."

"Roger that," Hemmele responded and got back to setting the device.

Madison and George both felt the anxiety. They had just lost two good men. But Krieger had not only made it to this point in the mission successfully, there was still enough time for Hemmele to engage the equipment.

Madison's executive assistant handed her a phone.

Madison listened, then turned to the president. "Sir, we have an urgent call for you from two of our European allies."

George looked at her, shook his head and said, "Tell them that due to the assassination attempt on the vice president, I can't be reached right now."

"Yes, sir." Madison nodded, smiled and walked a few feet away to convey the message.

A moment later she came back, and looked at George. "Good thinking sir."

George nodded and they all got back to concentrating on the mission.

Dr. Owen had her screens back to tracking all of the gold transports. Then, with a small sense of satisfaction, she turned to the president. "Mr. President, the images you see in gold are the ships and planes transporting the gold. Images in red are foreign entities attempting to locate the gold."

* * *

A few minutes later, the team listened as Owen communicated with Mauricio.

Finally, Owen said, "Okay, slow to idle and maintain course. Your rendezvous is ready. We're going to activate the equipment. Be ready for any kind of interference."

"What's this going to do?" Madison asked.

Hemmele responded, "Hopefully nothing major to the ship, but the gravitational field will be warped. Even though the ship and their rendezvousing submarine are both stealth, the highest likelihood of them being detected is when the sub surfaces and they start the transfer."

Hemmele and Owen communicated on a few more details and then Hemmele continued to explain to Madison. "We're going to warp the gravitational field around them and mask their whereabouts, so they'll be undetectable."

"Just like a UFO does," Madison added, as more of a statement than a question.

Hemmele didn't respond. When he felt eyes looking at him, he said, "We've never done this outside of this base."

* * *

Mauricio and Krieger had already reduced their speed. They had put themselves on the speaker.

After Hemmele actuated the equipment, he asked, "Do you notice any disruption?"

Mauricio looked around. "Negative, nothing of consequence…"

There was silence on both ends. After Mauricio and Krieger assessed their environment as carefully as they could, Mauricio said, "There might be a little different drift, that's all."

"The direction of the waves may have shifted a little," Hemmele said, "and that's good, it's exactly what we're looking for."

Hemmele was relieved there weren't any other ill effects he hadn't anticipated. He glanced from Madison to the president, to Owen.

A minute later, three hundred yards away from the drifting frigate, the ocean erupted with foam as the nose of a massive submarine emerged. The Pennsylvania was the largest submarine in the US Navy. It had been retrofitted with the most advanced technology of the day. In addition, there were some last-minute enhancements that had been made for this mission. The missile tubes had been engineered to accommodate room for storage canisters that extended the forward deployment time of the special forces teams for the mission. The other two Trident tubes had been converted to swimmer lockout chambers. An advanced SEAL Delivery System and the dry dock shelter were mounted on the lockout chamber, so the ship was able to deploy sixty-six Special Operations sailors or Marines, including Navy SEALS and USMC MARSOC teams. Updated communications equipment was installed during the upgrade that allowed the SSGNs (Ship Submersible Guided Nuclear) to serve as a forward, clandestine Small Combatant Joint Command Center. This was how some of the Special Forces teams and equipment got to their embarking points and now, this was how they were going to disappear undetected into the depths of the ocean. With the submarine being the stealthiest in the world, the gold that was about to be unloaded and the Special Operations teams would be home free.

Once the teams and the gold were safely loaded, Krieger knew the sub would speed towards the United States faster than anyone would think possible. The two turbines secretly provided over eighty-thousand horsepower and would quietly reach top speeds of over thirty knots.

As he sped away on the frigate, Krieger watched the submarine submerge with the Special Operation forces and gold on board.

* * *

Three hundred miles away, a smaller navy stealth ship slowed as it approached the open end of the oil tanker. As soon as the high-tech stealth with its fifty tons of gold pulled inside, the tanker throttled up to speed.

Less than five minutes later, two globalists' jets flew on the horizon. They were in search of gold that wasn't there.

CHAPTER 66

Rothmayer leaned closer to the speaker on his desk. "Hello, Mr. President."

The president had taken the call because this man was much more powerful than political figure heads of countries. After all, he and his banking friends were the people who had put most of them in place. The global banking cartel was the world's largest funder of political campaigns worldwide. They only supported politicians who continued to drive their countries into more debt, gradually giving the banking cartels more money from taxpayers.

Those who wanted to cut spending had their campaign funds cut off, almost ensuring they'd be voted out of office.

The president had never met this man before, but he knew the Rothmayers and the Vatican controlled the city of London and Wall Street, and personally appointed every head of every bank around the world.

George knew that whatever this man had to say, it wouldn't be in the best interests of the people of the United States.

George responded in an open-ended manner as he gazed at Madison who had just handed him the phone. "To what do I owe this phone call?"

"Mr. President," Rothmayer said, "I believe you have something of ours, and we'd like it back."

"I don't know what you're talking about, unless you're talking about some gold, I've heard that went missing."

The aged man boldly retorted, "That gold is ours!"

George wasn't having any of it. "You stole that gold from the people of the United States and several other countries, then you melted it down to remove the markings identifying the rightful owners and you blended gold from several parts of the world together to reduce the ability to trace it through mineral detection… No, you stole it and you've been hiding it. We just took back some of what you stole. If you leave us alone, we may let you keep some of the rest."

That was a response the globalist hadn't expected. That was why he hated George and everything he stood for. George wasn't a politician, and he couldn't be bought. Politicians were so much easier to control.

The globalist financier paused briefly before saying, "We have your vice president!"

George froze. His expression went from serious to one of grave concern. But he could only play the cards he had in his hand. This was something he had discussed with Adam and Krieger during conversations about contingency plans.

George gave the response Krieger had suggested, carefully keeping his voice casual. "No, I'm guessing you don't have him, or I'd be talking with him."

The banker was smug in his response. "It's only a matter of time. We have him located, and he'll be in our custody very soon. Unfortunately, with all the terrorist activity around here, I'm hoping he doesn't get caught in cross fire and killed."

"Caught in the cross fire with whom?" the president questioned, trying to tee up an open-ended question to see what he could draw out of the man.

"We have our UN resources surrounding a location as we speak," Rothmayer said. "We have every available resource deployed to protect the vice president, but it'll be hard to ensure his safety. If you could give us the locations of our gold, we could redirect more resources to save the vice president. It would be a shame to have him end up dead at the hands of the terrorists."

The message was clear. Rothmayer had people closing in on Adam's location and they were going to kill him, and when they did, his globalist-controlled media would report that the vice president had been killed by the same terrorists that had orchestrated the other attacks in London.

* * *

Meanwhile, Mafia families systemically worked their way through cities eradicating extremist elements.

Tonight, they were in multiple cities across the nation. The agreement was that, after getting rid of HVTs in over fifty cities across the country, the Mafia could target the supporting characters who'd be next in line to take their place, as long as they were foreigners.

Ferraro had given the names to the families. The Mafia families were many things, but they didn't want to cross the federal government, especially with this president at the helm. The Mafia, along with much of the country, had awakened to what was happening to them at the hands of the globalist bankers. They understood the country was in dire straits and there weren't enough resources for the government to eradicate all their enemies, both foreign and those from within.

This was their chance to not only help the middle class, but turn back the tide of power that had begun to shift. In a day or two, the government would take control. As it was described to Ferraro, when the Government came in, the Mafia would cease any and all violent operations, which would add to the perception that the US government had come to the rescue and immediately curtailed violence.

The ongoing presence of these new forces would stay in the cities, giving even more credibility to the assurance that cities across the nation no longer had to live with the magnitude of violence that had become the norm. It wouldn't be perfect, but it would be much better than before. The Mafia and the government would see to it.

But for now, the cities across the nation were exploding with violence as organized crime and gangs were being systematically eliminated with the kind of unchecked violence that had never been seen before.

* * *

Gabby's auburn hair bounced around the back of the cap it was weaved through as she pranced down the street like an excited college girl. The front bill of the hat was pulled down just enough so cameras couldn't easily see her blue eyes. All that showed of her face was her newly glossed plump lips and her perfect jaw. Her neck and shoulders were exposed.

She and Adam had been debriefed to keep their faces looking anywhere but up. The globalists would be using their cameras with facial recognition technology to identify them. The slight shadows cast on their face by the twilight also helped make a positive identification more difficult.

Gabby had a bounce to her gait. She was doing in on purpose to made her breasts bounce. She was scared. There were cameras everywhere for the next few blocks, and authorities would be watching. She had remembered Adam's dry humorous comment that nobody would be looking at her face. She was hoping that anyone monitoring the cameras wouldn't see enough of her face to identify her and her bouncing assets would distract any onlookers from identifying them.

Gabby did a little pirouette in front of Adam. She was acting playful, but it *was* an act. She took the opportunity to look behind them. The coast was clear.

***

At the police headquarters, a young man looked at camera footage. Suddenly he noticed Gabby. Her ultra-tight top revealed her assets. Her bouncing breasts were something that instinctively commanded his full attention. He enjoyed every bounce. He looked from the front and from the side.

Then a moment later, he snapped himself out of it. He had better not get caught gawking. The world was so politically correct, he could actually lose his job. After all, his superior was a middle aged, politically correct female who, deep down inside, harbored well-taught resentment for alpha males and almost anything that accompanied their instinctive traits. She was all about the things that had led the UK down this path of globalization. He and his kind were now prisoners in their own country. He was planning his get-away to the United States, but he wasn't ready yet. He needed to save more money and he needed his job to do it.

He took his focus off Gabby and looked around for anyone matching the descriptions of the two people he was searching for.

CHAPTER 67

Alexus walked up and stood at a polite distance from Madison. Madison motioned for her to approach.

Alexus stepped forward and stood to Madison's side. She paused. The president turned to face her. She said, "We have confirmation that one of our safe houses in London was just infiltrated by UN forces."

George's startled look cut through Alexus.

"The vice president wasn't there," Alexus quickly added, her eyes big.

The edge of George's tight lips turned slightly upward.

* * *

Francisco Gonzalez stepped down onto the back of the small fishing boat and handed the man a bag full of money. The owner-captain of the boat immediately felt it was heavier than usual.

The captain looked at Gonzalez. He opened and immediately closed the bag. He didn't stop to count the money. He nodded and noticed Gabby's womanly shape and a larger figure directly behind her. He wouldn't ask their names, he never did.

Gonzalez immediately turned, offering his hand to Gabby. She stepped to the side, allowing Adam to come on board. As she stepped past Mauricio, the captain handed her a long overcoat. "Here, put this on. It gets damp out there."

It was then that the distant light of the pier shone on Adam's face. It illuminated his profile enough for the captain to realize who he was. The captain froze momentarily. "Sir, you'd best have a seat over here."

"Help me cast off," the captain said to Gonzalez. "We'd better get out of here."

Gonzalez had led Adam and Gabby out of the city. Realizing the deep state would have every harbor and airport in the area covered, Mauricio had Gonzalez take Adam and Gabby northwest. They would cut across the straits to Ireland.

Knowing the English Channel was one of the most heavily monitored waterways on the planet, they wouldn't communicate with anyone. This chartered fishing boat was their best option. They needed to get off the island.

Dawn was a few hours away. The search for Adam and Gabby was undoubtedly expanding by the hour. They had to get underway before even these ports on the west side of the country were being watched.

* * *

Krieger looked at Mauricio. "Don't say a word."

The small stealth aircraft they were packed into had taken off from an aircraft carrier. Krieger was squished into the small fuselage like a sardine. The seat was too small for him. Mauricio looked at him and eyed his seat and smirked. This time he didn't say a word, he let his smile say it all. The only other two people with them were Special Forces. They were serious. They didn't say a word. There was no pilot.

When Mauricio closed his small computer screen, there was complete blackness again. Flying at just over 20,000 feet, they headed north by northwest.

Mauricio said, "Just a few more minutes."

The light above the door began to flash. They each turned on their small oxygen supply tanks on their suits. That flashing light illuminated the small area enough so the others could see the SEAL commander had pulled down his goggles. They did the same.

When the door began to open, the frigid outside air gushed in. The countdown started in their ear pieces. A few moments later the light changed color and the four of them jumped out.

The pitch-black night and the sea below them was disorienting. It took Krieger a moment to stabilize before he glanced at his wrist watch. He watched the readout of his altitude and the direction of the intended drop zone.

When the screen on his watch flashed at two thousand feet, he pulled his chute cord. Their locating devices allowed the small vessel to quickly pick them up.

On board, each of the men stripped while the crew gathered the chutes which were put into a bag and dropped into the sea. The homing device would allow the bag to be picked up by a small stealth sub.

Krieger and the team changed into local attire. Then they donned shoulder holsters, Glocks, and waist belts. They each took several magazines.

The boat headed towards the shores of Ireland. At a safe house, they'd meet up with Adam and Gabby, and escort them to a location where they could be picked up safely.

CHAPTER 68

Seeing Krieger when she walked into the safe house brought Gabby an immediate sense of security. The boat ride to the small port on the east coast of Ireland had been uneventful. Making it to this safe house in the south was a relief.

The deep waters off the coast of Waterford would allow them to be picked up a few miles off shore by a sub, which would take them to an aircraft carrier. From there, they'd be flown back to the States.

Gabby's sense of relief was short lived. The tone being used in the adjoining room was unsettling. Gabby finally heard the SEAL commander say, "Yes sir."

The next thing Gabby heard was the unmistakable sound of Krieger walking across the floorboards of the old house.

Krieger came into the room, followed by Mauricio. "The harbor is being watched. If they know we're here, it won't take long for them to find us. This town isn't that big. We'd better get you out of here now."

Mauricio looked at the local commander. He said, "We can get them out of the city, but I hesitate to make any electronic communications." Then he looked at Gonzalez and said, "Tell me you have some options or contacts here on the island?"

Gonzalez thought for a second and then said, "Only one."

***

About four hours later, Gabby walked into the adjoining room of the suite. She took a sip of her sparkling mineral water. She had just put on new clothes. Gonzalez's contact had gotten them for her from a shop on the grounds. It was a classy, fitted outfit designed for European women about thirty. This castle sure beat the past two safe houses.

To remain as undetected as possible, Gonzalez had checked into one room with Gabby. Adam was in an adjoining room as a guest of the women who had gotten Gabby her new outfit.

It had all been set up by Gonzalez, who had contacted Sonya Snyder, an old friend he could trust. Currently, Snyder was showing Captain Kurt Kimball around the grounds. He was actually doing reconnaissance. Snyder had retired early a few years ago, and was living out her dream of being in charge of a world class hotel. Here at the Ashford Castle, she was in her element. The woman was almost fifty, but still retained traits of her stunning beauty. Her green eyes sparkled and, though her hair was now dyed, she'd chosen the dirty blond color of her youth. It suited her. It was clear that she admired Mauricio who, through a personal contact, had gotten Snyder the initial interview here at the castle.

Kimball looked around warily as they walked. The expansive grounds covered almost four hundred acres. Once the home of the famed Guinness family, this historic world class five-star castle in County Mayo dated back to 1228. The grounds and the nearby town had formed the backdrop for many famous movies, including the John Ford film, The Quiet Man, starring John Wayne and Maureen O'Hara, which had received seven Academy Award nominations. The castle also drew some of the most powerful people in the world; both Ronald Reagan and Bill Clinton had stayed there.

Snyder directed Kimball's attention to the Cong river. It fed cold water into the forty-four thousand acres of Lake Corrib, well known for its brown trout, salmon and pike fishing. After walking the grounds, Kimball was satisfied that the presence of Adam and Gabby hadn't been detected... yet.

* * *

Early that morning Kimball shook Adam awake. "Mr. Vice President, you need to get up. We have company."

Sleeping in his clothes, in case a fast getaway was needed, Adam took a deep breath and got out of bed. He immediately headed for Gabby's room where she met him at the doorway. Krieger had awakened her at the same time.

There was a knock at Adam's door.

Kimball and Davis, the two Special Forces guys, took Adam and Gabby into the other room. Krieger positioned himself to the side of the door and pulled his pistol, then looked through the peep hole. It was Sonya Snyder, Gonzalez's friend.

Krieger let her in. He put the chain back on the door when it closed.

Snyder quickly stepped farther into the room. "The authorities have the road blockaded, and they're stopping every vehicle that's coming in and out of here. Our security cameras show they've also closed off the service entrances."

Krieger looked at Adam. "They're most likely British SRR."

"SRR?" Adam questioned. He wasn't familiar with them.

They're a relatively new special forces unit of the British Army, called the Special Reconnaissance Regiment. They specialize in close target reconnaissance and surveillance with eyes on intelligence."

Sonya now understood more of what was happening, and looked at Gabby. "Well then, you don't have much time." Her gaze switched back to Krieger. "There's a woman at the front desk reviewing records of everyone who has checked in over the past two nights."

Kimball said, "That must be them. They have very highly trained men and women. She's probably a member of a special detachment acting on a tip."

Adam turned to look out the window. Gabby followed and looked out over his left shoulder.

Adam turned back to Snyder. "What are the other options to get out of here?"

Snyder looked at Gabby and then to Adam and said, "Can you ride?"

"A horse?" Adam questioned.

"Yes sir," she said, "a horse."

As Adam, Gabby, Krieger, Mauricio, Gonzalez and the two secret service agents all huddled together, Snyder looked to Krieger. She explained, "The bike trails parallel the roads, but the equestrian trails go around the lake and through the woods. They cut across the most scenic parts of the grounds."

Krieger nodded. "It's better than going on foot. Sounds like our best option. How do we get there?"

Snyder began to point out the window and say, "It's just over…"

Kimball interrupted. "It's over a hundred yards away. They'll be exposed."
Snyder hadn't thought of that. She nodded in agreement.

Kimball looked at Adam and Gabby and added, "They'll be looking for you traveling together. We'd better split you up."

***

The two special forces guys tied the sheets together.

Mauricio said, "Dump your all electronics, any type of electronic device you have. These guys have the latest state-of-the-art electronic surveillance gear to eavesdrop and track their targets."

Gabby and Adam had dumped their phones in the safe house in London, but Adam had one that Mauricio had given him when they'd got to the castle. He passed it back over to Mauricio. He looked at Adam and then turned to Krieger and said, "We need to communicate with the sub. These devices should be clean, but there's no guarantee who's been compromised."

Krieger understood Mauricio's concern... They'd need to change the pickup point... again. "Affirmative." Turning to Captain Kimball he said, "You go with Gabby, and have Davis go with Adam."

Kimball turned and stepped over to the window. He opened it slowly and looked around. He motioned for Gabby to come over. He'd go down first. She'd follow.

As Kimball was lowering himself down. Adam gave Gabby a hug and a kiss. He held her waist and said, "I'll see you in a few minutes."

Gabby smiled and said, "The next time we stay here I want to be in the Presidential Suite."

Adam smiled, laughed and said, "Absolutely, as it should be... and we'll do some fishing."

"Of course." With that Gabby began to let herself down the sheet to the ground, immediately followed by Gonzalez. The SRR would be looking for two people, so Krieger had put the three of them together. He hoped that, with Gonzalez's stature, it would help them be overlooked.

Adam quickly changed again and Krieger handed him a hat.

"Wear this," Krieger said, "and keep your head down. Snyder, can you escort the vice president to the stables? Our best chance for him to get there is if he walks with you."

Snyder nodded. "Sure."

"When you get there, get the vice president and Gabby mounted up, and show them where to go. Shit, where do we meet up with them?"

Snyder thought for a second than had an idea. "There's a small town just on the other side of the estate. One of the equestrian trails comes out there. I can mark up a map, and you can meet them there."

"Sounds good," Krieger said.

Adam put on his hat and said to Snyder, "Sonya, you ready?"

"Ready as I'll ever be," she said with some trepidation. Then she took a breath and, with more confidence said, "Let's do this, sir."

Adam took a step towards the door and then turned to Krieger. "Bill, how are you getting out?"

Krieger had no misconceptions about his ability to make a stealthy getaway in broad daylight, so for better or worse, he had formulated a plan.

"I have an alternate plan… You'd better get going sir."

Adam knew they only had minutes, so he nodded, opened the door and headed out with Snyder.

CHAPTER 69

"How in the hell did they track that shipment?" President George Carnegie snapped at the General who was monitoring the extraction of the gold from the states.

The General hesitated with his response. The two largest shipments of gold were free and clear. However, the Pennsylvania, which was headed home with its hull full of gold, had been diverted to pick up the vice president. Another shipment that was on a stealth ship, had driven directly into an oil tanker undetected. The UN forces were currently tracking two decoy ships. The largest air shipment was also free and clear, and on its way to safety. Though this shipment was sizeable, it wasn't the largest by any means and the president had been apprised that most likely they all wouldn't get through.

The General relented. "We don't know how they traced it, hell they may have just used some deductive reasoning. We don't have much time, so let's focus on what we can do about it. They don't have it yet."

Dr. Owen's team had intercepted the communication that the SAS, Special Air Services, was going to catch up to the plane and force it down. When this British special services unit forced the plane down, they'd not only confiscate the gold, they'd use the capture as a political tool to whatever ends they could. The president knew the agenda of the globalists was to get him out of office before he got more done for the nation.

The president got the feeling that the General had something in mind. "You're right General; what are our options?"

The General had Owen hook him into another area of the Area 51 base, then he turned to the president. "They're tracking the plane by its transponder. We prepared for this, if it's not too late."

George had been briefed on the military's technology to change the transponder signals that identify aircraft, but he hadn't ever witnessed its use.

A moment later, the confirmation came through the speaker. They could do it.

The General explained, "We had each plane fly a path parallel to commercial flights. Hold on, this'll take a minute."

As the president and Madison listened, the General gave the orders and then listened as the plane began to encroach on another plane flying towards the US. Then, when the planes were relatively close, a woman's voice directed them by saying, "Switch."

There was a slight jump on the screen they were all looking at, and everything appeared normal. One plane headed south west, and the two images of the planes got farther apart on the screen. The General hadn't given an indication of success or failure.

Finally, the General listened with relief as the woman said, "It looks good from this end General, and it appears the SAS is following the decoy."

The General turned to George and said, "There you go Mr. President, another flight of gold is safely on its way home."

Madison hadn't put all of the pieces together. "General, so what just happened?"

"The SAS suspected our plane had gold in it and diverted a few of their fighters to intercept it and force it to land. So, we had a decoy plane already identified. When we got the word, our plane moved closer to the decoy plane and we switched their transponder signals."

"That's when we saw the blip on the screen?" Madison asked.

"Yes, Senator. Then our plane peeled off and resumed its original course under a different transponder signal. We just had to wait to ensure the fighters were following the decoy."

"Won't they know something's up when they force one of our military planes to land?" Madison asked.

"Well, it's not actually one of our planes." After a short hesitation, the General said, "It's a civilian plane."

"A civilian plane, isn't that…"

The General interrupted Madison in mid-sentence. "It's mostly full of media people who were returning from London."

George's forehead creased. "Don't you think I have enough problems with those media people?"

The General said, "We didn't plan it that way sir, but when we looked at the most viable flights to establish as decoys, this flight was the best choice for this plane and, well, we thought it was fitting. It must be fate. Maybe it's a good tweet in the making."

The president's smile could be seen half way across the room as he shook his head.

Madison nodded and said, "Well, good planning General. Gabby would be proud."

The president looked at the General. "Speaking of Gabby, has anyone heard from them?"

* * *

Gabby moved seamlessly around the stable area. She had been brought up around horses in rural Maine she knew what she needed to do. As soon as Adam and Sonya entered the stable, Sonya grabbed a map of the estate from the desk. She began highlighting the route. Gabby, noticing the look on Adam's face, began helping him.

A moment later, Sonya walked swiftly up to Adam and said, "Here, take this route. It'll lead you to the back of a small tavern."

Gonzalez added, "Mauricio and Krieger will meet you there with a car."

With that, Gabby mounted a huge chestnut and Adam mounted a black gelding a half a hand smaller.

The second Special Forces agent came into the barn. "The Colonel told me to cover you."

Kimball said, "Good, we can use the help. You follow me. Grab a horse."

Captain Kimball mounted a beautiful bay mare and said to Adam and Gabby, "We'll go at a brisk walk until we hit the woods. As soon as you're out of sight, get out of here as fast as you can. We'll stay back and cover your tracks. We'll cut across the path a few times. If anyone's following, maybe it'll slow them down."

In a flash, the three of them were off.

CHAPTER 70

As soon as they hit the woods, the Captain looked back. A few people were walking towards the stable. One was rather fit and large. You didn't see those kinds of guys at a castle. He continued into the woods until he came to the first fork in the trail. He and his partner dismounted. They stripped branches from a large tree and wiped the tracks clean from Adam and Gabby's horses. Then they turned right, went down the trail about fifty yards, then went off the trail, before doubling back and coming out at the fork again, where they went right again. Their horses were leaving hoof prints that now gave the impression that four horses went right.

***

The British SAS had deployed their entire D squadron of approximately sixty-five men and women to Ireland. Commanded by a Major, one of four troops was on the castle grounds. They were being commanded by a Captain. One of the other troops had been tasked with surrounding the castle grounds. The two remaining troops were following up on other leads.

***

Adam and Gabby had pulled up to the back of the bar. From the edge of the woods, they watched for vehicle pulling up that might be Mauricio or Krieger. None had shown up yet.

A moment later, the captain pulled his mare to a stop. He listened and said, "They're behind us."

The captain dismounted and pulled out his cell phone and dialed Mauricio.

He looked at Adam. "He'll be here in a few minutes, but we don't have that much time, these guys will be here in a minute," referring to whoever it was chasing them on horseback.

Gabby dismounted and wrapped her steed's bridle around the bridle post. She walked directly towards a young couple coming out of the bar.

A moment later, the couple looked at each other and nodded. Gabby reached into her pocket and handed them some money.

Walking up to Adam she said, "Okay hun, they've agreed to take our horses back to the estate for us so we can go in and have a few drinks. I gave them some money for their troubles and so they can get a ride back."

Adam's eyes got a little wider and he smiled and dismounted. "You ride pretty good?"

"Been riding our whole life," the one young Irish lad said as he and his companion both nodded.

As the two mounted their horses, Gabby added, "We do appreciate this. Like I said, the castle has strict rules against drinking and riding." Then Gabby added, "Oh, they're all warmed up, and this one really runs."

The young man looked at the Captain, realizing they were questioning his role. The Captain said, "Take that trail to the left and run them as hard as you want right now." Then changing up his tone to one a little sterner, he added, "But cool them down as you get to the castle."

The young man gleefully said, "Yes sir," and then turned to Gabby and Adam. "Thank you." He turned to his female companion, saying something, and she took off first, with him in chase.

The captain heard the thunder of approaching hooves. He turned to Adam and said, "Stay out of sight until Mauricio gets here."

Kimball and Davis rode off with the plan to catch up to the two guys and see if he could bait them into a race back towards the castle.

***

Krieger turned right into the pub, slowing as he went to the back. *I don't see any horses.*

A moment later he saw Adam's silhouette emerge from the concealment of a spruce tree.

Adam immediately recognized Krieger. He was squished into the small vehicle.

Just as Krieger stopped, another vehicle came skidding to a stop on the dirt parking lot, inches behind Krieger's vehicle. Mauricio bounced out of it before Krieger could pry himself from behind the wheel with a groan.

Krieger looked around as he approached Adam. "Sir, it's damned good to see you."

"Well, the feeling is mutual. How'd they ID me?" Adam asked.

"Somehow they got a lead that we may be at the castle," Mauricio answered. "Then they finally got enough of your face from when you mounted the horse at the stable."

"The stable?" Adam questioned. He had been extremely careful not to look up everywhere else.

"Sir, this is Europe, they have cameras everywhere." Mauricio knew it wasn't Adam's fault. It had only been a matter of time.

Krieger wanted to get moving. "So, here's the situation. We have a Special Ops team on their way, but they won't be able to get to your extraction point for about two hours and it'll take you about two hours to get there. Until then, it's the four of us, so we're going to have to split up."

"Split up?" Gabby questioned. "Colonel, I'm beginning to get the feeling that you don't like our company."

Krieger always appreciated Gabby. "Understood ma'am, but it's more the company you draw. The good news is we've got you a clean phone." He motioned to Mauricio, who handed Gabby a small phone in an unusual looking case.

Mauricio explained, "At least this time you'll be able to contact us, but realize they're tracking every electronic communication in this area right now, so don't use it unless it's an emergency. After you use it, even though it's encrypted, they'll have your location, so they'll be able to pinpoint you; it won't be long until you have company."

As Gabby started to open the case, Mauricio explained, "Keep the phone in that case before and after you use it. These guys have some of the best tracking technology available and that bag is designed to mask the signal. For most tracking technology, this case masks the phone, but then again, for every technology there's a counter technology, so that's why you should only use it if you absolutely have to."

"Understood," Gabby said as she secured the phone back in its case and put it in the pocket of her tight jeans.

"So, what's the plan?" Adam questioned.

Krieger had had a new extraction point chosen until they'd been compromised at the castle, necessitating yet another change. "While you drive to the new extraction point, we'll divert them to the location on the west coast. That way, while you're going east, we'll draw them west. We have an unsecure phone with us. We're going to take this second car and go west and begin communicating. That should match all the intelligence they currently have."

Mauricio handed Adam a map. There was already a circle on it. Mauricio pulled out a highlighter and drew another circle. He said, "We're here. You go east and follow this road about five miles and take your first right on 334, then your next right on 83. Just follow the highlight south and east and it'll take you right there. It's deep there, so the sub will be able to get close. There are only two numbers programmed into the phone, one is ours and the other will get you in contact with the operations commander. They should meet you in the parking lot, but just in case, their number is also in the phone."

Mauricio then handed Gabby another small device. "Take this. It'll show you a map just like directions on your cell phone, but it'll identify official vehicles, like police and official military vehicles. They'll be shown as a red dot." He then emphasized, "It won't show every under-cover vehicle from agencies like MI6, but it'll help."

Gabby took the device. "Thank you."

"Roger that," Adam said to Mauricio. He turned to Krieger and asked, "Is there anything else we need to know?"

"You have plenty of gas," Krieger said, "so don't stop for anything. Keep your heads down and drive normally. This car is from a friend, so it won't be reported stolen. You shouldn't have any issues. Just leave the keys in it when you get there. A small task force will meet you and get you down to the sub, but again they'll be just getting there about the time you do."

"What about you?" Gabby questioned.

"We plan on being there too. But don't worry about us, and don't wait for us. We'll improvise as need be. You just get on that sub."

Adam replied, "Understood." He knew Krieger would do whatever he could to divert the Special Reconnaissance Regiment towards himself.

Krieger replied, "Good luck sir."

After watching Adam and Gabby jump in their little car and head east, Krieger and Mauricio got in their vehicle and sped off to the west.

Adam gave the map to Gabby. "We're looking for the right turn."

Gabby looked at the map and said, "We're going to the Cliffs of Moore."

CHAPTER 71

Adam had just angled off to the right on route 83 when he and Gabby saw two cars speeding in the direction they had just come from. Gabby turned around and looked behind them. They weren't being followed. She turned back around and said, "That was a little too close for comfort."

The first half hour was tense though uneventful.

It was at about that point Adam and Gabby had their first indication that things were beginning to heat up.

Gabby studied the screen of the device Mauricio had given her. She said to Adam, "There's one of these red dots coming our way."

"How far out?"

"It could be two miles."

Adam knew neither of them had ever used the device before. The vehicle would drive right past them on this two-lane road. Even if Adam and Gabby kept their heads down, there was no guarantee they wouldn't rouse a second look. Adam thought it'd be best to hide, but he didn't see a viable option. He pushed the gas pedal to the floor.

"They look to be less than a mile out," Gabby said.

"Affirmative," Adam said as he navigated a turn as fast as he could. Then, up on the right, he saw a truck pulled over. He could see the highway up ahead in the distance. He'd never make the highway so he focused on the truck while looking for the vehicle coming over the horizon.

He hugged the right side of the road. As he approached the pull off, he followed the truck's path and slowed. The terrain dropped down several feet on the right. Adam pulled within inches of the truck's right tire. As he slowed to a crawl, Adam asked, "How much space do I have over there?"

Gabby opened her door a crack to look down. "About a foot."

Gabby held the tracking device up to Adam. He nodded, cracked his window and then inched forward. He could hear the gravel crunching below the weight of the tires. He could also hear an approaching vehicle.

Gabby noticed he was gripping the steering wheel tighter.

When the sound of the approaching vehicle reached the point where it was almost parallel with the truck, he had reached the front bumper. Adam cut it in front of the truck as close as he could and stopped.

The sound of the car faded in the distance. Gabby saw on the screen that the vehicle had continued.

She smiled. "Good job. I'm impressed."

He looked back at her. His grip relaxed and he smiled and got back on the road.

On the highway, Adam hid on the right side of two trucks as other cars approached, just in case. They were now half way to the extraction point.

Heading into Clarinbridge, Gabby looked as the screen and said, "There's another official vehicle behind us. It looks like there's a few more just appearing on the screen in front of us."

"How close are they?"

"This is crazy," Gabby said. "The ones up ahead are a few miles out and the one behind us is maybe a mile."

"Is he gaining?"

Gabby studied the screen for a few seconds and then gasped and nodded, saying, "He must be moving quick, because he's gaining fast."

Adam had been following Krieger's directions and going the speed limit, but now wasn't time to throw caution to the wind. Again, he pushed the gas pedal to the floor.

"How far?"

"Just under a mile. Maybe three quarters." Gabby turned around and looked out the rear window. "No sight of them yet."

Adam navigated a few turns as quickly as he dared. "Keep an eye out over the ridges."

Gabby was watching behind them when Adam said, "We're coming into the town. I'm going to have to slow down. Where are the other vehicles?"

"There's one on the far side of town," Gabby said, "and another one that looks like it's in town, but neither of those are moving. They must be parked."

"That makes sense. They're probably watching all the entrances and exits from the towns. The one behind us, who knows. It might have been following a lead out of town or something."

"Well he's gaining quickly." As Adam crested a hill, Gabby caught a brief glimpse of the vehicle behind them. Its lights were flashing.

She turned back around as they entered the town.

"I don't see another vehicle on this end of town, do you?"

She looked at her device. "No."

Adam slowed. "Let's hope they were watching this end of town and are heading back to their position."

Gabby agreed and added, "Or they have seen us and want to check us out."

"Good point," Adam said. "We need to get off this road before they catch up to us."

"There's only two other routes out of town," Gabby said. "And they both have surveillance."

"Look for somewhere to hide, anywhere."

Gabby looked at the row of buildings to their right. They must have been over a hundred years old.

Suddenly, Adam screeched on the brakes and skidded. He took a hard right into a parking lot.

He said, "Here, it's a good luck sign."

"What good luck sign?" Gabby looked around.

"Paddy Burke's restaurant and bar," Adam said. He straightened the car, then quickly turned right again and came to a complete stop.

"Shit, no place to hide," he said. He looked back at the road. "They'll be able to see us."

Gabby glanced back and realized he was right. She looked at her screen and then out of her window. In the distance she saw lights reflecting off windows. "They're coming."

Adam needed to react. The only place to go was down to the Clarinbridge River… by steps. A moment later Gabby realized what he was doing.

Adam said, "Hold on." The tiny car bounded down the steps, jostling them around. When he reached the bottom, Adam turned and looked out his window. "Shit, can they still see us?"

Adam turned right and there was a small boat ramp. "This is going to be close," he said. He turned left down the boat ramp.

"What are you doing?" Gabby screamed. She eyed the creek bed.

"They can still see us," he said.

Hitting the creek bed was like hitting a large pot hole. Water splashed and Adam turned left. The car bounced up and down as Adam navigated his way the fifty yards upstream. The creek bed was mostly dry, with an inch or two of water in places.

"If we can get under the bridge," Adam said, "they'll pass right over us."

The car bounced and jolted perilously. They both hoped it would keep moving. Wipers slapped at the splashing water. Adam pulled into the small opening under the bridge, and a moment later, the authorities passed overhead.

Gabby's screen showed the car pass overhead, then it turned around and passed back in the direction it had come from.

Adam didn't move.

Gabby said, "Shouldn't we get out of here?"

"That's what I'm thinking about," Adam said. "Let's think this through. They have a car stationed at the edge of the town in all three directions. They'll see us leave."

"So, we hole up here for a while?" she asked.

"We can't."

Adam's tone startled Gabby. She knew he was processing his thoughts, so she just let him think for another few seconds then he asked, "How far out of town are they?"

Gabby looked at the screen and held it so Adam could see. "It looks like less than a mile."

"See, there, they're just beyond that road going north east. If I remember right there was another road going northeast just before we pulled into town."

Gabby moved the map and pointed and said, "There it is. I remember passing it."

Adam looked at her and said, "It's time for you to send a text to Mauricio."

"A text? Won't they be able to trace it?"

"Absolutely, I'm counting on it." He looked in her eyes. "Text exactly that we just turned northeast out of Clarinbridge and are heading towards our rendezvous point."

Gabby got it. "They won't know which road we took, and they'll each take one of the roads."

"Exactly."

"You sure about this?" Gabby questioned.

"Well, the way I see it, if they believe the car pulling into town could have been us, we have less than two more minutes before they come looking for us. In this town, I don't see many places to hide."

Gabby's eyes got bigger. She didn't need any further convincing. She reached into her pocket and pulled out the phone. She opened it and sent a text to Mauricio, then she put the phone back.

Gabby watched her screen to see if the cars moved, and few minutes later, the parked vehicles begin to move. They each took a road to the north east.

She smiled and looked at Adam. "It worked."

They pulled out from beneath the bridge, their wheels spinning. Water splashed again as they bounced out of the dried creek bed. A few people were walking out of the bar. They had watched Adam pull out of the dried creek bed. They laughed and Adam waved and smiled as he passed them. He took a right on the road and was back on course.

"So, do you think we'll make it to the extraction point before they catch on?" Gabby asked after a few minutes of silence.

"I wouldn't count on it," Adam said. As soon as he said it, he realized he should have chosen his words more carefully. In his peripheral vision he could see the comment made Gabby flinch. Then he decided he'd better get her ready for what might happen. "I figure that if they believe we were five minutes out of town, then it would take them at least fifteen minutes to catch up to us. Then they'll probably go another few miles before realizing we may not be in front of them. They'll be communicating with their command the whole time and, about that time, they'll decide we may have slipped by them and they'll most likely send vehicles in this direction."

Just then Adam saw a road sign coming up. It read, County Clare. "So, what's the next town?"

"It's Bealaclugga. It's only a few miles up ahead."

Adam slowed his speeding vehicle as they approached the town. He was surprised to see there were no authorities in sight.

Gabby glanced between her screen and the road ahead. "It looks clear." A moment later she saw the town and, realizing how small it was said, "Maybe they don't have their own police force here."

"That could be," Adam said as he cautiously looked around.

The road was lined with neat stone walls. Gabby looked at the quaint homes. "Nice town."

Adam said, "Very nice." Then his tone changed and he pushed the gas pedal to the floor. "Now let's get out of here."

Upon exiting town and making it through one more town, Adam asked, "How far to the next town?"

"Lisdoonvarna, it's about ten minutes up ahead."

The silence after Gabby's explanation sent Adam's senses skyrocketing. "What's wrong?"

She kept looking and then said, "This one's a lot bigger. I mean, it's a real town. This one won't be as easy."

CHAPTER 72

"Any word on Adam?" the president asked as Air Force One reached cruising altitude.

The president was heading back to DC, and he was becoming increasingly concerned. He knew the reason Adam was being hunted by the globalists was because if they could capture him, they could use him as leverage to force the president to return the gold and the money that had been transferred to pay off the national debt. Those bastards had actually stolen over thirty trillion dollars from the US treasury, and the president had even tried to let them keep the rest of it if they walked away. But they were just too greedy. They wanted it all, including control of the whole country. If they captured Adam, George had no doubt they would most likely kill him. Then they'd have fake stories broadcast around the globe about how terrorists had killed the vice president.

Madison had just received the latest information on Adam. She said, "Sir, he's heading towards the alternative extraction point. But we believe he's been spotted."

"What can we do?"

"We've contacted Colonel Krieger and the General, and they're working with Admiral Halsey." Madison's face was grim. "They are doing everything within their power."

"Balls to the walls Halsey," The president said. "He'll get 'er done."

Madison added, "My line is open. They'll keep me informed about any developments."

George nodded. "Good. Now what about the status of the rest of the mission?"

***

Adam slowed to the speed limit as he entered Lisdoonvarna. "Here we go."

They drove down the picturesque main street of the town. Shops, taverns and hotels were painted in bright yellows, reds, blues, orange, lavender, purple and green.

Adam scanned every parking lot and side road.

"Keep your eyes peeled," he said.

"I am," Gabby said as they passed the Matchmaker Bar. Gabby had noticed the statue of the couple and signs that said the matchmaking festival was Europe's biggest singles event.

"There's a lot to look at."

As they passed by the sign Gabby said, "Nice town. It must be packed during the festival."

"I guess so," Adam said. His head swiveled from side to side.

"Look out," Gabby screamed suddenly as a box truck came through the narrow alley way between two buildings.

Adam pushed the pedal to the floor, but the small engine wasn't enough to pull them out of the way fast enough. The truck's bumper hit the rear quarter panel directly behind Gabby, and the impact sent the small car spinning in a full circle. The rear driver's side quarter panel hit a rock wall hard and they stopped.

"Get out!" Adam pushed at Gabby's shoulder as he shouted.

Gabby's door was jammed. She put her shoulder into it, to no avail.

Adam saw the door of the truck opening. "This way," he screamed, flinging his door open.

She unbuckled her seat belt, and he reached for her two hands. She clasped tightly to his wrists, and he clasped onto hers, his back arched as he pulled.

She moved her legs as fast as she could and crawled towards his open door.

They both landed on the ground, with the car between them and the truck.

Their small vehicle was suddenly riddled with bullets, and glass and debris flew.

"Over the wall!" Gabby yelled.

They dove over the short rock wall behind them, and suddenly, another box truck clipped Adam and Gabby's vehicle, and rammed into the box truck that had hit them.

They hadn't noticed the truck coming in from the north.

There was a car behind it, and men poured out of the front and back of the new truck on the scene, unleashing hell on the box truck so furiously that Adam wrapped his arms and a leg around Gabby. Fragments of rock were flying everywhere.

Then there was a moment of silence before two men approached in full tactical gear.

Adam and Gabby were trapped.

They couldn't move fast enough to get away. Adam looked up into the barrel of an automatic weapon.

"Mr. Vice President, I presume?"

"Yes."

"I'm Sergeant Kelly, and this is Ahola. We're from the Army Ranger Wing of the Irish Special Operations Force."

Adam and Gabby slowly got up, and climbed back over the rock wall.

A woman dressed in full tactical gear walked briskly up to Kelly and handed him some identification she'd taken off one of the men that had been shooting at Adam and Gabby.

"Who are they?" Gabby asked.

It was then that Kimball walked up, and Gabby's eyes widened. The two navy SEALs had come back; they'd been in the small car behind the truck.

Kelly extended his arm and handed Kimball the ID.

Kimball looked at it, and then at the vice president. "They're British SAS, sir. Disguised as locals. The president has information that they were going to assassinate you and set it up as a terrorist attack."

"Captain, it's good to see you," Adam grimaced noticeably as he reached out a hand. He was bleeding.

"Are you hit?" Gabby pulled up Adam's shirt to see blood coming out of his side. There appeared to be an entrance and exit wound.

Gabby looked at Kimball. "Can you get us out of here now?"

A medic immediately stepped up to look at Adam's side.

"It's not that simple ma'am," Kelly said. "We don't know who to trust. All of the police and authorities have been directed to report any sight of you.

That'll allow the globalists to send in more thugs like these. We need to get you two off the island as fast as possible."

The medic who had looked at Adam's side said, "It's a fragment sir. Hurts like hell, I'm sure, but you'll be all right."

He opened a medical pack and ripped open a bag of blood clot.

"It went right through. This will stop the bleeding," the medic said. "Take a deep breath, sir."

Adam took a deep breath.

"He's been shot? It's a bullet wound?" Gabby said.

"It appears to be a fragment of a bullet," the medic explained. "You'll be alright, sir. About forty stitches, maybe less."

He poured on the blood clot, and Adam grimaced. The medic repeated the same movements on the back side of the wound, then gingerly began to wrap Adam's mid-section. It was obvious he was being cautious with the vice president. Gabby reached out and grabbed the wrapping. "Here, let me do that. Don't worry, he won't break."

She yanked hard and began to wrap the wound tightly.

Adam looked at her. He could tell she was concerned. "Did I ever tell you that you've got a perfect nose?"

She mocked his comment with a smile. Then she gave an abrupt extra tight pull on the dressing, securing it. He gasped.

She looked up at him and said, "Did I ever tell you to suck it up?" Then she looked up at Kimball. "What's our next move?"

The captain had just received a report in his ear piece; authorities were closing in. He looked around and saw onlookers beginning to gather. "We better get going. Get in the truck."

Adam and Gabby hurried to the passenger side of the truck and the Irish Special Operation Sergeant said, "Head out of town, and with any luck, we'll meet you at the cliffs."

"Affirmative," the Captain said, and he got in the truck, then backed up onto the sidewalk and cut the wheel hard left and proceeded south.

"How much further?" Adam asked as he looked out the large side mirror. He didn't see anyone following them.

"Just a few miles, but we won't make it." The Captain abruptly turned down a side street and hid the truck behind a bar.

Kimball said, "Get out."

Kimball had left the truck running. He got out and ran back towards the rear. He threw open the door, turned to Adam and said, "Look out, sir."

Adam and Gabby looked up and saw a small car squeezed into the back of the truck. The side mirrors had been folded to get it in. The Captain hurried to slide two ramps out, and latched them in place on the rear of the truck. Then jumped into the rear of the truck and climbed over the trunk of the small car. From the top of the car and squeezed himself in the driver's window, started up the car, backed it out of the truck and got out. He had left the door open.

The Captain spoke fast. "Sir, they've got a description of the truck. There's no way we'd make it to the extraction point. You go right back to the street and get out of here. Continue north. The extraction point is only a few miles up ahead, but they're heading this way. There are coats in the back seat, put them on when you get out of the car... and good luck."

"Doesn't anyone want to hang around us for all the fun?" Gabby said as she got in.

Adam knew the Captain would probably drive north to draw off the authorities, then if there was time, he'd probably ditch the truck and take off by foot. Adam's eyes expressed all of that and the Captain understood when Adam held out his hand and said, "Good luck, Captain."

"You too, sir," Kimball said.

Adam jumped in and squealed the tires of the small car as he pulled back on to the road.

As they passed over another immaculately maintained stone bridge, they could see the cliffs to their right.

A few minutes later, Adam pulled into the parking lot on the left side of the road. There were a few security officials mulling around talking.

Gabby looked over at them. "They're not paying attention to us."

"Let's hope not," Adam responded as he looked for a parking space.

After Adam parked the car, Gabby turned around and reached in the back seat. She pulled out the two waxed cotton shell jackets by J. Barbour & Sons of England. They'd fit in perfectly.

"Here, take this, and make sure you look down," she said as she handed a jacket to Adam.

After getting out, Gabby put her arms through the classic European jacket. She kept her head down, pulled up the collar, and fluffed her hair around it. The jacket concealed her tightly fitted clothing. Someone would have to be looking directly at her to see her jaw line.

Adam got out of the car and flung his coat over his right shoulder, concealing the side of his face. He closed the car door.

They walked to the back of the car, and looked up.

Gabby positioned herself on Adam's right, and they began walking towards the path. All they had to do was walk down the sparsely traveled coastal walking trail, which wound its way down the north side of the cliffs. On the shore a small skiff would pick them up and take them out to deep enough water. There, with the help of a pair of Navy SEAL divers, they'd be escorted off the far side of the boat, out of sight from anyone on shore, and safely be taken below water to the submarine which would transport them to the carrier. From there, they'd be flown stateside.

The trail was steep and the path was narrow. Walking was a challenge. Adam and Gabby watched their every step. They paid little attention to the breathtaking views of majestic cliffs, the Aran Islands or Galway Bay.

Hope built in Gabby's mind as they descended, until she looked down the path and caught a glimpse of a woman walking up. The woman had looked directly at them.

A shiver of fear surged through Gabby's body like a lightning bolt. It was only a glimpse, but Gabby knew what she saw. She squeezed Adam's hand.

"I recognize that woman walking up the path," Gabby said. Then Gabby caught a better look at her, "She's one of the women agents from the safe house in London."

The woman's head was down as she approached.

Now, just a few feet away, Gabby was sure it was the woman from the safe house in London, the woman who had given her the skimpy clothes as a disguise to get out of London. She was one of Francisco Gonzalez's people.

The female agent was walking up the path with a sense of urgency. When Adam noticed her, she held up her index finger and pressed it against her lips. She was motioning for them not to speak. The woman looked behind Adam and Gabby. Seeing no one, she stepped close. The three huddled.

"They have listening equipment," she said.

Adam nodded once.

"Change of plan."

Gabby, rolled her eyes, *another one.*

"The shores are being patrolled, it's no good," the agent whispered. "And the SAS are coming up the path behind me. Turn around and walk quickly."

This wasn't shaping up to be the quick getaway they had planned. Adam quickly processed what was happening. The SAS was closing the parameter on their whereabouts, and if they found him, they'd most likely have a task force dressed up as terrorists to either kidnap him to use him as leverage to get their stolen money and gold back. Then they'd probably just kill him.

"Where do we go when we get up top?" Adam questioned.

"Mauricio's figuring out a way to get you off this rock." Rock was their term for the island.

Just then her phone beeped with an incoming text. It read, 'Meet me at the tower.'

"Head towards the tower. It's back up the trail to your right." The woman added, "Sir... be ready,"

Adam nodded.

"Be ready for what?" Gabby asked as she looked at Adam.

Adam clasped Gabby's upper arm, directing her to start walking back up the path.

"Anything," was all he said.

As the path curved, Adam looked down the trail. He could see a sharp turn about fifty yards down the path. There wasn't a soul in sight.

But looking past that, Adam noticed another bend a few hundred yards further. The men coming up the trail were agile, and they were moving swiftly. They were big. He put one hand on Gabby's waist and another on her back. He got close and quietly urged Gabby on. "Walk faster."

* * *

Madison was being diligent to ensure the president wasn't on the line. He stood next to her as she played the middleman. The lines of communication should be secure, but the deep state was everywhere. She was talking with Krieger and Mauricio, because they didn't want George on any of these emergency communications. If she was compromised, at least the deep state would have nothing on George for the upcoming election.

At first, it had appeared that Adam's extraction from Ireland was going to be quick and uneventful. Now, after two changes in the extraction point, Adam was on foot, being hunted. The small SEAL teams had done a good job before. But everyone was hesitant to engage anyone not directly under control of Krieger. For that reason, the president had some of the special forces teams that were heading stateside diverted to secure the vice president and Gabby. The teams would be there very quickly. The question was, would it be quick enough?

Exhausted from the stress, Madison finally hung up. It was up to the teams now.

Air Force One was about to descend. They would be at Andrews Air Force Base soon.

CHAPTER 73

Adam had just looked back, and had seen large men running up the path. "They see us," he said. "Run!"

Adam and Gabby reached the top of the path. There was an area off the shoulder of the road where people could congregate.

Gabby stopped. She had overheard a young woman tell the man she was with, "It'd be nice to take the ferry, but it's a little chilly."

Gabby walked up to the woman, smiled and said, "Here, why don't you take my jacket?"

"What?" the woman replied.

Adam froze.

"We're catching a flight out and our luggage is already at the weight limit. We have our regular coats in the car. It'll cost us as much to ship these as it would to buy new ones."

Gabby took off the coat and held it for the woman saying, "Here, try it on."

The woman looked at her boyfriend, smiled and put her arm in. The fit was fairly good.

Gabby smiled and said, "Turn up the collar. It'll keep the wind off."

The woman did and her eyes lit up as she looked at the man she was with.

"It's yours. We've got to run and catch a flight," Gabby said.

Adam followed her lead. "Here, take mine," he said. "They're almost a matching set."

The young man reached out and grabbed the jacket. "You sure?"

"Absolutely."

Recognizing the value, the young man immediately took the coat and swung it over his shoulder like Adam had.

Gabby pretended to check the time. Looking at the young woman who was almost gleeful, Gabby added, "You know, if you run, you can still make the next ferry tour of the cliffs. If you miss it, you'll have to wait three hours for the next one."

She looked at her man and said, "We can make it, let's go." Then she turned to Gabby and said, "Thank you so much."

The young man offered his hand to Adam. He made eye contact and the young man froze. He was thinking he was having deja vu.

Luckily, the woman touched the young man, her signal to get going. He looked at her, then with final 'thank you's, they ran off towards to the left to catch the ferry.

Adam and Gabby turned right. It was over a mile to the tower. Adam noticed a few parked bicycles, rentals he had noticed before. One was a three-wheeler for two. He ran up to it, and Gabby jumped on behind him, and they headed towards the tower. Neither of them looked back.

When they were fifty yards up the road, the SAS turned left towards the young couple who had taken their jackets.

* * *

The President and Madison were on the phone continuously as they drove to the White House.

Madison had been keeping tabs on Ferraro's progress through Melissa.

Melissa was commanding operations in several cities. Ferraro and his team were purging foreigners who were aligned with the globalists. It was a constant blur of activity.

The president had been in contact with John and the judges, who were allowing searches of key deep state operations.

Madison had also been in contact with the economic mastermind group. Their spokesperson, Haley, had kept Madison informed. They had their plans drafted and were just getting the presentation together. They'd be ready to present to the President within a day or two.

George had been working with other world leaders, and he wasn't the only one wanting to get rid of the globalists. Some leaders were shocked that the entire debt owed to them by the US had been paid off. Other deals with world leaders entailed shipments of gold in exchange for favors.

All Federal Reserves had been locked down. The private security agencies had been taken out, and the Marines and Army were securing the locations. There was a lockdown. Nothing was going out and nothing was going to go in until the gold arrived.

The president had deployed his teams of people to visit politicians. Most of the conversations started with the politician wanting to know what George wanted. The team of two would present audio, video and written evidence from the NSA database and other sources showing a variety of major infractions by the politician, including treason, insider trading, conspiring to overthrow the government and much more. The teams would explain that either a military team would enter the building and arrest them and they'd be prosecuted, or they could cooperate one hundred percent and pass bills that were already drafted to become laws. Without change, the president wanted an immediate passage of a surplus amendment to the constitution, funding the border wall, the repealing of the seventeenth amendment, and more. The visits usually ended with the message from the president assuring the politician that they would be able to retain their position and retire immediately after they cooperated fully. A few of the politicians referenced the dead politicians found at Arlington. No one knew anything about that, but it did appear to weigh on these politicians.

George had received information that a few final arrangements for gold were complete…

The entire time, Madison kept waiting for more communications on the dynamic situation of the vice president.

Now it was all coming down to one thing.

The biggest risk out there was still the safety of Adam. From a personal, political and economic standpoint, George and the country needed Adam to escape.

* * *

Adam heard a vehicle screech to a stop that had just passed them as it headed south. They'd been spotted.

"Pedal!" he yelled out to Gabby.

With stone walls on each side of the narrow two-lane road, there was only a small area for bikes on the edge of the road. Adam knew the car would have to back up at least once to navigate the U-turn. He eyed an opening in the stone wall.

Horns started blaring behind them.

Adam took a right turn into the Burren Way Trail entrance. The narrow entrance was just wide enough for a car to squeeze through. Up ahead, he could see another opening to a dirt path. A car couldn't navigate through that. They were so close to the ocean.

Adam took a left on the narrow dirt trail. He down shifted and they labored up the incline. He stood and pumped the pedals and his hands squeezed the handle bars. He pulled down to exert as much force on the pedals as possible. A sign had said 'walking trail.'

It was obvious that was all this trail was suited for. He was in first gear. They'd have been better with a mountain bike.

Gabby heard a car skid to a stop on the gravel and she looked back. Maybe three hundred yards away, men dressed in plain clothes were getting out. Their plain clothes were so no government would be blamed for Adam's kidnapping or murder.

When the first few shots were fired, Adam knew they'd come from a semi-automatic weapon. The sound of lead whizzing by was too close. Just ahead of them was a hill, and Adam pedaled harder than he ever had.

They disappeared over the crest of the hill. As Adam and Gabby gained speed, the bike bounced around wildly.

To their right, the majestic cliffs fell off to the sea. There was no way to navigate down those cliffs without rappelling.

Hills and valleys with rambling fields to their left. Taking the bike off the trail wasn't an option. The farmers had undoubtedly had their fill of wanderers, that's why the stone walls.

Up ahead were remains of stone buildings that looked to be hundreds of years old. Most likely from Neolithic and early Christian periods.

They headed straight for the shelter the remains of the buildings could provide. They needed to make it there before the team of assassins crested the hill behind them.

* * *

Rock fragments burst into the air like shrapnel as Adam and Gabby dove over a three foot high section of rock ruins. The advancing team shot in short bursts of three and four as they crested the hill. That was enough to tell Adam they weren't amateurs.

Adam took out the 9mm Krieger had given him. A few shots might slow down the advancing threat, but that was all the few magazines would do. Adam shot twice. From this range he may have not even been close with this pistol, but it did its job. The assailants took cover and started advancing in a cover and shoot pattern. This slowed their progress in half.

"What do we do?" Gabby asked.

Adam looked at the hill behind them. He knew they'd never make it to the top. The soldiers would take a knee, get a good bead on them and drop at least one of them. These soldiers were most likely carrying a C7A1 assault rifle, which was a favorite of the UK Special Forces. If not, they had something with similar accuracy.

"We can't make it to the crest," Adam said. "Call the number on that phone." He reasoned that their cover had been blown, so breaking communication blackout didn't matter.

Gabby turned on the phone and dialed. A moment later she said, "It's not going through."

Adam figured they were either being jammed or their connection was just out of service. He wasn't going to say anything. The soldiers were advancing.

Then he remembered the military tactic, shoot and move.

"Get ready to fall back to that wall," Adam said as he pointing to another wall about thirty yards behind them in the ruins, "and keep your head down."

Adam shot twice. They ran to the next wall. They could do this once or twice more, then they would be out of places to fall back to.

Adam looked up, and another group of men was coming over the crest of the hill now, two hundred yards behind the others. He took a few more shots at the closest group. He and Gabby fell back again.

He could tell that moving their location had bought them a few more seconds, but that was all.

Taking two to three shots at a time, Adam had emptied his first magazine. He slapped in another one of the three he had.

He looked at Gabby and said, "Ready?"

She nodded.

He peered over the rock wall, and rested his forearm on it to steady his aim. He took a few more shots.

They turned and ran as fast as they could, retreating to the next rock wall in the ruins. Jumping over the wall, Adam hit the ground, rolled and grimaced in pain. Gabby flinched at the sound Adam had made. It was telling: he was hit.

He had come to a stop on the ground behind the rock ruins.

Adam gasped, then took in a breath. He struggled, got up on all fours and crawled close to the security of the stone wall.

Gabby was freaking out. "Are you okay? Say something!"

Adam remained on all fours and inhaled through clenched teeth. "My back."

"Okay, okay." She took a deep breath. "Stay still."

Gabby peeled up his shirt and saw it.

"It's a piece of rock..."

He was trying to catch his breath. Before he could say anything, she said, "Hold still."

She pulled at the rock. He reeled up in pain, not ready for what she was going to do.

Her fingers had slipped off.

"Can you get it?" he asked.

"It's sticking out. Just hold still."

"Give me a second," Adam said. "Pull it as fast as you can."

Adam took a deep breath. He curled down, face between his knees. He nodded.

"This is going to hurt." Gabby gripped a four-inch piece of limestone protruding from just under Adam's left shoulder blade and pulled as hard and as quickly as she could.

It moved a little, but her right hand slid off. She looked at her fingers and palms of her right hand. They were scraped from losing her grip.

"Hold on," she directed.

He replaced the air that had expelled from his lungs from her first attempt, then held his breath and nodded again.

This time she put her left hand on his shoulder blade and pulled with her right hand. It was half way out when her hand slid half way off the rock. Without saying another word, she repositioned her grip and pulled hard and fast.

The sliver released. From the best she could tell, it had gone in just over an inch. Blood oozed, but it didn't gush. It hadn't hit an artery.

Just then, she heard charging footsteps. She saw the gun a few feet away, picked it up, peeked over the wall and began shooting. Her eyes watered.

They were being overrun.

Adam had taken a deep breath. It hurt like hell, but there was some relief. He pulled his shirt back into place.

He reached in his pocket and pulled out his last magazine. A few seconds later, Gabby was empty and she handed Adam the pistol.

He ejected the empty magazine, inserted the new one and slapped it into place. He had just handed the pistol back to Gabby when he heard, "Hold it. Put your hands up," from an accented voice to their left.

That was it, the soldier had worked their way around the ocean side of the ruins. Adam and Gabby hadn't seen him.

The man motioned for Gabby to put the gun down. Gabby hesitated. Defiance was written all over her face. But, seeing the resolve in the man's eyes, she opened her palm.

CHAPTER 74

The sound of the shot whizzing by was so close, Adam and Gabby could feel the impact of the sound waves cutting through the air. The proximity was frightening.

The soldier dropped to the ground. Dead.

Adam and Gabby both spun around. They saw a large figure flying over the wall. Another figure followed. It hit the ground and rolled.

"Colonel," Gabby said with a gasp of relief. "Oh my God." She was face to face with Krieger.

"Get down," Krieger said. He pushed Gabby's shoulders with well over a hundred pounds of force. She had no choice, she went down.

The firefight continued.

"Don, I haven't been this glad to see anyone since I can remember," Adam panted, wincing in pain.

"That's nice sir, but our time here is short lived." Krieger looked over the wall and fired a short burst in one direction, then at another angle.

Suddenly, a soldier dove over the stone wall. He rolled and got on all fours.

"Sir, all clear for a hundred yards plus, but they've got reinforcements coming." The soldier crawled next to Krieger. "We can't stay here long; our guys are ten minutes out."

That was what Krieger was just about to explain to Adam. "We can pin them down here, but they've got the whole rest of the platoon coming, and they'll be here before our reinforcements."

"What are our options?" Adam asked.

"There's only one. They're closing in from the north, south and east, and we're surrounded. Our only chance is to get you to the tower. Mauricio is going to get you off the rock and down to the sea before they close in." Krieger was dead serious.

"How long do we have?" Adam asked.

He expected something more optimistic besides Krieger's answer. "Maybe five minutes."

"Five minutes?" Gabby said. She looked at Adam. "What are we waiting for?"

Krieger and Adam both knew there was nothing more to say. "Take the path towards the tower and Mauricio will find you and get you to the sub."

Krieger looked at Adam and Gabby. "Ready?"

When they both nodded, Krieger pushed the end of his throat mike to communicate with his small team.

"Lay down cover fire for the vice president," he said. "On my three, two, one."

When the cover fire erupted, Gabby and Adam ran up the narrow dirt path as fast as they could. They were about midpoint of the cliffs when they reached the top of the hill and caught their first glimpse of a round stone tower. It was O'Brien tower, built in 1835 by Sir Cornelius O'Brien. It sat high on the cliffs, almost seven hundred feet above the crystal blue Atlantic Ocean.

Suddenly, a woman came running towards them yelling, "Get down!" It was Gonzalez's assistant.

In an explosion of activity, men came charging over the hill from behind the woman. Others came from the south. Shots began flying in every direction.

The woman pointed towards the direction of ocean and shouted, "This way, keep down."

They ran together and the woman had led them to a depression in the rocky terrain about fifty yards away. They were close to the edge of the cliffs and Gonzalez was waiting.

Adam and Gabby ducked behind the rocks.

Adam winced as he crouched.

Gonzalez's mouth hung open. He was looking at the blood that was running down Adam's side.

"Sir, you're hit," Gonzalez said.

Adam grimaced and forced himself to inhale. "It was a rock fragment."

Gonzalez knew it must have been all the movement and the lack of a bandage causing the bleeding. But, based on the amount of blood on Adam's shirt and pants, he had lost enough to compromise his physical skills. Gonzalez processed all this and more.

Adam was in more pain than he wanted to admit. He was also beginning to get fatigued.

Gonzalez could see it. "Let me look," Gonzalez said.

Gonzalez began to carefully peel Adam's shirt. It was sticking. Some of the blood had coagulated as it seeped through.

"At first, I thought it was a bullet," Gabby said. "But I pulled out a large sliver of rock fragment."

Gonzalez had seen enough wounds. He noticed that peeling that little bit of shirt away had caused fresh blood to pulsate to the surface. Not a good sign. He stopped and put the shirt back in place and held his palm on it. Then he placed his other hand on the front of Adam's chest and compressed.

The pressure sent a gasp of air out of Adam's lungs. He immediately took another deep breath.

Gonzalez looked back at Gabby.

They held eye contact for a split second. Gabby understood, and the look wasn't lost on Adam. He looked at Gonzalez and then at an apparatus.

"What's this?"

"It's a hang glider," Gonzalez said.

"A hang glider," Adam repeated.

"I couldn't find any rope."

Gabby looked at Adam and asked, "Do you know how to hang glide?" Adam shook his head, then heard shots hit the rocks they were hidden behind. He snuck a quick look over one that was giving them protection to the west. There were a few men trying to hold off twice as many coming to surround them.

He turned back around and looked at Gabby and smiled tightly. "This seems like a good time to learn."

Adam was wincing in pain from the injury to his back. The gunfire was getting closer and Gonzalez peered over the rocks and shot a few rounds. At this point he was concerned if Adam had enough strength to lift the hang glider. Even if they could manage that, they also needed to gain enough momentum to get it to glide.

Gonzalez's assistant had just taken her turn shooting. She turned around and said to Gabby, "You've got to get him out of here."

"How does this thing work?" Adam gestured to the glider.

"You run and jump when you get to the edge of the cliff," Gonzalez said. "You'll drop a little, and then the wind will catch you."

"That's all there is to it?"

"I guess," Gonzalez answered, before realizing his choice of words wasn't the best.

"You guess?" Gabby questioned. "Have you ever been hang gliding?"

Gonzalez had a blank look on his face. The answer was obviously no. Gonzalez shrugged. "But the guy I got it from said that's all there was to it."

The shots increased in volume and frequency and Gonzalez looked over the rocks, quickly turning back after one ricocheted close to them.

Adam lifted the edge of the glider and ducked underneath the right wing, then looked around the underneath of the glider. "Where are the other straps?" he said.

Gabby was next to Gonzalez's assistant, peering over the stone wall at the advancing men, and she turned around and looked at Adam.

Gonzalez began strapping Adam in. In a moment, it became apparent there were only straps for one.

"What's the weight capacity of this thing?" Adam asked.

Gonzalez frantically looked around. He found the label.

"Three hundred pounds."

One of the advancing men pointed. He appeared to be speaking through his microphone, likely alerting others close by.

Gonzalez's assistant urged, "We won't be able to hold them off very long."

"How far out is Krieger?" Gonzalez questioned.

She didn't know.

Adam looked Gabby in the eyes and then up and down and said, "Take off your shirt."

"What?" Gabby sputtered.

"No, not you." Looking at Gonzalez, Adam said, "Take off your shirt and tie Gabby's left hand to my right hand."

Adam held out his hand. Then he turned to Gabby and said, "We'll have to run side by side and, right when we get to the cliff, you reach around and jump on me and hold on for dear life. Use your legs to wrap around me."

Gabby nodded. She felt a knot forming in her stomach.

"We'll run and jump… then the glider will fall a little and catch the wind."

"Fall…" Gabby's eyes were huge and her face was pale, "how far?"

Gonzalez had taken off his shirt and wrapped part around Adam's arm. He had just finished tying Gabby's arm to Adam's and had pulled the knot tight with a quick snap, when automatic gunfire sent rock fragments from left to right. Krieger dove over the rock wall.

No one had answered Gabby.

Krieger could see Adam was grimacing in pain and noticed blood coming from his side. "You need to get to the sub."

Over a dozen men were advancing on their position. Gabby grabbed Adam forcibly by the upper right arm. "Come on. Let's go."

Adam was frozen with pain.

He looked out over the ocean. It was a drop of hundreds of feet below.

Gabby was waiting, but Adam hadn't moved. He just stared westward over the ocean.

Then, he noticed blue and green rays of light in the horizon. A feeling of calmness came over him. He knew it was a sign. He had seen these colors before. It was time to go.

He looked at her and grimaced.

He took a deep breath and said, "Ready."

"Together?"

Adam nodded. "Together."

Seeing the impending moment, Krieger yelled, "Cover fire!"

* * *

In unison, Gabby and Adam grabbed the cross-bar and took off running. With her last step before the cliff's edge, Gabby pushed off with her right leg.

She twisted, landing directly in straddling position facing Adam. She hung on for dear life. She was shaking with fear.

She squeezed the cross-bar tight as they fell. They were descending.

Then they felt the current change and the wind began to fill the sails. They began to glide.

Gabby looked at Adam and his eyes were wide and his lips tightened.

"Hold on," he said. "This is going to be close." Something was wrong in his tone.

Gabby turned her head around to the right as far as she could. She squeezed Adam tighter with her legs. They were headed directly at a huge rock structure sticking about two hundred feet out of the North Atlantic.

Adam gripped tighter. Gabby hugged him as tightly as she could. She closed her eyes for a moment.

Then she felt another change in the wind current, and she opened her eyes.

The glider began to level off. They were closing in on the huge limestone tower. It was getting bigger by the second. Adam pushed down with his right arm. He pulled up with his left, trying to get the glider to turn. The air flow seemed to be winding around the structure. Then, winds of providence began to fill their sails. The glider seemed to hesitate in the air, and it almost stopped moving forward. They began to climb, faster than they had descended. There were a few moments of hesitation, but Adam didn't move a muscle. He just held tight. Then they began to move forward, and soared just to the side of the huge rock formation.

Suddenly, up ahead, the ocean erupted with foam. A huge submarine had broken through the ocean's surface. That was it, they were finally going to be home free.

* * *

Now aboard the aircraft carrier, Krieger needed to speak with the president immediately. The Captain had set them up in his small secure conference room to make the call.

"Mr. President," Krieger began. "Thanks to some brave Irish, the vice president and Gabby are safe and sound."

Krieger took a breath and let the magnitude of what he said sink in. The submarine that had picked them up was under strict orders not to communicate, due to their large cargo of gold. This was the first time George had heard that Adam was safe.

The president's heart leapt. "Oh my God. Yes! Colonel … you don't know how good this news makes me feel His face beamed a huge grin across his desk.

Realizing he was on a speaker phone the president asked, "I'm here with Senator Madison Dodge, who's with you, Colonel?"

"Sir, it's myself, Mauricio and Gabby, just the three of us. I put the vice president on a fast mover with a four-wing escort. I know we're behind schedule, but they're headed back to DC and," looking at his cell phone Krieger said, "he'll be there in time for your review with the economic mastermind group."

"Hello Mr. President," Gabby said.

"Gabby, it's good to hear your voice," Madison said.

"Hello Gabby, it's a relief to have you safe and sound again," the president responded. "Colonel, from what I'm hearing, you're telling me we're a full go for the State of the Union address and the meeting afterwards?"

"Absolutely, sir. I only wish I would be there for the State of the Union. But I wouldn't miss the meeting afterwards."

"Colonel, I can't think of anyone I'd rather have at that meeting than you," the president said with a tone that went from relief to reverence. He fully understood what would happen in the meeting after the State of the Union. Now, it was beginning to sink in what Krieger and his team had just accomplished.

"Colonel, let me commend you and your team for accomplishing this feat. What you've done for your country is unparalleled in modern history. You've given the country a chance."

The president looked across the desk as the Senator. Her eyes were filled with the same emotion he was feeling.

He continued. "I don't know how everyone got out of there. You'll have to tell me about it later."

The president knew that Krieger was a true hero. He deserved the respect and adoration of the entire nation. If the people ever knew what he'd done, they'd be in awe. He and Madison were. Now, with the gold on its way back to America, and with the transfer of money Adam had orchestrated, the entire national debt would be paid off.

The president even planned to send some of the gold to other countries it had been stolen from in turn for peace and a truly better world. Even now, some joint military forces were getting smaller stashes of gold from several locations across the globe.

Until that very moment, the president hadn't thought about if he'd ever tell the country about Krieger or Adam had done. That would be something to think about.

The Colonel had masterminded almost every Special Forces team from every branch of the military to reclaim stolen gold from across the globe. Krieger grinned with satisfaction as he reflected on Gabby and Adam soaring away on a hang glider, while he'd held the position until reinforcements arrived. When the SAS realized Adam had gotten away, they'd dispersed. Then, Krieger and the rest had rappelled down the cliffs to be taken to the sub. After it had surfaced, Gabby and Adam had soared almost directly over it. Not wanting to overshoot the sub by too much, they'd let go of the hang glider and dropped into the North Atlantic. They were in the water several minutes before the sub stabilized and a team come out and got them. When Krieger, Mauricio and a few others made it to the sub, they were all transported to rendezvous with the carrier.

"Absolutely sir," Krieger said, "and let me say that I believe Gabby has a few stories of her own to tell."

Madison hadn't felt so relieved and hopeful about the country since she could remember. "We look forward to hearing them," she said.

The president knew the carrier had sent out a team to look for Tim, the pilot, and The Shadow.

"What about Brooks?" George asked, not wanting to use his alias.

Gabby hadn't heard anything about the dog fight Tim and Brooks had been involved in to take out Sordid and The Cleric. She looked at the Colonel. He hesitated and leaned down closer to the speaker on the table.

In a slow, somber tone he said, "Sir, we're sorry to report, Brooks didn't make it."

CHAPTER 75

In the State of the Union address in front of the joint session of Congress, the president gave the most important and inspiring message a president had ever given in modern times.

It had been a week since Adam had gotten back. The cities had been calm for the past few days. Special task forces dressed in blue and white uniforms with red accents had begun their patrols. The newly designed attire was a cross between the standard police uniform and a marine uniform. The people's first impression of these patriots would be that safety and security had returned. With many large gangs taken out, the streets in major cities were now as quiet as a country town.

The president laid out how these newly created military-type police would pull back shortly, but would be available to deploy to any city where crime began to escalate uncontrollably.

With that put to bed, the president addressed political and economic topics. "This is the start of a new age, an age of enlightenment leading to a new and invigorating age of freedom and opportunity for all. Before I get to that, there has been some house cleaning here in Washington I'd like to address."

The room was dead silent as the president continued. "We have texts, cell phone calls and other data to indict well over a thousand people. I'd like to thank the special task force that has not only extracted this information from the NSA database, but they have also mapped the contacts these people had with many political appointees who have burrowed into a variety of government positions. Because of this, we have let go of several thousand individuals in the CIA, FBI and other organizations. We already have dozens of people with ankle bracelets on. Immediately following this address, we will be recalling trustworthy retirees to take their place. They'll also be watching for any residual deep state activity. I ask those of you who are contacted to join us in helping get your country back on the right track. Your country needs you more than ever. In addition, we will be notifying more than a thousand people that if they continue their nefarious activities, they'll not only be prosecuted to the fullest extent of the law, they will lose their pensions.

"I'll be filling you in more this week from the new media room. Let me explain our new media room. We are converting our current media room into a high-tech room where we'll be able to communicate directly to you, the American people. We'll have regularly scheduled updates, which will include fireside chats and more extensive updates complete with guests who'll be helping on important initiatives.

"The reason for this is, we have evidence that the media has been complicit with foreign entities to destroy our culture and the financial well-being of the American worker. Coinciding with this move, we have the votes to pass a new Truth in Media law. It will be described to you in the coming week. This move will not only allow us to talk directly to you on a regular basis without anyone filtering the truth, it will greatly reduce the false narratives the mainstream networks previously engaged in."

George waited for the light applause to wane.

"Now for the best news. A cross-functional group of patriots, consisting of entrepreneurs and visionaries from across the country, have been working diligently in secret. Their job was to outline some dynamic changes that will set the country on a path to be free and prosperous for the next two hundred and fifty years. I'd like to thank two of our visionaries who've joined us today. Heading up our grand strategy advisory group are James Haley and Robert Szegda. They led the efforts to integrate these practices, which will ensure the people of this country keep the power intended for them to have as we eradicate the establishment from every nook and cranny of our government. To do this, the following things are being put into place and into law to ensure the establishment doesn't rise again."

Even those known to be establishment politicians clapped joyfully. Those of them who were there, had been visited by a few of the president's team of two. The president wouldn't say anything today about that, or the empty seats. That wouldn't be disclosed publicly for a few days. But the president already had the bills drafted and the votes counted. Each law would pass easily.

The president went on to outline a myriad of solutions that came from the team, starting with how political freedom began with public funding elections; now elections would be publicly funded again and politicians could no longer take money for campaigns. This would put an end to the two-party tyranny that established the elites as a ruling class. It would virtually eliminate the control huge multi-national companies had on politics. This would also ensure that the middle class would again be duly represented in Congress and the presidency.

The president went on to describe how they had found that electronic ballot machines were designed for fraud and most were hackable, so he was going revert to paper ballots, which would be counted publicly on site.

"Another unique insight the team came up with is that political debates need to be fair. We have a debate commission, which has been compromised. Let me explain that the debates were once planned and managed by the League of Women voters, who did an excellent job. They are the epitome of what good, civil citizenship is all about. For that reason, we're going to have them take back control of political debates."

The entire congress was on board. Some were patriots, others had been presented with information that they would either be prosecuted immediately, or they could vote for each of these improvements and then retire. They had heard of multiple deaths of their associates. Some had been blamed on health reasons, but most of that wasn't the real reason. The president had orchestrated a counter coup on those trying to finalize taking control of the country, and they knew any communications would be tracked now that the Special Forces teams were back state side.

"It's my pleasure," the president continued, "to let you know that we have paid off the entire national debt. We have the votes to pass a multi-year budget, which will ensure we run a surplus for the next few years to come. We also have the votes to pass a surplus amendment to the Constitution, ensuring financial strength for the country forever.

"You may ask yourself what all this will do for you. Well, your take home income will increase in two phases. First, you'll see an immediate reduction in your payroll tax. An average income earner paid three hundred dollars per month in interest to the Fed. This money will be given back to you in the form of a tax reduction. We'll post shortly how to calculate the additional money you'll be taking home. We estimate the average household to have a tax reduction that will exceed that three hundred dollars per month."

George was excited to reveal the thing that would have the biggest impact on the middle class. "Let me say, you won't have to worry about the federal income tax structure for long. For phase two, we are going to eliminate the federal income tax. It was never intended to be permanent. This tax will be replaced with tariffs and an automated transaction tax, which will fairly tax every person, business and entity in proportion to the money they exchange. This will end all other federal taxes as we know them. The founders never intended for us to be taxed by the federal government."

George went on the explain that the current tax system did not tax Wall Street and all the foreign entities and investors beholding to the current system. This new transaction tax would include taxing foreign exchanges and stock transactions, where it was intended. He also explained that huge companies would no longer be getting away with not paying their fair share. George explained that, after this passed and was implemented within the next few months, the average middle-class American would be paying less than half of the federal tax that now burdened them. He knew it would be much less than half.

The applause was so loud and long; the president hadn't realized until that point that all of those people advocating higher taxes for individuals had never thought of this as a viable option. He could see it in their eyes. Using his hands to motion for them to sit, he thought to himself, *I thought this speech would be one of the shortest in history, but if I let them keep applauding, it may end up being one of the longest.*

The president made eye contact with Madison. She had helped him with the speech. He was ready for the next rocket on the resurgence of the middle class.

"Article one, section ten of the Constitution says, 'no state shall make anything but gold and silver coin a tender in payment of debts.' Article 1 section 8 says, 'to coin money, regulate the value thereof.'" The president went on to explain how the government would transition to a gold and silver backed currency.

The president had one more thing to undo. "We have the votes, and we're going to repeal the seventeenth amendment. The Constitution says the states were to appoint the senators. The seventeenth amendment was put into place by the banking families so they could control the senate. Repealing this will ensure that we get new blood in congress every time a governor changes over at the state level."

Across the country people suddenly realized their paychecks were going to get significantly larger. Tears of joy and jubilation were flowing. Attitudes were softening. Men and women who had become cold towards the country and each other opened their hearts. It was if a divine hand of providence had sent the retribution so the country could return to the spirit it had once enjoyed.

CHAPTER 76

George followed Adam into the small room. George looked around and saw Krieger stoically standing in one corner. A few other large men stood like giant pillars around the room. It had been George's idea to have the meeting here, off the coast of Georgia on Jekyll Island. This was retribution.

This group of the world's most elite banking families was relatively small. They all knew each other. Usually, they only got together in side rooms at their annual conferences that started at the Bilderberg's hotels. Today the heads of the banking families were here.

In past years, they might have sent one of their minions, because the president had no power or authority over them. Prior to this, any president trying to marginalize their power wouldn't be long for this world.

The president headed towards the front of the room.

One head of a banking family was comfortable enough to stand and step towards Adam. He said softly, "We should wait for Lord Rothmayer to arrive before we start the negotiations."

Adam looked at Krieger and the president. They had uncovered the evidence that the attempt on George's life at his mountain house had been ordered by Rothmayer and his network of cohorts. At the same attack, George's family and both Adam and Gabby had almost lost their lives. Several secret service and friends had paid the price to keep the globalists from taking over the presidency once again.

Adam waited for George to be escorted to the front of the room. It wasn't his place to be first to speak, but in this relatively small room everyone had heard the comment. Adam decided then and there to address it and establish the tone for the meeting.

"The Lord will not be coming," Adam said, loud enough for everyone to hear. "We have confirmed that he and his family have been assassinated. We all know they have made many enemies. People who have evidence of such have finally fought back. The world is transitioning to one of peace and prosperity for all. The president will describe our next step in that direction."

Adam's message stunned the group and the quick transition to George didn't give them time to respond.

The president's tone was direct and forceful. "These will be very straightforward. Today, we're announcing that we will be calling in every Federal Reserve note worldwide. After that, we will never recognize a Federal Reserve note as a currency. Furthermore, you and all of your associates will be leaving the country within forty-eight hours." George paused. "Any deviation from this timeline will elicit grave consequences."

Stunned, the globalist bankers momentarily sat frozen. They had never been spoken to in this manner. A few looked to their right and left to check the expressions of the others.

George wasn't waiting for comments or questions.

"As soon as you leave here," he said, "we will issue a joint press release that states that the US treasury note will now be the new standard currency of the United States to align with the Constitution."

"Sir, I must…"

George cut him off. The reason George had called the meeting here was first for nostalgia, and second, the White House hadn't been cleared of all deep state surveillance yet, so this location offered no risk of leaving a recording. Krieger had had a team clean the room, and every attendee was fully clean of any electronic devices.

George said, "You were called here so I could tell you in person that a group of our most elite Special Forces has been given a large sum of money for the patriotism they have displayed over the past few weeks. A select few of these are being given an additional substantial sum of money to be on retainer for the rest of their lives. In exchange for this substantial retainer, they have their orders. If at any time, something should happen to me, Adam or any other patriotic president, they are automatically activated, without personal contact, and with predetermined targets."

Now George's eyes scanned the room as he said, "You and your families are among their targets. Their individual mission is to each eliminate their targets and any associates deemed to be in cahoots with you and your kind. We have covered all our bases."

George was looking at faces that had never before known real fear. "After successful completion of their mission, they will be given another sizeable, seven figure sum. There are two separate groups to take out each target, if those targets are still alive." George spoke with purpose. "Should the United States government ever be solicited by any entity for another such deceptive scheme where you make money on interest or you start paying off politicians again, or anyone proposes a global tax, the people behind it will be viewed as having declared war on the people of the United States, and will be dealt with in the same manner.

"If you're thinking about reaching out to your political allies within our government, forget it. We've not only purged over a thousand people, but just before this meeting began, we cancelled the continuity of government program." George shook his head and looked at their startled faces. "That was a nice name," he said, "to cover up the truth that all the people you pay off could keep their top-secret security clearance and stay embedded within our government to push your agenda against the American people. Stopping this program is cutting off several of the heads in your deep state operations."

George smiled in a way that conveyed his feelings more than words could.

"Gentlemen, I leave you with this thought: leave us alone and be careful what you say to the media and any political or business affiliates. We have eyes everywhere, and for decades we will be listening in on almost every minute of your lives. If you crawl into some sound proof area by accident, it will be the last such place you'll ever be in. We will have no tolerance for anything but people who will help the sovereignty of the United States of America and help us grow the middle class to again be the beacon of hope for the world.

"In case you were wondering how we're going to do this, some of the deep state gold that was being used against us to fund deep state activities is now being used to fund *these* activities, designed to ensure the sovereignty of our nation."

George wasn't going to tell them about the teams of various military personnel who were at that time being deployed to confiscate more of the untraceable gold around the world. "As you leave here, remember, be careful of every word you speak to the media and in your personal lives. If you don't align with a sovereign United States, realize we have a decentralized network that will ensure risks to our sovereignty are eliminated."

George gave the room one last nod, turned right and walked out the door. Adam followed.

Krieger stayed behind. When he opened up his jacket, revealing his automatic weapon, the other guards standing around the room all did the same. The message was clear.

Before the day was out, the financial control of the country had been restored. The US treasury was making the money again. It was backed by gold again. George had ensured that no state shall make anything but gold and silver coin a tender in payment of debts.

The president had positioned the middle class to be flooded with wealth beyond their wildest dreams, the way it was intended to be by the Founding Fathers.

EPILOGUE

With the president winning the reelection by three hundred and forty-seven electoral votes, he would maintain control of the gold long enough to put it where it belonged.

The President rang the bell, opening the stock market. The market had continued its surge with the new US currency backed by gold and silver. The additional few trillion dollars that the president had confiscated from the South Pacific and the Far East would trickle into the market for a few years to come.

* * *

The country would not be aware of all the work and harrowing adventures that took place for all of this to happen. One day, some of it would come out.

As for Adam, he often thought of that premonition he'd had over ten years ago about a yellow haired president who was a billionaire running for, and becoming president, declaring in an interview that he would "pay off the entire national debt in a year" and there would be "no more Federal Reserve."

* * *

Ferraro's vehicle suddenly died in his driveway. It had no electrical response.

They were fifty yards from his house. His two body guards in the front seat looked at each other. Ferraro heard something behind them. He turned around. A heavy duty Chevy pickup had pulled just inside the gate. The gate hadn't closed.

Ferraro's two men drew their weapons as they got out of the front seat. With weapons up, they walked cautiously.

Ferraro walked behind his men as they approached the truck. The driver's side door was open and the truck was running. No one was at the wheel.

There was a note under the wiper blade.

Ferraro pulled it out. He looked around, and unfolded it at the crease.

It read, "Enjoy the ride and clean out the back."

"No one in sight," one of his men said. They were all scanning the area.

Ferraro cautiously walked around the vehicle. A hard top covered the entire bed. It unlatched with a click. Ferraro slowly lifted the top a few inches. He froze, then slowly lifted it higher. With an abrupt motion, he lifted it until his arm was extended fully.

Neatly stacked rows of gold bars filled the bed. The sunlight glared off them and reflected on his face.

Ferraro felt eyes on him. He had a sense that someone was watching.

He looked behind the truck.

Across the street on the edge of the woods there was a figure. Ferraro only caught a glimpse. He looked closer. It was gone.

The figure had disappeared into a shadow.

THE END

NOTES

1 Sterling & Peggy Seagrave, Gold Warriors, ... Page 272

2 https://www.cagw.org/reporting/2017-prime-cuts accessed Sept 12,2018

3 http://www.pewresearch.org/fact-tank/2018/03/22/u-s-tariffs-are-among-the-lowest-in-the-world-and-in-the-nations-history/ accessed June, 2018

4 http://www.pewresearch.org/fact-tank/2018/03/22/u-s-tariffs-are-among-the-lowest-in-the-world-and-in-the-nations-history/ accessed June, 2018

5 http://www.pewresearch.org/fact-tank/2018/03/22/u-s-tariffs-are-among-the-lowest-in-the-world-and-in-the-nations-history/ accessed 2018

6 https://www.youtube.com/watch?v=7H6KzMGRlSQ, accessed March 14,2017

7 https://www.youtube.com/watch?v=7H6KzMGRlSQ, accessed March 14,2017

8 Gary Allen, None dare Call it Conspiracy, Copyright 1971, Second Printing:2013 by Dauphin Publications Inc., page 33

9 https://www.youtube.com/watch?v= sJzPDOUvZE, Dark Legacy – JFK and The FED, accessed March,2017

10 https://www.youtube.com/watch?v= sJzPDOUvZE, Dark Legacy – JFK and The FED, accessed March,2017

11 https://www.youtube.com/watch?v=VSXQYvm57YM , Former FBI Agent Reveals Who Really Killed JFK, accessed June 28,2015

12 https://www.youtube.com/watch?v=VSXQYvm57YM , Former FBI Agent Reveals Who Really Killed JFK, accessed June 28,2015

13 https://www.youtube.com/watch?v=VSXQYvm57YM , Former FBI Agent Reveals Who Really Killed JFK, accessed June 28,2015

14 https://www.youtube.com/watch?v=7LbNWUNfnaA , The Men Who Killed Kennedy- Part 2 – The Forces of Darkness, accessed June 28,2015

15 https://www.youtube.com/watch?v=7LbNWUNfnaA , The Men Who Killed Kennedy- Part 2 – The Forces of Darkness, accessed June 28,2015

16 https://www.youtube.com/watch?v=7LbNWUNfnaA , The Men Who Killed Kennedy- Part 2 – The Forces of Darkness, accessed June 28,2015

17 https://www.youtube.com/watch?v=7LbNWUNfnaA , The Men Who Killed Kennedy- Part 2 – The Forces of Darkness, accessed June 28,2015

18 https://www.youtube.com/watch?v=7LbNWUNfnaA , The Men Who Killed
Kennedy- Part 2 – The Forces of Darkness, accessed June 28,2015

19 https://www.youtube.com/watch?v=7LbNWUNfnaA , The Men Who Killed
Kennedy- Part 2 – The Forces of Darkness, accessed June 28,2015

20 https://www.youtube.com/watch?v=7LbNWUNfnaA , The Men Who Killed
Kennedy- Part 2 – The Forces of Darkness, accessed June 28,2015

21 https://www.youtube.com/watch?v=7LbNWUNfnaA , The Men Who Killed
Kennedy- Part 2 – The Forces of Darkness, accessed June 28,2015

22 https://www.youtube.com/watch?v=7LbNWUNfnaA , The Men Who Killed
Kennedy- Part 2 – The Forces of Darkness, accessed June 28,2015

23 https://www.youtube.com/watch?v=7LbNWUNfnaA , The Men Who Killed
Kennedy- Part 2 – The Forces of Darkness, accessed June 28,2015

24 https://www.youtube.com/watch?v=7LbNWUNfnaA , The Men Who Killed
Kennedy- Part 2 – The Forces of Darkness, accessed June 28,2015

25 https://www.youtube.com/watch?v=7LbNWUNfnaA , The Men Who Killed
Kennedy- Part 2 – The Forces of Darkness, accessed June 28,2015

26 https://www.youtube.com/watch?v=7LbNWUNfnaA , The Men Who Killed
Kennedy- Part 2 – The Forces of Darkness, accessed June 28,2015

27 https://www.youtube.com/watch?v=7LbNWUNfnaA , The Men Who Killed
Kennedy- Part 2 – The Forces of Darkness, accessed June 28,2015

28 https://www.youtube.com/watch?v=7LbNWUNfnaA , The Men Who Killed
Kennedy- Part 2 – The Forces of Darkness, accessed June 28,2015

29 https://www.youtube.com/watch?v=7LbNWUNfnaA , The Men Who Killed
Kennedy- Part 2 – The Forces of Darkness, accessed June 28,2015

30 https://www.youtube.com/watch?v=7LbNWUNfnaA , The Men Who Killed
Kennedy- Part 2 – The Forces of Darkness, accessed June 28,2015

31 https://www.youtube.com/watch?v=7LbNWUNfnaA , The Men Who Killed
Kennedy- Part 2 – The Forces of Darkness, accessed June 28,2015

32 https://www.youtube.com/watch?v=7LbNWUNfnaA , The Men Who Killed
Kennedy- Part 2 – The Forces of Darkness, accessed June 28,2015

33 https://www.youtube.com/watch?v=pDe6QCqFu4c , OMG!!! (HIDDEN
SPEECH) JFK CONNECTED THE DOTS…, published May 13,2012.

34 https://www.youtube.com/watch?v=pDe6QCqFu4c , OMG!!! (HIDDEN
SPEECH) JFK CONNECTED THE DOTS…, published May 13,2012.

35 https://www.youtube.com/watch?v=pDe6QCqFu4c , OMG!!! (HIDDEN
SPEECH) JFK CONNECTED THE DOTS…, published May 13,2012.

36 Gary Allen, None Dare Call It Conspiracy, Copyright 1971 by Gary Allen, Second Printing 2013 by Dauphin Publications Inc., page 23

37 John Perking, Confessions of an Economic Hit Man, Copyright 2004 by First Plume Printing, January 2006, page XI

38 Parry, Allison, Skousen, The Real George Washington, Copyright 1991, 2008 by National Center for Constitutional Studies, Eighth Printing 2010, page 221

39 Parry, Allison, Skousen, The Real George Washington, Copyright 1991, 2008 by National Center for Constitutional Studies, Eighth Printing 2010, page 222

40 Parry, Allison, Skousen, The Real George Washington, Copyright 1991, 2008 by National Center for Constitutional Studies, Eighth Printing 2010, page 222

41 Parry, Allison, Skousen, The Real George Washington, Copyright 1991, 2008 by National Center for Constitutional Studies, Eighth Printing 2010, page 222

42 Parry, Allison, Skousen, The Real George Washington, Copyright 1991, 2008 by National Center for Constitutional Studies, Eighth Printing 2010, page 222

43 Parry, Allison, Skousen, The Real George Washington, Copyright 1991, 2008 by National Center for Constitutional Studies, Eighth Printing 2010, page 223

44 Parry, Allison, Skousen, The Real George Washington, Copyright 1991, 2008 by National Center for Constitutional Studies, Eighth Printing 2010, page 223

45 Parry, Allison, Skousen, The Real George Washington, Copyright 1991, 2008 by National Center for Constitutional Studies, Eighth Printing 2010, page 223

46 Parry, Allison, Skousen, The Real George Washington, Copyright 1991, 2008 by National Center for Constitutional Studies, Eighth Printing 2010, page 223

47 Parry, Allison, Skousen, The Real George Washington, Copyright 1991, 2008 by National Center for Constitutional Studies, Eighth Printing 2010, page 223

48 Parry, Allison, Skousen, The Real George Washington, Copyright 1991, 2008 by National Center for Constitutional Studies, Eighth Printing 2010, page 228

49 Kotter, a sense of urgency, Copyright 2008 by John P. Kotter, page 13

50 Kotter, a sense of urgency, Copyright 2008 by John P. Kotter, page 58

51 Kotter, a sense of urgency, Copyright 2008 by John P. Kotter, page 59

52 Sterling & Peggy Seagrave, Gold Warriors, Copyright 2005, by Seagrave, verso, page 251

53 Sterling & Peggy Seagrave, Gold Warriors, Copyright 2005, by Seagrave, verso, page

54 Sterling & Peggy Seagrave, Gold Warriors, Copyright 2005, by Seagrave, verso, page 96

55 Sterling & Peggy Seagrave, Gold Warriors, Copyright 2005, by Seagrave, verso, page 3

56 Sterling & Peggy Seagrave, Gold Warriors, Copyright 2005, by Seagrave, verso, page xi

57 Sterling & Peggy Seagrave, Gold Warriors, Copyright 2005, by Seagrave, verso

58 Sterling & Peggy Seagrave, Gold Warriors, Copyright 2005, by Seagrave, verso

59 Sterling & Peggy Seagrave, Gold Warriors, Copyright 2005, by Seagrave, verso

60 Sterling & Peggy Seagrave, Gold Warriors, Copyright 2005, by Seagrave, verso, page 147

61 Sterling & Peggy Seagrave, Gold Warriors, Copyright 2005, by Seagrave, verso

62 Sterling & Peggy Seagrave, Gold Warriors, Copyright 2005, by Seagrave, verso, page 3

63 Sterling & Peggy Seagrave, Gold Warriors, Copyright 2005, by Seagrave, verso, page 3

64 Sterling & Peggy Seagrave, Gold Warriors, Copyright 2005, by Seagrave, verso

65 Sterling & Peggy Seagrave, Gold Warriors, Copyright 2005, by Seagrave, verso

66 Sterling & Peggy Seagrave, Gold Warriors, Copyright 2005, by Seagrave, verso

67 Sterling & Peggy Seagrave, Gold Warriors, Copyright 2005, by Seagrave, verso, page 9

68 Sterling & Peggy Seagrave, Gold Warriors, Copyright 2005, by Seagrave, verso, page 5

69 Sterling & Peggy Seagrave, Gold Warriors, Copyright 2005, by Seagrave, verso, page 38

70 Sterling & Peggy Seagrave, Gold Warriors, Copyright 2005, by Seagrave, verso, page 61

71 Sterling & Peggy Seagrave, Gold Warriors, Copyright 2005, by Seagrave, verso, page 63

72 Sterling & Peggy Seagrave, Gold Warriors, Copyright 2005, by Seagrave, verso, page 46

73 Sterling & Peggy Seagrave, Gold Warriors, Copyright 2005, by Seagrave, verso, page 67

74 Sterling & Peggy Seagrave, Gold Warriors, Copyright 2005, by Seagrave, verso, page 67

75 Sterling & Peggy Seagrave, Gold Warriors, Copyright 2005, by Seagrave, verso, page 70

76 Sterling & Peggy Seagrave, Gold Warriors, Copyright 2005, by Seagrave, verso, page 78

77 Sterling & Peggy Seagrave, Gold Warriors, Copyright 2005, by Seagrave, verso, page 83

78 Sterling & Peggy Seagrave, Gold Warriors, Copyright 2005, by Seagrave, verso, page 90

79 Sterling & Peggy Seagrave, Gold Warriors, Copyright 2005, by Seagrave, verso, page 99

80 Sterling & Peggy Seagrave, Gold Warriors, Copyright 2005, by Seagrave, verso, page 99

81 Sterling & Peggy Seagrave, Gold Warriors, Copyright 2005, by Seagrave, verso, page 118

82 Sterling & Peggy Seagrave, Gold Warriors, Copyright 2005, by Seagrave, verso, page 148

83 Sterling & Peggy Seagrave, Gold Warriors, Copyright 2005, by Seagrave, verso, page 149

84 Sterling & Peggy Seagrave, Gold Warriors, Copyright 2005, by Seagrave, verso, page 179

85 Sterling & Peggy Seagrave, Gold Warriors, Copyright 2005, by Seagrave, verso, page 186

86 Sterling & Peggy Seagrave, Gold Warriors, Copyright 2005, by Seagrave, verso, page 209

87 Sterling & Peggy Seagrave, Gold Warriors, Copyright 2005, by Seagrave, verso, page 202

88 Sterling & Peggy Seagrave, Gold Warriors, Copyright 2005, by Seagrave, verso, page 227

89 Sterling & Peggy Seagrave, Gold Warriors, Copyright 2005, by Seagrave, verso, page 235

90 Sterling & Peggy Seagrave, Gold Warriors, Copyright 2005, by Seagrave, verso, page 241

91 Sterling & Peggy Seagrave, Gold Warriors, Copyright 2005, by Seagrave, verso, page 248

92 Sterling & Peggy Seagrave, Gold Warriors, Copyright 2005, by Seagrave, verso, page 275

93 Sterling & Peggy Seagrave, Gold Warriors, Copyright 2005, by Seagrave, verso, page 268

94 Sterling & Peggy Seagrave, Gold Warriors, Copyright 2005, by Seagrave, verso, page 248

95 YouTube video – the international banking cartel 1 – (1 minute 30 seconds into video).

96 YouTube video – the international banking cartel 1

97 https://www.youtube.com/watch?v=0Z6cstiuu4s, September 28, 2019

98https://www.globalresearch.ca/the-federal-reserve-cartel-the-eight-families/25080

Accessed April 14,2018

Made in the USA
Monee, IL
22 June 2021